Pictures *of* You

**Center Point
Large Print**

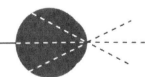

**This Large Print Book carries the
Seal of Approval of N.A.V.H.**

Pictures *of* You

CAROLINE
LEAVITT

CENTER POINT PUBLISHING
THORNDIKE, MAINE

This Center Point Large Print edition
is published in the year 2011 by arrangement with
Algonquin Books of Chapel Hill,
a division of Workman Publishing.

Portions of *Pictures of You*, in slightly different form,
appeared in *The Bellevue Literary Review*
and *The Best of the Bellevue Literary Review.*
This is a work of fiction. While, as in all fiction,
the literary perceptions and insights are based on
experience, all names, characters, places,
and incidents either are products of the author's
imagination or are used fictitiously.
The text of this Large Print edition is unabridged.
In other aspects, this book may vary
from the original edition.
Printed in the United States of America
on permanent paper.
Set in 16-point Times New Roman type.

ISBN: 978-1-61173-022-7

Library of Congress Cataloging-in-Publication Data

Leavitt, Caroline.
Pictures of you / Caroline Leavitt.
p. cm.
ISBN 978-1-61173-022-7 (library binding : alk. paper)
1. Women—Fiction. 2. Life change events—Fiction. 3. Domestic fiction.
4. Psychological fiction. 5. Large type books. I. Title.
PS3562.E2617P53 2011
813′.54—dc22
2010050669

For Jeff and Max,
the loves of my life,
for all of my life

~ ONE ~

THERE'S A HORNET in the car. Isabelle hears a buzz and then feels a brush of wing against her cheek. A grape-size electric motor sings past her right ear. What's it doing out in this weather? she wonders. It rumbles past her again, and she practically jumps. She tries to wave it outside, but instead it kamikazes to the back of the car, navigating among her cameras. Which is worse, she thinks, waiting for the sting, or the sting itself? She opens all the windows wider.

September fog is rolling across the highway, westbound US-6. Isabelle's windshield clouds. At first, she doesn't panic. She's been driving for twenty years already. She's a good, careful driver, and right now all this cloudiness is just an unwanted surprise. A trick of weather.

She switches on the headlights before she sees how much worse the lights make everything, how they reflect the fog. She tries the parking lights instead, which are a little better. They cut a small visual path on the road for her. Already, she feels a headache the size of a hard, shiny dime, forming behind her eyes.

Isabelle strains to see the road, checks her gas gauge, which shows half empty. She slows down. She wants to keep driving but might have to get off at an exit in Connecticut to fill up her tank.

Isabelle rubs at the window. She can still see. In the backseat, she's got money she took from the bank to help get her resettled until she can find work. All her cameras are here, and one small suitcase stuffed with clothes. Let Luke toss the rest. Let him give them to Goodwill or his new girlfriend.

Or his new baby.

She knows this is crazy, but right now she's capable of anything. She could reinvent herself. She could blot out her past.

A green sign, LEAVING CAPE COD, flashes by, and she starts to breathe. People sit in traffic for hours just to get here. They come from Boston and New York to spend two weeks in a tiny cottage and bread their bodies with beach sand and tanning lotion and absorb more sun than is healthy. Tourists collect the beach glass like it was diamonds instead of chipped pieces of soft drink bottles, and though everyone always tells her how lucky she is to live here, she's never wanted anything more than to leave. Every time a visiting friend gets ready to leave, she's had to stop herself from begging them to take her with them.

This isn't the first time she's run away, but the first time was a lifetime ago, back when she was sixteen and God knows that doesn't count. Now she has a little money, a profession, and a dirt-cheap illegal sublet in New York City that's available for as long as she wants it, courtesy of her friend Michelle. She yearns for cities where people don't make you feel there is something wrong with you because you live there year 'round.

She tugs at her thin necklace, lapis on a gold chain that was a gift from Luke for her last birthday, and in a flare of despair she yanks it off in one brief rip. She throws it out the window and lets the fog swallow it up. She tugs off the wedding ring he gave her, too, a broad gold band wide enough to have her name scratched on the inside, and bounces it onto the highway. She checks her rear-view mirror, wondering if Luke will come after her.

She squints at the sky. Maybe the fog will lift. There're still rays of sun out there, shooting through breaks in the clouds. God startling people into paying him some attention. That's what her mother used to say. A sign.

Isabelle glances up at the sky again. If you want to talk about signs, talk about how the sky had looked just this way the first time Isabelle had brought Luke home. She was just fifteen and he was twenty-five and working at the local gas station, a job that didn't exactly go over big with her mother. Of course, Luke's age made it even worse. She was so in love it was like being insane. She couldn't breathe when she was near him, couldn't eat or sleep, and her brain felt rewired.

Luke was the one who cleaned her mother's

windshield without leaving a single smear, who put gas in the car and checked the tires and the shocks. She knew his name because it was embroidered in red on his pocket. He had a green bandana that he wore like a headband in his long, glossy hair, and he always rolled up his sleeves, so Isabelle could see his muscles. When he smiled at Isabelle, his eyes were full of light. He looked at her like she was the most interesting thing he had ever seen.

When her mother was paying inside, he told Isabelle that he wanted to go live on the Cape, right by the ocean, and he almost had enough money to do it. He had asked Isabelle for her phone number and suggested they go to a movie.

"Not on your life," her mother said, coming up behind him. "She's way too young for you and way too smart and she's going to college to be somebody."

Keeping her eyes fixed on the road, Isabelle opens the glove compartment and takes out the Saint Christopher medal her mother gave her, needing its reassurance. Impulsively, she loops it around her neck. Nora, her mother, would be stunned to know that Isabelle had kept it, that, in fact, this necklace is something she truly treasures. Everything had seemed like a wide open road back then, and of course that was before she knew that everything she had ever hoped for was impossible. "Safe travels," her mother had told her, fastening the chain about Isabelle's neck, even though Christopher's sainthood was stripped a long time ago, even though Isabelle no longer believes in saints.

Isabelle and Luke came home one evening, when Nora was supposed to be at work at the library. They had been seeing each other a year then. It was a summer evening, and Isabelle wanted to pick up money so they could go to dinner. But as they pulled up, her heart sank, because there was Nora's little red sedan in the driveway. "Cheeze it, the cops," she said, trying to stay light, and then, as they got closer, she saw all these bright bolts of color scattered across the front lawn. "What the fuck?" Luke said. He started to laugh. "Is this her way of spring cleaning?" he said, but Isabelle gripped his arm.

"They're my clothes." Her voice was a rasp. There was her favorite blue dress, her winter coat, and all her junk jewelry sparkling among the dandelions. Her shoes were thrown on the bushes, her straw hat on the walk, her Saint Christopher medal gleaming on the lip of the lawn. The yard was a Jackson Pollock of clothes. Then the door banged open, and there was Nora, tall and beautiful back then, in the sleek green suit she had worn to work at her job in the library, her hair caught in a pin. Her arms were full of clothes and she stared hard at Isabelle and Luke, then opened her arms so the clothes tumbled out onto the front steps.

Isabelle leaped from the car. "Mom!" she cried.

"You don't follow my rules, you don't live under my roof," Nora shouted, slamming the door shut so fiercely that Isabelle began to cry. "Mom!" she wailed.

She made her way to the front door, grabbing up the Saint Christopher medal, picking up her sweaters, her skirts, bunching them in her arms. Her heart was racing so fast she was dizzy. She banged on the front door, rang the bell, but there was no response.

She dug out her key and then she saw the new, shiny lock. "Mom!" she cried, slamming her hands against the door. "Mom!"

She was banging on the door when she felt Luke touching her. *"Shhh,"* he said. He led her away, and when she bent down to get her clothes, he said, roughly, "Leave them. We'll get you new ones. Better ones." He guided her back to the car and then there was nowhere else for Isabelle to go even if she had wanted to, except with Luke.

All she had with her were her cameras. "Drive slow," she told him. She said it was because the cops around here were such hard-asses, but it was really because she wanted to give Nora a chance. She kept expecting her to run from the house, to call *Isabelle, Isabelle,* to stop Isabelle before she did something that couldn't be undone.

Isabelle and Luke drove to the Cape, landing in a tiny town named Oakrose, a place right outside

Yarmouth, that all the signs said was famous for its sunny beaches and fried oysters. The beaches, though, were small and crowded, and Isabelle didn't like oysters. Almost immediately Luke got a job at a local bar/café called Josie's. Isabelle got a job taking pictures at You Must Have Been a Beautiful Baby, a cut-rate child photography place where no one cared if the shots were artistic or you had a degree, as long as you were fast and could focus a camera. No one had come looking for Isabelle. Her mother had never called. Then the owner of Josie's died, and Luke took all the money he had saved and got a loan to buy it, renaming it Luke's. In that moment Isabelle somehow knew her mother would never come for her and Luke would never leave.

She wore the Saint Christopher medal all through her new high school, forging her mother's name on the paperwork, getting her records transferred, not really making friends because who else at sixteen lived with their boyfriend and not their parents. Who else worked every shift she could at the Leaning Tower of Pizza in order to save some money for film instead of going out and having fun? She wore it through the times she'd called home and gotten no answer, gripping it for comfort and hope. She'd worn it while she worked at the photo studio, loving the feel of it against her skin, the slide and flash, as she adjusted a child's hair or repositioned her light meter. She swore the medal made her customers behave better because they thought she was a believer, when really, she had no idea what she believed in.

And now here she is, thirty-six and married, and no longer a child, with no child of her own. There was never enough money for her to get the college degree she thought she'd have. Though she works at her photography, she's never sold a photo or had a show. The necklace brings her bright, glimmery hope, and ridiculous as it is, it comforts her to feel it around her neck. It still makes her feel that things can change.

She rolls up the windows and turns on the air conditioner. The car clicks and knocks. Luke had spent the last few years trying to get her to buy a better car, a little compact in a bright color instead of this black box that was always breaking down.

"How can you love something that never runs right?" Luke always said. And her joke response was always, "Well, I love you, don't I?"

Three hours later and she's still driving. She knows she has to stop for gas, so she gets off I-95 South and heads deeper into Connecticut. The weather is muggy and strange, as if it doesn't know what it wants, can't decide if it's going to rain or turn sunny.

She's in a white summery dress, but still, sweat beads on her back. With one hand, she tries to gather up her hair, so long she's practically sitting on it. Sometimes at the photo studio, the kids stare at her and ask her if she's a witch with all that black hair, if she can do magic. "A good witch," she says, smiling, but today, she's not so sure. The wire-rimmed glasses she needs to drive slide heavily on her nose; when she takes them off, there's a red mark on the bridge, like someone's underlined her for emphasis. "You're too sensitive for your own good," Luke had always told her.

And well, she is, isn't she? She feels the cold more than Luke does, bundling in sweaters as soon as the fall chill hits. The heat makes her wilt. She feels hurts more, too. The way, even after all this time, the cards she sends her mother always come back in the mail, scribbled across them in her mother's hand: *addressee unknown*. The way Luke sometimes looks at her when she surprises him at his bar. Though he says he is happy to see her, his blue eyes go cloudy, like an approaching storm.

People comment on her sensitivity at work, too. Sometimes people say that she actually sees things that aren't quite there yet. She'll capture a serious, thoughtful look in a usually sunny child. Or make a delicate little girl look steely. Some people say that Isabelle captures the very spirit of a child, that it's downright unearthly how you could look at one of Isabelle's images and somehow see a child's future. Years later, parents come back to the studio just to tell Isabelle how the serious and lawyerly looking baby she had photographed now wanted to be an actuary. How the delicately posed baby had signed with the Joffrey Ballet. How did you know? parents would ask. How could you *know?*

"I don't know," Isabelle would reply. Or sometimes, because it would make the customers happier, she'd lie and say, "Ah, I just know."

But she didn't know. She didn't know anything. She didn't even know what was happening in her own life. Within the past year she had found a white filmy scarf in the laundry basket, a silver bracelet in the kitchen, and once, a tampon in the wastebasket when she wasn't having her period. All of them Luke insisted belonged to friends of his from the bar who'd dropped by. "Don't you think if I was hiding someone, I'd make sure to hide her things, too?" he asked. He acted like she was nuts.

She came to his bar some nights and saw him surrounded by beautiful women, laughing, letting their arms drape about his shoulder, but as soon as he saw Isabelle, he shook them off like raindrops and kissed her. But still something felt off, like he wasn't really there with her.

Three nights ago, a call woke her from a deep sleep, and when she grabbed for the receiver, reaching across Luke, she swore she heard a woman quietly crying. "Hello?" she whispered and the line went dead. And when she looked beside her, she saw to her shock that Luke's eyes were open and wet. "Baby, what is it?" she asked, alarmed. She pulled herself up, staring at him.

"Just a dream," he said. "Go back to sleep." And he had rolled toward her, one arm on her hip, and in minutes he was asleep, but she lay awake, staring at the ceiling.

Then this very morning, when Luke was at the bar, a woman called her, blurting her name. "Isabelle." And then the woman told Isabelle she was Luke's girlfriend, how she had been his girlfriend for five years. "I know all about you, Isabelle," the woman on the phone said. "Don't you think it's time you knew about me?"

Isabelle braced one hand along the kitchen counter.

"I'm pregnant and I thought you should know," the woman said.

Isabelle's legs buckled. "Someone's at the door," she managed to whisper and then she hung up the phone, ignoring it when it rang again.

Pregnant! She and Luke had wanted kids desperately. She had tried to get pregnant for a decade before all the tests and herbs and treatments ground her down. Luke brushed away talk of adoption. "Is it the worst thing in the world if you and I don't have kids?" he said. Isabelle thought it was, but she didn't know what to do about it. She made Luke help her turn the spare room that was supposed to be a nursery into a darkroom, and the only children who lived there were those whose faces she photographed.

At first, when she found out about Luke's pregnant girlfriend, she thought it was the end of the world. And then she told herself it was only the end of one particular world. She surely deserved better than what she had. She would shed this life like a cocoon.

Now her back aches and she stretches against the seat. Last month, she had gone for a massage, and the masseuse, a young woman with a yellow ponytail, had tapped along her body. "You carry stress here," she said, thunking Isabelle's shoulder blades. "Here's anger." The sides of her hands wedged against Isabelle's neck. "Here's sorrow," she said, touching Isabelle's spine, and Isabelle gripped the edge of the massage table, wincing.

Here's sorrow.

Smile and you'll feel like smiling, her mother used to tell her. God rewards happiness. At You Must Have Been A Beautiful Baby, people always commented on her smile, bright, glowing, drawing kids to her like iron to a magnet. But she can't smile now no matter how hard she tries.

Isabelle glances at her watch. It's midafternoon and she's getting hungry. Her cell phone rings, but she doesn't pick it up, half afraid it's Luke's girlfriend again. I don't even know her name, Isabelle thinks. By now Luke is home and has found her letter. Maybe he's upset, maybe he's grabbing his jacket and his keys and he's gone off looking for her, desperate to find her. Maybe he's furious, smashing dishes on the kitchen floor the way he did when she first told him she wasn't happy living there, that she felt the Cape was suffocating her. In all the years they've been together, he's never hurt her, never raised a hand or even his voice, but he's smashed five sets of dishes, broken several glasses and a figurine he had bought her as a joke, a Scottish terrier with a tiny gold chain.

Maybe he isn't mad. Maybe he's just relieved. But really, who is she kidding? Of course he isn't home. Of course he hasn't read her pathetic letter. *Dear Luke, I want a divorce. Find a lawyer instead of me. Isabelle.* Of course he's with this new woman.

With this new baby.

Angrily, she swipes at her eyes. She sees a baby, small and glossy as a pearl, with Luke's eyes and not hers, and then she shuts her eyes, just for a second, and when she opens them, suddenly, she doesn't recognize where she is. The road is unfamiliar.

Isabelle turns on the radio. Even though it's a rock station, Tammy Wynette wails out at her. Oh, good. A heart as battered as hers and all she has to do is sing along as loud as she wants. If Tammy can survive, then so can she. She thinks of the money in her pocket, of her cameras settled in the

19

back, maybe of her mother, welcoming her back, the prodigal daughter. "I never liked him," her mother will say about Luke, and Isabelle will hope to hear, too, "but I have always loved you." Her mother has lived outside of Boston her whole life, endured her husband dying of a heart attack when he was only thirty, coming out of a Superette carrying groceries, continued on through Isabelle running off with the man who fixed their car, a man she said she knew was trouble from day one.

The fog is heavier now, the visibility terrible. Damn. She knows she's lost now. It was a mistake to take a side route, but she can always turn around and get back on the highway. Maybe she can stop at a diner, treat herself to a late breakfast, eat everything that's bad for her, everything she loves: eggs, bacon, sausage.

The darkness gets to her. It doesn't feel natural at this time of the day, and even though she knows it's just fog, it feels spooky. Squinting, she tries to see more than a few feet ahead of her, but the fog's enveloping her, making her increasingly uneasy. She flicks the parking lights on and off to try slice through the darkness and then the fog moves again and she sees, almost like pieces of a torn photo, patches of what's there. Something red. A glint of chrome.

A car stopped in the center of the road, turned the wrong way, its lights completely dark. A fillip of red dress. She jolts. She knows the stopped car is not moving, but it still seems to be speeding up toward her, anyway, growing larger and larger even as she tries to pull away from it. The road's too narrow, ringed with tall, thick trees. Her eyes dart on the road, but there's nowhere to go. There's no space to turn around, not enough length to stop in time, no matter how she's pumping her brakes. *Oh, Jesus.*

Isabelle veers, trying not to hit the trees. The car slows, lurching her forward. Time turns elastic, stretching out, slowing. Then, shocked, she sees a woman with short, spiky, blonde hair, a red dress frilling around her knees, coming into sharp focus, rising up like one of Isabelle's negatives in the milky developing fluid, and the woman is just standing there, in front of her car, not moving, staring as if she knew this would happen and she was somehow waiting for it. And Isabelle swerves again, harder this time, the tires screeching, her heart clamped.

"Get out of the road!" Isabelle screams. Frantic, she grips the wheel. "What are you doing!" she shrieks, but the woman seems pinned in place. In the distance she can hear a voice, like a splash of pennies, and then she sees a child—a child!—a boy with dark flying hair and when he sees her, for a moment, he freezes, too. His eyes lock onto hers and for one terrifying moment, Isabelle feels hypnotized, for one second Isabelle can't move, either. And then, she smashes on the horn and he startles and bolts across the road, disappearing into the woods, and her car's going too fast and she can't stop it. She can't control it. Her heart tumbles against her ribs. Her breath goes ragged. She's losing control, and despite herself, she's praying: *God. Jesus.* Then she hears the hornet again, which flies past her out into the night and then the woman finally moves, pressing herself back closer to the sedan, and it's too late, and the two cars slam together like a kiss.

～ Two ～

CHARLIE NASH KNEELED in his backyard, his hands covered with dirt, the fog all around him. His neck was filmed with sweat and the air had a strange, clammy feel, but he wanted to get these plants, the bright showy annuals, the dwarf pear trees with their roots diapered in purple burlap, in the earth to surprise April and Sam when they came home.

Plants want to grow, he always told Sam, all they need is just a little extra help sometimes. He crouched lower, touching the leaves of the strawberry plants. The soil should have been sandier for them, and there were some weeds poking up that he needed to tend to, but all in all, the strawberries would do fine. Well, he thought, plants do their best to stay alive wherever you put them. Just like people.

He got up now and stretched, glancing at his watch again. Nearly six. April would be done with her shift at the Blue Cupcake and just picking Sam up from After School. They'd be home soon.

He felt a prickle of unease. He and April had had an argument that morning and all day it had stayed with him, like a sour taste in his mouth.

Right after breakfast, he had been rushing to get to a job, running late. April was following him from room to room, so that he actually stumbled into her, knocking his funny bone against the doorjamb. When he got to the bedroom and bent to grab his jeans, she snatched his arm, making him stop. Her breath came in little skips. "You fell asleep last night while I was talking to you," she said. He looked at her, bewildered. She was usually so understanding when work exhausted him. She'd turn down the bed and plump the pillows, and then kiss him sweetly goodnight. "You didn't hear what I said to you last night, did you?"

He zipped the fly of his jeans, and reached for a black T-shirt. She was pale and lovely in the light, but he had no time. "We'll make it up," he told her.

"When?" She stepped back from him, her face closing like a door. "I try to talk and you don't listen."

"Honey, it's just a busy time right now. What's with you today?"

April shook her head. "You have your own company. You could turn jobs away once in a while! You don't need to work that hard, you just want to." She tugged his arm. "Sometimes I feel like I'm not even married anymore."

His nerves were fraying, his stomach burned, and his elbow throbbed. He had three jobs that were late and the clients were furious. He had to call several different suppliers because his usual brought him grade two wood even though he had specified grade one. Ed, his foreman, wanted to show him some problems with the central air that was being installed on yet another job. Charlie couldn't have this argument right now. And he certainly didn't want to have it in front of Sam.

"Charlie, I'm right here talking to you!" April cried, her voice taking on an edge.

Charlie went back into the kitchen, where Sam was staring down at his cereal. "Go get your school books, kiddo," he told Sam, "You don't want to be late." He ushered Sam out of the room, and as soon as Sam was gone, he turned back to April. "You know what," he said, "I don't know what's with you today, but I can't deal with you like this."

She looked at him askance. "Fine. Then don't. Just go if you're going. Just drive and don't come back."

When she turned her back to him, he bumped his elbow again. He was so irritated that he couldn't help it; he snapped. "If it wasn't for Sam, maybe I would just keep driving," he said. It didn't make him feel any better, barking like that, but he couldn't shake his annoyance enough to apologize, to make things right. He found and kissed Sam, and then stormed off to his car. Of course, he felt bad as soon as he got in the car. What did she think, that he liked being this tired? That he hadn't wanted to talk to her last night, to make love to her? He had wanted to. God, he had. Last night, he slid her nightgown from her beautiful shoulders, kissing her breasts, her stomach, the soft swell of her thighs. He fought his exhaustion, but then just as he was stroking her back, she said, "Charlie, let's talk," and his desire switched off. He sat up, had done his best to listen, but Jesus, he was so tired. So tired. Why did they have to talk? Why couldn't they just feel? Her voice lulled him, the rhythm of it, and he fell asleep.

He hadn't slept through the night, though. He stirred at four in the morning and April wasn't in bed. He got up, looking for her, and when he walked past Sam's room, he saw the door was open and she was sleeping, pale and beautiful, nested in a chair that she had pulled close to Sam's bed. The two of them looked so peaceful and perfect that he hadn't wanted to wake her up.

It was an argument, he told himself. It meant nothing. All married couples argued, didn't they? They fought and made up and then they grew closer.

What was love? What was it really? Sometimes he felt as if he didn't have a clue. He had fallen in love with April the second he had seen her and they had married within months, the two of them giddy with joy and surprise, hurtling toward their future. They had a child together, and a whole life, and maybe it was stupid to question anything that good, because the truth was that he couldn't imagine his life without her.

All day he had wanted to call her to apologize. He grabbed for the phone at ten, and then it rang, and it was the suppliers trying to argue with him about the grade of wood they'd given him. "I see what I see," he told the supplier. "And it isn't right." He was going to call April again at noon, but then he got a call from Ed, who told him that another job—a kitchen renovation that was supposed to have taken only three days—was running late and Charlie had to go on site and take care of it. By the time things had calmed down, it was time for him to go home. Well, tonight he'd treat his family to someplace special for dinner. He'd woo April back and things would be fine.

Charlie studied the lawn. There, by the fence, he'd put in a little goldfish pond for Sam. Maybe give Sam his own garden. "What do you want to grow?" he had asked his son. Charlie had brought home books filled with pictures of plants, and for the past few evenings, all they had been doing was looking at and exclaiming over the pictures. Judging from the ones Sam had lingered over, Charlie was sure Sam was going to say roses or azaleas, but instead Sam wrinkled up his nose. "A dog," he announced.

Charlie's heart crumpled. April averted her eyes. He put one hand lightly on his son's silky hair. "We'll see," he said quietly. It was a lie and he and April both knew it, though Sam, eyes gleaming, bounced about him like a ball. *We'll see*. We'll see what? It was the kind of thing his own father used to say when Charlie had begged for a dog himself, and Charlie had never gotten over thinking his father just might mean yes, even after time had gone on and on and the dog he had yearned for had never materialized. But while Charlie could have cared for a dog, could have slept with the dog, cuddled it, and kissed his fur, Sam had asthma. Put him in a room where a dog had even strolled through and Sam would have an attack. Feed him ice cream that was too cold, give him a day that was too muggy, something that made him laugh a little too hard or cry a little too deeply, and suddenly, terrifyingly, Sam's lungs clamped shut.

There were too many days at the emergency room, where Pete, Sam's pulmunologist, would look up and spot Sam and tease him, "Hey, Buddy! Hey, Sam! You missed me? You like us so much you came to visit again? You look too healthy to be here, sport!" And the thing was, he did look healthy. He was a sturdy nine-year-old boy, with creamy skin and navy blue eyes and a sheath of thick chocolate hair. Looking at him, you wouldn't know anything was wrong.

People died from asthma. Isn't that why he and April took Sam for checkups and monitored his breathing with the peak-flow meter every morning? Charlie still marveled that here Sam was, alive in the world. "Where in the world did I get such a wonderful boy like you?" Charlie asked.

"Mars," Sam said. "Jupiter. The planet Zyron."

Some doctors said the salt air of the Cape was good for asthma. Another doctor told them to move to a drier climate. The doctors warned to keep Sam's visits to New York, where his grandparents lived, short because of the pollution.

The doorbell rang, loud and insistent. Even from back here he could hear it. April had her key. He bet it was Jimmy, their paperboy, a kid who had a crush on April and blushed and dropped the change every time he saw her. The doorbell rang again, more insistently. "Hold your horses," Charlie said, and headed for the door. He tripped on one of Sam's Legos and put it in his pocket and opened the door.

Two cops were standing in front of him glancing awkwardly at each other.

"Charles Nash?" one asked, and Charlie nodded. A thought flew into his head. Maybe he was about to get sued. It had never happened before, but he knew it could. There was a client who tumbled into a pool he had built and made some threats. Once a man insisted that the grass Charlie had planted had attracted a gopher that bit his dog. But servers brought papers, not police, so why would they be here?

"There's been an accident."

The youngest cop was talking. Charlie couldn't concentrate. He nodded, but he didn't know what he was nodding at. He stood out in the heat-soaked day and the cop's words were an undertow, tugging him under.

"That's what we think happened," the young cop said. "The accident was in Hartford."

"Hartford? That's three hours away . . ."

"The cops there have jurisdiction, but as a courtesy, they called here and we came to tell you."

"Where were they? What are you talking about?"

"They can tell you more, but we know that the accident happened just off Interstate 84. It's the east side of Hartford. They're both at the hospital there."

"They? Both of them?" Charlie couldn't breathe. "No, no. My son's at After School. He stays there until five or six and then my wife picks him up from work."

The older cop stared at Charlie, narrowing his eyes as if he were trying to figure something out about him, something hidden or suspicious, almost as if Charlie were suspect. "The car's pretty totaled," the cop said. "Anything in it burned."

"What?" Charlie looked at the cop, who was studying his shoes.

The cops glanced at each other. "You know where they were headed?" one asked.

Charlie felt a cold clutch about his ribs. "They were headed home."

The cop shook his head. "According to the Connecticut cops, it doesn't appear to have been the driver's fault," he said.

Charlie tried to stop whatever was banging against his skull. "Which driver?"

"No alcohol. Fog, but no speeding. Crystal-clean record."

"My wife's a great driver," he said. "She's never had a traffic ticket."

The cop leaned forward as if he were going to tell Charlie a secret. "Your wife's car was in the middle of the road with no lights. No flares or signals. It was facing the wrong way. Your wife was in the center of the road and the boy ran into the woods. There was a 911 call, an asthma attack."

"My son has asthma. Is he all right? What does my wife say happened?"

The younger cop hesitated. "We don't know," he said, finally.

Charlie grabbed the handles of the railing.

"You okay?" the cop said, leaning forward, and Charlie's air pipe squeezed shut even more. He thumped himself on the chest, and for a moment he wondered if he were having one of Sam's asthma attacks. "Fine," he said, and then he grabbed for his car keys and one of the cops took his hand. "Can you have someone drive you? You don't look in any condition to drive three hours."

"It's three hours," Charlie repeated. Just hearing the number hurt.

"We have time," the cop said abruptly. "We'll wait with you until you can get someone to drive you."

He called a few friends, but no one was home. Then he called his foreman, Ed, who came right over, got Charlie in the car, and then drove as fast as he could. Neither one of them spoke and there was only the roar of the highway.

The car didn't seem to be going fast enough for Charlie. The motor knocked, and he clamped his hands together and then unclamped them. The streets were crowded with people, but they all were moving in slow motion. A young woman stretched sluggishly up on tiptoes to reach for a magazine at a newsstand. An old man splashed a bottle of water onto the street, laughing, "Ya ya ya."

Everything's all right, Charlie told himself. People got things wrong all the time. Ask three witnesses about a crime and you'd get three different answers.

Finally, they reached Hartford Hospital. Solid and red brick. An ambulance whined past him and Charlie felt suddenly nauseous. He dug his fingers into his palms, hunching over, sweating. It was a mistake. That was what it was, a mistake. He'd get to the hospital, see his wife and son. They would all go home and this would all be an amazing story they'd laugh about later.

• • •

THE HOSPITAL WAS BRIGHT and noisy. Ed walked with him, close by. In the elevator, the woman next to him clutched a bunch of oddly yellow daisies, sighed repeatedly, then backed away from Charlie, as close to the wall of the elevator as she could get. Charlie looked closer at the flowers. Dyed, he thought in wonder. The flowers were dyed. He leaned across the woman and punched the floor button and she sighed again. The dyed petals fluttered with her breath.

When the doors opened, he nearly stumbled. "I'll wait for you here," Ed said, nodding toward a waiting room. He sat in one of the orange chairs and put his head in his hands.

Charlie tried to snag a nurse, a doctor, to ask, Where are they? Where are they? But every time he approached a nurse, she glided past him like quicksilver, shoes as whispery as cat paws. Every time he cried, "Doctor," the doctor glanced at him and then was pulled away. Charlie headed for the main desk; a flurry of people were around it. A nurse looked up at him. "April Nash. Sam Nash," he said breathlessly.

The nurse blinked at him. "Oh, Mr. Nash—"

"Where can I find my son? Where's my wife?"

She touched his arm, making his heart skitter. It was never a good sign when they touched you. He had seen far too many television hospital dramas to imagine what was going to come next: the

33

lowered voice, the steady gaze, the bad news. He jerked his arm away. "Let me get the doctor for you," she said.

"No, no, you tell me." he said, but she started walking and he followed her, and then there, at the end of the corridor, sitting up on a gurney, swimming in an oversized blue hospital gown, was a boy. Charlie strained his eyes, trying to make out a face, but he was too far away to tell who it was. There was a nurse beside the boy, banding a cuff about his arm.

The floor was black, with blue and green and red lines to follow to different departments, and Charlie's shoes skidded on it, but he still ran as fast as he could. The boy was getting bigger, more detailed, and then suddenly, Charlie saw the pale skin, the dark brown spill of hair, all the elements that added up to Sam. He started to cry as he ran toward his son. "Sam!" he called, thinking, Look at me, *look* at me, as if his son's seeing him would make Sam real. "Sam!"

Sam didn't move. And then Charlie saw his arm, held out stiff, stitched from the wrist to the elbow in neat black crosses that made Charlie's head reel. "Daddy," Sam said. "I got stitches." Sam winced when Charlie touched his cheek. "Daddy," he said. "It hurt."

"He had quite a gash," the nurse said. She took off the blood pressure cuff and patted his shoulder. "You'll have a scar. Like a little souvenir," she told him. "Something to make you special."

Sam stared down at his arm.

"We gave him a nebulizer for his asthma," the nurse said.

Charlie hugged Sam tight against him. He could feel his small chest rising and falling, the rapid birdlike beat of his heart. He could smell his sour breath. "Daddy," Sam whispered. His voice sounded funny. Charlie pushed back his son's hair to check his face, shoved up the sleeves to check the bones, the skin purpled here and there, each bruise like a punch to Charlie's gut. "You're okay," Charlie said, in wonder. He hugged Sam again as tightly as he could, but Sam felt cold and clammy, and Charlie noticed his lips were a little blue. He looked up at the nurse.

"He's going to be *fine*. This is one strong boy, I'll tell you that fact." The nurse's voice was loud and strong, but then she tapped Charlie and drew him away, where Sam couldn't hear. "He's in shock," she said quietly. "He might feel and act stunned for a while. Just give him lots of love and he'll be fine."

Charlie turned back to Sam, hugging him close.

Sam struggled free. His eyes were enormous, the pupils dark and glassy, but distant, too, as though he wasn't seeing Charlie even though he was looking right at him. "I ran," Sam blurted. "I ran from the car."

"That's all right. That's good. I'm glad you ran, otherwise you might have gotten hurt in the car."

"I didn't know what else to do!"

"You ran and you're all right." Charlie swallowed. "What were you doing in the car, kiddo? Where were you and Mommy going?"

"They won't let me see Mommy," Sam said.

"My wife—" he said to the nurse. Another stretcher, pushed by a man, wheeled past.

"You'll have to find a doctor," the nurse said. "Lots of people here tonight."

"You sit tight," Charlie said to Sam. "Stay with the nurse and I'll find Mommy." He couldn't wait to see her. They'd hug and cry, and in the light of this, their morning argument would be no more than a piece of lint they'd brush away and forget.

Everything was fine. Sam was okay. April was probably bruised or bandaged, too scary for a little boy to see, and of course, Sam would need preparation for a thing like that, explanation and reassurance.

He was only a quarter of the way down the hall when a voice called, "Mr. Nash!"

Charlie turned. A doctor, bookended by two cops in uniform resembling Canadian Mounties, was coming toward him. All their faces were drawn, like coin purses. "Mr. Nash."

The doctor was in green scrubs, a mask slung about his neck. "Where's my wife?" Charlie asked the doctor.

"Mr. Nash."

Charlie looked around. "Is she on another floor?"

He noticed, suddenly, a faint splotch of mustard on the doctor's sleeve.

"I'm so sorry," the doctor said.

LATER, THIS IS what he remembered. The cops asking him the same unanswerable questions the Massachusetts cops had asked him. The cops asking his permission to talk to Sam, and Sam refusing to say anything, even with Charlie standing there beside him, holding his hand. A nurse handing him a small plastic bag of April's belongings. Her wallet, her comb and a handkerchief, everything so familiar. Two doctors asking him about the donor card they had found in her wallet, wanting him to sign papers so her organs could go to someone else. Someone else would touch April's skin. Someone else would see through her eyes. They asked him about signing papers for an autopsy, and then about a funeral home. He stood there, staring. "We can refer you to someone in Oakrose," the social worker said gently, and he nodded. He remembered going into the room to see her. An ordinary empty room with a long table and his wife lying on it, casually, as if she were just resting, her face relaxed, her skin as pale as stationery, a faint smile on her lips as if, even with her eyes closed, she knew he was there and she was happy to see him. He touched the hem of her dress, one he had never seen before. For a moment, he thought, Maybe it's not April. There was a triangle of skin on her cheek that was gray. He cupped her face, stroked her arms, her legs. "Breathe," he said.

He got up on the table and lay beside her, wrapping one arm about her. He shut his eyes and then he heard the door open, steps coming toward him. "Mr. Nash," a voice said, and he opened his eyes and saw the damned social worker again, but he couldn't move, couldn't make his legs work. She touched his arm again and this time he stiffened.

"Is there someone I can call for you?" she said.

"Call April, my wife."

She was quiet for a moment. "Is there someone else?"

He shook his head.

"I know how hard this is. I know how you must feel, but you can't stay here," she said.

He thought of Ed, sitting in the waiting room, his head in his hands. "How do you know how I feel?"

She put her hand on his shoulder. "My daughter died when she was ten. She choked on a piece of bubble gum."

He shut his eyes. If he kept still, she might go away.

"I'm going to call a funeral home for you. They

can make arrangements to transport your wife home. Is that all right?"

He felt a card touching his hand and he opened his eyes. She had printed on it *Roland Brothers' Funeral Home.* "She wanted to be cremated," he said, and she nodded.

"I'll tell them," she said. "But you need to take your son home."

Slowly, he lifted himself up off the table. He followed her down the corridor, along the red line and then the blue, and then to a small room and there was Sam, fully dressed, a bandage along one arm, chatting away with one of the nurses. Sam took one look at Charlie's face and went silent. "Come on, we're going home," he said quietly, and Sam slid off the hospital bed and took Charlie's hand, holding it tight.

The police were waiting, their hands awkward in their pockets. "You have a way to get home?" one cop asked.

Charlie nodded. Then he went to find Ed and as soon as Ed saw Charlie's face, Ed stood up and did something he had never done before. He wrapped both arms about Charlie and squeezed. "Come on," Ed said. "I'll take you both home."

IT WAS LATE. The neighborhood was dark, curtains were drawn. Down the block, the Gallaghers' yellow tabby was yowling in heat. "Are you going to be all right?" Ed asked, and

Charlie thought of Ed's wife, a lean, pretty woman with red curly hair, who must be up worrying about him. Charlie rubbed Ed's shoulder. "You've done more than I can ever thank you for. Go home," he said.

Sam staggered a few steps on the sidewalk. Charlie picked him up, a bundle of warm, sleepy boy with a jagged cut all along one arm. It would leave a scar, he thought. Charlie took Sam into his room, gently laying him on the bed. As soon as Sam's head rested on the pillow, he was asleep.

Charlie sat down on the bed beside Sam. He couldn't go into his own bedroom. He couldn't move about in his own house. The phone rang and he let it.

The bed was narrow, but Charlie gently lay down beside Sam and threw one arm about him, drawing him close, watching his son's chest rise and fall. He bent and kissed his cheek.

I ran, Sam had told him. Ran where? Ran to what? What was Sam even doing outside the car? What was April doing on that road three hours away? Where were they going and why hadn't he known anything about it? *He's in shock,* the nurse had said.

Charlie lay awake, staring into the dark, listening to the creaking of the house. Then he got up and went to get the plastic bag of April's belongings that he'd left on the front table. He upended it on the living room floor. Her wallet, a spray of change, and some makeup. Everything was tinged black, edged in smoke. He felt as if he had been sucker punched. He sank to the floor, feeling sick.

He used to laugh at those movies where men would lift their wives' clothes and inhale. Now Charlie held April's blue handkerchief to his face, but it smelled only of smoke. He let it drop.

Charlie's hands began to shake. He shoved the bag to the far corner of the floor. Why didn't she tell him she was going someplace with Sam? Was she still angry about the argument? Was this her way of cooling off, go someplace and come back before he even knew she was gone? He strode to the bedroom and opened her drawers, flinging out the brochures she kept for places and sites she wanted to visit. The Frank Lloyd Wright Falling Water House in Pennsylvania. The Whetstone Park of Roses in Ohio. Was that where they were headed?

She hadn't left him a note. She hadn't told him anything was wrong. Everything was still here, but dear fucking Jesus, she had stood in the middle of a road with the car turned around the wrong way, and she had taken Sam.

Love you. The night before she left, when they first got into bed, before they had argued, she had said that to him, whispering it against his neck. *Love you.* Most mornings there was a quick kiss because they were both rushing off, because Sam was going to be late for camp or school. He had touched the tip of her nose, smiling at her. "Say it back to me," she always said, and he always said, "Don't you know by now?" Every morning, like a dear, familiar routine.

But they had fought that morning. He had said terrible things he hadn't meant. She hadn't given him a chance to fix it.

When he stood up, his head reeled. Everything looked different to him now, as if the colors were all a shade off. The air had a strange metallic taste and he was suddenly shivering. Charlie yanked open the bedroom closet. There were the dresses she never wore, the jackets of his that she lived in. He grabbed up handfuls and threw them to the floor. He wasn't sure what he was looking for, what he thought he'd find, but he looked through her pockets. Nothing, nothing. There was nothing but this huge pile of her clothes and the only thing wrong was that she wasn't in any of them.

The closet was just about empty when he saw the suitcases.

They had bought four of them just last year, a matched set of red leather because April thought no one else might have red. "A snap to find in the airport," she told him.

There were only three suitcases in the closet. The biggest one was gone.

~ THREE ~

THE FIRST TIME Charlie saw April, she had a black eye.

He was at the Leaning Tower of Pizza. The place was a big, cavernous barn, with wood tables covered in red oilcloth that the waitresses were always wiping down. Red nets were slung across the ceiling, and the blackboard listed thirty-five kinds of pizza.

Of course, he knew it was a tourist trap, but they had great pizza, they were open twenty-four hours a day, and Charlie knew all the waitresses. Charlie liked sitting at the communal tables, making conversation with the summer people. He liked feeling like a native who could tell people the best places to go for crabs, the best movie theater, and why aloe was a natural healer for the sunburns they almost always had. And sometimes, too, he liked bringing dates here, though lately, he'd been coming alone more and more.

Tonight, the place was packed and it was all he could do to find a tiny table wedged in the corner. The waitresses in red-checked aprons speed-walked past him, and Charlie lifted his hand, trying to get their attention.

He was about to go to the counter and get his order to go when he heard a tray crash. People catcalled and stamped their feet. He looked over and saw a shimmering diamond field of broken glass and ice chunks, and right in the center was a waitress he had never seen before, tall and pale, with vanilla-colored hair cut short and as shaggy as a boy's. She was crouched over the plates, her back a curve. Usually, the waitresses got upset when such a thing happened, but this woman seemed completely unconcerned about the chaos. She didn't seem to hear the uproar around her. He couldn't stop looking at her graceful neck, the spiky points of her hair. He wanted to stroke her back, and he got up and walked over to help her. It wasn't until she looked up, turning her face to his, that he saw her black eye. Startled, without thinking, he plucked up some ice from one of the spilled drinks and brought it to her eye, and when he did, to his shock, he felt heat radiating from her skin, melting the cube so it dripped along his hand. She gazed at him calmly, and he dropped the ice cube.

"Butterfingers," the waitress said. Her voice was low and had a hint of a drawl. The corners of her mouth curved up. She turned and went into the back, cinching her apron tighter about her.

Charlie felt as if he had been struck. Black eye or not, he had never seen a more beautiful woman. He forgot the pizza he had wanted. The whole world seemed to have narrowed down to her: all pale and black and blue.

After that, it was pizza every night. Charlie

always sat at the same table and watched her. She never bothered to hide the eye with makeup, never looked away when anyone stared rudely. What was her story? he wondered. Was she a runaway wife and the black eye was her ex's good-bye? Had she walked into a door? Gotten into a fight with a rival for some man's affections? There were a million things that could have happened to her, and all he wanted was for her to happen to him. He just wasn't quite sure how to make that so. He told himself it was ridiculous. What did he know about her, really? Was she smart? Did she read? Did she even want a relationship? He chewed thoughtfully at an end of crust.

She was the only one of the waitresses who didn't have a name tag, who didn't joke with the customers, who moved about the restaurant like a guest who was just taking orders as a favor. "What's that new waitress's name?" he asked Judy, one of the oldest servers.

"Why, did she do something bad?" Judy asked.

"No, no, I just want to know," he said, and then Judy grinned and told him. "Her name's April. And she's a royal pain in the ass."

April nodded at Charlie when she spotted him, but she never came over to talk, too busy juggling plates and glasses and pizzas and demanding customers. When she disappeared for her breaks, it unsettled Charlie. But one day, instead of running out, April whipped off her apron and settled at a table, taking out a notebook and furiously writing. He watched her, his heart knocking.

It was ridiculous not to ask her to dinner. All she could say was no and he had dealt with no's before. He left his mushroom and green pepper slice and walked over. "April," he said. She looked up at him, as if she had been expecting him. Her eye was nearly healed, only a faint blush of yellow at one corner. He glanced down at her notebook: "Why can't I be like that?" she had written.

And then, "April," said another voice, and April looked up, past Charlie, her face lighting up. She quickly crumpled up the piece of paper. "There you are, Mick," she said, and Charlie withdrew. Mick was beefy and tall, with a black leather jacket slung over his shoulders even though it was almost eighty degrees outside. Mick tugged April close to him. "Come on, kitty cat," he said. "We've got miles to go tonight," and April flung off her apron and wiped her hands on her hips. She put down her order pad and followed Mick outside just as if she were hypnotized. Charlie sat back at the table, watching from the window. April settled herself on Mick's motorcycle, hooping her arms tightly around him. She rested her cheek against his back, her beautiful eyes half closing. The bike zoomed off in a loud roar.

Charlie pushed his pizza away. He wasn't

hungry and he felt foolish. He had a crush and that was all. She was just a waitress at a pizza joint. He hadn't had a single conversation with her except for the thousands he carried on in his mind, and really, whose fault was that? I'm a fool, he thought. A grown man acting like an idiot. Suddenly, the noise and chaos of the place got to him, the couples holding hands, the families teasing their children, the summer people in their touristy Cape Cod T-shirts. Everyone was spinning and moving and he felt as if he were standing still. He put down a few wrinkled bills for a tip, and then he left, too.

After that, Charlie stopped going to the Leaning Tower of Pizza. Instead, he went to Pie in the Sky three blocks away, where the pizza was more gluey, the atmosphere less lively, but at least he didn't have to see April. He didn't have to picture her getting on the motorcycle with Mick. He went out with his friends or he simply went home, sitting on his front porch and waiting for her to fade from his imagination.

ONE NIGHT, A FEW weeks later, Charlie went to the beach. It was a cloudy, unseasonably cool night. Kids piled into cars and honked the horn as they passed Charlie. It was the kind of weather that tricked you into thinking the summer was already gone. Charlie walked the deserted beach, hands deep in his pockets. It was a private beach and he was the only one on it, so when he heard a splash, he imagined it was a fish of some sort, come too close to shore. When he heard the splash again, he turned, and that's when he saw, at the other end of the beach, April, in a thin, short summer dress, wading into the water and then suddenly breaking into a swim. For a moment, he thought it was just a mirage. He looked around for Mick, but the beach was empty. It was crazy to swim alone, even more so at night when no one was around, when you'd blend with the sky and disappear. Even from here, he could see how far out she was. "Hey!" he shouted, but she didn't seem to hear. He waved his hands wildly in the air. He shucked off his jeans and T-shirt, kicked out of his shoes, and headed for the water himself.

The cold shocked him, making his teeth chatter. Waist deep, he stepped on the edge of a sharp rock and his toes recoiled. Damn, damn. What was he thinking? What was she? He began to swim, fast, until he was out over his head. He couldn't see her. "Hey!" he shouted again, treading water, turning around. What had happened to her? He shouted, "April! April!" And then, suddenly, there was her head, her hair dark and slick with water, smooth as a seal, and when she turned to him he saw that her eyes were as shiny as moons and full of surprise. "Leg cramp," she panted. She winced as he pulled her to him. Her dress, soaked with water, tugged around them both. Putting one arm about her, drawing her close, he swam to the shore. "I've got you," he said.

It was freezing on shore. Shivering, he snatched his black T-shirt and handed it to her. And then he dragged on his jeans, which grew damp as soon as they touched his skin. He rubbed at his arms and then turned to look at her. "Are you okay?" he asked. "What were you doing out there, swimming alone? Why did you go in wearing your dress?"

"What are *you* doing alone?" she said. His T-shirt was long on her, like another dress. Her black eye was gone, but somehow, she still looked wounded to him.

"Thinking," he said.

"So was I. And I thought a swim would clear my head. I didn't have a suit handy so I thought I'd make do with what I had." She smoothed the shirt down over her body.

"Let me buy you dinner," Charlie blurted.

"Dinner. It's past midnight. And why would I let you do that?"

He suddenly felt awkward. "Because I think I just saved you."

"I wasn't in danger. It just looked that way." She looked down at her body, as if she had just noticed she was wearing his shirt, then she looked back at him. "Thank you."

He held out his hand. "Charlie Nash. From the Leaning Tower of Pizza." He felt like an idiot.

Why would she remember him from all her customers?

She nodded and then briefly took it. "April," she said finally. "April Jorgan. And I should get home."

"I'll walk you."

"I don't live in such a great area," she said.

He walked beside her, his hands in his pockets, letting her direct him through the shortcuts. He couldn't help it; he felt ridiculously happy even though he was freezing and damp. A collie chained to a front fence barked wildly, straining to get free. "Right here." She stopped in front of a small gray apartment building. There was a rusted fence surrounding it. Some of the windows had green paper shades. "Thank you for the rescue." She smiled at him, and he felt that sudden shock again. "Have dinner with me next week," he said.

She studied him. "Anything but pizza," she said.

A WEEK LATER, he took her to River Nile, a little Ethiopian place where you sat on the floor around low, round tables and shared the food, eating with your hands. He had thought it would be intimate, but as soon as the food came, he was suddenly embarrassed. He couldn't stop watching her fingers folding the different purees into the spongy *injera* bread. His mouth went dry.

Neither one of them ate very much. She told him how she'd moved here when she was twenty and had never left. "I'm happy being a waitress," she told him. "No matter what anyone says, waitressing is good money. Especially with summer people who tip like there's no tomorrow. You make enough and then you can just pack up and go somewhere new. A customer makes a stink, you may never see him or her again. You don't have to deal with it. And there's always work." She grinned at him.

She said she had many acquaintances but no close friends. She had no family anymore. Her parents lived in Florida and had died recently, one within days of the other. "True romance," she said. "They were always holding hands, so I was always trailing behind them." She had left at seventeen, the last week of her senior year, packing everything she had in a backpack, including the savings she had managed, and she didn't care if she ever went back. The cruelest thing about it was her parents never asked her to come home. "They never seemed to even notice I was gone," she said.

Charlie thought of his parents, who had a chilly sort of relationship. When he was a kid, he was always worried they were going to get divorced, and one day he simply came out and asked. His mother had slapped his face. "Don't you ever say such a thing!" she warned. "You keep saying it, then your father and I will really divorce and leave you and you'll be all alone forever and it will be your own fault." He rubbed his stinging face and began to cry. His mother's face softened. "How much do you love me?" his mother said. He stared at her. "Go on, tell me," she urged, and she wouldn't stop until he had spread his arms wide. "This much," he said, choking, and then she nodded, satisfied, and he cried some more.

He studied April, the wistful way she spoke about her parents. She rested her head in her hands. "They're gone," she said simply. "My mother died of a heart attack when she was just fifty. Keeled over at the hairdresser's while she was getting highlights, and my father was right there because God forbid she should go someplace without him. When I went home for the funeral, my father could barely move. He cocked his head to the side when he saw me, like he needed a minute to place me. I did everything for him. I kept telling him how much I loved him, but he just kept saying, 'Now, I have no one.' Was I really no one to him?" April rubbed one hand over her face. "Two days later, I got up early to surprise him with blueberry waffles for breakfast. The whole house smelled wonderful. I went to wake him and that's when I found him. Her nightgown laid out beside him, his arms wrapped about it." Charlie heard her swallow.

"I never want to feel like that again." April looked at him so intently that for a moment he thought he had lost her and he felt a sudden, overwhelming sadness. "Let's go home," she said, standing, reaching for the light sweater she had brought with her.

"Of course. I'll take you," he said.

"To *your* home."

As soon as he opened the door, he wished he'd hired a housekeeper. He wished he had remembered to stack the newspapers neatly, to put away the plates from breakfast, to put fresh flowers from the garden in one of the countless vases he had. He was embarrassed by the pile of books in the corner that he should have reshelved by now, by his worn bathrobe he had flung on the couch this morning. But she didn't seem to notice. She was quiet in his house. She looked at his books, picking up one on orchids. "Can I borrow this?" she asked, and he brightened because when someone borrowed something, it meant you'd see them again. She picked up the snow globes he collected and put them back. She didn't speak when she led him to the bedroom and turned to him and began unbuttoning her blouse, taking everything off except her earrings. Her skin shone. They tumbled onto Charlie's bed. She leaned across him to turn off the lights. "I like it dark," she said. He was used to women making noise in bed, asking for what they wanted or whispering what they were going to do to him, but April was so quiet, he worried that he was hurting her, or that she wasn't having a good time. He kept searching for her face, trying to see her in the dark, but when he reached out, he felt her lids fluttering beneath his fingers, tightly closed. "Do you like this?" he whispered, trailing his hand along her back. "Does this feel good?" She sighed and put her hand against his mouth.

Afterward, they lay together, his arm about her. He held her tight, waiting. His eyes had grown used to the darkness and he could see her now. He could feel her breathing against him, weightless. He put one hand on the top of her head, almost as if he were protecting her, keeping her safe, and then she looked up at him. She finally saw him. "You," she said, and touched his face.

EVERY DAY AFTER work Charlie would go and pick up April from the restaurant. He waited for her to close up, watching her tally the register, admiring the easy way she wiped the counters clean.

One day, she got in the car, looked Charlie in the eye, and said, "Let's drive."

"Where?"

"For miles. Let's just see where we end up." He thought of Mick, the way he had said to April, "We have miles to go tonight," and how she had taken off. He shook the image off. She was with him now. This was different.

He put on the music, but she shut it off. "Let's just listen to the night," she told him. She made him stop after an hour because she said she wanted to drive, and when she did, he began to doze off. When he woke up, he didn't know where he was. The road was ink, the sky dark. Charlie sat up straighter. "Where are we?"

"On the road to Paradise." She laughed.

"Put on the headlights," he said. "Really. This is dangerous."

"I can see perfectly fine," April said, but still, she flipped a switch and the road became illuminated. "The first time I noticed you, you put ice on my black eye," she said. "Why did you do that?"

"I wanted to help."

"But you didn't know me."

"I knew you."

"You're a kind guy, you know it, Charlie?"

She put her hand on his knee, just for a moment, before returning it to the wheel. "You never asked me what happened."

"I thought you'd tell me when and if you needed me to know."

She was quiet.

"You can tell me."

"I wasn't doing something fast enough for Mick."

Charlie looked at her, shocked.

"That day at the beach. I had just left him. I wasn't sure where to go or what to do. And then you showed up." She gave him a half smile. "I wasn't trying to kill myself, if that's what you're thinking. I just felt a little lost. Haven't you ever felt that way?"

Charlie didn't know what else to do but take her hand and kiss it.

"You haven't said you love me. Do you?" April asked.

Even in the car, he could smell the scent of her hair, cherrywood and maple. He thought of his mother, demanding, "Say you love me," her arms spanning wide. He shook the image off. He thought of the way he could make April happy just by bringing her one small, perfect pear, the way he sometimes caught her looking at him like she couldn't believe her luck. "Can't you tell?" he asked. "Don't you know what you mean to me?"

She looked at him. "I make you really happy, don't I," she said, and when he said yes, her face bloomed into a smile. The road swam before them. Charlie saw the signs. They were only a mile away from the house. "I love you. And I think we should get married," April said. "Then wait until you see how happy we're going to be."

THEY WERE MARRIED in the fall by a justice of the peace. Charlie's parents hired a car to come up, baffled and affronted because this was the first time they had met April and because Charlie wouldn't have the wedding in Manhattan where all their friends were. Charlie's father handed him a sizable check in a pale blue envelope and his mother stared at April, who was in a simple, long white dress, a rose Charlie had grown himself tucked behind one ear. "That's what she gets married in? It looks like a nightgown," Charlie's mother whispered to Charlie. But still, she embraced April. "Mom!" April said, and his mother sighed. Ten minutes later, Charlie and April were husband and wife.

Oh, but married life was wonderful! They cooked elaborate dinners and ate them by candlelight. They made love for hours. She always slept with her arm draped over him, and the one time she didn't—when a bout with the flu had him up all night—he came back to bed to find her cradling his pillow.

Of course, they both wanted kids. "We'll be a *family,*" April said. "A family!" They sat up nights listing all the ways that their family would be different from the ones they had grown up in.

Two years later, on the coldest day of the year, Charlie crouched beside April in the delivery room, holding her hand, watching Sam being born. When the doctor held Sam up and Charlie saw his small face, the blue eyes wide open and looking right at him, he burst into tears.

"Why are you crying!" April asked, alarmed. "Is everything all right with the baby?"

"Everything is wonderful," Charlie told her, wiping at his tears and kissing her.

Charlie's mother offered April a baby nurse as a gift. "With a baby nurse, you can get out. You can have your life back."

April was horrified. "My life back! The baby *is* my life," she said.

"You let me know when she changes her mind," Charlie's mother said. "And believe me, she'll change her mind. I know I certainly did."

"April's not you," Charlie said.

April might not have taken Charlie's mother's advice about baby nurses, but she pored through baby books, tomes she piled up by the bed and underlined in blue highlighter. She couldn't walk in the park or the beach without cornering other young mothers and asking their advice, without plunking herself down next to a nanny and whipping out her notebook. She talked calmly to Sam while she diapered him, telling him about books she was reading or what was on the news, and when Charlie teased her, she shrugged happily. "It doesn't matter what you say," she told Charlie. "Babies just need to hear your voice." She sang to Sam in his bath, and when he squalled in the middle of the night, she was up and by his side before Charlie even reached for his robe. "I was born to do this," she said.

For the first time since they'd been together, Charlie began to worry that she was a speeding train and he was a sputtering car, falling behind. He'd never tell her, never want to mar her happiness, but the thing was, though April seemed to have embraced motherhood, he wasn't so sure about being a father now that he had a baby. He knew it was selfish, but April was spinning away from him, into her orbit of babies. He couldn't help thinking that he hadn't had her to himself long enough. At night, April remembered Charlie like an afterthought, reaching for him at night while he slept, ruffling his hair as she glided by, lost in her own thoughts. She used to be voracious for sex, but now she was tired or she just wanted to read one of her parenting books. When they did make love, she seemed far away, her eyes open and watchful, one hand on her stomach. Afterward, he reached for his wife and held her. When the baby cried, Charlie said, "No, let me."

He got up and stood in the baby's room. It was flooded with moonlight and Sam smelled of powder. Sam had deep blue-black eyes and a dusting of dark hair, and as Charlie rocked his son, Sam put a tiny hand on Charlie's shoulder and Charlie felt a shock. His son. He was holding his son. "Sam," he said, "Sam," and the baby yawned and then studied him, as if at any moment they might share an incredible secret.

Charlie took two weeks off to be with his infant son, but most of that time he ended up doing the housework, tackling laundry piles that seemed to be mating and breeding; cooking whatever was fast and easy and wouldn't use much cutlery or dishes; tidying up and vacuuming the rugs. Then he'd stand over the crib with April, the two of them mesmerized by Sam, who slept and cried and wet his diapers with astonishing regularity. Charlie would bend low into the crib, inhaling. He'd lift his son up and burrow his face into the baby's soft belly.

"Me and my men," April said.

"Does he look like me?" Charlie asked. "Do you think he has your eyes?"

April laughed. "Don't be silly. He's the image of me."

The first week Charlie went back to work, he thought he'd feel relieved. No laundry to tend to, no meals to cook. But, while putting up sheet rock, he kept thinking about the color of Sam's eyes, as blue as a brand new pair of jeans. He kept imagining his son's face. "Take over, I have to leave," he told his foreman.

He drove home taking the shortcuts. He bounded into the house, and when April and Sam weren't there, he went to all the places he thought they might be. The park. The playground. And finally to Johnny Rocket's, where he found them in a booth. He was hot and sweaty, his heart skipping. "God, you look terrible. You feel okay?" April said. Charlie sat down and took his son's tiny hand. "Now I feel just fine," he said.

The Nash family. He loved to say it. He put it on the answering machine: "The Nash family isn't home right now." The Nash family went for pizza every Friday at The Leaning Tower of Pizza. All the waitresses knew April and gave the Nash family extra cheese on their pie. They fussed over the baby and teased Charlie. The Nashes went to drive-in movies (the Cape being the one place where they still existed), and while Sam slept in the backseat, Charlie and April held hands, stuffed themselves with popcorn, and watched double features. If the movies weren't very good, they didn't really mind. They went to the beach, spreading out soft blankets under a huge umbrella. They went to Manhattan to visit Charlie's parents, who cooed over their grandson and pushed his stroller all through Central Park, from the zoo to the duck pond. They hugged April and told her she was too thin, even for New York City standards, and had she seen how great the parks were here? Had she thought about going back to school?

April laughed. "This is my school," she said, smiling down at Sam. When her friend Katie started up a new bakery, the Blue Cupcake, April took a job to help out, just for a few hours a day. The place was small and homey, with wood tables and comfortable chairs, and every time Charlie walked in, the air seemed soaked in sugar. April could bring Sam in his carrier, and he'd sleep or play with his toys. She could sit at a table and have muffins and sip tea and talk to the locals.

· · ·

AT FIRST, SAM GREW like a tumbleweed. At three he was reading. At four, he was the smartest one in his preschool, a small, sturdy boy in a Mickey Mouse T-shirt, curled up in a chair, trying to write a story with a pad of paper and a blue crayon as thick as his thumb. He liked musicals, especially *Grease*, and he would sing for hours into the toy tape recorder April and Charlie had bought him. You'd never look at them and think, This is a family with a problem.

You'd never look at Sam and think, Oh, what a shame, he's so sick.

~ Four ~

ISABELLE'S EYES JERKED OPEN. She gulped air and gave a good long cough. Her mouth tasted as if she had been chewing on cans. Everything was blurred and white—walls and curtains and ceiling, the starchy sheet and waffled blanket thrown over her, a faint blue stain on the hem, all of it swimming in front of her. She blinked at two bolts of orange before she could remember the name for what they were. "Pitcher," she said aloud. Her voice sounded funny and faint, as though it had been smothered in cotton batting.

A hospital. She was in a hospital room.

She tried to move and pain shot through one leg. She felt like throwing up.

A crash. She had driven into a car accident.

She tried to sit up, wincing. She reached for the pitcher on the right, and her hand touched air. Someone had put her in a hospital gown, and her right leg was throbbing, but before she could examine it further, a doctor with a bright red T-shirt under his lab coat strode into the room, a young nurse trailing behind him. He smiled brightly when he saw her, as if they were old friends. "What day is it?" he asked her.

"Saturday," she guessed.

"Give the lady a prize. You got here Friday." His smile broadened. "You are one lucky woman.

Your car crashed and you managed to get out and walk away," he said cheerfully.

She started pleating the sheet with her fingers. "I walked away?"

"Oh now, now, don't look like that," he said. "You're going to be fine, Isabelle."

He knew her name, but she hadn't the foggiest idea what his was. Isabelle struggled to remember him, to remember anything, but all there was, was here, in this hospital room. "My eyes," she blurted, panic fluttering through her. "I'm seeing double."

He nodded casually, as if she had told him she were having baked chicken for lunch. He took out a tiny flashlight from his pocket and shone it in her eyes, and when she drew back, startled, the nurse put one hand on Isabelle's back and kept her still. The doctor clicked the light off and popped it back in his pocket. "You bumped your noggin. We'll run some tests. Tomorrow, if your vision's okay, you can go home."

"What happened to the other people?" she asked. She saw them, the woman in the red dress, the boy, running.

"What other people?" He studied her leg. "Those bruises? They'll fade in a week."

"The other people in the crash. What happened to them?"

He scribbled something on a chart. "You'd have to ask their doctor."

"Who's their doctor?" she said, but he turned abruptly, striding out of the room.

"Wait!" Isabelle grabbed at the nurse's sleeve. "Can you get me a newspaper?"

"Reading would strain your eyes right now. You just concentrate on getting some rest," the nurse said, patting Isabelle's shoulder.

"Someone can read it to me—" Isabelle said, and then seeing the look on the nurse's face, blurted, "What about a TV? Can I get a TV?"

"I'll send someone," the nurse said, and then she was gone.

Isabelle slept on and off through the night, riding a wave of painkillers. She dreamed she was freezing in Siberia. People were stuffing snow around her so she couldn't move. She jerked awake. Nurses were packing ice under her armpits, along her thighs. "It's to bring your fever down," a nurse said.

"Where are they?" Isabelle said, her voice a rasp.

"I'm sure your family will be here in the morning," the nurse said. Isabelle felt a prick in one arm. She fought, struggling to stay awake, but then the world went cold and white again.

When she woke the next morning, she was cool and dry. Someone had put her in a clean gown. The sheets and a soft white blanket were pulled over her. Her sight was still doubled, and she had a throbbing pain orbiting her head.

A specialist came in to look at her eyes, a woman so disinterested that Isabelle felt affronted. "Follow my finger," she ordered Isabelle, waving her hand around in a blur so that it was all Isabelle could do not to get dizzy. "Touch your index fingers together." She shone a light in Isabelle's eyes and then stepped back. "Your sight should be fine tomorrow," said the doctor. "You just rest now."

Rest. How was she supposed to rest? She couldn't read, no one had come around about the TV, and she didn't have her cell phone to call anybody.

Luke. Had anyone called him? Had they even been able to find him? Was he too busy screwing his girlfriend? He wouldn't know she had been leaving him, not unless he'd been home and had seen the note. And even then, he wouldn't believe she could ever leave. He couldn't imagine there was ever anything he could do that he couldn't talk her into forgiving him for.

He was dead wrong.

She begged quarters from a nurse and made her way to the hall. She passed a newspaper and picked it up, but the nurse was right, the words were a blur.

She called her friend Michelle first and as soon as she said her name, there was an intake of air. "Oh my God, Izzy! Luke just told me. I've been frantic. How are you?"

"Luke told you?" Isabelle asked. How did Luke know? Two tables spun in front of her. "I'm fine. At least I think I'm fine." Her voice grew small, as curled as a fist. She was about to say it again, louder, with more impact, because Michelle hadn't responded. "Can I stay with you for a while?"

"Of course you can. God, when I heard about it—"

"What did you hear? What did Luke tell you? I don't really know anything. Are the other people okay?"

There was an odd, funny silence. Isabelle twisted the phone cord around her hand. "Michelle?" she said.

"All that matters is you're all right," Michelle said finally. "I'm coming right out there."

"No, no, I'm coming home soon. There's no need."

Behind Isabelle, a man coughed and sneezed. "Tell me what you know," Isabelle said.

"I don't know what happened to the other people," Michelle said. "I just know it was a terrible accident and we're all so lucky you're okay."

Isabelle turned and the man tapped his watch. "Did the newspaper have anything?"

"I didn't get the paper or see the news."

Isabelle held the phone closer to her face. Michelle was a news junky. She would no more think of not buying two different newspapers every morning than she would consider not brushing her teeth. "Can you turn on the news now?" and then she heard the dial tone. Michelle had hung up.

She called her other friends, Lindy, Jane, Ellen, and asked immediately what they knew about the crash, and though they all knew Isabelle was in the hospital, the rest of the details were fuzzy. "So there was nothing in the papers?" Isabelle asked. "No one told you anything?"

"I didn't see a paper," Jane said, and Isabelle felt something snaking up along her spine.

"Can you turn on the news now?" Isabelle said.

There was that funny clip of silence again. "Doorbell," Jane said. "I have to go."

"Wait!" Isabelle cried, but Jane was gone.

Isabelle pressed the phone against her cheek. She managed to make her way back to her room and sank into the bed, suddenly exhausted. She rolled onto her side, her lids drifting shut. Maybe she'd wake up and, just like the bad TV movies she sometimes watched, it would all turn out to be a dream.

"Hey."

She rolled over and opened her eyes. Luke. Blurry Luke. She could make out a stuffed bear with a polka dot bow in his arms.

"I am so sorry," he said, his voice pained, and she averted her face. She didn't know if he was talking about the accident or about them, but really, what did it matter? She thought of all the times he had been nice to her after she had found earrings in the house or sworn she smelled perfume. How he had taken her out to a fancy dinner, how he reeled her back in so tenderly that she didn't notice the sharpness of the hook. She hated herself for the sudden sharp pang of yearning she felt, the way she wanted him closer. *Go away.*

"The cops called me." He set the bear on the bed. "A detective wanted to talk to you, but the doctor nixed that, and good for him. There's time for that later."

"A detective?" Isabelle said. She tried to sit up more.

"Routine. Lay back down, baby."

"Don't call me baby. What was the detective's name?"

Luke shrugged. He made the bear's head swivel. "Izzy, feel better soon," he made the bear say in a high, squeaky voice. He lifted both the bear's paws so it seemed as though the bear were waving at her. "Do you want me to call anyone for you?" he asked, and Isabelle shook her head. "Do you want me to call your mother?"

Isabelle shook her head. Her mother would think this was God showing Isabelle the error of her ways. Her mother would take one look at the situation and say I told you so, and Isabelle wouldn't really be able to argue with her.

"What happened to the other people?" Isabelle asked. "What did the cops tell you?"

"I don't know," he said. "I didn't ask."

"You didn't ask?" She looked at him, astonished, and tried to sit up. "Why didn't you ask? I need to know if they're hurt, if they're *alive*—" As soon as she said it, she felt an electric current of panic. He took her hand and she yanked it from him. "What do you know?" she accused.

"I read your letter," he said quietly. "That's what I know."

"I don't want to go home with you," she said. "I know what you did. I know who you are now. I didn't know before, but I know now." She shifted so that the bear tumbled to the floor. Luke picked it up, hesitated, and then tucked it under one arm. "You're a liar and a philanderer and a cheat," she said. "You're a *father.*"

Luke looked away but he didn't say anything. He sat in the chair beside the bed. "Of course you'll come home with me," he said. "We can work this out."

"No we can't. Not this time." She looked away from him. And then she couldn't help it. She looked back. "How could you do this, Luke?" she said.

"Let me make it up to you," he said. He tried to take her hand again, and she made a fist and slid it under the sheet away from him.

"Your car's totaled," he said. "The doctor said

you're lucky to be alive, that it's a miracle you got out of the car." He leaned toward her. She looked at him, then shut her eyes and tried to sniff his neck to see if he had the other woman's scent on him. "Come here," she ordered, and he did. She could smell his aftershave. Pine and musk. She had always loved it, but now all she could think about was someone else's nose pressed up against Luke's neck. "You wear too much aftershave," she said, and he frowned.

"I went crazy. I was so worried. So scared . . . it all made me realize—" Luke said.

"Don't. Please don't." She waved her hand at him. "I'll rent a room. I can get my job back until I have a place to go."

"Isabelle, please listen to me." He reached over and grabbed her foot under the sheet. "Stay with me until you find another place. I'll stay in the spare room. I'll stay in the kitchen if that's what you want. Please. Just come home. Let me take care of you."

"I know how you take care of me," she said bitterly. "I'm staying with friends."

"But *I'm* your friend. I'm more than your friend, I'm your husband. I'm the one you need to stay with." He leaned closer. "I'm not seeing her anymore, I swear," he said. "There's no one in my life but you."

"You're not seeing the mother of your child?" She gave him a stony stare and he stood up from the chair. "Okay, then. You stay in the house and I'll be the one to leave," he said. "I'll find a place. I can stay in the back room at the bar if I have to. Look at you. You've been in a terrible accident. You can't look for an apartment now. The only thing that makes sense is for you to come back to the house."

"I don't want you there," she said. "Can you do that?"

He lifted his palms. "Anything. Anything you want."

"Fine. Now will you please leave?"

"I'm not leaving you," he said. "I'm staying right outside. You need me, you tell the nurse to come get me. I'll be right here."

With whom? Isabelle thought, but she kept her mouth shut.

He set the bear on the bed again, settling him so it looked as if the bear were watching over Isabelle. "He's not leaving, either," Luke said.

That afternoon, while she was pouring herself some water, she noticed her vision had cleared. There was just one pitcher now. Startled, she looked around the room, at the orange chair, the door, the window. Everything was singular again. One hospital bed. One pitcher. One glass. One Isabelle.

She could see. She could get up and look for the woman and the boy. She started to gently swing her leg over the bed, when a resident came in.

"Leaving so soon? Was it something I said?"

Defeated, she lay back against the bed. "I see only one of you," she announced.

He smiled and took blood. He made her touch her fingers again and follow his tiny flashlight with her eyes. "I have good news," he said. "Your husband can take you home tomorrow morning."

No way was she going to let Luke take her home. Instead, she called Michelle, who came that Monday morning with a light summer dress, underwear, and bright green flip flops for Isabelle to change into. She also brought her new baby, Andi, held against her in a Baby Björn. "I'm glad I didn't see Luke here. I'd have had to slug him," Michelle said.

"I'm glad he's gone," Isabelle said, but she couldn't help wondering where he was. "I'll be here," he had said, and then he had left her alone in the hospital.

"Oh, isn't this adorable!" Michelle picked up the stuffed animal.

"Andi can have it."

"Let's get you home," Michelle said, handing the bear to Andi, who gummed its ear.

Isabelle couldn't wait to get out of the hospital, but as soon as she was in Michelle's car, panic set in. Her skin felt clammy. She couldn't catch her breath, and her arms and legs had turned to rubber. A car zipped past them and she flinched. The road seemed crazily curved, and she felt tiny cracks opening up throughout her body. It was all she could do not to jump out of the car and keep running. She'd do anything to feel safe again. She looked around the car. This is how lives are ruined, she thought. This is how people die.

She felt Michelle watching her and dipped her head, biting down on her lip. "It's okay," Michelle said. Her friend reached across and took Isabelle's hand for a moment and squeezed it. "I'll go really slow," she said quietly. "We can stop anytime you need."

Michelle drove as carefully as she could. She stopped every half hour at the rest stops, and as soon as she parked, Isabelle leaped out of the car, panting, rubbing her arms as if to make sure they were still there, intact. "We're almost there," Michelle promised. "Just a bit more."

By the time Michelle pulled up at Isabelle's, Isabelle could have crouched down and kissed the pavement.

ISABELLE DIDN'T KNOW what she expected, but not that everything would look and feel so different. She thought the house would be as she had left it three days ago. Luke's casual mess, a dish or two still in the sink, maybe all her things neatly boxed up. She hadn't thought what it would be like to come back to the house without Luke in it.

The sharp tang of citrus cleaner permeated the

air. Luke had cleaned for her. She tried to imagine him paying attention, swiping at grime, and shook her head. Maybe he hired someone. Maybe his girlfriend did it. The floors were gleaming, even the rugs had been vacuumed, and there was a pot of daisies, the flower he had courted her with, on the table. She hobbled into the room. There was a card with a picture of Saturn on it—her favorite planet, the rings lit as if by moonlight. Inside, it read, *Call me if you need anything. Love, Luke.* She dropped it into the wastebasket.

On the kitchen table were more cards from friends who had heard, from the studio. The answering machine light was glowing. Fifteen calls.

Slumping on the couch, Isabelle looked around her. The first time she had walked into this house with Luke, she had been barely sixteen. Oakrose. Luke loved having a baseball field right in the town and that every summer there were concerts right on the beach. "Look at this great house!" he said, but it was really only a tiny one-bedroom, all the rooms cramped together, the lawn nothing but pine needles. She loved it only because she was there with Luke.

The two of them had walked into this living room holding hands, spiffed up for the realtor. Luke was in a sports jacket and tie and he had slicked his hair back so it looked shorter. She was wearing a long yellow summer dress and had pinned her hair up so that she might look older. She had worn a cheap rhinestone ring they had bought at a Rite-Aid, and though they had both laughed at it, Isabelle had felt different the moment she'd slid the ring on. The house! God, she had thought it was a palace. She'd stood in the center of the empty living room and shut her eyes, dizzy with joy. She could go into any room she wanted and no one could tell her not to! She didn't have to shut a door and push a heavy dresser up against it to have privacy! Imagine, sixteen years old and getting to live in her own house, all courtesy of Luke's savings account. "Who are your parents?" a new neighbor asked and Isabelle laughed out loud and showed off her wedding ring, while the neighbor looked at her in surprise. "You look so young," the neighbor murmured.

"I'm twenty," Isabelle lied. Neighbors could be won over. Friends could be made. Marriages could happen when both parties were old enough and bigger houses could be bought when enough money was saved. *Who are your parents?* What kind of a question was that? She should have quipped back, "Well, who are yours?"

"You aren't going to have any wild parties, are you?" one neighbor asked.

"My husband manages a restaurant," she said, though the truth was Luke had just got a job at a local pub, "and I'm a photographer," as if that explained everything.

She would walk into the small room in the back and picture a baby crawling on the floor toward her. In the kitchen, she imagined the clink of forks at a dinner party. And one day they'd build her a darkroom. Her own darkroom! She'd get her GED and take some courses, or maybe she'd just start working. What did it matter? All of life was spread out in front of her like a picnic blanket and all she had to do now was pick out the refreshments.

Luke retiled the crumbling bathroom and kitchen in a bright ocean blue. He patched the drywall and repaired the hole in the stairway. Before he did, she had slipped in a brown paper packet of photos of the two of them, a time capsule someone might find years later. Imagine, they might think, such a nice young couple and so in love! Look at them holding hands! Look at the way he looks at her.

They lived in the house for two years and when she was finally eighteen, old enough to get married for real, she put her rhinestone ring in a drawer and exchanged it for a thin gold band they bought at a jeweler. She had called her mother, telling her they'd gone to a justice of the peace. "Married," Nora finally said. "God help us all," and then she had hung up. The only thing Isabelle kept from her past was her last name.

She and Luke had come back here to the house, the two of them as dressed up as they could afford, and he had lifted her up and carried her across the threshold and everything had felt new for a very long time. Every time she walked through the front door, she smiled.

Now, though, the house felt broken. Her sorrow must have gotten into the floorboards, because now they creaked when she walked on them. Her disappointment made the cupboards sag. The neighbors had changed so many times she no longer knew some of them, and no one would consider them a young couple anymore, nice or otherwise. Luke was just a guy who had worked his way up in a local pub until he owned it. He spiffed it up and got a decent menu of food, a chef who could whip up four different kinds of pastas, some soups and sandwiches, but no matter how fancy the tablecloths, how pretty the menu, everyone in the area knew it was still really a bar, a place with dark lighting where you could sit for hours and not get kicked out, or kiss a complete stranger, and that's what they came for.

Well, she should have known better. She should have seen what was coming. Isabelle got herself a bottled water from the refrigerator and sat in the kitchen, sipping, trying to think what to do next, when the doorbell rang.

A MAN IN A DARK SUIT was at the door, and for a moment, Isabelle thought he had the wrong address, until he flashed a badge, a glint of silver in the chilly air. Her mouth went dry and she couldn't speak. She had felt better since she was home, but now her leg began to throb. "Detective Harry Burns. I'd like to talk to you about the accident, if I may," he said. He glanced at her. "Is this a good time, ma'am? You feel up to it? I tried to talk with you in the hospital but the nurses were pretty persuasive that I wait."

Isabelle eagerly led him into the living room, nearly toppling, and he quickly offered a hand to steady her, holding her tightly. He helped her to sit and then pulled up the black leather chair of Luke's for himself. "What happened to the other people?" Isabelle blurted. "Please, you have to tell me."

He looked at her mildly. "Let me get some information down, first," he said. Her stomach twisted. He pulled out a dime-store notebook and a black pen that had chew marks on the tip, and Isabelle was suddenly conscious of her matted hair, and she wrapped it into a clumsy knot. "Your husband gave us your insurance information," he said. "So we don't need to go there." He nodded at her, expectant. "Why don't you tell me what happened."

She looked at her hands, which were still jeweled with bruises. There was a thin white band of flesh where her wedding ring had been. She wanted to get it over with, so she started to talk. Every once in a while he asked her a question, but she kept noticing how bored he looked, and more than a few times he glanced at his watch. "What was your speed?" he asked. "What was the visibility?"

"There was so much fog," she said. She swallowed. "I was only going about thirty."

"Uh-huh."

"What happened to the woman and the boy?" Isabelle said.

He looked up at her and for the first time she noticed that his eyes were a soft, mild blue, like cat's eyes. "I thought you would know. The woman died instantly," he said.

The air around Isabelle turned to ice. Her skin prickled. The detective was still talking, his words swimming toward her. "The boy's okay," he said. "Scratched up, but he'll live." He tapped his pen against the pad. "From all we could gather so far, looks like you're in the clear. Appears that you did nothing wrong and the other woman was negligent." He told her they checked the skid marks and saw that Isabelle wasn't speeding. They'd seen how heavy and dense the fog was firsthand, and it was clear that no driver could see through the soup of it. "You did everything right, to my mind. You weren't talking on your cell phone, being distracted?"

"There was a hornet in the car," Isabelle whispered.

"A hornet?" He looked at her, but he didn't write anything down.

"It wouldn't leave."

He glanced down at his notes. "The coroner's report isn't in yet," he said. "If she was dead already before the accident, or on drugs, that would rule out homicide charges."

"Homicide!" Isabelle cried. "She was alive! I saw her standing in the middle of the road!" She wept into her hands and he shut the notebook. She grabbed for a tissue on the table, blowing her nose.

"You weren't speeding," he said. "You didn't flee the scene and you weren't drunk or on drugs. I'm filing the case as a formality, and I'll tell you what. I know what's going to happen before I even do it. The DA's going to reject it. The woman's car was pointing the wrong way and the lights were off. She was in the middle of the road. She was negligent. There'd have been no way you'd have been able to see the car in all that fog, no way you could have stopped. We didn't even see the smoke from the cars at first because of all the fog. Worst that'll happen is your insurance rates'll jack up."

Isabelle tried to keep track of everything he was saying, but his words seemed to be slurring.

"Forget wrongful death," he said. "There's not enough evidence for even a civil suit. And for a criminal case, we'd have to have witnesses." The detective stood up.

"The little boy—"

"He doesn't count as a witness. He was deep in the woods when we found him. Sick with asthma. Highly unlikely he saw anything." He stood up. "We'll be in touch," he said. "Don't get up. I'll let myself out."

Isabelle felt frozen to the chair. Wrongful death. She heard the door open and then close.

The woman died. She covered her face with her hands. She wouldn't kill flies. When Luke had found a mouse in the kitchen, she wouldn't let him call an exterminator and insisted on getting one of those humane traps and freeing the mouse outside after they had caught it.

She had killed a woman.

She cried harder, great tearing sobs that made her feel as if someone had punched a hole in her heart. They had all known. Luke. Her friends. She'd call them and they'd deny it, or they'd tell her they were just protecting her.

She managed to stand up, though her legs had turned to water. She should have known, too. She went into the kitchen, where her laptop rested on the table. She turned the computer on, found the local paper, and went back three days, to Friday, when the accident had happened. Nothing. It had probably happened too late to make the evening edition. She swallowed and hit the link for Saturday's paper and there it was, spilled across the front page.

Was Mysterious Murderous Crash
a Snap Judgment of Local Photographer?

Isabelle stood up and then sat down again.

A terrible fog may have led to a mysterious two-car accident Friday that killed a local woman, say the sheriff's investigators. The woman, April Nash, 35, of 134 Mayfield Street, a waitress at the Blue Cupcake, was apparently driving the wrong way on a one-way road. Her Mercury sedan was parked in the center of the road when it was slammed into by a Honda driven by local child photographer Isabelle Stein. Ms. Nash was instantly killed, and her son and Ms. Stein were both taken by ambulance to Hartford Hospital and later released in good condition. Friends say Ms. Stein was traveling to New York City, but what Ms. Nash and her son were doing on the road was unclear.

County Sheriff Lt. Bob Saldo said an investigation was pending. "We don't have witnesses, but clearly something was out of the ordinary here and we intend to get to the bottom of it." Saldo encouraged anyone with information regarding the crash to call 555-987-5940. An investigation is pending.

There was a black-and-white photo, as shocking as a slap, of two crumpled cars on a lonely road. There was her car, her little Honda, smashed like a metal toy. Pointed toward it was the other car, ruined beyond recognition. For a second, Isabelle covered her eyes. She forced herself to look again, and there was an inset of a beautiful woman laughing, her light hair artlessly cropped, her eyes big as dinner plates. Isabelle began to shake.

April Nash. Her name was April Nash and she was lovely and a mother and a wife and she was only thirty-five years old. Younger than Isabelle. She worked at the Blue Cupcake, where Isabelle sometimes went to get coffee. She had probably seen her lifting trays and chatting with customers. They could have passed each other on the street all the time. They could have been friends.

Isabelle touched the screen with her fingertips and started crying again.

When the phone rang, she almost didn't answer it. She had fallen asleep on the kitchen table, her face pressed against the wood. The wall phone was so close, it seemed to be ringing in her ears. She sat up, reaching for the receiver, desperate for the sound to stop. "Hello?" she rasped.

"You're all right?" The voice was sharp. It had been years and years of calls unreturned, letters come back in the mail. But she knew who it was and she gripped the phone. "Mom. It's so great to hear your voice. You can't imagine—"

"Your accident is in the Boston papers. Everyone is talking about it. I nearly died when I saw your photo. I called the hospital and they told me you were all right, so I didn't have to come down there."

"I'm all right," Isabelle said. She felt a sudden tug. She felt ten years old, wanting her mother there to smooth her hair back and tell her that she was Nora's baby girl. Her mother snorted. "Well, I shouldn't wonder about this mess. That's you all over, barreling ahead, getting into trouble, never thinking about the consequences. I tried to stop you when you got involved with Luke, but you wouldn't listen. And now what? You've killed a woman and ruined your life."

The floor was moving under Isabelle's feet. Her tongue felt as if it were weighted with stones. "Mom," she whispered. "Don't do this."

"Do what? You never understood anything that I was trying to do for you," Nora said. "I'm glad you're all right, but that doesn't mean I approve of your life," and she hung up the phone. Isabelle held the receiver against her forehead and shut her eyes.

~ FIVE ~

THREE DAYS AFTER April died, Charlie woke up on the floor of Sam's room, a toy airplane cutting into his shoulder. He was drenched in sweat, still in the same clothes he had worn to the hospital. He hadn't intended to sleep here, but last night Sam had shouted in his sleep and Charlie had raced in, switching on the light. "Mommy!" Sam had cried, and he looked so small and fragile that Charlie had held him until Sam fell back asleep. Charlie couldn't bear to leave him. And more than that, Charlie couldn't stand to be in his own bed alone.

For the past two days, the two of them had done nothing but sleep. He had left Sam only once, calling a sitter so he could go and take care of the paperwork for the funeral home to have April cremated. When they asked what he wanted to do with the ashes, he went blank. "Let us know," the funeral director said.

Today, though, he had to get them back in a routine. He had to call people. And he had to tell Sam that April was dead.

He was about to stand when he caught a whiff of beach salt. His head reeled. The room smelled like April. For one crazy moment, he imagined her coming into the room. He heard footsteps and he glanced up, sickeningly expectant. "You big silly. It was a mistake," she would say.

"April?" he said. Every detail of that morning rushed back to him. The smell of the coffee. The way April kept winding around him. They had argued and he'd been in a bad mood, but was that enough for her to snatch up their son and leave?

Sam coughed. The April smell vanished and Charlie looked at his son. Right now, he felt as if Sam were the only thing anchoring him to the earth, that without him, he might dissolve into a thousand pieces. You breathe, I breathe, he thought.

Charlie tucked Sam in and walked out of his room. He'd tell Sam after breakfast. He went to the kitchen and stood there for a moment. He drummed his fingers on the counter, and then he jerked open the kitchen cabinet to get plates for breakfast. When they fell out of his hands, smashing on the floor, he began to cry. April. Oh Jesus, April. His wife was dead and he didn't know why.

"Daddy."

He looked over. Sam was wavering in the doorway. Charlie crouched beside him. "Are you okay?"

Sam nodded.

"No asthma?"

Sam shook his head. "Where's Mommy?" he asked, and Charlie gently pushed Sam's bangs out of his eyes.

"Where were you going with Mommy in the car?" Charlie said carefully.

Sam didn't move. "Is Mommy still at the hospital?"

"Did you pack clothes for winter or for summer? A lot or a little?"

"I didn't pack anything."

Charlie tried to swallow the panic rising along his spine. "Mommy packed for you?" he asked. "Where were you going? Why did she take you out of school?"

Sam stepped back. "I don't know!" he said.

Sam shut his eyes and Charlie heard him humming, low and deep, the way he did when he wanted to shut people out. Today, it was one more closed door that made Charlie feel he was about to break into pieces. "Come on, Sam. You do so know! You were there! What did your mother say? What did you talk about before you left? What did you talk about in the car? Look at me when I'm talking to you!"

"You're hurting me, Daddy!" Sam cried, and instantly Charlie loosened his hands. He stood up, his body shaking. Oh God, what kind of a man was he to grab his own child like that? What kind of a father? "Sam, I'm sorry. Sam—" he said, but Sam ran out of the room, back to his bedroom, and when Charlie got there, he wouldn't open the door.

Never had Charlie hated himself so much. He stared at his hands and then he tapped on Sam's door. When there was no response, he tried to open it, but the door was locked. "Please open the door," he begged. "I'm so sorry. Please. I'm right outside."

He waited outside Sam's door for ten minutes and then finally tried the door again. This time it opened, but Sam was asleep again, sprawled on his bed. Charlie lifted him up and slid him under the covers. He bent down to kiss his son's cheek.

Charlie went back into the kitchen and put the kettle on. He didn't feel like coffee or tea. He didn't feel like straightening the house. Sick with grief, Charlie called his parents. As soon as his mother answered, he started sobbing.

"Honey." His mother never called him honey. She had never cared for April, but as soon as he told her, she got efficient, the same way she was with her garden clubs and book groups. "We'll be there tonight," she said. "We'll help however we can."

Charlie didn't know what that meant. With his parents, it usually meant money—taking care of the bills, going out to eat, hiring help, all of it somehow under their rules, as if he were still a boy instead of a man. It always ticked him off, but right now, he was frankly too exhausted to be anything but grateful. Money wasn't a problem, but he could use the help. And Sam could use the extra attention, two adults who weren't tearing apart at the seams the way Charlie was.

Charlie picked up the broken plates; he swept

and washed the floor. When he got to April's clothes, he didn't know what to do with them. He couldn't hang them in the closet, but he couldn't bear to throw them out, so he put them in a bag and stuffed it deep in the closet. In a few hours, the house was tidy, but Charlie still wasn't tired. He was cleaning up the spare room when he heard Sam in the kitchen.

"Hi, Daddy." Sam was setting the table, clumsily folding the paper napkins, anchoring them with forks, all the while his eyes glued to the little TV on the counter, which showed a cartoon hand wearing a pair of pants and dancing around. Sam moved his bandaged arm awkwardly. "I set the table, Daddy," Sam said. Charlie saw the three plates, the multicolored cereal bowl April loved. His head reeled and he sat down. "You don't have to do that," Charlie said quietly. He cupped Sam's head in his hands and tried to sit him down.

"It's my job," Sam said. "Are you going to eat with me, Daddy?" Sam carefully poured some soy milk into a puddle on his cereal. He picked out a handful of blueberries and carefully spelled out "Hi!" with them across the top of his bowl. Then he took a spoonful of cereal and lazily chewed.

"Sam." He put a jar of honey on the table and Sam looked up at him. "We have to talk," he said. "Your grandma and grandpa will be here soon. Other people are coming, too, and I want us to have some time together first."

Sam nodded, his eyes flickering. He tapped his spoon on the edge of his bowl, a disjointed rhythm. "Guess what song this is?" Sam said.

"We have to talk about the accident." Charlie swallowed. Give him time, the nurse at the hospital had told Charlie. He's in shock. "I'm sorry I yelled at you. I was just upset," Charlie said.

Sam banged his spoon to the table, refusing to look at Charlie. "I don't want to talk. What are we going to do today?"

Charlie got up from his chair and went and kneeled beside his son. He could smell Sam's breath, sweet and milky from the cereal.

Charlie felt something sharp nicking at his throat. "You know there was an accident. A terrible accident. You know how lucky it is that you're alive."

Sam nodded. "I know Mommy got hurt," Sam said, his voice small.

Charlie swallowed. "Mommy died," Charlie said.

Sam twisted away from Charlie and dug his spoon into his cereal. "No, she didn't."

"There was a crash—"

"I know that," Sam said, letting the spoon clatter. "I saw it." Sam got up from the table. Sam walked to the sink, his back to Charlie.

"Sam—" Charlie said, but Sam clapped both hands over his ears, shaking his head, refusing to turn and look at him.

Charlie stared at Sam, trying to swallow down his grief. He got up and gently turned Sam to face him. Sam's eyes were squinched tight, and Charlie carefully peeled Sam's hands from his ears. "Look at me," Charlie said.

Sam's eyes opened. "I saw her after the accident," Sam said, his voice strained.

"Sam, no, you didn't see her. You couldn't have."

"I did so. I was there and you weren't. I know what I saw." Sam drew his mouth into a thin, tight line. "I'm not hungry anymore," he said. "I don't want the rest of my breakfast."

Charlie waited until Sam left the room, and then he shut the TV off and collapsed into the chair. He put both hands over his face. He thought about what it would do to Sam when he really understood his mother was dead, when the grief would really hit. Was it so terrible if Sam was in denial—at least for a little bit longer? Wouldn't Charlie do anything to be able to be that way himself?

His cell phone rang and Charlie reached for it automatically. His mother. Friends.

"Mr. Nash?" The voice was clipped with irritation. "It's nearly ten."

He pressed the cool plastic of the phone against his cheek. "Charlie, were you planning on coming today or not?" the voice said.

His mind skipped, and he glanced at the Humane

Society calendar hanging on the kitchen door, a picture of a white kitten mewling. Oh, Christ. Today was Monday, wasn't it? Work and school and normal life and he had planned to put in a kitchen for the Liversons. Oak cabinets, adobe tiles. Was his crew there already? Ed would never tell clients personal business. And Charlie hadn't told Ed he wouldn't be coming in. "My wife—" Charlie said and then stopped. How was he supposed to do this? "An accident," he said finally.

There was so much silence on the line, he thought she might have hung up, but then he heard her breathing. "God," she said. He heard her waiting. "The crew's there?" he said, and then he had her put on Ed.

"I'm sorry," Ed said. "I didn't know how to handle this."

"Stud the walls," he told Ed. "The sheetrock should be there, too." He looked down at the notepad by the phone, flipping the pages idly, and then he saw April's handwriting: *Library. Shoe store.*

He couldn't think anymore. "Please take care of it for me," he said, and then, because he didn't know what else to do with it, he put the notepad in a kitchen drawer.

CHARLIE KEPT WAITING for Sam to have an asthma flareup because strong emotions could set him off, but Sam was now quietly reading in the dining room. "You're okay, kiddo?" Charlie asked, and Sam nodded.

You never knew with asthma. Sam had been fine until he was four and then one day he'd started clearing his throat, which turned into a cough, and next thing they knew they were in the ER.

The doctor had seen Sam immediately. He took one brief listen to Sam's chest and in minutes a machine appeared. "It's a nebulizer," the doctor told April and Charlie. "It'll open his lungs right up. Breathe," he told Sam, handing him the mouthpiece. Sam, who looked as fragile as a pearl, breathed and coughed and noisily wheezed, his shoulders moving up and down.

"Asthma," said the doctor. He waved his hands. "Good you brought him in." He glanced at Charlie and April.

"Asthma?" Charlie said, astonished. The doctor scribbled something on a chart. He glanced at Sam, who was slumped over, holding the mouthpiece. Flutes of steam wafted from the other side of the mouthpiece, stopping only when Sam inhaled. Never had Sam looked so frightened. April folded her arms tightly around her, but Charlie abruptly picked up a few of the tongue depressors on the counter and fashioned them into a kind of figure, making them march on Sam's leg until Sam gave a wobbly smile.

"No one in our family has asthma," Charlie said quietly to the doctor.

The doctor shrugged. "They don't have to. It's not always genetic. It's an autoimmune disease and sometimes just appears and no one knows why." The doctor scribbled something on a prescription pad, and though April held out her hand, the doctor gave the sheet to Charlie, along with a pamphlet about asthma. "You can all go home and get out of those pajamas," he said, half smiling. "Here, you take this." He handed Charlie a blue inhaler in a bag, like a party prize, and then Charlie scooped Sam up from the table, letting the tongue depressors fall to the floor.

The night they discovered Sam had asthma, they lay awake in bed, holding each other and talking. How could something like this happen so suddenly? Why hadn't they seen it coming? April hadn't touched a salt shaker or had a drink the whole time she had been pregnant. She had even made herself take walks every day to keep strong. She took vitamins and never missed a doctor's appointment. Why couldn't her little boy breathe?

The older Sam got, the worse his asthma got. But it wasn't just the disease that derailed Sam, it was the way it made him feel different. It broke their hearts when they saw the way he yearned after the other kids and their dogs, how he thrust his hands deep into his pockets because he knew he couldn't touch the animals. They hated taking him to a birthday party and seeing everyone else eating sugary cake; Sam couldn't have any because he was allergic to chocolate.

"It's not right," April said. When Sam was seven and he came home crying because he wasn't chosen for the soccer team at school, April marched right into the Blue Cupcake and persuaded them to sponsor a soccer team. "I'll do all the paperwork and publicity and the only thing I want is to have Sam be on the team," she told them. The team made Sam the water boy and he was so happy, he slept in his Blue Cupcake soccer shirt. She brought home two tiny blue fish in a glass bowl and set it right on his dresser. "Who needs a dog or cat? Bet you're the only boy with these rare beauties," she said. Sam's mouth formed an amazed oh, and April wrapped her arm about him.

"Oh, asthma," she said, waving her hands as if it were nothing. "Why should we let that stop us?" When he was wheezing, she'd tell him the prince and the pauper story, acting out the parts in different voices. She made faces until Sam smiled. Charlie leaned against the doorway, watching them. "You're amazing," he told her, when she finally left the room, but she shrugged. "He's the amazing one."

When Sam grew sicker, April got on the Internet. She started calling doctors and then healers and miracle workers. One day April told him she had seen a woman who told her that people with respiratory problems were troubled souls.

"What? Sam's not troubled!" Charlie said. "He gets happy just seeing dandelions sprouting in the grass."

"Well, she said these souls are unsure if they want to remain on earth. Breathing is our contract to remain here on this planet."

Charlie felt chilled.

"We have to give him an incentive to stay. The woman told me that I'm his mother, that I should know what to do."

Charlie dismissed it as a crackpot theory, but that night he woke and April wasn't in the bed. He got up and found her sitting beside Sam, holding his sleeping hand. "Please stay," she was whispering, over and over again. He went and sat beside her and she rested her head along his shoulder. "Ask him to stay," she whispered.

April read article after article about how doctors didn't always know the right thing to do. "Doctors make assumptions," April told Charlie. "They can misdiagnose."

"He has to go to a doctor!" Charlie said. "He has a chronic condition!"

"I'm not saying that," April said. "I'm just saying that doctors aren't the gods they'd like us to believe they are. We have to think for ourselves a little here."

Charlie remembered when he was sick as a boy,

his father still left at six in the morning to go to work, and his mother had the maid look after him. His mother ducked her head in to say hello to him, calling, "I'm not coming in! I don't want to get sick, too!" and then she was gone. April might be spending a lot of time with theories he considered nuts, but she still hovered over Sam. Anyone could see how concerned she was.

Charlie got rid of the drapes in Sam's room, the carpets, the books, anything that might gather dust. He cleaned the cabinets of all the foods that might jumpstart an attack, and when Sam cried bitterly, Charlie took him in his arms and promised him he'd take him to the movies.

One day, April gave him the Pulmicort inhaler. Sam put his hands to his chest. "My heart's all jumpy," he said. April rushed him to the ER for the second day in a row and called Charlie, who arrived to see her pale and shivering, leaning against the wall. "The doctor's with him now," she said.

Sam had to stay in the hospital for three days. He seemed lost in his little bed, a blue striped curtain around him, but April refused to leave his side. All April could talk about was that woman who'd told her that some souls pick up and leave because they aren't sure they want to stay. Was asthma Sam's way of wanting to leave? But why wouldn't Sam want to stay? What hadn't she given him? Why wasn't it enough?

02/03/2017

Items checked out to   p1202983x

Engleby : a novel / Sebastian

Barcode   3 7526 00100 2063

Due   **02-24-17**

The brethren [large type] / by John

Barcode   37526001269126

Due   **02-24-17**

Pictures of you [large type] /

Barcode   37526001245894

Due   **02-24-17**

Go to www.ccls.org and take the Love
Your Library Survey between Feb. 1 &
28 and be entered to win a $50 Wawa
gift card!

"Sweetie, stop," Charlie said, but April shook her head.

"You're a terrific mother," Charlie insisted.

She looked at him, her eyes huge pools. "Really? Then why do the doctors always want to talk to you instead of to me? Shouldn't they want to talk to the mother? I'm right here!"

"It's because I'm calmer, that's all."

April shook her head. "No, it's not that."

He had tried to comfort her, but he had begun to notice, too, that she was right. The nurses gave her funny looks. He went out to get lunch and when he came back, she was in the bed with Sam, holding him tightly. "I'm right here with you," she said.

A nurse came into the room and stopped. "You're pulling at the IV," she said. April shifted on the bed. "You can't be in the bed with him like that," the nurse said.

"Don't tell me what I can't do," April said. "This is my son." She hugged Sam harder. "Ma'am," the nurse said, but April wouldn't budge. Finally, the nurse reached over April and adjusted the IV.

That night, Charlie slept in the orange plastic chair by Sam's bed, but April slept in the bed with her son. Every few hours, a nurse would come in, and before they could tell her to get out of the bed, April would glare and say, "I'm not hurting him." They woke Sam to give him antibiotics. Charlie held Sam's hand, but April snapped at the nurses, "Can't you be more gentle?" Two days later, the hospital released Sam. The whole ride home, April rode in the back with Sam, holding him close. "I'll do my best so we never have to go back there," she told him.

Every year, Sam got worse. They were almost always at the hospital. When Sam first turned eight, he was so sick he was in an oxygen tent. "Every dream I had ever dreamed for him seems like it's dying," April said.

"Come on, you don't mean that," Charlie said, but April shook her head.

"When he was a baby, when I was in the house all the time, I kept telling myself, just you wait, because soon I could take him to the beach. We could ride horses. I could give him the kind of childhood I wished I had had. Now the best I can do is get him on a soccer team." She took Charlie's hand and laced her fingers through his.

"You aren't alone," he told her.

"I worry all the time. That something will happen to you. That something will happen to Sam. Nothing's forever, is it?"

Charlie lifted up her hand and kissed it. "We are," he said.

"Are we?" she said. "Are we, really? Promise me that we are."

"I want my stuffed bear," Sam said, through the tent. "I want Ricky." His eyes welled. April turned her wedding band around and around on her finger. "Oh, cookie," she said, and her voice rose an octave. Charlie touched her arm and then she curled against him.

Later that evening, Charlie came back from getting coffee and went to check on Sam. He heard the rasp of Sam's breathing. The eerie blue light of the hospital machines glowed in the dark room. April was gone.

A nurse walked by. "You looking for your wife?" she asked. "I saw her get in the car a while ago."

Charlie grew rigid. How could she have left their son when he was so sick?

An hour passed. He walked up and down the corridor twice and then went back in the room, and there was April, her face flushed, her coat open, snow dotting her hair. She was laughing. "Where were you?" he said, and then he saw that Sam was hugging his stuffed animal, Ricky, to his chest. "What's this?" he said alarmed.

April turned to him. "It's just for a few minutes," she said, her voice low. "Look how happy he is. I went home to get him."

"He's in the hospital, April. He's in an oxygen tent!"

Her face changed. He saw it, how she telescoped away from him. She turned and gently took the bear from Sam, just as a nurse glided in.

"No stuffed animals in here," said the nurse.

"He was just leaving," April said. She slid the bear into her pocket.

"Ricky. I want Ricky," Sam started to cry.

The nurse shot April a look. "Now, now, you don't want to give yourself an asthma attack, do you, Sam?" the nurse said.

April drew herself up and walked into the hall and Charlie followed her, touching her arm, making her stop and turn and look at him. "He was *happy*. For five minutes. Is that so terrible? Is that such a crime for him to be a normal boy for ten minutes? He's had that bear for years without problems. His own doctor said it was okay as long as we kept it clean. He's not wheezing from his bear."

Charlie's mouth opened and then closed.

"Where were you?" he said. "It didn't take that long to just go home and come back."

"I went for a drive," she said.

"You went for a drive? Now?"

She took off her coat. "I had to get out."

"You couldn't tell me? April, do you realize what's going on here?"

She handed him her coat, damp from the night. "I'm back now and don't you criticize me. Don't you dare tell me I'm not a good mother."

She walked back into the room to look at Sam again. Charlie followed her in, and they sat together beside Sam, who'd fallen asleep. Just outside the doorway, the nurses were talking.

"What a pain in the ass," one nurse said. April looked at Charlie. "Why do the nightmare moms have to be on my shift?" the nurse continued.

"Remember that woman here with the little girl who had Munchausen's by proxy?" the other nurse said. "Sweet and pretty, everyone liked her? She couldn't do enough for her daughter? If we hadn't called social services, that kid would have died."

April froze. Charlie stood up. April had told him that the nurses didn't like her, but he had thought she was just being oversensitive. This remark, though, seemed uncalled for. He knew what Munchausen's by proxy was: parents who deliberately made their kids so sick that they had to be hospitalized—monster mothers who sacrificed their kids' lives to fill their own need for attention.

"Let's go for a walk," Charlie said to April, and April followed him into the corridor.

The nurse was folding towels on a cart. Charlie tapped her. "What did you say about my wife?" Charlie said sharply.

The nurse stacked the towels. "Excuse me, I'm very busy here."

"We heard you. Munchausen's by proxy. What are you implying about my wife?"

The nurse piled the towels on the bottom rack. "I've been here for six years and I've dealt with a lot of parents. All I'm saying is you don't bring stuffed animals to a child with asthma in a hospital. You don't give him a peanut butter sandwich when he's allergic to it."

"What peanut butter?" Charlie said.

"Like I said, I'm very busy," she said pointedly, and wheeled the cart away.

For a while, after she left, neither April nor Charlie spoke. April leaned against the wall. She reached out for Charlie and then let her hand drift back down. Charlie couldn't stop looking at her, as if she were a door closing on him. "You gave him peanut butter?" he said finally, and she waved her arm.

"He wouldn't eat his lunch," she said softly. "It was just the thinnest layer and he ate every bite. You should have seen how happy he was and it didn't give him asthma."

"April, do you know how serious this is? Are you crazy? Are you out of your mind?"

"Out of my mind?" She drew herself up. "How can you speak to me like that? I don't sleep anymore, worrying about Sam. I can't think about anything else all day. I'm on the computer for hours every day trying to find answers, to fix this. If I'm out of my mind, I'm out of my mind with worry. What have I done to those nurses? I try to make sure everything is done right and because I make one mistake, they act like I'm deliberately trying to harm my son!"

He touched her arm but she jerked away.

"I can see dust in the air in his room here!" she said. "What about that? Why doesn't the hospital do something about that?" She drew her sweater tighter around her. "Thanks for being on my side."

"I am on your side! Of course I'm on your side!"

"Are you?" she said, and before he could reach for her, she was gone.

He told himself that she meant well. So she questioned authority. Was that so terrible? Was any parent perfect?

THINKING BACK TO those times made Charlie feel a little desperate now. Asthma mom, April used to call herself. Asthma mom. When she fought the soccer team to let Sam be the waterboy, if not a player. When she had to explain to him why he couldn't go to a kid's sleepover because it was held at a house with two cats and a dog. He knew Sam's asthma wore her down, but why had she taken him out of school the day of the accident? Where were they going?

He looked over at Sam, engrossed in his book, and then he went into the bedroom and shut the door so he could make some calls in private. Charlie called the school first, and spoke to Miss Patty, the principal. "I've been meaning to call you," she said. "We're all so sorry."

"What time did April pick up Sam on Friday?" he asked.

Charlie heard a hum radiating through the wires.

"She didn't pick him up," she said. "I told the police that."

"What? You told the police?" Charlie felt something burning in his stomach. "Wait . . . you just let him leave? Do you realize how serious this is? Don't you watch out for your kids? Don't you check where they are?"

"Mr. Nash," she said. "Your wife often came and got Sam, sometimes in the middle of the school day, often without signing him out. We had spoken to her about it."

"What are you telling me?" He thought of April, impulsively showing up, taking Sam somewhere. But where and why?

"I have it on record that someone from the school did call the house to ask where Sam was and there was no answer. And that was—around lunchtime."

Charlie couldn't speak. He gripped the receiver, his knuckles growing pale. "And you just let that go?" His voice splintered. "You didn't follow up? You didn't think to call me?"

"Mr. Nash," said Miss Patty, "I don't know how this happened, but I assure you, we watch every child and something like this will never happen again. We are all so sorry and very glad that nothing happened to Sam."

"Something did happen to Sam," Charlie said, and then he hung up the phone.

He called the Blue Cupcake, and when Katie,

the owner, answered, the first thing she asked was if they got the food basket she'd sent over.

Charlie had no idea, but he thanked her. "Did April come in to work on Friday? She didn't quit or anything, did she?"

"No on both counts. I called the house around ten when we were getting busy, but there was no answer. I ended up waiting the tables myself."

He wanted to ask her if anything seemed wrong with April, if Katie noticed anything different lately, but the words jammed inside of him.

How did things happen? He'd never been a religious person, though his parents had made him sit through church and had told him about God. He thought there might be something out there, some ordering force, but it certainly wasn't a man in a beard who doled out punishments or who tested the innocent to see just how faithful they were. Still, he lived by a kind of code. He tried to be a good man, to do the right things, to make the world a little better than it had been before he had put his stamp upon it. You could be generous with the love you gave, with the care you took with others. You could follow all the commandments that made sense to you and still the world could sideswipe you. There was no cause and effect. There was no karma. The truth was that he wasn't so sure he understood how the world worked anymore.

He and April had fretted so over Sam. Charlie

shouted at cars that didn't stop. He scolded the crossing guards for not paying good enough attention. He worried about Sam all the time.

And maybe his mistake had been that he had never worried about April.

"Daddy?" Sam's voice flew into the room. "Can we have lunch?"

Charlie put the phone back in his pocket and walked out of the bedroom. He couldn't imagine eating anything, but Sam should.

Around six, Charlie's parents arrived, honking the horn of their rented car, a Lincoln town car of all things, and then rapping on the screen door, their faces expectant. They were dressed as if they were going to a party, his father still in his business suit and tie, his white hair swept back, his mother in a fancy blue dress, her bobbing reddish curls cut to her chin. They hugged him and then Sam, and then Charlie's mother took his arm. "We'll stay as long as you need us," she said. "I'm telling you, you're going to have to throw us out."

She tilted Sam's chin. "You poor baby," she said. Sam studied the ground. Charlie shot her a warning look. "Don't you look tall!" she said quickly, and Sam stretched up to show her and Charlie felt a flash of relief.

He gave them the spare room, new sheets for the double bed. He kept waiting for skirmishes that evening, but to his surprise, there were none. Sam seemed delighted they were around, and didn't wait for affection but claimed it for himself, trailing after his grandma, taking his grandpa's hand. Sam wanted to show them the garden in the backyard, his computer games, puzzles, and the books he was reading. "Whatever you need to do, you go and do it," his mother told Charlie. "We'll watch Sam."

"He acts like he doesn't believe she's dead."

"What do you mean he doesn't believe it?" his father said. Both his parents stared at him.

Charlie raised his hands. "He's in shock," Charlie said. "In denial. He was in the car with her. I tried to tell him, but he refuses to talk about it."

"You know, I read in the *Times*, recently, that even infants grieve," his father said. "They experience loss. They may never remember their mother or their father who died, but on some deep cellular level, they know—and they grieve."

Charlie was exasperated. His father always pulled something out of the newspaper instead of discussing his own emotions. The few times when Charlie had come to his father as a kid, wanting advice, his father just quoted other people. "How do scientists know that?" Charlie asked, his voice rising. "How could anyone say that was for sure?"

"I don't know. They just do."

His mother took his hands. "Well, then, Sam doesn't have to talk about it right now," she said.

She shook her head. "Poor baby," she said, and, for a moment, Charlie didn't know whether she was talking about him or Sam.

Charlie stopped trying to talk about things with his parents, but he discovered right away that it was a godsend to have them there anyway. He took a nap that evening and woke to find his mother doing the laundry, though in Manhattan she had a laundress. Meticulously, she separated whites and darks, she poured in fabric softener and bleach at just the right time. "What, you think I never did this?" she said.

His parents helped get Sam to bed, his mother reading Sam a story in a funny voice, his father making Ricky Bear dance. As soon as Sam was tucked in, his mother took Charlie's arm. "Come on, let's sit out on the front porch," she said. "You need to relax. I brought some wine from our cellar, a perfect little red."

The night was cooling down and there were stars in the sky. Charlie's mother opened the wine and poured it into glasses she set on the porch table. "Let it breathe," she said, and then she moved her chair closer to Charlie, patting his arm encouragingly.

"Does he seem okay to you?" Charlie asked, and his mother shrugged.

"Leave the kid alone. Plenty of time for misery later," said his father.

"We haven't talked about the funeral," his

mother said. "I know this is upsetting, but you can't just leave the body at the funeral home. Would you like me to call people for you? Have the arrangements been made? Are you going to let Sam come? I think you should."

"No funeral," Charlie said. He had only been to a few funerals in his life and every single one of them had seemed barbaric to him. "She was cremated."

"Cremated! But you still have to have a ceremony. People expect it. They need it."

"I don't want a memorial. We'll scatter the ashes when we're ready."

His father studied him. "Charlie," he said finally. "What are you telling us?"

Charlie felt a flash of helpless anger at April. They had never even had a will until after Sam was born, and even then, it had been like pulling teeth to get April to do it. "Nothing's going to happen to us," she insisted. The day they had drawn up a will, she had stashed it deep in a drawer.

"You need to have a ceremony. Have people there when you bury the ashes," his mother said.

"No."

"Why are you being so stubborn about this?"

Charlie thought of April's ashes, dust in a box. He wondered how long funeral homes held ashes, if he could leave them there forever, as if they didn't exist. Why would you want to make yourself hurt more by making a ceremony out of them?

Charlie's father picked up a small plastic figure from the porch table, a Hawaiian hula girl swinging her hips that Charlie had bought to make April laugh. He studied it and then looked at Charlie. "You were only one when my mother died, so you don't remember her, but I do. Even now. When my mother died, I visited her grave every single week for five years. You have no idea how much comfort it gave me. I don't go so much anymore, but I like knowing she's there. Knowing I could go if I wanted." He touched Charlie's arm. "You need to have a place for your feelings."

One place, Charlie thought? What about in the supermarket buying pasta and remembering how April made necklaces for Sam out of macaroni? What about driving to the gas station and remembering how April was always having trouble with the car but he never did? What about, even now, walking into the house and, for one terrifying and wonderful second, smelling the soap she used?

Charlie took the hula girl from his father. "She wouldn't be there, not in a grave."

"That's where you're wrong," said Charlie's father. He threw up his hands. "I'm going to shower and then hit the hay," he said, rising heavily and going into the house. As soon as he was gone, Charlie's mother leaned toward him conspiratorially. "I don't understand it," his mother said. "I've heard the story three times already, but still, I just don't understand it. What was she doing on that road, anyway? Why would she let Sam run out of the car?"

"Maybe she didn't let him."

"What do you mean, she didn't let him? What did Sam tell you?"

"I told you, he won't talk about it. Maybe it's good that he forgets."

"Oh, sweetheart," his mother said, touching his shoulder. "You think he can forget?"

"Did you like her?" he asked quietly. He half expected her to say "who," but instead she shut her eyes for a moment. "What difference does it make?" she said, finally.

"It makes a lot of difference to me."

His mother picked up her wine and sipped. "This wine is heavenly. I don't know why no one is drinking it but me."

"What do you remember about her?" he asked. "Do you remember she used to always wear her cardigan sweaters with the buttons at the back? That she didn't eat ice cream, but she could easily go through a box of Mallomars all by herself?"

"Stop this," his mother said. "Please."

"Tell me about when she came to visit you that time in New York. What did you talk about? She was so excited. She spent days figuring out the perfect gift to give you, planning the things you could do together. She so wanted you to like her. Did you?"

"Charlie," his mother warned. "Why are you doing this?"

"Don't you have memories of Dad in your early days? Don't you go over and over them? Relive them?"

"Sometimes," she said evasively.

"You're lucky you still have each other," Charlie said. "You're lucky you're so close." He looked thoughtfully at his mother. "You know that one thing April and I had in common. We both spent our childhoods being jealous of our parents."

"What are you saying?" His mother put her wineglass down, resting it carefully at the center of the table.

"You and Dad. You've always been this unit with me on the outside. I felt so left out sometimes. I remember you kissing in the audience when I was in a school play once. I was so scared you wouldn't look up in time to see me sing my song, and when you did I was so relieved I almost cried. I felt like my whole childhood was me shouting, *Look at me! Look at me!* I kept trying to get you two to notice me instead of each other."

"You've got the story wrong."

"How have I got it wrong? I know what I remember."

She lowered her voice. "You know what you

want to remember. You saw what you *wanted* to see. Your father and I have had our moments, let me tell you. It hasn't been all peaches and cream."

"What moments?" Charlie leaned forward. His mother was in her seventies, but she was still beautiful, her hair thick and lush and copper as a penny, her skin dewy. All her clothes were expensive, simply and beautifully cut, and she still turned heads when she walked into a room. She had once shown him pictures of herself when she was nineteen and had won Miss Coney Island, a gorgeous young girl in a polka-dot two-piece, the silky championship band draped across her. His father, a Columbia law student on summer break, had taken one look at her and that had been that: two weeks later, they were married and living in a two-bedroom Upper West Side apartment with a doorman. Love at first sight that had lasted.

She waved her hand. "I shouldn't have said anything. I don't want to talk about this anymore. People have all sorts of things going on in their lives and they stay together because they love each other, or they have kids to consider, or they just think it will be worse if they leave." She touched Charlie's sleeve. "You don't have to worry about your parents," she said. "We're doing fine. Subject closed. It's you we're worrying about now. You and Sam."

All the next day, Charlie watched his parents. He knew his mother. If she said she wouldn't talk about something, you could pack a case of dynamite beside her and even light it, and she'd still keep mum. His father was even worse, so calm and unflappable, his face unreadable. When he was growing up, Charlie was never sure if his father was angry with him or not unless he came right out and told him. Even now, he could count on his hands the few personal stories his father had ever shared. The anecdotes were brief, but they were also perfect surprises, like the after-dinner mints he sometimes carried in his pockets, little jolts of sweetness that lingered.

Once, Charlie's father had taken him along to court, and Charlie had been astonished at his father's passion. His father whirled his arms in the air like eggbeaters. He practically grew ten inches as he begged the jury not to convict his client. "He's an innocent man!" he shouted. Charlie had felt his skin tighten, bursting with love and pride and excitement, but as soon as the case was over, his father had returned to his plain old ordinary self, speaking to Charlie as calmly as he did to his potted plants.

THAT EVENING, THEY all went to dinner at Derby's, a small kid-friendly pasta place Sam liked. Charlie couldn't concentrate. His parents were sitting so close together, their elbows touched. He watched his father kiss his mother on the cheek. His mother rested her hand on his shoulder when she reached past him for the salt. Sam tried to spin his fettuccine on a fork and, giving up, took small, delicate bites.

They were on dessert, sharing vanilla and strawberry sorbet, when Charlie's father excused himself. "Got to scout out the rest room," he said. Charlie watched him striding across the room; he excused himself a lot these days. Prostate, his mother had told him. The man got up five times a night because he had to pee. But he was still handsome, Charlie thought. Still had all his hair and most of his muscle tone, and of course, those steely blue eyes that had so intimidated Charlie as a child.

But now Charlie wanted to talk to his father, to be reassured that everything between his parents was all right.

"You okay?" his mother asked. "You look like you're on another planet."

"Earth to Daddy," Sam said, nibbling a spoonful of vanilla sorbet.

"Must be catching," he said. He put down his napkin and went in the direction of the restroom. He found him in the hallway, leaning against the wall. He had his back to Charlie and was on his cell phone. Business. His father was still working. He *loved* his job, and if you even mentioned retirement, he practically got apoplexy. Well, Charlie thought, good for him, and then his father sighed. "Darling," his father said, and Charlie froze because there, for a moment, he heard the same passion his father exuded in court.

Charlie put his hand on his father's shoulder and felt him stiffen. "Gotta go," he said, and snapped the phone shut, and when he turned to Charlie, his face was composed. "Who was that?" Charlie asked.

"Business. Clients. It never ends." His father tucked the cell phone in his pocket. "You know how it is," he said, but he didn't look at Charlie.

"You call your clients darling?" Charlie said.

"You must have misheard me," his father said evenly. "I said nothing of the kind. Now, if you'll excuse me, I should get back to my grandson before he polishes off all the sorbet without me."

Charlie leaned against the wall. He saw his father back at the table, feeding his mother some sorbet from his spoon, the two of them laughing, their heads bent so close they were almost touching. Anyone watching them would never in a million years think anything was wrong with such a handsome couple. "You didn't want to know," his mother had told him. "You saw what you wanted to see."

They went home and Sam went to bed, and then Charlie's parents, but Charlie stayed up. The house was quiet. The world outside was winding down. He picked up the newspaper, reading every page because what else was there to do? It was stupid, but he began to read the obituaries. He hadn't put one in for April. They broke his heart, all those others suffering the way he was. The photographs showed a smiling beefy man, a beautiful young woman, and one little kid. Each piece told a story. A love story. Charlie felt his cheeks growing hot. He didn't bother to brush away his tears, because, when you came down to it, he could have written any of those lines. And each one said the same thing: *Come home. Come home.*

IN THE FOLLOWING DAYS, the house was filled with casseroles from neighbors. The phone never stopped ringing. There were calls from his friends and one or two of Sam's pals, quiet, bookish boys who were somehow on the outside, just like Sam. Sam's teacher, Miss Rivers, called and the school sent over a big fruit basket wrapped in pink cellophane. Margaret from down the block stopped in to meet Charlie's parents and offered to sit for Sam, though she knew nothing about asthma or kids. Dan, over on Pearl Street, told Charlie that he and the wife would love to have Charlie's whole family come for dinner, any time they wanted. "Thank you," Charlie said, but how could he tell people that all the casseroles and plants upset him more, that right now it was all he could do to take care of his son, let alone be sociable?

Charlie grieved hard, and it began to worry him

how detached Sam still seemed. Charlie cried in the shower, the water storming down on him. He wept in the middle of the supermarket when he saw the packets of soup April loved. Little things made him flare with anguished fury: a couple kissing on TV, or a newspaper stand being out of the mints April had loved. But Sam—Sam moved as if in a dream. Charlie's parents didn't seem to make note of it, but it unsettled Charlie so much that, one day, he went into the backyard where no one in the house could hear him and called Sam's teacher to ask what to do. "He doesn't cry," Charlie said. "I told him his mother was dead, but he acts as if he doesn't believe me. Could he still be in shock?"

Miss Rivers was quiet for a moment. "Kids grieve in their own way and work on their own time," she said. "You just let him be."

Charlie hung up and came into the house, into the kitchen, where his father was cooking and his mother was playing with Sam. His father was a gourmet cook, who liked to putter in the kitchen and be liberal with exotic spices. At first, Charlie was a little worried about the meals his father had insisted on cooking, but now, he could bless him for the kid-friendly menus he concocted: hash browns and hot dogs, hamburgers and plain old spaghetti, mashed sweet potatoes and the creamy mac and cheese he was now popping into the oven.

He was grateful for his mother, too, for the way she took care of everything. "Museum, beach, movie, that's where we're going to go," she said, ticking them off on her hands, smiling conspiratorially at Sam. Charlie liked all the noise and fuss over Sam, the exhortations for him to eat, to wash his face, to stop biting his nails like that, did he want to bite them right down to the knuckles?

"How about we put those hands to use while we wait for lunch?" Charlie's mother asked, and drew out a box of modeling clay in bright colors. Sam looked suddenly greedy. The two of them sat at the kitchen table, and Charlie watched his mother trying to make a dog with her long manicured nails. When a nail broke, she didn't say anything but kept on working the clay. Charlie wanted to go over and hug her, but he couldn't make his legs move.

A few days later, his parents returned to Manhattan, urging Charlie and Sam to come, too. "I wish we could stay longer," his father said. It was a relief that they'd stopped talking about a funeral or a memorial service. His mother hugged Charlie tightly. "Don't do anything stupid," she said. "Don't you dare try to be brave."

Charlie wasn't quite sure what she meant, but he kissed her and then he let Sam fill her arms. "It breaks my heart to leave this boy!" she said. She hugged Sam. "What can I buy for you? What do you want?"

"He doesn't need anything," Charlie said.

"Don't be silly," she said. She leaned closer to Sam. "Sugar, your mom's an angel now," she said. She lifted one hand like a barrier against Charlie. "She's in Heaven watching over you. She sees you and you can talk to her."

"Mom . . . ," Charlie said.

Sam broke free of his grandmother's grip and gave her a glassy smile.

Charlie missed his parents as soon as they had left. The house felt strange and quiet in their absence. He would have to go back to work. Sam would go back to school. He'd have to somehow muddle through all of this. He picked up the newspaper, riffling through the first few pages and then, there, like a physical blow was April's photograph. Why was this still in the news? Why did he have to be reminded this way? She was standing in the sun, wearing a flowery dress. "Runaway Mom," read the headline. "Three Hours from Home." Had she really been running away?

He stared down at the newspaper again. There beside his wife's picture was a photograph of a woman he remembered seeing about town. All that curly black hair. "Did photographer's road rage cause accident?"

~ Six ~

SAM WAS HAPPY his grandparents had visited, but he was glad they were gone, too. He didn't believe his grandma when she said his mother was an angel. He knew that wasn't true, but she still kept saying it, over and over again. He didn't love it that they kept asking him about that day, either, and when they did, he made his mind a blank sheet of paper. He felt his voice growing smaller. "What happened?" they asked. "Do you remember?"

He told them it had been foggy, too hard to see. He didn't tell them that it was his fault. Sooner or later, everyone would know that and then he would be in trouble.

"He doesn't remember," Sam's dad said. But the truth was Sam did remember. All of it, so clear and sharp he could feel it happening all over again.

THAT DAY, THE DAY of the accident, he had come into the kitchen dressed in his favorite blue-and-red striped jersey. Usually, his mother was up, singing along to the radio and making them breakfast. "Sleepyheads arise!" she'd call. But today, his mother was sitting in the dark at the kitchen table, in her flowery blue nightgown, and she wasn't saying anything at all.

"What are you doing in the dark?" his father said. He snapped on the light and then they both saw the smudges under her eyes, the wobbly line of her mouth. His father bent to rub his mother's shoulders, but she moved away. His hand floated in the air.

She rose slowly, and gave a half smile to Sam. "I'm just tired," she said, bending down to kiss him. She cooked them breakfast, but she seemed as if she were in another world, sleepwalking from the stove to the table. She opened the refrigerator and stared inside, and then shut the door without taking anything. She burnt the edges of the French toast; she spilled the orange juice in a pool on the table and stared at it, biting down on her lip. "You look like you're going to cry," Sam said, worried, and she ruffled his hair. "Don't be silly," she said.

Nothing tasted right that morning, and the whole time they were eating, his mom didn't take a bite herself. She just leaned against the counter and watched them. His father glanced at his watch. "How could it be this late?" he said, jumping up.

His mother trailed his dad when he put his plate in the sink. She followed him when he put the juice back in the refrigerator and when he left the room to go get dressed. Sam could hear them arguing, their voices dark and angry, though he couldn't make out the words.

Sam's appetite was gone, and he pushed away his plate. His father came back into the kitchen, dressed, rubbing his elbow, his mother at his heels. "Go get your schoolbooks, kiddo," he told Sam. Sam fled to his bedroom, pulling his math book from under the bed, his science book from his desk. He hummed so he wouldn't hear the angry voices, and then his father was suddenly in his room, kissing him good-bye and leaving so quickly, Sam didn't have a chance to ask him if everything was okay.

By the time he came back into the kitchen, his mother was sitting at the table again, her head in her hands.

The teakettle whistled and his mother started, as if the whistle were directed at her. "Why are you taking so long with breakfast?" she asked, pointing her finger at his plate of French toast. "Eat. The doctor says you need protein." He didn't want to tell her he couldn't eat—that the toast tasted like rubber tires and the juice had too sharp a tang. She tapped fingers on the counter, then ran them through her hair. "It's cold in here," she said quietly, but she didn't turn down the air conditioner, which was always set on high because it helped him breathe better. Instead, she shivered. She went and got a sweater and put it on over her nightgown. "Please, please finish," she said, and he heard something new in her voice that scared him.

He got his lunch and his books and went to the front door. "I'm allowed to go by myself now,

125

remember?" Sam said, but she threw on a long coat over her nightgown, sliding her feet into a stray pair of loafers by the door. "Let me walk you, today," she said. Oakrose Elementary was just three blocks away. The whole walk, she stayed silent, and Sam thought it was better for him to be quiet, too. When they got to the school, it was already crowded with parents and kids. The door was open and a teacher was greeting all the kids, smiling at them as they came inside. Sam was about to go in, when his mom tapped his shoulder. "Wait just a minute, buster," she said, and he turned and she kneeled in front of him and looked deep into his face, almost as if she were searching for something. Her breath smelled dark like coffee. He patted his pocket and felt the lump of his inhaler. "I have my inhaler," he told her, because she always asked. "And I know where the house key is."

"Let me look at you," she said, and then she studied his face.

"Mom," he said. The other kids were rushing past him. "You're staring at me."

"Yes, I am." She smoothed back his hair. "I'm sorry I'm not myself this morning," she said quietly, "Sam, it's not you. Or your dad. It's me. It's just me." And then she hugged him so tightly, his ribs ached. "Mom—" he said, and she hugged harder and then finally let him go.

"Good-bye, Sam," she said, and then she stood

up and began walking back home. He waited for her to twist around, to give him a final wave, and when she didn't, he headed to the teacher and walked into the school.

He didn't know why he decided to go home early from school that day. It was just before lunchtime, and he was on his way to the bathroom. It was the first week of school—fourth grade! You had to be responsible and not dillydally. You had to come right back to class. He wasn't really a dillydallier, but that day, he took his time, taking the long way, exploring the bulletin board of Masks of the World, reading some of the essays about "What I would do if I were Robin Hood today." Most of the kids said things like they would get a better costume instead of those stupid tights or they'd steal candy instead of money and they'd keep all the candy for themselves. He stopped reading and idly walked to the long glass doors to the outside, and he didn't know why, but that day, he experimentally pushed the main door open, without even stopping at his locker first to get his things. You weren't supposed to go outside by yourself, not ever, and he didn't know why but he always thought if you did, a bell might go off, or Miss Patty, the principal, might run out and then you'd have to listen to one of her lectures about good behavior. He stepped out into the morning heat and then he was suddenly running, heading home, exhilarated.

He was very careful. He knew how to cross streets. He knew if anyone talked to him, he should keep on walking, and if anyone touched him, he should kick and yell "fire" because more people would respond than if you just yelled "help." No one was going to kidnap him or hurt him, not if he could help it. He bet if he begged them, his parents might even let him skip After School from now on. There was only one thing that could hurt him and that was his asthma.

Right, then left, and then left again and there was Mayfield, his street, and that was when he started to feel anxious, worrying that he had done something wrong. He wasn't sure, but would his mother still be working at the Blue Cupcake or would she be home? What would his mother say? She'd have to call the school, or maybe she'd make him go back and apologize the way she had when he had taken some bubblegum at the market, not really thinking. "All thinking is thinking," his mother told him. "That's no excuse." And his dad had said, "Give the kid a break, for God sakes." They had argued furiously, the way they always did these days, and then he had started to wheeze. "Great, just great," said his father.

"You think this is my fault?" she said, her voice breaking.

He knew the extra key was tucked in a fake rock, hidden in the hydrangeas, because his mother was always losing her keys, but when he got to his house, to his surprise, he saw his mother's car in front, the blue of it shiny, as if it had just been washed, and the front door wide open, like a mouth talking to him. She was home. For a moment, he stood perfectly still, halfway between the front door and the car door. Down the street, he heard a motorcycle backfiring. He headed for the car, and when he got closer he saw there was a big suitcase in the back, which alarmed him. As far as he knew, no one was going anywhere. He jumped into the backseat and tried to open the suitcase, but it was locked. He glanced toward the house, waiting. Where was she going?

The car was getting warmer, the air felt heavy with rain, which usually meant he was going to wheeze. Experimentally, he took a breath. It felt all right, but you could never tell. He was at the mercy of the weather. A winter chill could send him to the hospital. The summer heat wasn't good for him. His doctor gave him something called a peak-flow meter, blue plastic, with a red and green marking on the numbers. He'd breathe into the mouthpiece as hard as he could, and his breath would push a little arrow up toward the row of numbers, and if the numbers went to the green, he was fine, but if they moved to the red, then he'd have to see the doctor and no one was happy about that.

He scrunched down on the floor of the car. There was a light cotton blanket folded there and he drew it over him. He'd surprise her, jumping out and calling *"Boo!"*

It seemed like a long time. He turned around twice, he changed his position and wished for a drink of water or one of the biographies he loved to read, but that would spoil the game. He liked stories where people had something wrong with their bodies that they overcame, like Helen Keller, but when he said so in class, Bobby Lambros hooted, "Big deal, she got famous. But she's still *blind* and *deaf,* dummy!" Then Bobby shut his eyes and waved his arms around and made grunting noises, saying *"wa, wa"* like in that movie they made about her, and Sam turned away, disgusted.

Yawning, he curled up in the corner of the car, the blanket tented over him, and then, despite himself, his eyelids began to droop, his muscles lightened, and there he was, on the floor of the car, rolling into his dreams.

THE CAR WAS MOVING. Sam heard the rivery sound of the road under him, and he sat up, rubbing his eyes, pulling the blanket from him. Cars were zipping past in a blur of color. And there was his mother in front, singing along to some song on the radio. "You are my spec-i-al someone," she sang, and because Sam thought she meant him, he grinned. Her voice sounded bright, like it was full of bells. The air seemed full of happiness. With one hand, she picked up the cell phone and dialed, listened, and then she put the phone away.

His neck hurt, his legs hurt, and he was now deeply thirsty, so sluggish with sleep that he didn't feel like saying boo anymore or playing any game. "Mom?" he said, and he saw her start, felt her slamming on the brakes, pulling over to the side of the road. She jumped out of the car, tugged open his door, and made him get out, too. Her face was white.

She grabbed him by his shoulders, hard. "What are you doing here?" she demanded. "How did you get in the car? Do you know how dangerous this is? How stupid?"

Her eyes were as bright as mica, and she was wearing a red dress and the long hanging earrings he had given her for her last birthday. She looked different to him, as if the old her had been scrubbed clean.

"Why aren't you at school?"

"Where are we going?" he cried.

She was quiet for a moment. She took a step toward him and wobbled, and then he saw she was wearing heels instead of her usual sneakers. "Sam," she said, "we have to get you back to school, right now." Her voice sped up. She glanced at her watch and her face drooped. "It's nearly three," she said in amazement. "How did it get to be nearly three already? Maybe we can call a sitter," she said hurriedly, reaching for the phone.

"Why do I need a sitter? Why can't I stay with you?"

She dialed, cocked her head. "You can't come with me," she told him, and turned back to the phone. "Come on, come on, come on," she said, and then she finally hung up. "What am I going to do?" she said, and he heard the panic in her voice.

"Why? Why can't I go with you?"

"Because you can't," she said sharply. "Not just now." She paced back and forth. She picked up her cell phone and put it down. Her lower lip quivered.

"Mom," he said. "Are you crying?"

"What are you talking about?" she said. She pointed to her eyes. "Dry. See that? Dry. Nobody's crying." She stared down at her watch and then back at him, as if she were deciding something.

"Mom?"

"You'll have to come with me now," she said finally. "We'll figure something out."

He nodded doubtfully. "Where are we going?" he asked.

"Never you mind. Just get in the car and buckle yourself up." He started to get in the back but she stopped him. "Sit in the front where I can see you," she said.

"I thought I wasn't supposed to. I thought I can't sit in the front until I'm twelve—"

"Just do what I say and don't argue," she said. "Everything doesn't have to be by the book, does it? Sometimes the book is wrong." She got in and snapped on her seat belt and took a deep breath. Sam got in and pulled on the seat belt, and the whole time she made this restless tap with her fingers on the steering wheel. Being in the front seat felt funny, wrong. The sky seemed too large, the road too close.

Usually his mother drove carefully, checking the lights, keeping under the speed limit, always waving another car forward. Now, though, she wound in and out of lanes, beeping her horn, checking her watch every few minutes. The radio was off and all he could hear was the highway and his mother's breathing, and his own, which was beginning to feel a little jumpy. His mother passed a car that beeped at her and the man driving shouted something. "Oh," his mother said. "I can't even hear myself think."

Breathe, he told himself. Breathe slowly. Doctors were always telling him he had to relax, that learning to breathe right helped kids with asthma.

It felt to him like they were driving forever. "Where are we going?"

"What?" She glanced at him and then, distracted, peered back at the road.

"Mom?" he said.

She was silent for a long while and he was about

to ask again. "I don't know who I am today," she said quietly. He heard her swallow. "This will be a big adventure," she said, her voice taking on sparkle. "Don't you worry."

His mother was great about inventing big adventures.

He saw the blue sign that said a fuel stop was ahead. "I have to pee," he said, but instead of taking the exit, she pulled over along the side of the road. "Come on, you can go here," she said.

"Why can't we go to the rest stop?"

Her face furrowed in worry. "Because there'll be way too many people. There will be lines. And we don't have the time."

"Why not? Where are we going and why do we have to rush?"

"Pee," she ordered. "Please, please. Pee." Distractedly, she got out and looked around her.

Cars were whizzing by. Reluctantly, he stepped out onto the grass. "Go there, behind those trees," she said, tottering on her heels. "No one can see you. I won't look." She looked past him at the road, the blur of cars. "Quick before a cop comes," she ordered. "It's all I need, getting arrested for your indecent exposure."

He stepped back from the road and unzipped his corduroy pants and then quickly peed and zipped himself up again. When he came out, she had a bottle of water. "Hands," she said, and splashed the water on them like a fountain.

She shooed him into the car and then got in herself.

"I'm hungry," he said, and she dug into her purse and gave him some cheese crackers.

"I don't know what we're going to do with you," she said quietly, and she rested her hand on the top of his head and she got that worried look all over again, which made him feel smaller than he already was. "Please don't look at me like that," she told him.

He flinched and looked at her, but she was staring straight ahead at the road.

"I played endless games with you," she said. "I let you play hooky and took you out to movies that weren't age appropriate." She glanced at him and then looked back at the road. "The whole time I was pregnant with you, I sang you the same song every day, 'Got To Get You Into My Life' by the Beatles. I rubbed you through my belly and talked to you. You were small as a minute and I loved you. I did. And I do. How many times did I take you the emergency room? How many nights did I sleep on the floor beside your bed and argue and plead with all your doctors? Your dad adores you. He'll do anything for you, anything so you'll be safe and happy." She turned the wheel. "I do what I can. Everybody deserves to be happy, don't they?" she said, but she wasn't looking at him when she said it.

He knew enough not to ask too many questions.

Especially not now, when she had that look on her face. He watched the road ahead, the world turning into something unfamiliar and strange.

He touched her arm and she pulled it away. "Let me just finish this," she said, but he wasn't sure what she meant. She never finished anything, even when Sam did his best to help. She started painting a mural of trees on his wall and stopped after two walls, so that Charlie and Sam finished it on their own. She started writing a mystery about a librarian who commits a murder, and gave it up after chapter four. "I know the ending, what's the point of writing it?" she said.

His mother beeped at another car and changed lanes. He studied the clock on the control panel. One hour passed, then two. They had been driving over two and a half hours when the fog came in. "Damn," she said, craning her neck. "How am I supposed to see through this?" He opened his window so the fog came in. "Don't do that!" she said, and he shut it, but the cool air collected and his lungs tightened.

He sat up straighter, stretching his lungs so they could take in more air, the way the doctor had told him to do. He glanced at the signs. "Hartford," he said. "Bob's Big Boy Burgers." He swiveled to the other direction. "Gas, Food, Lodging!"

He couldn't help it. He coughed and his mother turned toward him. "Take your inhaler," she said automatically, and then he reached into his pocket, pulling out lint, two pennies, and then he felt for the plastic tube but instead of his inhaler, there was a Batman adventure figure. He glanced at his mother in horror. She was frowning again, hunched over the wheel. Then she turned to him.

"You don't have it?"

That morning he had checked for it, he had felt the plastic in his pocket, but it must have been this toy. Instantly, he felt panicky. "You didn't take your inhaler?" His inhaler was supposed to go everywhere with him. The school nurse had an extra one locked in her cabinet, but he avoided her at all costs when he saw her in the hall, because he didn't want her embarrassing him by asking him loudly "How's the old asthma today?" like she had the last time, making all the other kids laugh. "How's the old asthma?" they asked him, like the asthma was a person. Extra inhalers were in the house—in his room, in his parents' room, even in a special drawer at the Blue Cupcake. "Aren't you glad we have inhalers to make you feel better?" his dad always asked, but Sam wasn't so sure. His inhalers were everywhere and nowhere because he'd never let anyone see him use one. If he felt wheezy, he'd tell the teacher he had to pee and then he'd go into one of the stalls in the bathroom and even if no one else was in there, he'd flush the toilet to mask the whooshing noise the inhaler made.

"Are you sure it didn't fall out? Is it in the

backseat?" She slowed the car and felt around in the back with her free hand. "It's all the fog, the damp," she said. "I'll turn on the air conditioner. That should help. You wait and see." She shut all the windows and turned it on, but all it did was make them both cold, and this time, when he coughed, the wheeze was louder.

"Can you hold on?" she asked him. "We can call your doctor and get a new prescription phoned in somewhere. How about that? Can you wait?" She glanced at her watch. "It'll be fine," she said, "I'll call your doctor, have him phone in a prescription."

He coughed again, felt his lungs narrowing, which always made him panic. "Mom—"

"We'll find a hospital, then. We'll go to an ER."

"I can wait," he said. He hated the emergency room. You never knew if they were going to make you stay overnight, and they put in an IV needle, which he hated most of all because you were attached to it and the medicine they gave him always made his heart speed like a bird wildly flapping in his chest.

"I'm fine," he said, but he could barely get the words out. They both heard the accordion sound of his lungs, the thin gasping wheeze, and his mother seemed to deflate.

"Oh, baby, you're not fine," she said.

She wrenched the car around in a U-turn, startling him, making him bump back against the seat. She made a left onto another road. "Okay," she said. "Okay. We'll go back and find a town. Then we'll come back. There's still time," She picked up her phone and dialed. "Pick up, pick up," she said, and then she clicked the phone shut and looked at the map again and suddenly she was spinning the car around, changing direction on the road again, and all they could see was the fog. "If I could just see a bloody sign . . . ," she said, and then he coughed again.

The fog was so heavy now, he couldn't see the road in places. "Mommy," he said, "I'm sorry!" and then he coughed, and it was like breathing through a straw.

"I'm sorry, not you," she said. "I'm the one who's sorry." She grabbed her phone again; she punched in three numbers: 911, the numbers he was supposed to call if he was in trouble. She shouted into the phone. "If I knew where we were I could drive to a hospital!" she yelled, and then she suddenly threw the phone out into the fog. "Okay," she said, drawing herself up. "Okay." She looked at him. "Someone will be here," she said. "You're going to be all right."

"Who's coming?" He wheezed, trying to suck in air.

"Someone," she promised.

They both heard the car. She leaped outside. When he started to unbuckle himself, she reopened the door and shook her head. "Stay in the car," she ordered, "Don't get out until I tell you to. I'll make sure they see us," and when he moved to the door, she jerked his hand away. "I said, stay in the car! Don't make yourself sicker!"

Then she drew herself up, like she knew what she was going to do, and for one moment he couldn't see her. He unbuckled his belt and ran out by the car door. She was swallowed up in the fog. And then she moved closer and looked back at him and then there, coming toward them, were headlights, and she lifted one arm and waved and for the first time that day, he saw her smile, blooming like a flower, full of hope.

The headlights were coming too fast, so that he ran toward her, forgetting all the things she had told him never to do, calling her name, calling Mommy, and then she turned to him, not moving, standing still until it was too late, and then she had only a moment to stare at it, too, as though she couldn't believe it was finally here.

There was a great terrible noise, like the air screaming and breaking apart. Something slashed his arm and Sam cried out, and then he was running. And then he knew the sound screaming in the air was him. He could see that his arm was bleeding, gashed open as if someone had poured red poster paint into it. It hurt but he tried not to cry because sometimes crying just didn't do any good. "Mommy!" he screamed, but he didn't see her in the fog. What if she was hurt? Hysteria bubbled in his body. Where was she? Why wasn't she calling to him? He ran. His feet skipped over twigs and brush and the air suddenly grew hot. He ran into the woods, panting, and then crouched, his hands over his head, his eyes squinched tightly shut. He kept hearing the crash, over and over. His arm burned, and no matter how he gripped it, it wouldn't stop bleeding. He couldn't breathe! Couldn't catch his breath! Don't cry, he told himself, panicking, because he knew crying, like laughing, could make it worse, but the sobs kept heaving from him. Shaking, he curled himself into a tighter ball, he tried to purse his lips, suctioning the air up like a straw. Any minute his mom would call his name. Any second she'd wrap her arms about him. "Where've you been?" she'd say.

Don't look. Don't you dare look.

And then he glanced up, and for a moment, he saw a woman standing there, in a white dress with long black curls racing about her head and she looked just like the angels in his Sunday School book and his breath stopped. An angel, he thought, amazed, a real angel, and then, he thought, did that mean his mother was dying and the angel was taking her to Heaven? Tears flooded his eyes and he sobbed harder. The angel looked right at him so that he began to shake, and then she looked toward the place where his mother had been, as if she were motioning him. He tried to move toward them, but the angel and his mother both vanished

141

into the fog, as if they were together, leaving him behind. "Wait!" he screamed. "Don't leave me! Come back!" Then he heard another car, a door slamming and a voice calling, "Jesus," and then Sam came out from the woods, his airway so tight he felt lightheaded and he didn't see his mother at first—*don't look, don't look*—just two cars crashed together, and the angel was gone, and then he saw flames, hot and white, and an ambulance and two men in white were standing there, and when they saw him, one man moved toward him. "There's a kid!" he said. Everything was moving so quickly. Sam took a step, too, and he tried one last labored breath, as loud as a warning whistle, before he collapsed into the man's arms.

He woke up and he was moving in an ambulance on a small white cot. The two men were beside him There was a battery-operated nebulizer for him to breathe into, the bubbling, familiar sound of it, and he felt his lungs grow bigger. "That's it, breathe," said one of the men, and Sam did. His lungs opened, and even though he felt better, they said he had to go to the hospital.

"Where are they?" Sam cried, panicked. The two men looked at each other.

"Where's my mom?"

"She's following us in the car," one of the paramedics said.

"John—" the other man said to him sharply.

"I knew it! I knew she was fine!" Sam said. He craned his head to look out the front window, but all he saw was the fog.

"You'll be fine, too. Good enough to pitch a little league game."

"I don't play baseball."

"What? Now that's a crime!"

"Soccer," Sam said, though that was partly a lie.

Rest easy, they told him. They explained that he just had to see a doctor at the hospital, to make sure he was all right, and that his father had been called and was coming right away.

"Just a little asthma attack," said the paramedic. "Happens to the best of us."

"Does it happen to you?" Sam asked, but the paramedic shrugged. "My cousin gets them," he said. "Had them since he was your age and he's in his fifties now."

Sam lay still and thought about the fog, and how it could fool you. He thought about what he could tell his dad when he saw him. He thought of his mother turning toward him when she could have stepped out of the way, and he thought of the angel looking at him and then at the place where his mother was, and he folded his hands tight.

He felt a whip of fear. He couldn't see his mother following in any car from where he sat. Was she really there? "Is my mom still behind us?" he cried, and the paramedic gave Sam his hand and let him hold it. Sam heard one of the men swallow.

"Of course she is," he said. "Of course. Don't you upset yourself now. Your job is just to relax and to feel better."

SAM HADN'T FELT BETTER. Not back then, and not right now, either.

His grandparents hadn't helped. His father didn't help. His father watched him. Every time someone mentioned his mother being dead, he shut his eyes and hummed. He pressed his hands against his ears, or he quickly left the room so he wouldn't have to listen a second longer, he wouldn't have to think about why his mom wasn't with him. *Don't say it. Don't say anything.* Inside, he felt flooded with tears, but he wouldn't let himself cry because he knew if he did, he would never stop.

The people who came to the house looked at him like he had a secret. *What happened, what happened, what happened?* Sam didn't have many friends, but his father had let him invite Don over to play chess, but Sam had the feeling that Don was letting him win every game because he felt sorry for him. "You don't have to let me win," Sam said.

"Who's doing that?" Don said, but shortly after, Don said he wanted to go home. Sam saw the relieved way Don ran to his mother when she came to get him.

He thought of his mother watching him when she should have been watching the car coming toward him. It was his fault. All of it. "Where were you going? Why did she have a suitcase?" his dad kept asking.

"I don't know," he always answered.

"God helps those who help themselves," his grandma had said to his father, and his dad had snorted, but Sam kept turning that phrase over and over in his mind. How could he help himself so God would help him and his mom? He shut his eyes. Think, he told himself. Think. He had seen an angel with his mom. Maybe he had to find out where she had taken his mom and if his mom was all right there, and then maybe there could be a miracle and none of this would have happened. But how was he supposed to do that?

"Sam! Want to go to the library?" Charlie called.

THE OAKROSE LIBRARY was cool and quiet and one of Sam's favorite places. "Take out as many books as you like," Charlie told him.

Sam picked out three books on his favorite superheroes, Silver Surfer, Flame Boy, and Mr. Invisible, guys who could change quickly and do anything, who could save the world in seconds. He was about to go find his father when he bumped into a stack of books, banging his elbow. As soon as he saw them, his hands began to tremble. Angels with big wide wings flew across the cover. He was mesmerized by their calm faces. They looked as if they knew a great secret. It was as if this book was meant to be here, as if it was a message for him specifically. He traced the faces of the angels with his fingertips. "Knowledge is power," his dad always told him. Sam scooped up the books. Maybe there were clues in here.

His dad only casually glanced at the titles of the books Sam checked out, but as soon as they got home, Sam felt anxious about opening the angel books right away, as if he might be pressing his luck, so instead he leafed through the superhero books. All that afternoon, Sam read, but he didn't feel as happy as he usually did when he read. Mr. Invisible could escape evil, but he still was haunted by the death of his wife who'd died in the chemical fire that had made him invisible. Sam threw that book on the floor and reached for another. Flame Man got rid of a man-eating robot that was terrorizing the city, but he ended up losing his daughter.

He picked up one of the angel books and began flipping through the pages, skimming the story. His heart felt like it was pulsing through his skin. He read a whole book about a boy whose guardian angel helped him win a baseball game. It was a good story, but it didn't really help any. He leafed anxiously through the next one. None of the angels had black curly hair like the one he'd seen. They were blond and pale and gold bands of light circled their heads. He turned the page, his hands shaking. *Angel is the Hebrew word for messenger,* he read. A messenger! He knew it! *Angels sometimes appear to people when their loved ones are about to enter the Ever After.*

The Ever After. Sam's mouth went dry and he felt tears pushing at his lids. But where was the Ever After? Sam flipped the pages and he saw a drawing of a weeping man looking up at an angel floating in the sky and just above the angel's head was a smiling woman who seemed to be reaching out to the man. He searched for the caption. *Angels can be a kind of telephone through which we can talk to those who have passed on. Angels can even manifest those loved ones to us.*

Sam felt as if the world were tilting. He could talk to his mom! He could hear her voice! But manifest. What did that mean? Sam jumped up from bed and ran to his student dictionary, thumbing through the pages so wildly, he tore one of the edges. *Mad. Magpie.* There, there it was. *Manifest—to appear.* His mother could appear to him, like a hologram, like a dream. He could see her again and tell her he was sorry and she would hear him and talk to him. He cupped both hands over his mouth.

Sam grabbed up another angel book and opened it, sprawling across his bed. He had to learn more, he had to know everything he could about this. There was a sentence jumping out at him in bold black letters. "It is not man's place to question angels or to demand anything from them," the book warned. "All power comes from God and angels are simply God's messengers. It is up to angels to show you signs and it is your job to decode the meaning. Above all, be humble and full of gratitude."

Sam shut the book, thoroughly confused. What was this, that even if he saw the angel again, he wasn't allowed to ask her anything? And what signs was the book talking about?

He heard his dad rustling in the other room. Had an angel come to his dad, too? He didn't know what his dad would say if Sam told him he had seen an angel and his dad hadn't. Would his dad even believe him? Would he tell him there was no such thing the way he had when Sam had absolutely known for a fact that there was a monster under his bed, even after his father had shone a flashlight there and showed him the clean, empty floor? Would his dad try to change his mind? And even worse, would his dad start asking more questions about the accident that Sam didn't want to answer? "Be humble," the book had said, so did that mean if he told his dad or anyone, it would be bragging? Sam closed his eyes and pressed the book to his forehead.

Later that night, he went out on the back porch and looked through his telescope at the stars. He didn't really think Heaven was in the sky, like some big playground. He didn't think you could look up and see angels waving at you from the clouds. He didn't know whcre people went when they died, only that it was somewhere, and he had never needed so desperately to know where it was until now.

He stared up at the stars. No one knew what was on some of the stars. There was the Big Dipper. There was Orion. He squinted and readjusted the lens. There were people who found new stars all the time, and he wondered, What if angels live on those stars?

Suddenly he felt terrible, like any moment he might cry. He knew that the light from stars was light that was dead already, that what you were seeing was the past, not your present, and certainly not your future. What if the angel never came back to him again? Sam knew a few prayers from Sunday school, but instead, he shut his eyes and took a deep, long breath. *"Please,"* he said out loud.

A FEW DAYS LATER, his father went out and came back with a box. He looked a thousand years old to Sam, and his eyes were red. Sam saw his father put the box high up in the closet and then he got on the phone. Sam heard his father say his grandparents' names and then right away there was arguing. "It's not wrong," his dad said. "It's the best I can do right now. I'll have a service when and if I'm ever ready." Sam heard his father talk about how Sam would be going back to school, how he would be going back to work. Sam turned up his music so he couldn't hear. He reached for another book, this one set on another planet, and when Bud, the main character, shot off in his rocket into space, Sam glanced out the window as if he might actually see it.

~ SEVEN ~

THE DAYS FOLLOWING the accident, Isabelle stayed in the house, curled on the sofa, a blanket thrown over her. She didn't eat or answer the phone. She didn't change her clothes. She couldn't bring herself to shower. Every time she shut her eyes she saw April Nash standing in front of the car, her dress furling in the wind, her mouth moving, as if she were trying to tell Isabelle something important.

The phone rang, jolting Isabelle awake. Sweaty, she pulled her damp shirt away from her skin. She listened to the answering machine. "Baby?" Luke was calling again, but she didn't get up.

He sounded so upset. She had seen him cry only once, after their first failed pregnancy. They hadn't told a soul that she was pregnant, not until the first trimester was over, and then, they told everyone. Isabelle had mailed Nora a little note: "You're going to be a grandmother!" believing that this, finally, was the thing that would make her mother forgive her. When it didn't, she thought, well, surely when the baby was born. Imagine that. Driving up to Nora's with a baby in a car seat in the back. Nora might be able to resist Isabelle, but who could resist a grandchild? "Babies are gifts from God," Nora always said, and if babies were the gifts, surely their moms were the wrapping.

Luke had come home with tiny little shirts and socks so small they could fit dolls. He bought a little leather jacket that said BORN TO WEAR DIAPERS on the back. Every night, they lay in bed, holding hands, whispering names to each other, like mantras, each one so beautiful it could break your heart just saying it. *Cecile. Adriana. Wyatt. Cody.*

Every night, Isabelle put her hands on her belly. "Mommy's here," she whispered, and then she laughed out loud.

She was four months pregnant when it happened. She had gone to her appointment alone that day, in a new bright blue cotton maternity dress, even though she hardly had a belly at all. She couldn't wait for the doctor to examine her, a no-nonsense stick-in-the-mud who nevertheless had the reputation of being the best doctor on the Cape. She was spread across his examining table, naked under a paper gown, and she felt ripe and happy. He spread the imaging gel on her stomach and ran the ultrasound probe across her skin. It was Isabelle's favorite part of her visits now, seeing her baby on the screen, having the doctor point out the rapid little heartbeat. Even the doctor would usually manage a smile, but this time, he had gone silent, frowning so darkly, Isabelle propped herself up on her elbows. "What is it?" she had cried. He had stood straighter, and then he had carefully wiped off the wand and set it down, without once looking at Isabelle. He glanced at the nurse, who seemed to Isabelle to visibly flinch.

"What is it?" Isabelle whispered. The doctor wouldn't meet her eyes.

"There's no heartbeat," he said quietly.

Isabelle couldn't stop crying. The doctor kept spinning platitudes at her. He told her this was nature's kindest way of making sure an unviable baby wasn't born. He told her that she could always try again, that in fact, it would be easier next time, because time and time again, he had seen how after losing a baby, a woman would get pregnant right away, and the next baby would often be perfectly healthy. And then, for the first time since she had been coming to him, he touched her shoulder, a gesture so simple that she cried even harder. "We have to remove the fetus," he told her quietly. "A more elaborate D and C. I'd like to schedule you for outpatient surgery tomorrow," and then she looked up and saw the sadness in his face, and that was when she really felt frightened.

She walked out into the waiting room, and the blonde she had laughed with caught Isabelle's face and then her own face went pale. Then Isabelle was downstairs in the hospital lobby, sobbing on the phone to Luke to come and get her.

No one even looked twice at her. It was a hospital, Oakrose General, full of misery.

When Luke came, his face was terrible, and as soon as they got home, he hugged himself around her. He hid his face against her shoulder, but she could hear and feel his deep sobs. His body shook, like millions of tiny earthquakes. He took her to bed and lay holding her. "I promise. Nothing but good things from now on," he said.

For you, too, she thought, but she was too empty to say a single word.

Good-bye. Good-bye, good-bye, good-bye.

THEY HAD TO WAIT six weeks before they could try again, a date she marked on her calendar, determined, but they never became parents. She did yoga to soothe her nerves. She ate vegetarian and cut out chocolate and salty snacks and took her vitamins. She woke Luke up at four in the morning to have sex because her expensive ovulation kit told her it was optimal timing. Every time her period came, she wouldn't allow herself to feel bad. She saw her child, floating above her, like an angel spirit. "Come on down," she encouraged.

After six months, she stopped buying ovulation kits because it was too stressful. After a year, she quit taking the vitamins; she stopped going to the fertility specialist because the yearning in his waiting room was too palpable and their bank account was just about depleted. Finally, when the doctor told her that she couldn't have children at all, she cried for weeks and then told Luke she wanted to adopt.

She imagined a little Chinese baby with satiny black hair and almond eyes, but Luke looked at her as if she were crazy. "I don't want a child if it isn't mine," he said.

"Of course it will be yours!" she said, horrified, but he shook his head. "I don't even want to discuss it," he told her. "I'm sorry. I love kids and I want them as much as you do, but I want my own. That doesn't make me a bad person, Isabelle, so stop looking at me like that."

Maybe that was when things started to really go wrong for them, when a rift grew that couldn't be repaired. Every time they made love, she couldn't help but feel a dark cloud descending over them. When he reached for her, she always felt as if a part of her were pulling back; she couldn't separate making love from making children, neither of which seemed to be really happening.

Luke grew quieter and quieter. He began coming home later, calling her from the bar, where he was now having musicians come in and play late sets, music so loud, Isabelle never wanted to go. "Be home soon," he told her, and when he was, he smelled of smoke and beer. And sometimes perfume.

It began to seem like the worst kind of cruelty

that her job was to photograph kids. She fell in love with their faces and got upset when parents didn't fuss over them enough, or hug them, or seem to realize what a blessing it was to have children. A woman came in with five kids and sighed to Isabelle, "I feel like the little old woman who lived in a shoe," she said. "I don't know what to do with them."

"I'll take them," Isabelle said, and the woman laughed, but she didn't realize that Isabelle was only half kidding.

Isabelle wished every child were her own. She developed the pictures and studied the images and there, in the background, she could almost see the ghosts of her own children. She came home too tense to notice how Luke was drifting away from her, how he seldom told her about his day or kissed her mouth anymore, until he, like her babies, was gone.

He's only around now because he doesn't like losing, Isabelle thought. She had seen how angry he got when his team lost, how sour he was when the bar wasn't mentioned in *Boston* magazine as one of the best bets, how he had called up the editor and extended an invitation for a free dinner and wine flight, how he had persisted until the editor came and wrote the bar up in the magazine. "I'm coming over there," he had told her on the phone, but she was too numb to even know how she felt about it.

Her phone continued to ring, but she let the machine pick up. "Isabelle, I know you're there," voices said. *Isabelle, Isabelle*. The voices chanted her name like an incantation. Jane called, and then Lindy, and when Michelle called, Isabelle heard Andi babbling in the background. There was an almost constant rapping at her door, and sometimes notes slid through her mail slot. Call me. Let me know you are okay. Friends wanted to make sure she was all right. They told her how lucky she was to be alive, how fortunate they were to still have her. What an awful thing, they said. How horrible. I don't know what I would do if I were you. It wasn't your fault, they said. Don't even think it. It wasn't your fault. And as soon as she heard that, well, of course, she thought it was her fault because really, who else's fault would it be? Who else was there to blame?

"Whose fault was it, then?" she asked out loud. The house ticked around her. Her mouth felt dry. It felt like the first time she'd spoken in days.

Luke called twice a day. She could hear the clatter and clink of glasses behind him, the constant sound that began early because there was always someone at the bar who wanted a drink, even at six in the morning on a bright sunny day. She never picked up any of Luke's calls, but she couldn't help listening to his voice. He asked if she wanted to talk. If he could come over. "I can take care of everything for you," he said. She burrowed deeper into her blanket. "I'm still your husband," he said. *Hang up,* she told herself. *Hang up now.*

When the phone rang again, she automatically screened the caller. "Isabelle, this is Harry Jaspers from *On the Cape* magazine." His voice was soft and jolly, as if he had just been listening to the funniest joke. "People are interested in your story," he said. "You wouldn't believe how many people! And you wouldn't believe the misconceptions they have about you. I believe that you should have a voice. Call me on my cell. Let's do it before things get out of hand." Isabelle shut her eyes. The click of his hang-up seemed to reverberate inside her. What things were getting out of hand? She shivered.

Sleep. All she wanted to do was sleep for months and wake up and have all this be over. She shut her eyes, willing her breathing to steady, her heartbeat to calm, and then, soon, she fell asleep again.

She began sleeping more, and the more she slept, the more she wanted to sleep, deep and dreamless, as if she were drugged. She didn't need food or water or a hot shower or clean clothes. No, all she needed was this blessed sleep. She kept the blinds drawn so she didn't see the outside world, and she slept.

HANDS WERE LIFTING her up, and she swatted at them. There was a buzzing sound swarming in her

158

ears. "Sleep," she said out loud, burrowing deeper into the couch, but someone was pulling it from her, taking it out of her hands. She shut her eyes tightly. It was daylight. Bright, shiny hot. The blinds were up and a window was open and she smelled cut grass. She willed herself to tumble back down into her dreams.

"Isabelle. Jesus. Come on, wake up, baby."

She smelled him first and then her eyes fluttered open. Luke was beside her, staring at her in real concern. "Go away," she said. Her mouth was dry. Her tongue felt thick and pasted to the roof of her mouth.

"I will not," he said. "You don't answer your phone. You don't come to the door. Your friends called me, worried about you. Michelle even came to the pub to find me. They must have been worried because they sure as hell wouldn't contact me otherwise."

"You used your key," she accused.

"No, I came in through the window. Of course I used the key. I was worried."

He helped her up, and when she winced, he stopped, waiting for her to catch her breath. "Get your sea legs," he told her.

"Where are you taking me?" she asked.

"Shower," he told her.

She flapped her hands. "I don't want a shower."

"Yes you do. Maybe you haven't noticed, but you smell a little ripe. Plus, it'll wake you up." He

159

helped her into the shower, sitting on the toilet while the water rushed over her. She gasped at the hot spray. He poured shampoo into her hand. He handed her liquid soap. She was surfacing, fighting it, but every time she tried to shut her eyes, to sink back down, the water propelled her back up.

He reached for her hand as she gingerly stepped out, and then wrapped her in a towel. "Clean clothes, then a sandwich," he said. "I bought groceries. That fancy French cheese you like. Fresh tomatoes. A purple onion."

"I don't want it. I don't want you here."

"Yes you do."

She let him wiggle a long dress over her head, even though she almost never wore dresses anymore, preferring her jeans and sneakers. She was limp when he pulled on her bikini panties and slid on the red stretch shoes she loved. He led her into the kitchen, folding her onto a chair. "Sit," he ordered. She heard the rustle of bags, the clink of dishes. "I'm not hungry," she said, but when he set the plate in front of her, she smelled the sandwich and was suddenly ravenous. "Eat," he said. "You need to eat." He put one hand on her shoulder, just for a second. "I'll clean up."

"I don't want you cleaning—"

"Shhh," he said, and grabbed the mop.

She ate both halves of the sandwich he had made and polished off a glass of juice, too. Her head cleared and she smelled the bright lemony tang of the cleaner he was using. Her scalp tingled from the peppermint shampoo. "What day is it?" she asked him.

"Thursday."

"I need to go back to sleep."

"You need fresh air," he told her. "You can throw me out later, but right now, you're coming with me. Just out on the porch. It won't kill either one of us." And then he took her to the swing and even though it was big enough for the two of them, though they used to spend hours on it, talking, holding hands, now he sat on the steps, giving her space. She took long, even breaths. He didn't once reach to touch her. He didn't speak but looked at her, waiting. "So," he said. "What's the story, morning glory?"

"Why didn't you tell me she died?" Isabelle finally asked.

"How could I tell you that?" he said quietly.

"You didn't, but a detective did. He came here and told me. Then I saw the newspaper article. She was only thirty-five."

He folded his hands in front of him and looked down at them.

"I could have killed her little boy."

"But you didn't. He's alive and so is his father. And so are you. And that woman was in the middle of the road. Her car was turned around. What was she thinking?"

"But the newspapers say—"

"Oh, the newspapers," he said. "They get everything right, don't they?"

"I keep thinking if I hadn't gone on that road, or if I had left the car, taken a plane or a bus. If a million other things had been different—"

"Don't do this, Isabelle."

"Don't you ever feel that in your life?" She thought of his affair, of the inadvertent way he had ruined their marriage, of their lost babies. "Luke," she said, "why are you here? I'm not coming back to you and you already have someone else."

He glanced at her. "I fucked up," he said. "And maybe I'm doing penance. And why wouldn't I be here? A terrible thing happened."

He stood up, brushing his hands against his pants. "How do you feel about Chinese for dinner?" Luke said. "I'll even cook."

That night, he made spring rolls and chicken chow fun. He cleaned and made up the bed for her with fresh sheets and blankets. "In you go," he said. She was too tired to argue. She lay down. Her lids fluttered shut. "Thank you," she said, but when she lifted her head, he was already gone.

Isabelle woke with a start, clammy, unsure of what she had dreamed but having a feeling that it was bad. She was holding one of the pillows against her, and she pushed it away. She heard something. She quietly got up from the bed and listened.

Snoring. She walked to the living room. There on the couch was Luke, bundled into a blanket, half hanging off the couch, his mouth a small, damp O. She watched him. For a moment he looked like the boy she'd fallen in love with, the young grease monkey working at a gas station, uncomplicated, steadfast in love, a boy who loved her enough to run away with her. She thought of him at his bar, so proud he'd shine the counters the way other men shined their cars. His eyes opened and he saw her, but he didn't move. He kept silent, as if he were waiting for her. Then she turned from him and went back to bed.

In the morning, Luke was gone. Isabelle was soaked with sweat, and her feet itched, but there was music playing in the living room. He had set the table for her breakfast, cut up some fruit for her, left cereal in a bowl. There was a note: "I'm sorry. Call me any time. Eat. Shower. Live your life."

BY THAT AFTERNOON, three reporters had called her, and she ignored every one of them. She waited for her bruises to heal, and though she told herself she wouldn't, she kept reading the papers online. Instead of understanding more, she understood less. People loved this story. They loved the mystery, the human interest. Isabelle didn't like reading about herself—she flinched every time she saw a photo—but reading about April was something else.

Today there were photographs. There was April in jeans and a sweatshirt, hugging her son. There was a photo of April wearing a Blue Cupcake T-shirt, cheering in the stands of a soccer game.

Isabelle scanned the page. There, at the bottom, was a photograph of her. She felt sick. It looked like they had doctored the photo, darkening it to make her look sinister. "Photographer refuses to speak," the caption read, which made it seem as though she had something to hide, when instead, she just didn't know what to say. "What Was the Real Accident?" the headline blared.

Was the mysterious crash that occurred outside Hartford one week ago a tale of two suitcases? The two-car crash occurred on Crescent Road, a back road recently closed for repairs. Unnamed sources say that remnants of suitcases were pulled from both vehicles.

No formal charges have been filed against Ms. Stein, who was driving below the speed limit, and, according to reports, had tried to stop. Investigators still have no clues why April Nash's car was turned around on the road, or why her child was outside the car.

Grieving husband and father Charlie

Nash refused to comment on the accident or on the charred suitcase later found in the car. "It's a personal matter that we are doing our best to get through," he said.

Neighbors say the couple was happily married and there were no signs of trouble in the family. "I don't know," said a neighbor and friend who wished to be anonymous. "They always seemed to have the perfect life to me."

Isabelle stared down at the article. April had a suitcase, too. Where was April going? There was another photograph, and as soon as she saw it, she knew who it was.

Charlie Nash. The photo was a snapshot, and a little unfocused, but he had a nice, regular face, and all you had to do was look at it to see how filled with grief it was. "Charles Nash leaving the police station." She touched the photograph as if she could comfort him.

She googled Charlie Nash. Isabelle had heard of him, the name sounded familiar. The screen flooded with entry after entry, and every one seemed to jump out at her like warning flares. She forced herself to focus. He had such a life and it was all here, line after line after line. "Oakrose Housing Works Honors Charles Nash." "Charles Nash Home featured in *Cape Cod Homes*." She clicked on it, and a photo of Charlie Nash appeared, beaming in the middle of a construction site, his long hair gleaming and shiny in the sun, and then she thought, of course. Charlie Nash. She had seen him around town. "The One Contractor People Love" the article was titled. Fingers pressed against her temples, she read. " 'Renovating a house is like falling in love, discovering all its secrets and loving the house anyway.' " There was another photo of Charlie covered in sawdust. " 'I love them like they are family,' Nash laughs. 'When the job is done, it's done, though sometimes, I admit, I drive past the houses to see how they're doing.' "

She clicked off the computer. Oh, fuck, he was a good guy. He was the kind of man people wrote articles about, and even worse, all she had to do was look at one picture to see just how much the camera loved him. You couldn't fake a smile like that, or that look in his eyes, mischievous and intelligent. She clicked on a few more photos and in every one he was beaming, like a man who knew his life was wonderful. Isabelle's hand froze on the keyboard. She couldn't look at any more, no matter how much she wanted to, because the more she knew about him, the more she wanted to know, and the more she knew, the more it hurt.

Isabelle put her head in her hands. Nash Homes. She had seen the signs, the logo of a house with smoke coming out of a chimney, a blue picket fence and flowers, the kind of house everyone wanted.

She got out the phone book and, hands shaking, opened it.

Charlie Nash lived just six blocks away from her.

She'd probably seen him a million times, at the beach, the supermarket, getting pizza. She had most likely seen April and Sam with him, a family splashing beside her in the surf, buying ice cream cones at Jelly's. They all lived in the same small town, and yet they were somehow strangers.

SHE STAYED INSIDE for a few more days, and then, on Tuesday, a week and a half after the accident, Isabelle cautiously went out. The summer people were all gone, and the streets were emptier. She kept a low profile, hidden behind dark glasses. At first she kept to the more deserted areas, the line of beach, too cool for swimmers now; the wooded areas; but gradually, she ventured to the shopping district. She tried to walk with a purpose.

She didn't know what she expected, but to her surprise, no one did more than occasionally glance at her.

Isabelle walked from one end of town to the other. She went into stores she didn't really have any business in—a glass store, a candle shop— just for the pure pleasure of being out in the world, of moving around. When she bumped into Laney, an old client, at the greengrocers, Laney simply hugged her, and said, "So glad to see you," as if nothing had happened.

That night, when there was a knock at the door, she was surprised that she wanted to answer it, that she yearned for company, even if it was a two-minute chat with someone canvassing for money. She peered through the window expectantly. Michelle and Jane were standing there, talking intently to each other, their arms full of packages.

She pulled open the door and, instantly, Jane reached for her. "Don't even think of sending us away," Michelle said gravely. "We brought Indian takeout and a video and we're staying until you kick us out."

Isabelle looked at Michelle's flushed cheeks, at the sunflowers tucked under Jane's arm. She was surprised when she felt tears stinging her eyes.

"Oh, Izzie, I know," Michelle said.

Isabelle shook her head. "No, no, it's just—well, I'm just so happy you're here." She opened the door wide.

That night, Isabelle ate half a carton of veggie tandoori. "Have more," Jane kept urging, but she could really only pick. Isabelle tried to concentrate on the film, a comedy about two girlfriends in love with the same guy. She laughed when her friends laughed. She felt them watching her, making sure she was okay, and when Michelle asked if she wanted them to stay the night, Isabelle shook her head. She was tired, but it wasn't the same kind of exhaustion she had been feeling. Before they were out the door, Michelle turned and gave Isabelle a hug. "Just remember, you're not alone," she told her.

MORE AND MORE, people gave her advice. Take it easy. Take your time. Don't rush back into work. Figure out what you want to do. She called Dora, Michelle's friend in New York, to see if the illegal sublet was still available. "If you make a move in the next two weeks, it is," Dora told her.

She felt something warming in her stomach. She could still have a new life. She'd leave and all this would fade, like a stain she'd bleach from a shirt.

The day the insurance company processed her claim, Isabelle went to get a new car. Lindy had offered to go with her, but somehow it seemed important to Isabelle that she do this on her own. She remembered how anxious she had been driving home from the hospital with Michelle, but that was because it was all so soon. She had been so raw.

She took her bike, figuring she could put it in the trunk of whatever new vehicle she came home with.

The bike glided into the lot. No one was there except for two bored-looking young men in white shirts and ties, their hair slicked back. When they saw her, they perked up and whispered something to each other, their faces ruddy from the heat. The taller one came toward Isabelle. "No one comes here on a bike," he said cheerfully.

"I do," she said. "But I want to leave in a Honda."

"Let me show you," he said.

He touched the back of her shirt, guiding her toward some cars, and she flinched a little.

She slid her hand along the side of a blue car and felt a little queasy. "Get in and see how this baby feels," the salesman told her, opening the door. Isabelle got inside. He was standing outside, grinning at her, all lips and bright white teeth. At first, she felt the same unease she'd felt riding home from the hospital, but she shook it off and turned the key in the ignition. The motor rumbled and then, suddenly, she felt a hard, thick piece of glass slam down between her and the salesman. He was saying something, but Isabelle couldn't hear it. It was ninety degrees outside, but her skin was cold and she shivered. She swallowed hard, fighting the ball of panic rising in her throat.

He opened the door and leaned toward her. "Are you all right?" he asked. "If you don't mind my saying so, you don't look so good." He leaned closer. "You aren't going to throw up, are you?" he asked.

Her hands flew to her head. His voice was coming from underwater. Panic was thumping so hard in her body, it felt as if it were going to break through the skin. She knew if she moved she might die.

"Ma'am?" the dealer said doubtfully.

She began to shake all over. She couldn't do this. She gripped the wheel so tightly, her knuckles grew pale. She was going to die and she knew it and there was nothing anyone could do about it.

"Ma'am!" The dealer's voice was sharp this time and then he touched her and she felt something breaking and she managed to move, jolting out of the car. As soon as her sneakers hit pavement, she felt her heart slow. She wouldn't have been surprised to see shards scattered on the ground. She stared at the car as if she'd never seen one before.

The dealer's smile had gone funny and stiff. She pretended to study her watch. "Oh, look at the time," she said. She nodded like an idiot. "I'll come back. I have to run now." She couldn't look at him. She grabbed her bike, but her legs were too wobbly to get on it. Her whole body felt like a rag doll, limp and useless, and she began to walk her bike, leaning on it for support, the two miles home.

Isabelle had never really been afraid of anything in her life. She'd never had a phobia, never had to sleep with a nightlight, and heights didn't bother her. She had climbed up scaffolding to get a shot she wanted; she had waded into freezing waters and when a power line snapped and snaked toward her, sparking with current, she calmly took its picture. And of course, she hadn't been afraid of running away with Luke. Now, she was terrified of something. She had been driving since she was fifteen and suddenly, just the thought of getting into a car made her feel as if she were dying. She couldn't imagine even being a passenger in a car. Not after what happened. She tapped her hands on the counter. She wouldn't let this beat her. She'd fly to New York, then. She'd live in a city where you didn't need to drive at all, where you could walk everywhere.

THAT EVENING, WHEN the sky was clear, she took a walk, hoping to break up the long night ahead of her. She mindlessly wound in and out of the streets, and when she found herself walking down Mayfield, Charlie and Sam's street, she didn't question it. She didn't wonder if it was her subconscious guiding her here or if it was a simple coincidence. She knew she couldn't have stopped going this way if she had wanted to. Her legs kept carrying her forward, stopping only when she saw their house.

All the lights were blazing inside, the same way hers always were because it made the house feel less empty. She could hear music, something with a thumping beat, a bright chime of singing voices that she didn't recognize. Kids' music. For a moment, she stood in front of the house, unable to move. There was a yellow toy truck parked on the front lawn. She felt her body listing toward the light of the house. She took a step, trying to steady her balance. She moved up on tiptoe, craning her neck. She hated herself for what she was doing, but she couldn't stop. She saw someone move past the window and her heart slammed in her chest. She jumped back, toward the hedge next door, crouched behind it so she wouldn't be seen. The front door suddenly flew open. She heard a man's voice call, "Sam!" and then she saw the little boy on the porch, his shoulders heaving, his long hair in his round, dark eyes. He threw something into the air, panting. A small green blur in the sky. A plastic dog. She heard it clattering on the street, and then something bounced toward her. A tiny red collar. She stepped back.

Charlie came outside. "Sam," he said, only now his voice was so sad that it made Isabelle ache. Sam folded his arms tightly about his chest. He hunched over. His shoulders moved up and down and then Charlie walked toward the object and picked it up and handed it to Sam. "You don't want to do that," Charlie said quietly, and Sam wrapped both arms about the plastic dog. "Better?" Charlie asked and Sam nodded. "Come on, let's go inside." Charlie started to put one arm about Sam, but Sam moved past him into the house and Charlie's arm hung there, for a moment, in the air. And then he turned and looked out across the lawn, right toward the hedges where Isabelle was, and she froze, but he didn't see her. When the door shut, Isabelle sprang forward and came around the hedge. She bent and picked up the collar. She quietly put it in the mailbox, where they might find it.

Then Isabelle took off. She walked again, faster, until she had rounded the corner, telling herself that this was not her business and that she would never walk down that street again.

But she couldn't keep her promise. Isabelle always had an errand to do. Grocery shopping. The cleaners. To buy film she wasn't using. She walked toward Charlie and Sam's house with her eyes down, and the closer she got to it, the more terrified she was, and the more ashamed, but she kept walking, and every night she learned a little more. From the takeout boxes she saw in the trash can, she learned that Charlie didn't cook. She learned that Sam liked balls and trucks and that he liked to throw things on the lawn. It was a house full of music. Blues, classical; once, someone sounding like Bessie Smith wailed that just like a flower, she was fading away.

One night she went by later than usual, and even from across the street, a few houses away, she saw the lights were not as bright and she felt a clip of fear. And then she took another step and stopped because there was Charlie on the porch, a glass of wine in his hand. Isabelle fell back in the shadows, crouching behind an SUV. She knew that what she should do was turn around and walk the other way, but she couldn't take her eyes off Charlie.

Charlie didn't drink the wine. He was standing so still she didn't dare move. He rubbed his face with his hands, stared at the sky for a moment, and then began to weep. Isabelle turned on her heel and began running home, and by the time she got there, she was crying, too.

GRADUALLY, THE NEWSPAPER stories stopped. Every morning, she got online and thought about making airline reservations and getting the hell out of there, but she never did. In town, she didn't feel as though people were staring at her anymore. She saw her friends, she got outside. Life went back to normal, but still, she walked down Charlie's street. One night, a neighbor came out of the house, an old man in bright blue running shorts and a sweatshirt, a pedometer strapped to his waist. He waved happily at her and Isabelle started. "How far today?" he asked.

"How far what?" It was strange to hear her voice in this neighborhood.

"How far do you walk? I always see you!" He patted his chest. "Six miles," he said proudly.

"Five," Isabelle whispered.

"Good for you!" he stood there, moving from foot to foot and she realized, with a shock, that he was flirting with her. "We ought to start a neighborhood walking club!"

"Good idea," she said lamely, and he nodded.

"See you tomorrow!" he said, "I'll look for you!" He sprinted off.

He knew her. He recognized her. He was going to look for her. She had never seen him before. Isabelle had thought she was the only person here, but while she was busy watching Charlie's house, people were busy watching her. She couldn't come back. And yet she couldn't leave.

The New York City sublet was gone, but Isabelle called Luke and told him the house was his, that she didn't want to be in it anymore. She found a cheap one-bedroom apartment, a one-floor walk-up over on Broom Street, just a block away, and let Michelle and Lindy help her move in.

She thought of those stories Nora had told her. Nora believed that spirits who had unfinished business stuck around people's houses, haunting them until someone pointed them toward the light. Every time she heard the house creak, she would nod at Isabelle. "That's your father," Isabelle's mother would say. "He loves us so much, he can't leave," and Isabelle would roll her eyes. Now, Isabelle felt like a ghost herself, drawn to Charlie and Sam's house. But who would point her to the light?

• • •

AT THE END of September, nearly a month after the accident, Isabelle went back to work. She hadn't picked up a camera since the accident, hadn't been able to think of anything she might like to photograph, and the one photo she tried to take, of two old women talking on a bench, had come out so terrible, she hadn't bothered to keep the print. She thought she could do the work at the You Must Have Been A Beautiful Baby studio easily enough. Parents pretty much told you what they wanted, and creativity usually wasn't a big factor. She had called Chuck, her boss, and told him she'd like to come back. "Good, we can use the help," he said.

"Isabelle!" Emma, another photographer, who often complained that Isabelle got all the good jobs, gave her a brief hug. "Let me get you coffee."

"Isabelle!" Ted, the lighting guy, strode toward her, crushing her in a hug.

Isabelle stood around while Ted fixed the lights. "You wouldn't believe the weeks we've been having," he said. "A woman wanted her poodle's portrait done. When I reminded her we only photographed children, she huffed that her poodle was her child." He winked at her. "Guess what, we did it for her."

She laughed halfheartedly. "There," he said. "All done." He tipped an imaginary hat at her and left the room, and then she realized that neither he nor anyone else had asked her a single question about the accident or about Luke.

By early afternoon, customers began trickling in. This was easy, by-rote work. She was brisk and efficient and it made the hours fly. Only one person seemed to know who she was, a mother in a powder blue dress with a freckle-faced little girl. She frowned at Isabelle and then said, "Maybe we won't get our picture taken today," and left. Isabelle saw her leaning across the counter, arguing with Rick. She heard her name. She heard. "It's not right. Kids are involved."

Isabelle moved deeper into her studio, away from the door, and away from Chuck. She shut the door so she wouldn't hear any more, but truly, all she could hear was the sickening thud of her heart.

⁓ EIGHT ⁓

IT WAS THE FIRST week of October and Sam was finally going back to school. He had just started his first week of fourth grade before the accident, and now he had to go back, start a routine again, pretend to be normal. Sam felt disoriented. He had been in his new classroom, but now everything looked different, as if there had been a time warp. The soft red couch that had stood below the window was now against the far wall. All the tables were separated and put in the corners and the red and purple braided rug that had covered most of the floor was gone and the wood had been painted deep blue. The map of Native American Tribes that had been on the back wall was gone, along with the Make Your Metaphor worksheets. Instead, there was a big wall map of China and Sam hadn't the foggiest reason why. There were reports on the parts of a cell hanging up, and every name was up there but Sam's.

"Make yourself at home," Miss Rivers said kindly. She put an arm about him and gave him a quick hug. She showed him the friendly-looking tables where everyone could work at the seat they chose; the class schedule marking off math, reading, science, and free work time; and the list of rules she had put up. "You're in fourth grade now, so we have some privileges." He could go outside and get a bottled water if he wanted or a snack from one of the vending machines. He was allowed to go to the office and the school library himself, without a partner. "You know everyone," Miss Rivers said, and Sam nodded. He noticed that the other kids shied away from him, as if he had cooties or something.

Sam hung his book bag on a hook and slunk to a seat at a table. All day, he felt out of sorts. His pen leaked during free writing period and stained the tips of his fingers, so he had to go the bathroom and scrub and scrub. During reading, he couldn't find anything in the school library that really interested him, so he was stuck reading a book about farming that was so boring, he finally closed it and doodled pictures of dogs on a piece of paper instead.

Everyone treated him differently. His friend Don, who had come over to play chess after the accident, just nodded at him but didn't ask Sam if he wanted to come over for a playdate. Annie, Sam's science partner from last year, who everyone said had a crush on him, didn't even look up at him when Sam said hello. "Annie," he said louder, and this time she met his eyes and then looked away.

No one mentioned his mother or where she might be. They didn't have to.

Only Teddy Boudreaux treated him the same as he had last year, sticking a leg out when Sam was walking to sharpen his pencil before free-writing period, so that Sam tripped. "Walk much?" Teddy hissed, keeping his eyes on him so long that Sam felt unnerved.

Sam knew he shouldn't take it personally. No one wanted to be friends with Teddy. Teddy lived with his mother, but because she was never home, he ran wild all over town. He was always in the principal's office, and last year he had been suspended for two weeks because he had taken a hammer to school and threatened to hit any kid who bothered him. Teddy's favorite target was always Sam. He made wheezing sounds to humiliate him. "Asthma Boy," he hissed. Just last spring, Teddy had stolen Sam's inhaler right out of his pocket and thrown it in the toilet in the boys' room. By the time Sam found it, he was already wheezing and panicked, and even though the water in the toilet looked clean, he had had to run it under the hot water for a long time before he dared to use it.

To Sam's relief, Miss Rivers came right over and put her hand on his shoulder. "You take it easy today," she said.

"Everything's so different," said Sam, meaning the room.

"Well, we're all friends here," Miss Rivers said, guiding him back to his seat.

Sam stared at the blank paper in front of him. He had no idea what to write about, but he knew the teacher would get mad if he didn't put down something, so he wrote a few sentences about a movie he had watched on TV. Then, because he couldn't think of anything else to write, he got up to go outside and get himself some water.

It was cool having privileges, being out in the corridor without a teacher or a partner. The hallways were long and empty and smelled like disinfectant, and for a moment Sam wondered if he could run down them and not be stopped. The vending machines were around the corner, filled with healthy, boring snacks like nuts and raisins. As soon as Sam reached the machines, he saw Teddy, and he stood perfectly still. How had Teddy gotten here so fast and how come Sam hadn't seen him leave the classroom? Teddy gave Sam the once-over, and then crouched by the snack machine, his hand up in the mouth of the machine. He tugged out a bag of pretzels and pocketed it and then looked defiantly at Sam, narrowing his eyes. Then he thrust his arm up into the machine again.

"What are you doing to that machine?" Mr. Morgan, the sixth-grade science teacher, suddenly appeared. Teddy jumped up, pushing his hands into his pockets. "Teddy, didn't we talk about this? Don't you have any respect for school property? Do you like going to the principal? Do you want us to call your mother? Three strikes you're out and this is strike three."

Teddy stayed silent, his face flushed. He looked so miserable that, despite himself, Sam felt a pang of pity. "My snack got stuck and Teddy was trying to get it for me," Sam said. As soon as he said it, he felt shocked.

As soon as Mr. Morgan looked at Sam, his whole face seemed to soften. He looked from Sam to Teddy doubtfully. "We have privilege," Sam said weakly.

"Not for hours at a time. Get back in class, the both of you," Mr. Morgan said. He watched them round the corner, and as soon as they did, Teddy's hands curled into fists, and Sam leaped back, banging into the lockers. Teddy gave him a long glare and then vanished into the classroom.

The bell rang at two thirty, and Sam's stomach lurched. He half expected to see his mother. She used to meet him at the front of the school in the car, revving the motor, her radio so loud, everyone could hear it. She never looked like any of the other mothers. She'd be wearing a pretty, bright-colored dress while the other mothers were in shorts and T-shirts, their hair in ponytails. The other mothers were as brown as nuts from the sun and the beach, but his mother was as pale as a piece of paper. The other mothers also huddled together and chatted about school and their kids, but Sam's mother stood apart. When someone said hello, she looked surprised, as if they had said hi to the wrong person, and barely turned her head.

When she zoomed up to the curb, she jumped out like a chauffeur for him. She held the door of the car open like it was a chariot. "Let's vamoose," she'd say, with a flourish, and he couldn't wait.

Now, he hung out on the sidewalk. He folded his arms, he tried to make himself a small, tight ball. He felt the other mothers watching him.

Someone tapped him. "How are you doing, Sam?"

He turned and there was Archie Simpson's mom. He and Archie weren't friends, though they had been in the same class since kindergarten. Archie was big and freckled and he picked his nose, something that always made Sam want to sit as far away from Archie as he possibly could. "Fine," he said forcefully. "Just fine!"

She looked at him doubtfully. Her eyes filled with sympathy that made Sam want to cry and scream at the same time. "Is your dad coming to get you?" she said. She raised one hand up like a visor over her eyes. She squinted down at him. "Because I'm just waiting for Archie, and I'm sure he'd love to have you come over."

Sam squirmed. Archie didn't read or draw or like to do anything but Pokémon, which bored Sam. "Really," said Archie's mother. "Would you like to come with us?"

"No, thank you. I'm allowed to walk home by myself now," Sam told her.

• • •

CHARLIE WAS IN the supermarket, stocking up on fruits and vegetables. Neither he nor Sam had any appetite, but it was still important to have family dinners, to brush your teeth and act normal, even if you felt you could never be normal again. Charlie wheeled down the pasta aisle, grabbing sauce and ziti, a green cylinder of grated cheese.

Maybe he'd buy some wine, have a glass at dinner to tempt an appetite. He knew that you could stay lost forever if you wanted, if you didn't fight it every second. Charlie had seen it with his clients. Husbands or wives whose spouses had left them in the middle of the renovations would insist on moving forward even though they couldn't walk into a room without bursting into tears. A couple whose baby had died of SIDS would repaint every room in their home except the baby's. He remembered them. The unhappy ones. The ones whose lives had crashed like comets into solid earth.

Last night, when his mother had called, she'd told him to act as if he was happy and then he would be. She insisted it was a whole philosophy her book group had been discussing.

"I can't act as if April is still alive," he snapped, and then, hearing his mother's hurt silence, felt instantly sorry. "I'm sorry," he said. "It's just a little hard right now."

"You never listen to me. No one is saying that you should act as if April's alive," she said. "Of course you can't. Of course it's horrible and tragic. But just act as if you have hope. Can you do that one little thing? Can you do it for Sam?"

Charlie thought of how, every day, sadness would build up inside him but he'd tamp it down, waiting until Sam was asleep, and only then would Charlie cry. "I'll see what I can do," Charlie said.

He bought the groceries and put them in the car, and then as he was driving home, he spotted the sign: Henderson's Detective Agency. Impulsively, he pulled the car in. Maybe they could find out what happened, tell him where April was going on that road.

When he walked in, the main room was empty, and almost every inch of wall was covered with maps. When Charlie walked closer, he saw they were maps of Spain and China and Germany. They were beautifully framed, and in the far corner was a clock divided into six time zones. All Charlie could think was, Look at all the places where you can be lost. Look at all the places you can disappear.

Charlie didn't know what he expected, probably a dumpy guy in a badly cut suit, who smelled of cigarettes. A door in the back of the room opened and a man strode toward him, in an expensive dark suit and silver tie, as polished as the flat-screen computer humming on his desk. "Hank Williams, and no relation," said the man. "I don't even like country music."

"Charlie Nash," Charlie said. Williams held out his hand for Charlie's and pumped it, nodding with recognition. He sat down behind his desk, looked at the computer, and then motioned to Charlie. "So, tell me," he said. "I know about the case from what I've read in the papers or heard on the news. So, what are we really looking at here? What's this about?"

At first, he took a lot of notes, which reassured Charlie. He asked a lot of questions, but then gradually, Hank began tapping his fingers on the desktop, and then he folded his hands and studied him so intently that Charlie sat straighter in his seat.

"Let's start with the facts. Your wife is dead, Mr. Nash. You know she's not coming back and nothing you find is going to change that."

"Of course I know that."

"And you know I may not find anything, or what I find might not make you feel any better. And you know you still have to pay me for my time." Hank met Charlie's eyes.

"I know that," Charlie said.

"You don't have much to go on," Hank said. "You don't have a description of anyone she might have been seen with. All you know is that she was three hours away from your home with your son. You saw each other every day and you said she wasn't unhappy."

"She wasn't." Charlie thought of April beaming at him when he came home. He thought of the way she always hooked her legs around his when they went to bed at night. He felt something snaking up his spine. "Isn't it your job to find out all these things?"

Hank settled back in his chair. "I just want you to be sure you want to know."

"I want you to find out why my wife left. I want you to find out where she was going and why she took our son with her."

"I can take your case," Hank said. "I can call all the people in her address book, and track down some leads. Ask the right questions. Everything's computerized these days, so my expenses won't be that much. But even so, I'm not cheap. $5,000 for the month. That should be enough to see if there are leads here." He tapped his fingers on the desk.

Charlie thought of the bills he had to pay, the jobs he hadn't worked because he had felt too stressed. "Whom do I make the check out to?" Charlie said. "I'll take a month."

CHARLIE MAILED HANK pictures of April, her address book, even samples of her handwriting. He told Hank about her waitressing at the Blue Cupcake. He gave him phone bills and Master-

Card receipts. Every day, Charlie waited for the phone to ring. He imagined different scenarios. April had been running away to California with Sam to see a specialist, another one of those quack doctors who did quantum touch or qui therapy, the ones April knew made Charlie nuts and that's why she hadn't told him. April was going to call him as soon as they got there. Or April had bought tickets to visit one of the friends Charlie had never met, to show off her son and then come home.

None of it made much sense.

He thought of April and Sam stepping into another life without him. Once he had overheard them talking in the backyard, pretending to be other people, talking about all the places they would go, and at the time, he had thought it was funny.

He didn't think it was funny now.

He tried to think what he had done, how he had failed her. Had that one argument really been enough to derail them? Hadn't he come home with little gifts for her all the time? A velvet scarf, a pair of amber earrings, a gleaming silver bracelet as thin as a wedding band. He couldn't walk down the street without holding her hand. At dinner, he reached across to touch her hair, her chin, the curve of her shoulder. He couldn't sleep at night without making his body a comma around hers. Wouldn't he know if she had been unhappy? And Sam. What had she told Sam when he got in the car with her? What had they talked about as they drove, and where did Sam think they were going? What had he ever done to Sam that would make Sam able to leave him, too—or had Sam even known?

WHEN THE DETECTIVE finally called, it was nearly Halloween. No one knew anything. There was no trail. There was no reason. The airlines had no listing for April Nash. "Do you want me to keep looking? Was there another name she might have used?" Hank said.

"I don't know . . ."

"Look," Hank said. "Sometimes I have people who disappear and I can't find them. They just don't want to be found, for one reason or another, and that's their right. They step right into another life, like it was another dimension on *The Twilight Zone* or something. Sometimes they show up all on their own, they come back as if no time had passed at all, as if nothing had happened. It's the same with peoples' secrets. Sometimes secrets just want to stay secrets. They don't want to be unlocked."

Charlie pressed the phone against his ear. Was Hank right?

"Her life is over. You still have yours and you should get on with it." Hank was quiet for a moment. "I can call you again, if I have any other leads, but truly, I'm sorry."

"So am I," said Charlie. "But please keep looking."

IT WAS THE end of the day and the whole fourth grade was going a little nuts because they'd brought in their Halloween candy, and even though it wasn't allowed in school, everyone had been sneaking bites. Sam had brought red Twizzlers, the one candy his father hadn't edited out of his bag, but they tasted gluey and unsatisfying.

Sam walked home from school that day alone, as usual. He had given up trying to talk to his old friends because they looked at him like they were about to cry or they ignored him, as if having a dead mother was something that might happen to them, too, if they stuck around him.

He was glad he didn't have to go to After School anymore, where more kids would act weird around him. He had begged and promised his father he'd be responsible enough to walk home and stay home by himself, that he wouldn't answer the door to strangers, that he'd call if he went to a friend's house. "I don't know if that's such a good idea," his father had said doubtfully, but then Sam had blurted, "Mom let me do it all the time," and his father's face had changed, and he had slowly nodded his okay.

Sam roamed through the park and sat on one of the swings, pumping his legs, trying to stretch out the time before he had to go home. Every time he opened the door, he thought this might be the day and a miracle would happen. He would open the door and the whole house would smell like sugar and the angel would be standing there, smiling at him, thanking him for being so patient.

"Hey."

Sam spun around, and for a moment he couldn't breathe because there was Teddy. "That was nice what you did. That thing with the snack machine. Thanks." Teddy squinted at him.

Sam shrugged.

"Why'd you do it? Because you're scared of me, right?"

Sam hesitated. "Nuh-uh. Because you were hungry."

Teddy flushed. "Yeah. How'd you know that, Asthma Boy? You psychic?"

Sam looked past Teddy. No one else was in the park where they were. If Teddy beat him up, no one would probably see or even hear him shout. Sam swallowed. "Because I was hungry, too. My mom used to remind me to take my lunch."

Silently, Teddy considered him. Sam wondered, if he got up really fast, if he ran, whether he could make it to the end of the park before Teddy caught him.

"So, you want to come to my house?" Teddy asked.

· · ·

THEY HEADED TO Teddy's house, crossing Lark Lane and then over to Jason, and suddenly the soft pine-needled lawns gave way to scrubby grass. Sam was radiant with excitement. He loved the way he felt, like he wasn't Asthma Boy or Accident Boy anymore. Like he was as invincible as Teddy, who no one dared to mess with. They crossed over to Defray Street, and two older boys Sam didn't know nodded at Teddy, and then they actually nodded at Sam, too.

"Here we are," Teddy said.

Teddy's house was smaller than Sam's. The front lawn was balding in spots and the paint on the house was chipping. When Teddy opened the front door, it was dark inside.

Teddy clicked a switch. The living room was cluttered with newspapers and dirty dishes and there wasn't a rug on the floor, which was scuffed blue linoleum. Teddy opened a wood cabinet and took out something and waved it at Sam, a small package of whiskey sour mix, a picture of a couple clinking wine glasses. Sam startled. "I'm not putting any whiskey in, dummy," Teddy said. "You mix it with soda water. It tastes better than lemonade. Trust me. I've had it a million times."

Sam wasn't thirsty, but he took the fizzing glass Teddy offered him and sipped, and to his shock, he liked the tart, sour taste of the drink.

"What time does your mom get home?" Sam asked, and Teddy shrugged.

"Whenever she feels like it. Six. Ten. Midnight. What about your dad?"

"Five."

Teddy's face darkened. "Yeah, well, I get to do whatever I want here. I usually have pizza for dinner every night, if I want. And I watch whatever I want on TV and no one tells me not to." Teddy drained his glass. "Come on," he said. "Let's get some money."

Sam couldn't believe it when Teddy led him into his mother's room. When his own mother was alive, she never let Sam's friends play in her room, and Sam wouldn't have wanted to bring them in anyway. It was too private. When Teddy started to rummage through his mother's dresser drawer, Sam hung back. Teddy pulled out quarters and nickels and placed them in a pile on the bed, which was still unmade, the sheets kicked to a corner. "You do the closet," Teddy ordered, and Sam wandered into the sea of Teddy's mother's dresses and skirts. All of his own mom's things were gone from her closet. He fingered a silky red blouse and then a cotton skirt, and there, over in the corner, was a blue printed dress just like one his mother had worn to Sam's Blue Cupcake soccer game. She had stood up and cheered, even though he was just the water boy and no one even wanted any water to drink. The clothes seemed to whisper around him.

"We have enough money," Teddy called. "Let's go get some pizza. It's on my mom." Teddy shoved the money into the pockets of his jeans. "I do this every day," Teddy said conspiratorially. "And you can come over anytime."

Sam thought about being home alone. "Okay," he said.

~ NINE ~

ISABELLE GOT LORA Jones's name from the Yellow Pages, choosing her because the office was within walking distance, right off Deeder Road by the beach, and mostly because Lora Jones was a psychiatrist, not a psychologist, and might be talked into giving her pills to help her sleep without dreaming about the accident every night. She hadn't been a big believer in therapy in the past, because what was it but talk and couldn't you do that better with your friends who loved and knew you? Didn't she do that with Michelle and Lindy and Jane? But she knew she couldn't keep calling up her friends and crying to them. "It's time to move on," they said gently, as if she were a stalled car that only needed a little push.

Isabelle was surprised she had gotten an appointment, but she had liked Lora's voice on the phone, like a pour of honey. Now that she saw her, she liked the way she looked, too, the startling white hair cut to her chin, the draping velvets of her clothes. She smelled of cinnamon, and, to Isabelle's surprise, Lora hugged her when she walked in.

"Dr. Jones," said Isabelle.

"Call me Lora," she told Isabelle, and the hem of her long blue dress swayed against her ankles.

When she turned, Isabelle saw a blue butterfly clip sparkling in Lora's hair.

They sat in the chintz chairs, and the whole time Isabelle spoke about the accident, Lora was still. "I'm not surprised you're feeling discombobulated," Lora said.

"I can't drive anymore," Isabelle said. "It's stressful for me to even be a passenger."

Lora nodded. "Why, of course you would feel that way. I can give you some Valium. Take it a half hour before you get in a car. Just for the time being."

Isabelle wrapped her arms about her chest.

"You're going to have to get in a car sometime," Lora said. "Nobody's saying you have to drive now. You can start slow, with baby steps, and with a little help."

Lora sympathized with everything that Isabelle told her, that she couldn't eat, that her dreams were filled with the accident, that every time she saw a newspaper, she felt sick. Isabelle twisted the strap of the pocketbook on her lap. "There's something else," she said. She looked at her lap and told Lora that she was sneaking over to Charlie and Sam's house, that she couldn't stay away from them. Lora studied Isabelle with an even gaze.

"You're spying on them," Lora said.

"I just want to make sure they're all right," Isabelle said.

"You can't do that. You can only make sure you're all right," Lora said. She held up a finger. "I have an idea for you," she said gently. "Write a letter that you will never mail. Write it to Charlie and Sam. Tell them how you feel about what happened that day," she said. "It's just to get your thoughts out on paper, to see the power those words have and then to let them go. Afterward, you can just rip up the paper or burn it, if you want."

"I don't know . . . ," Isabelle said doubtfully.

"Why aren't you more angry? The man's wife was negligent. You were injured. You were ready to leave here and now you can't."

"What?" Isabelle shifted on the couch.

"Why aren't you angry, too? His wasn't the only life derailed. Yours was, too."

"A woman died. There was a little boy involved. He could have died, too."

"And he didn't. And the accident wasn't your fault." Isabelle stared at her. "Write the letter, Isabelle," Lora said, and then before Isabelle could respond, Lora stood up, smoothing her skirt.

She scribbled something on a pad and handed a prescription to Isabelle. "Valium. Really mild." Isabelle had hoped for something stronger, but at least it was something. "Next week, same time," Lora said, and then showed Isabelle the door, a curl of her perfume winding around them both.

• • •

THAT NIGHT, ALONE in her house, Isabelle took out paper and a pen.

"I am so sorry"

It didn't sound like enough to her. What was sorry?

"Dear Charlie,"

She forcibly crossed it out and wrote instead:

"Dear Mr. Nash,

"I just wanted you to know that I am so sorry for what happened and so glad your son is all right. If there is anything I can do or any way I can help, please let me know."

Lora had promised her that she would feel relief, but instead, Isabelle felt like screaming. She bunched the paper up in her fist and then dropped it in the wastebasket. A letter was nothing. Then she took a Valium and lay in bed, the sheets pulled up to her chin, waiting not to feel anything at all.

SHE WOKE UP groggy, dreading going into work. Maybe today would be slow. Maybe no one would come into the studio at all. She'd take a brisk walk to wake herself up, come home and shower, and then go to work.

She passed the supermarket, the park. The air was getting cooler. A wind had picked up, and she wrapped her coat tighter around her. She dug for her sunglasses against the bright glare of the day. There was a playground with a wire fence, a spill of noisy kids, flocked by teachers in fall coats, with careless hair, laughing and talking together. Long ago, when she was so desperate to have a child, Isabelle had avoided playgrounds and parks. She hadn't wanted to be reminded of what she didn't have. She didn't want to listen to the mothers complaining about how tired they were, how busy their schedules, while Isabelle sat there with her arms wrapped around herself, sick with envy.

She stood on the outside, fingers hooked onto the links of the fence. In the corner, a group of girls were holding hands in a line, the last girl clutching the wire fence, the rest winding in and out of one another's open arms, until they were all twisted, with their arms crossed tightly. All of them were singing, spelling out in a kind of raucous chant, "R-a-t-t-l-e-s-n-a-k-e spells rattlesnake." Over and over, almost hypnotic, in this strange, sad little minor key. Rattlesnake, rattlesnake. The chant got to her, as if it were directed at her, as if she were the snake. Isabelle released her fingers from the fence, and just as she stepped back, a boy ran across her field of vision.

She knew him right away. She knew the shock of chocolate hair, the hunch of his shoulders. "Sam." She didn't realize she had actually said his name out loud. She looked around. Where was his teacher? She hoped he had a friend on the playground, that he wasn't just by himself, although he appeared to be. She hoped he was happy, that he liked school. "Sam," someone called, and Sam looked right at Isabelle, meeting her eyes like a jolt of electricity. Isabelle's heart was thundering, and her coat flew open in the wind. She ducked her head and sprinted away. Sam. She had seen Sam.

And he had seen her.

SAM WATCHED HER running away. He felt a bolt of heat. The air sparked in his lungs every time he took a breath. There was that splash of light, and that sound, like a rustling of heavy wings. He pinched the skin of his wrist hard to make sure this was no dream.

The moment he had seen her he had known who she was. When he looked at her, the sun shimmered behind her. He narrowed his eyes, trying to keep her in focus, his heart rocketing in his chest. Then her coat opened up in the wind and he heard the flapping of huge, heavy wings, beating so loudly he had to reach up his hands and clap them to his ears.

He looked around, dazed. The teacher wasn't looking at him.

The angel. She was the angel from the accident and she could help him contact his mom!

But all of a sudden, she turned and ran away, looking back once, as if she were telling him to follow her, to hurry. This was his chance! He glanced behind him to make sure the teachers weren't watching, and then he sprinted after her. He followed her past his house, past the Fro-Zen ice cream place.

When he crossed the street after her, the cars seemed to stop as soon as Sam's foot left the curb. The angel didn't turn around to see him. The light stayed green not just for her but for him as well. He put his hand up in wonder, and he felt it pulse.

The angel turned down Broom Street and stopped in front of a small apartment building. She didn't see Sam, a few houses down, breathing heavily, pausing to watch her next move. He was spinning with excitement. Did she live here? Six blocks away! Did an actual angel have a real house? She stepped inside and closed the door. He ran over and touched the door, wondering if she would come out again with a message for him from his mother, or if he was just supposed to be patient, the way the angel books had said. All good things come to those who wait. His grandma told him that. Maybe that was what he was supposed to do.

He gave it a few more minutes, just to be sure, and when the door stayed shut, he headed back to school; but without the angel, everything was out of whack. The lights stayed green for only a second, so he had to run across to avoid getting hit by a car. Suddenly, all these angry dogs were around, straining on leashes and barking at him.

Hurrying, Sam breathed through his nose so he wouldn't wheeze, still dizzy with excitement. He put his hand on his pocket, readying himself to take out his inhaler, but to his surprise, his lungs were clear. The angel had found him, and that meant something. All he had to do was put on his thinking cap and pay really good attention and then he'd figure out what to do next.

He got to the playground just as the kids were slowly making their way back into the building, and stealthily fell back in line with them, triumphant.

THAT NIGHT, SAM lay on his bed, one of his angel books spread across his chest. "Angels are here to comfort and protect us, to give us hope and a glimpse of the world to come," he read. "They walk among us and we may not even know how we have been touched by them."

The world to come. Where his mother was. Was it like Heaven, which always seemed sort of boring to Sam, with nothing to do all day but play harps on clouds? Maybe it was like Earth, only without wars or bad stuff in it. Was his mom happy? Did she miss him the way he did her?

He had to figure out how to see the angel again without it seeming like he was asking her for anything. He could hang around her house, watch for her and see where she went.

Sam shut his eyes. His mother used to appear

when he least expected it. He remembered one day she had rapped on the glass of his classroom door. His teacher, Miss Horton, went outside and talked to her. Sam watched the way his mother's head tilted, as if she were listening to what Miss Horton was saying. He saw, too, the way Miss Horton frowned, and then his mother's head shook. *No.*

Then Miss Horton turned around, her face as pinched as a drawstring purse, and she opened the door and his mother came in, her shoes clicking on the floor. "Sam," she said, motioning to him.

"He'll be back tomorrow," his mother said, and her voice was so full and sorrowful that Sam began to worry.

"Is everything all right?" Sam asked.

His mother glanced meaningfully at his teacher. "We'll talk when we're in the car."

Sam felt the ball of worry in his stomach rolling into something bigger and bigger. He went and got his books, and the other kids snickered. As he made his way out of the classroom, someone poked him in the side and Sam flinched. As soon as they were outside, Sam tugged on his mother's sleeve. "What's wrong?" he asked.

His mother grinned at him. "Who wants to go for a ride?" she said.

"What's wrong?" he asked.

"Nothing's wrong. Can't a mother want to spend some quality time with her son? Put on your happy face. We're going to have an adventure."

An adventure! Instantly, Sam perked up. She reached into the glove compartment of the car and pulled out a map. "Put your finger down," she told him. "Where it lands is where we're going." She pulled out her yellow sunglasses and put them on the top of her head. Sam put his finger in the air, hesitating. "Go ahead. Close your eyes and put your finger anywhere on the map and that's where we'll go." She had that little line between her brows. She was serious! He closed his eyes and stabbed his finger on the map. "Boston!" she said.

In a crowded diner near Boston, she turned to him and said loudly, "Don't feel bad you didn't get that movie role. Bruce Willis is insane not to have chosen you."

The man next to his mother looked up with interest and Sam's mother gently nudged his side. "Let's hold out for a film with DeNiro. We'll talk to your agent today."

Sam grinned. "I want the Lord of the Rings role," he said, and this time, the woman next to him glanced over. She stared at Sam, who giggled.

"Excuse me," the strange woman said. "Do I know you?"

"You should," said Sam's mother, and she paid the check. "We have to go," she said politely, and the whole way out, Sam felt the woman's stare on his back.

Oh, it was so much fun to be someone else. His mother was full of surprises. They spent the day at the museums in Boston, coming home just a half hour before his father did. When his mother saw his car pull up, she slid her finger across her mouth like she was closing a zipper. "Our secret," she said.

"Have a good day today?" his dad asked when he came inside, and Sam had to pinch himself to keep from laughing. "The best," he said.

His mother began showing up more and more when Sam was at school, and Sam never knew when it would happen. "Are you sure this is okay to do?" Sam asked, and his mother laughed. "What can the school do? I'm your mother." She took him to fancy restaurants, and museums, and once she took him to New Hampshire to look at the mountains. Everywhere they went, she called him by a different name, Frank or Jamie and once Rocko, and she gave herself new identities, too. "We can be anyone we want," she said.

Once she came when Sam's class was about to study the Revolutionary War. He loved school, and just seeing the pictures of the British in their snappy red uniforms had made him excited. "I don't know if I want to leave," he told his mother. "We're going to see a movie about the Revolutionary War."

"Oh," his mother said. "The Revolutionary War. I see. Get in the car." She drove to Lexington. "Lexington and Concord. Part of history and you get to see it firsthand, not like they would do in that stupid school." She stumbled on the cobblestone sidewalk. "If I'd known we'd be walking, I'd have worn flats," she said. They walked and she told him about the battles fought there. They stood in front of the statue of the Minute Man and she told him they had to be ready at a minute's notice, that's where they got the name. "Like us," Sam said, and his mother laughed. She ruffled his hair. "Yeah," she said. "Like us." She looked around. "Had enough education?" she asked, and when he nodded, they headed for the car. "Me, too," she said. The next day, Sam couldn't wait to get home to tell her that he had been the only one in the class who had known how the Minute Men got their name. "What did I tell you?" his mother said.

Two weeks later, she showed up again, but this time, in the school hallway, he told her he wanted to stay in school. "We're having science," he protested. "I love science!"

She got a funny look on her face.

The sky had a dirty wash to it, like laundry that hadn't quite come clean. His stomach was rumbling and he didn't feel like going to another diner, didn't feel like being Nick or Thomas or Bob or anyone but who he was, which was just Sam. He wanted to stay in his own classroom, and then to go home and eat his own macaroni and soy cheese. "Mom," he said, tugging at her shirt. "It's time for my science class."

"David," she said. "Or you could be Timothy today."

"Sam. I'm Sam now," he said.

"Yes," she said quietly. "Yes, I suppose you are."

She stepped inside and told his teacher that she had gotten the date wrong, that Sam's dentist appointment must be for the next week and not this one. And when Sam got home from school, he couldn't wait to tell her about the experiments they had done, how thrilling it was to see the jump and jolt of electricity, but his mother was flushed, her eyes as bright as pennies. "You should have seen it!" Sam crowed.

"And you should have seen what I saw," she said.

Something prickled along Sam's back. "You went without me?"

There was a space growing in his belly that he didn't know how to fill. "Next time," she told him. "Now, tell me about your science day in school."

After that, Sam's mother never came to take him out of school, no matter how many days he kept staring at his classroom door waiting for her. He hadn't gone on an adventure with her ever again, not until he had snuck into the back of her car.

Now, he thought of his mother, floating away like dust. He thought of the angel. He thought of the door in his classroom, the long empty hall. Maybe tomorrow, instead of his mother, the angel might be the one to come for him.

~ TEN ~

SAM AND TEDDY were roaming the Giant Eagle supermarket, moving in and out of the aisles, past the Thanksgiving displays of canned pumpkin and cranberry sauce, until they got to the cookie aisle. The Giant Eagle had been part of their routine all month, the two of them bolting out of school, stopping here, and then winding up at Teddy's, where Teddy almost always had something fun to do. As long as Sam was home before his father, he saw no reason to tell him where he spent his time these days.

Teddy glanced around the empty aisle. "We could eat down the aisle and nobody would know a thing." Teddy lifted up a bag of Strawberry Ripplies. "Whoa, these are the best. Want some?" he asked, his eyes lighting up, and Sam hesitated. Sam wasn't allowed to have that much sugar because of his asthma, but he could already taste the cookies in his mouth. "Come on, what do you like?" Teddy scanned the shelves. "Ho Hos? Yodels? Want to go check out the candy next?"

Sam reached for a package of Vanilla Chewies and then, grinning, Teddy took it from him. He elusively clasped the package to his stomach and turned toward the aisle. Then he coughed extravagantly, ripping the package wide open. Instantly, cookies flew from the bag, spilling into

Teddy's hands and onto the floor. Sam leaped back, amazed. Teddy wolfed one down. "What are you waiting for?" Teddy barked, stuffing cookies into his mouth and into his pockets, "Help me here."

"That's stealing—"

Teddy rolled his eyes. "Who's going to want to buy this bag after it's open? They'll just have to throw them out and that's waste and that's even worse than stealing. Come on, I won't do it again."

Sam hesitated and then, just as he decided that maybe Teddy was right, that as long as the bag was open, they should take some, a manager in a red apron rounded the corner. "Hey, you kids!" he shouted.

Sam froze. Panicked, he looked at Teddy, but Teddy wasn't running or even looking guilty. Teddy just stood there with the bag of opened cookies right in his hands. The manager put his hands on his hips.

"I've been watching you kids. Are you going to pay for those cookies?" the manager asked.

"We don't have any money," Teddy said.

"Then that's stealing," the manager said. He reached into his pocket and pulled out his cell phone. "You kids can't just come in here and take whatever you want. I'm going to have to call both your mothers."

A bubble of grief welled up in Sam. The

manager looked at him. "You first. What's your mother's number?"

Teddy pointed at Sam. "His mother died in the car accident!" he blurted. "He saw it happen! It was in all the papers!"

The manager took his hands off his hips. "You're that boy," he said quietly, but it wasn't a question.

Sam felt his ears burning. He couldn't look at the manager.

"He even got a scar from it! Show him, Sam! Go on, show him!" Sam couldn't move, and to Sam's horror, Teddy jerked Sam's sleeve up, showing the scar, as jagged as a lightning bolt.

"I read about it," the manager said. Sam wrestled his arm away from Teddy, pulling his sleeve down.

Teddy tapped Sam. "Don't cry," he told Sam. "It's going to be all right. Please don't cry." He nudged Sam harder. "Once he starts crying, he never stops," Teddy assured the manager. Sam quickly put his hands over his eyes. He wasn't faking. Hot, salty tears sprang from his eyes.

The manager sighed. "Go," he said, finally. "Just get out of the store right now." He wagged a finger at the boys. "But I catch you doing this again, next time I won't be such a softie."

The boys ran, Teddy laughing as soon as they were outside the electronic door. "You should have seen his face!" Teddy whooped. "And you were great! The way you looked like you were going to cry for real!"

Teddy dug into his pockets as he ran, pulling out cookies by the handful, showing them to Sam. Sam knocked the cookies out of Teddy's hands, scattering them on the ground. "Hey, what's with you?" Teddy said.

"I'd rather go to jail than have to talk about the accident," Sam said, his voice hard.

Teddy stuffed another cookie in his mouth, surveying Sam. "Okay, okay, sorry. Next time, I'll think of something else." He pulled out another cookie. "Truce," he said, and Sam took it, popping the cookie into his mouth, shutting his eyes as the sugar dissolved and spread across his tongue.

They went to Teddy's house. As soon as they got inside, they took off their jackets and flung them on the couch. Then they took down Teddy's mother's Scrabble set, but after a few turns, Sam's heart wasn't in it. He was still too angry at Teddy. And anyway, the only words Teddy came up with were three-letter ones like cat or dog, which wasn't much fun. Meanly, still smarting from what Teddy had said in the supermarket, Sam put down the word "veneer." Teddy scowled. "Yeah, like that's a real word," Teddy said. "Don't try to act smarter than me, because you're not."

Teddy stood, stretching, and went over to a cabinet, prying open the door. He held up a DVD, grinning.

"What is it?" Sam said, and Teddy popped it into the DVD player. The words Red Hot Enterprises flashed on the screen and then there was a man and a woman in an empty Laundromat. She was wiggling around, taking off her funny socks, which were lacey and reached high up on her legs, and putting them in a washing machine and the man was moving his tongue in and out like a lizard. Then the man grunted and ripped the woman's dress off and pushed her onto the table, laying her back among the towels.

Sam startled. "What the heck is this?" he asked and Teddy laughed.

"It's what people do," he said. "It's called fucking."

Sam stared, amazed.

Teddy was hysterically laughing. "Look at the guy's big hairy butt!" he screamed. "And look at her boobs!"

"This is weird" Sam said, but he couldn't stop watching. The woman's face was pinched, as if she were in pain. And the guy kept snorting.

Just then the door opened, and Teddy jumped up.

A woman came into the house, her hair flying, her face a scowl. Sam stood up, feverishly hoping Teddy would snap the movie off with the remote. But the woman wasn't looking at the video. Instead, her eyes were scanning the room, the discarded snack packages, the abandoned

Scrabble game in the middle of the floor. She turned to Teddy, her eyes dark.

"What's going on here? Who told you you could have company over?"

The moans from the DVD seemed louder than ever now. To Sam's astonishment, Teddy suddenly looked smaller, as if he had shrunk six inches. Sam could hear his own breathing, the faint wheeze that made him put his hand in his pocket to make sure his inhaler was still there.

The woman swept her arms. "What's this mess? You don't pick up around here? You think I like working three jobs so you can live like a pig?" Almost casually, as if they had been watching the news, she reached for the remote and turned the DVD off.

Teddy's voice grew smaller. "I was going to . . ." he said. He stepped back from her.

"I should have given you away at birth," she snapped, and then she walked over and slapped Teddy in the face.

Sam gasped, stumbling backward against the couch, and the woman twisted around and stared at him. "Who's this?" she said flatly.

Sam looked to Teddy for help, but Teddy was pasted to the wall.

"I'm Sam." He could hardly get the words out. "Teddy's friend. Sam."

She snorted. "Well, lucky you," she said. She grabbed Teddy's hands away from his face. "You send your little friend home and then get in the kitchen. You and me are going to set up some new rules around here."

Teddy's mother dropped her coat on the couch and strode into the kitchen. He heard her banging things around and then Teddy suddenly shoved Sam. "You better go," Teddy said. He opened the door, and the rain dotted his shirt.

"Maybe she'll calm down," Sam said.

Teddy shook his head. "You have to get out of here." He gave Sam a push.

"Can I call a cab or my dad?" Sam asked. He looked around for his jacket and grabbed it up, sliding his arms into the sleeves.

There was a crash. "Teddy! Get in here!"

"Can I at least have an umbrella or something?" It was cold and dark outside, and the rain was pelting down.

"I said go! What are you, deaf or stupid?" Teddy shouted, and then shoved him out, so that he tripped and fell on the front steps, tearing the knee of his new pants. Then Sam heard the door lock.

SAM LOOKED BACK at Teddy's house, but the curtains were drawn. The neighborhood was deserted. His mom had never yelled at him the way Teddy's mom had yelled at Teddy. She'd never hit him, and once, when she had seen someone on the street hitting a kid, she had pulled her car over and threatened to call Child Services.

The rain slicked Sam's hair down into his face. In the downpour, the whole neighborhood looked different, and for a moment, he wasn't sure where he was.

It was getting dark outside and by the time he got to his house, Sam was soaking wet, shivering so hard his teeth were clattering. He reached into his pocket. There was his inhaler, his tissues, which were now sodden. Where was his key? Tears sprang from his eyes and he couldn't help it, he was crying full force now. He forgot his key! He couldn't go back to Teddy's. Not with Teddy's angry mom there. Not with the way Teddy had booted him out. He ran to the back, to the fake rock that held the extra key. Fumbling, he turned it over, but the key wasn't there.

All along his street, the houses were in shadows. Not even the neighbor's dog Spike was out, barking his head off. The air had a strange, metallic taste to it, like pennies on his tongue. "Hey!" Sam shouted, "Hey! Anyone!" His voice was muffled by the wind whipping through him. He sniffled. He ran next door to the Andersons' and rang the bell, but no one was home, so he ran to the Rogers' house. No one came to the door there, either. And then Sam was running, one block and then two, until he was in front of the small blue apartment house on Broom Street and there was a thin string of lights twinkling on it, and then, without thinking, he banged and banged and banged on the door.

ISABELLE SAT AT the kitchen table, watching her tortoise slowly make his way across her table. It still amazed her that she had actually bought him at a store and brought him home. She couldn't help admiring the smooth brown of his shell, the scalloped edges that came to a point front and back. Even the slow, dinosaur-like way he walked across her table, his tiny black nails clicking on the surface, gave her a thrill. She'd never had a pet, because her parents thought they were too much trouble and Luke hadn't wanted one, and even if she had gotten an animal, a tortoise would never have been an obvious choice.

The moment she had seen him, something about him had gotten to her. She'd been walking home from Beautiful Baby, past the pet shop, and she saw him through the storefront window, wedged into a glass tank that was too small for him, without even room for him to turn around. He looked so unhappy, Isabelle had marched right into the store to complain. "That tank's too small for that tortoise," she said. The pet store owner, an older man in a bowling shirt, just shrugged at her. "He's got a brain the size of a pea. He hardly moves. What does he need room for?" he said.

Isabelle looked back at the tortoise, at the tiny tank that didn't even have a bowl of water. The tortoise had his eyes closed, and his legs were tucked tightly into his shell. "I'll take him," Isabelle said. "Can you deliver the tank to me if I pay you extra?" Before she knew it, she had spent a hundred and twenty dollars and she was walking home with a nine-inch tortoise in a box and a book called *Get to Know Your Tortoise!*

As soon as the tank arrived, the tortoise looked happier. She had lifted the tank—big enough for a small pan of water he could soak in if he wanted—onto her long wood table, and lined it with newspaper. She gave the tortoise a saucer of cut-up tomato and apple, placing it right near him, and she fit in the hollow wood log the pet store had recommended, because tortoises loved to burrow. As soon as he had smelled the food, he had opened his amazing eyes, deep, lustrous brown, ringed in orange. "There you go," she soothed. She had fed him from her fingers, even though the book cautioned that tortoises could bite. "Nelson," she christened him. It sounded dignified and hopeful.

"You are so beautiful," she told him, and he stretched his neck out for the first time, making a long, lovely curve. Nelson yawned, showing the pink of his mouth, and then he met her eyes, unblinking, as if he were taking her measure. "That man was wrong. You don't have a brain the size of a pea," she told him, and it seemed to her that he understood.

The buzzer sounded and she scooped Nelson up and put him gently back into his tank. He rustled in the newspaper, burying himself under a layer so that only his tail stuck out.

Isabelle pressed the intercom button, "Who is it?" she said. She was just about the only person here who ever asked who it was. No answer. The buzzer rang again and then Isabelle heard a faint buzz that meant someone else was letting the person in.

When the frantic knock came on her door, Isabelle cautiously peered out the peep hole.

For a moment, she didn't see anyone, which was unnerving. "Anyone there?" she said. Then she looked down and there was Sam. He was crying, shivering so hard his teeth were knocking. She unhooked the chain and the door swung open. He couldn't stop shaking, and when he looked up at her, she felt staggered. "Sam," she said, astonished, and then he flung himself into her arms.

IT TOOK HIM a while to stop crying. "Are you all right?" Isabelle asked, and he nodded but kept crying. He was soaking wet. She brought out a blanket and wrapped it around him. His small shoulders, like bird wings, were heaving, and he dug in his pocket and breathed into an inhaler, which made her worry even more. "Let's get you warm," she said, "and then we'll figure this out."

He trailed her as she rounded up an old Harvard sweatshirt Luke had bought her. She found an old pair of black sweatpants that he could roll up and gave those to him, too. "Go put these on," she urged. "I'll throw your wet things in the dryer." He swam in the clothes, but at least he stopped shaking. Then she led him to the kitchen and heated up some soup. She saw him staring at the tortoise. "I just got him today," she said. "Isn't he great?"

"You know my name," he said.

"Well, of course I know your name," she said, and then she stopped because she didn't want to mention the accident or the newspaper accounts that had been plastered with news of him.

"Do you have a name?" he said. He stared at the soup, licking his lips.

"Of course I do. Isabelle. Isabelle Stein."

"I didn't know your name, but I know who you are, too."

"You do? But how do you know me?"

He looked at up her, locking eyes. "I saw you," he said.

Isabelle braced her hands on the counter. Sam took another spoonful of soup. "You were there with my mom," he said.

Isabelle was suddenly nauseated, turning away so Sam wouldn't see her distress.

She stood by the counter, listening to him eat, the two of them completely silent. When she heard his spoon clatter, she turned and then sat down across the table from him. "Where's your father? Why did you come here?" she asked him.

He stared down into his soup, making circles with his spoon. "You can look at me, you know," she said quietly.

He glanced up and met her eyes.

"Where were you? Where's your father?"

"I forgot my keys!"

"But why would you come here? How would you even know how to find me?"

He sneezed into his hands. Isabelle handed him a napkin and he blew his nose. "I followed you once," he said quietly. Isabelle thought of all those nights she had crept to his house and hidden like a burglar in the shadows, watching for movements behind the windows, straining to hear music that might let her know more about them, that might help her to know that they were all right.

"Why would you do that?"

Sam fiddled with his spoon.

Isabelle crouched beside him so she was eye level. "Why would you go looking for me?"

Sam stayed silent.

"We're calling your dad right now," she said, finally.

She thought she should call, but Sam shook his head. "No, I'll do it," he said. He was so skinny, she thought. He looked so little. "All right," she said. "That's probably a better idea."

He turned his back toward her, cradling the phone. He punched in the numbers, his small shoulders heaving. "Daddy?" he said. "I got locked out." He half closed his eyes. "None of the neighbors were home, but I-I came here."

Sam turned farther away from her. "I don't know!" Sam said. "I am. I don't know why. I'm sorry. No, this is the first time." Sam acted like he was confessing a crime, and Isabelle had a sinking feeling that Charlie would think she was responsible.

"Tell your father I'm on Broom Street," she said to Sam. "Six forty-four, apartment four B."

Sam hesitated and then repeated the address. "No," he said. "I told you I don't know! Just come get me!" When he hung up, his shoulders were sloping. "He's coming now," Sam said, and it was then that Isabelle realized that Sam hadn't once said her name to Charlie.

"Why didn't you tell him you were with me?" she asked and he shrugged. "I forgot," he said, but he wouldn't meet her eyes and Isabelle suddenly felt afraid.

AFTER BUZZING CHARLIE IN, she heard his steps on the stairs. She started for the door but then froze. Sam got the door and there was Charlie, hunched into a denim jacket, his long, black hair flying, his eyes so dark she couldn't see the pupils. She expected him to recognize her, to say something, to shout at her or be angry, but he looked past her, his eyes lighting on Sam. "Are you okay?" he asked, patting Sam down as if he might have broken bones.

"I'm fine, Daddy!" Sam shook his father off.

"Do you want to come in?" Isabelle asked, but it was as if Charlie was in some bubble where he couldn't see or hear her. The tortoise made a clicking sound in his tank.

"Where's your jacket and your pants? Whose sweatshirt is that?" Charlie asked Sam.

"She gave me these clothes. Mine are in the dryer," Sam said.

"Can you just wait in the hall for a second?" Charlie asked him. "Don't go anywhere. Just stand right outside."

Charlie waited until Sam was outside before he turned slowly to Isabelle and then, for the first time, he met her eyes. He looked different suddenly, as if all his features had fallen. "You're that woman," he said quietly. "I recognize you from the newspapers."

"I'm so sorry—"

"Why would my son come here?" Charlie interrupted.

Isabelle hesitated. She looked out in the hallway and saw Sam rolling one hand along the small wooden banister by the stairs, head dipped so low, his hair covered his face. "I don't know," she said.

"How would he even know where you lived?"

"He said he followed me once. I didn't know until he told me tonight."

"He followed you? When did he even see you?"

Isabelle hesitated. "I happened to pass by his school one day on my way home. I didn't speak to him—and I didn't know he had followed me."

Charlie shook his head. "You can understand why I don't want him here, can't you?" he said quietly. "I don't know what crazy ideas he has about you, but he's had a very hard time of it and you're the last person in the world to help us."

Isabelle was surprised by how much that stung. She stepped back.

"Sam came *here*," she said. "He was cold and wet and he didn't have his key. I got him out of his wet clothes and gave him some hot food. I made sure he was all right. And we called you." She looked toward the kitchen. "I'll go get his things." She went to the dryer and pulled out Sam's clothes, folding them as she walked toward Charlie. "They're dry now," she said. "You can keep the sweatshirt and pants."

Charlie took the folded clothing, looking down at them. His eyes scanned her long table, where Sam's drained glass was, his empty soup bowl.

"He finished the soup," Charlie said quietly. "He hasn't really been eating much these days. I didn't even know he liked soup that much."

"He had two bowls."

224

He met her eyes, and self-conscious, she stepped back.

Charlie's shoulders straightcned. "Thank you," Charlie said quietly, and then he stepped out into the hallway, putting one arm firmly about Sam. Sam stared up into Isabelle's eyes, and she couldn't help it. She smiled at him. Charlie pulled Sam closer to him. "We appreciate this, but Sam won't be back here," Charlie said, and then he started down the stairs and they were gone.

ON THE WAY HOME, in the car, Sam kept studying his fingers. Charlie felt his stomach roil and there was a dark, sour taste in his mouth. "I'm so sorry the extra key wasn't there. From now on, I'll double-check." Sam nodded but still wouldn't look at Charlie.

"Why did you go to that woman's house?" he asked carefully.

Sam looked out the window, as if he were considering something. "I remembered her from the accident," he said haltingly.

Charlie suddenly felt sick. Of course. Isabelle was the only other person who had seen what Sam had seen that day, who had been there. Sam probably felt some weird kinship with her or maybe it was a way he was processing his grief, to go and seek her out. He glanced over at his son, and he looked so fragile that it was all Charlie could do not to stop the car and take Sam in his arms.

"I don't want to talk about it," Sam said.

Charlie turned the car down their block. "Listen," he said carefully. "You don't have to, but I think it's best if you stay away from her."

"Away from her! Why?"

"She's a stranger and you don't talk to strangers. She shouldn't have approached you. That was a very wrong thing to do. You tell me if you see her again."

As soon as they got home, Sam stormed into the house, marched into his room, and firmly shut the door. What was he supposed to say to Sam? Charlie wondered. That if it wasn't for Isabelle, Sam's mother would be alive? That if Isabelle had gotten better directions, she might not have been on that road, might not have struck his wife? The papers said she was local. That was what really bothered him. After such an accident, why hadn't she moved away? Why did Isabelle have to live here, where they both would see her and be reminded of what had happened? He didn't even want to breathe a mouthful of the same air she was breathing.

TEDDY DIDN'T COME back to school all that week. Sam tried calling him the next few days, but the line was always either busy or no one bothered to pick up, and they didn't seem to have an answering machine. Once, after school, Sam even gathered up his courage and biked over to

Teddy's, praying the whole way that his terrifying mom wouldn't be the one to answer the door; he positioned his bike for a quick getaway, just in case she was. He kept remembering the narrow slit of her eyes, the pinch of her mouth when she looked at him. He rang the bell three times, then four, standing at the door so long, a neighbor finally came out next door and yelled at him, "Go away! They're not home!" She shooed at Sam with her hands like he was a stray dog.

SAM BEGAN TO BE a target at school for bullies. Before he had been friends with Teddy, no one had really paid him much attention. But once the kids knew he was hanging out with Teddy, there had been that sudden burst of respect. Kids made way when Sam passed. No one mocked him when he began to cough and wheeze in class and had to ask to be excused, because if they did, Teddy would shoot them a threatening look.

Now, Sam felt punished for his friendship, like the kids knew that without Teddy, he wasn't so big, certainly nothing to be afraid of. A spitball pinged against his back, but he couldn't risk turning around. He brushed at the back of his shirt, ignoring the titters, and when the lunch bell rang, he took his time getting up. He was starving, but the thought of going to the cafeteria for lunch was terrifying, especially since yesterday Bobby Rocket had stolen his sandwich and thrown it in the trash, giving his friend a high-five after he did it. So Sam crept to the art room and shut the door, slowly eating his baloney and mustard sandwich until he heard the bell.

The longer Teddy was absent from school, the worse it got for Sam. "What are you going to do about it?" Billy Adams sneered, tearing Sam's homework out of Sam's hands. When Sam raised his hand because he knew what the periodic table was and proudly gave his answer, he heard muttering behind him, dry and hot on his neck like a heavy wind. There were repeated kicks to the back of his chair. "You think you're so smart," someone hissed.

He stopped doing his homework, because then it couldn't be taken from him. "See me," Ms. Rivers wrote on his papers. She called him to her desk, which made the kids snicker. "Is there anything you want to talk about?" she probed, and he shook his head, keeping his eyes down, focusing on the red laces of his sneakers. When Miss Rivers called on him for an answer later, he stopped saying it because then no one would kick his chair. He made his mind shut like a slammed door.

"Sam," sighed Miss Rivers. "Are you with us, Sam?"

"Asthma Boy," someone whispered, loud enough for the whole class to hear, but he didn't turn around. He squinched his eyes tightly shut.

He knew that sometimes, what you didn't see couldn't hurt you.

RIDING THROUGH TOWN on her bike, Isabelle thought about what a mess she had made of things. She told herself it was over. She had tried her best to do the right thing, but look how terribly that had all gone.

She swerved, heading for the park. She didn't have to be at Beautiful Baby for another hour, to photograph newborn triplets. Imagine being that lucky, she thought.

She took her camera from her bike pack. She snapped the front of the local deli, which was being torn down. She loved the sign: FRESH SANDWISHES. GET THEM WHILE THEIR HOT. She was angling for another shot and, to her surprise, saw Sam in the lens.

Isabelle lowered her camera. A raw pang traveled up her spine. He had appeared out of nowhere and he looked so skinny and pale, as if someone had rubbed him with a gum eraser. His hair was too long and shaggy, falling past his collar, and he had faint purple circles under his eyes, as if he hadn't been sleeping. But when he saw her, his face lighted up. "Hey, kiddo," she said, trying to sound casual, not to let him know how upset she felt at seeing him.

"Is your father here?" she asked, and Sam shook his head. He kicked at a stone in front of him, once and then twice. She wanted to stroke his hair back, to give him her scarf, to feed him the package of butter cookies she had in her pocket, but she kept her hands on her camera. He's not your child, she told herself. Not your responsibility.

"You aren't supposed to be with me," she said simply. "You know your dad wouldn't like it." He kept staring at her, and she began to fiddle with the lens setting, rotating the lens aimlessly.

"I'm in the park. I'm not with you."

"That's a technicality."

Sam studied her camera. "What were you taking a picture of?"

Isabelle pointed to the sign.

"Why?" Sam asked.

"The sign's funny. Sandwishes. I want to remember it after they tear it all down."

"Wishes," Sam said abruptly. "My parents used to hug me and call it a Samwich." He moved closer, peering at her camera. "The camera looks cool."

"It's a Canon." She showed it to him. "Film, not digital."

"How come it's not digital?"

"I like shooting with a film camera. It's richer," she said. "It shows more, I think. Plus, I'm stubborn and old fashioned. I just like it better." She showed him how the lens could turn. "This is for focus. You turn this focusing ring here for the aperture and it lets in more or less light," she said. She noticed his lashy eyes, the splash of freckles on his cheeks, and she suddenly wanted to touch every one. She felt her eyes watering and had to lift the camera to hide her face. She turned her flash on. "You want the flash in the daylight because it actually opens up the shadows." She took his picture.

Sam grimaced. "I hate the way I look in pictures. I always look like I'm sick."

Isabelle lowered the camera again. She studied him. "I don't think you look sick at all," she said. "Sometimes photographs show things that aren't there. You have to learn to look deeper, to see what might be hidden."

He looked at her, considering. "Can I take a picture?" he asked.

"Sure you can." She handed him the camera. "Brace it with one hand on the bottom, and then use your index finger and your thumb to focus it." She moved his arms close to his chest. "That's to keep it all steady, so your movement won't give you a blurry picture." She showed him how to look through the viewfinder, how to see the needle in the middle. "That's your light meter. Today you probably want it right smack in the middle."

"I see it!" he said, his voice rising in excitement. "But it's to the right."

Isabelle pointed to the aperture scale. "You want to change your f-stop then. Go to, oh, f-eight, I would say. In the business, we say f-eight and be there!"

"Is that, like, photographer talk?"

"It is indeed."

He changed the f-stop and then peered through the camera, holding it gingerly. "Okay," he said. "Now what do I do?"

"It's okay. Don't be afraid of it," she told him. "What do you want to take a picture of?"

"I don't know yet."

"Well, take your time. See what catches your eye." Isabelle had no idea what Sam might take. You could never tell with kids. She had once taught a kids' photography class at Beautiful Baby. She'd spent hours gathering interesting things she thought they might like to photograph: stuffed animals, bags of candy, even a rubber chicken she had found in a joke store. To her surprise, the kids had ended up taking pictures of their own nostrils or their feet and one little girl had taken nothing but shots of her own hair that she was holding out in front of her. Isabelle was amazed by their creativity, and the kids had been thrilled with their pictures.

Sam held up the camera in both hands and peered through the lens. He was facing her and she heard the shutter click.

"Wow, that was fast."

He nodded, happily. "Go through the whole thing again," she told him. "Cock this lever to get to the next frame. Then check the light meter." She watched him fumble with the rings and then he held the camera up and snapped another picture of her. "Don't you want to take anything else?" she asked, and he shook his head.

"When you develop the picture, can I have prints of the ones I took?" Sam asked. "Can you mail them?"

"Sure. I print them myself."

How would she manage mailing him pictures when Charlie had asked her to stay away, Isabelle wondered. She glanced at her watch. She couldn't believe she was here with Sam. She wanted to call Beautiful Baby and tell them she'd be late or that she wouldn't be there at all, but she knew she couldn't. "I've got to get going," she said, holding out her hand for the camera, and for a minute, her hand touched his; then he turned and took a picture of the street, and then gave the camera back to her.

She took off on her bike, looking back as she turned the corner. Sam was already gone.

AS SOON AS SHE got to work that day, Isabelle went to see Chuck. He had his feet up on the desk and one hand was buried in a bag of chips. There was a spot of grease on his tie. "Oh, hi," he said casually, motioning to the chair with a nod. "What can I do for you?"

"You could give me a raise," she said. Chuck

took another chip and then laughed at her, as if she had told him a hilarious joke. "Oh, sure, how about a million more dollars?" he offered. The chip crunched. "Maybe I'll give myself one, too."

"I'm serious," she said quietly. "I haven't had a raise in over a year. I deserve one."

"Excuse me, you deserve one?" He frowned and sat up straighter. "You don't have a college degree."

"Give me time off and some financial help and I'll get one," Isabelle blurted, but he lifted his hand.

"Let me refresh your memory, Isabelle. You weren't here for three weeks of our busiest season. We had to really scramble to get things done."

She looked at him, astonished. "I was in a car accident." The words wounded her. She didn't like saying them.

"It's not so busy now. Do you see people lining the streets to get in here? Do you even see them in the waiting room? Tourist season's ending. Beautiful Baby's going to get slow. You know that." He tapped a finger on the desk. "Besides," he said. "People aren't crazy about you taking their kids' pictures anymore."

She flushed. "That's ridiculous. Who told you that?"

"Is it ridiculous?" He picked up a potato chip and gestured at her. "I may think it is, and you may think it is, but if our clients don't think it is, then we have a problem. People know you as the woman who killed a mom."

"It wasn't my fault." She tried to stare him down. "Some people don't even know who I am."

"Oh, yes, they do. This is a small town with big memories. People believe whatever they want to believe. They do know who you are, because I've heard them talking about you." He leaned toward her.

Isabelle felt a pulse beating in her neck. "I'm the only decent photographer you have here and you know it."

"How good do you have to be to work here?" he said. He dipped his hand into the bag and pulled out another chip and studied it before popping it into his mouth.

Isabelle got up and walked out of his office. Was Chuck right? Was it the accident? Was it that people didn't want to be photographed by her because she had killed a mother, because she could have killed Sam?

Maybe I don't blame them, she thought.

She had wanted to be a photographer since her father had given her her first camera. She was always taking pictures, always reading books about photography and sending her work to magazines. She never got anywhere, but people had told her that she had promise. What did that mean? It was a false word, like *plucky*. How and where did you go with it?

IT WAS THE BEGINNING of December, and Charlie was at yet another meeting with Miss Rivers. "I'm still worried about Sam," she told him, tapping her pencil on the desk. She told Charlie that Sam was a smart boy, but all of a sudden he was doing terribly in school. "He seems to have lost interest in everything," she said. "He doesn't turn in his homework, he's failing his tests, and he doesn't pay attention. He used to be the smartest boy in the class and now it's as if he's not there anymore. He's always daydreaming."

"He does his homework," Charlie said. He remembered Sam hunched over the table, concentrating so hard that he didn't even hear Charlie come up behind him.

Miss Rivers pursed her lips. "Plus," she said. "He doesn't have any friends."

Charlie started. "Of course he has friends," he said.

"I'm just saying that at school, he keeps to himself and reads," said Miss Rivers. "For a while he was friendly with Teddy, but Teddy hasn't been back to school because of a personal family matter." The teacher leaned forward. "Actually, I thought Teddy was part of the problem."

"Teddy?" Charlie said. He felt suddenly bewildered, trying to place the name. "Who's Teddy?"

Miss Rivers gave him an odd look. "Teddy. His

best friend, Teddy." Miss Rivers pursed her lips. "Mr. Nash," she said. "Maybe he needs to talk to somebody." She scribbled something on a card. "No one can deny he's had a hard time. He's been through a trauma. And kids can be cruel. This woman is supposed to be just excellent." Numb, Charlie took the card and tucked it in his pocket.

The whole way home, Charlie brooded. Sam had a best friend named Teddy and Charlie didn't know a thing about him.

He pulled the card the teacher had given him from his jeans. Talk to somebody, the teacher had said. Sam had seen more than enough doctors in his lifetime. He thought of his son sitting in a room while a stranger leaned toward him and asked him questions. He thought of all the jobs he had to do, but what was work compared to his son? Charlie picked up his cell phone and called his foreman. "I'm taking a few days off," Charlie said. "Personal family matters."

ISABELLE STOOD IN her darkroom, hands on her hips, looking at the photographs Sam had taken. Photographers always talked about the law of thirds. You were supposed to divide up the shot into three sections for compositional interest, putting the main subject a third of the way into the frame, but here she was, smack in the middle and it was one of the most arresting photographs she had ever seen. He had captured her, and the most curious thing was that he had somehow photographed her so that her shoulders were dark and burly, as if she had wings under her dress and any moment she might spread them to lift off the ground and fly away. She studied the picture as critically as she could. Well. This was really a good picture. For a kid and for anyone. She clipped it onto the clothesline in her darkroom. She'd find a way to get it to him.

She picked up the one shot she had taken of him. His face was arresting, his eyes so luminous she couldn't look away. He was gazing right at the camera, right at her, almost as if he were trying to tell her something.

SAM WAS HOME alone when a big brown envelope came through the door addressed to him. He didn't get mail. At least not real mail. You couldn't count the junk mail that somehow got addressed to him, offers for time shares in Florida or subscriptions to magazines he really didn't want, like *Popular Boating* or *Muscle Man Today*. He took it to his room and sat on the bed before carefully tearing open the envelope. There was a small blue card that said only "Sam, I know you wanted these. They are good." And then there was Isabelle's name. He traced his finger across it.

There were three pictures, two of Isabelle and one of the street, but she had blown them up so they were large and glossy. As soon as he saw them, he had to bring the photos closer to his face to make sure he was really seeing what he thought he was seeing. She had told him that pictures showed things that sometimes seemed hidden, and now, he understood that what she had been telling him was another message. There. Right there. Look at that. Her coat was bunchy, hiding her wings. And her face was turned as if she were guiding him to look in a certain direction and when he did, he saw a blurry spot in the photograph and his heart leaped.

His mother. He knew it. It was a sign, just like the angel books had said.

"Sam." He heard his father and quickly put the photographs back in the envelope and slid it into the bottom of his drawer under his sweaters.

For the next three days, Charlie took off work, put his cell phone away, and did nothing but be with Sam. "Everyone deserves to play hooky once in a while," Charlie told him. They went to four movies in two days. They went bowling, and afterward, they walked along the main street. "Let me buy you something," Charlie said, stopping in front of Laughs toy store.

Sam brightened and, to Charlie's surprise, shook his head. He met Charlie's eyes. "I want a camera," Sam said.

CHARLIE WAS SO relieved that Sam wanted something, that he showed interest, that he immediately took him to Gray's Camera Store, where the clerk started pulling out digital cameras. "How about those?" Charlie asked, but Sam shook his head.

"I want a film camera," he insisted.

"Really? Film? But digital is so much easier. That's what everyone uses now," Charlie said.

"Film shows more," Sam said.

"I bet you're right," Charlie said, impressed. The clerk brought out some film cameras, heavy and more substantial. "You sure?" Charlie asked, and Sam studied the cameras.

"Do you have any Canons?" he said. "That's what I want."

"You and ninety percent of the business. They've got different models and lenses to go with every budget. And you're in luck because I've got a used one," the clerk said. "At a good price for a Canon, too."

The camera came with a strap that Sam could slip over his neck and an instruction booklet as big as Sam's fist. When Charlie saw the price tag— three hundred dollars—he blanched. He was about to guide Sam back to one of those little automatics, but then he saw how Sam's face was lighted up, how excited he was. "Sold," Charlie said. "It's your early Christmas present."

For the first few days, Charlie got used to flashes of light in his eyes, making him blink so he couldn't see.

The camera seemed to transform Sam. He stopped reading obsessively. He stopped sitting in the dark, and instead, he couldn't wait to get outside with his camera. All he wanted to do was take pictures. Charlie couldn't wait to see the pictures Sam had taken. He took three rolls to the photo shop and two days later went to pick them up, but when he opened the folder, his jaw fell.

Charlie had bought Sam black and white Fuji film, the best, which wasn't all that cheap, either. He remembered Sam snapping pictures of him at dinner, or when they were in the park. He knew Sam had taken a posed picture of Charlie watering the lawn and working in the garden, but where were those and what were these?

He spread the shots out. All of the photographs were of cars speeding away, or the backs of people, their heads turned as if they were about to tell you an important message. It had been a brilliant sunny day when Sam and he had gone out to take pictures, but all these shots were dark.

He didn't know what to say to Sam. Not that he was any expert on photography, but shouldn't the pictures be brighter? Shouldn't they have something in them other than cars and the road? He didn't want to ruin Sam's obvious enthusiasm, or to put a damper on the first thing that had made Sam excited in weeks. He thought he'd get him some books on how to take pictures, maybe he'd talk him into a class, but to Charlie's shock, when Sam saw his photos, he was delighted.

"Look how great they came out!" he said. He pored over the shots as if they were masterpieces, holding them up to the light, squinting, and when he handed them to Charlie, he stood so close that Charlie could feel the warmth of his skin. Sam hung all the pictures up on the bulletin board in his room, carefully thumb-tacking around the edges, and later that evening, when Charlie walked by, he saw Sam looking intently at the pictures, one after another, as if a wonderful drama were unfolding in front of him.

THE CAMERA MADE Sam brave, as if it had secret powers. He took the camera to school, and almost instantly good things started happening. First, the camera was like a stop sign. It was one thing to trash Sam's lunchbox, to throw his sandwich, but all you had to do was look at the camera to know it was expensive and special. Sam tensed when Billy approached him. He put his arms around his camera, ready to shout for the teacher if he had to. Billy eyed him and said, grudgingly, "Cool camera."

The next incredible thing that happened was that Teddy walked back into the classroom, his arm in a sling. "What happened to you?" Sam asked.

Teddy scowled and acted as if he didn't even know Sam. "None of your beeswax."

Sam heard Teddy tell the other kids that he broke his arm while riding on the back of a motorcycle, that he had been going 70 miles an hour when the bike swerved and crashed, but all Sam could think of was how Teddy's mother had raged into the room.

At recess, it was too cold to go outside, so they all went into the big gym. Teddy followed him, tapping Sam on the shoulder. "Take my picture," Teddy said, and posed with his arm.

"Hey, me, too," said Billy, and he held up his arms as if he were a muscle man on the beach. Then all the other kids wanted their pictures taken, and because taking their picture was better than getting pushed around, Sam did as he was told. When he was behind the lens, no one touched him.

Miss Rivers made Sam let her keep the camera for him. All day, he kept looking over at her desk, and every time he did, he felt a strange new surge of power. He looked up and saw the world in pictures. He made mental frames about Miss Rivers, around the window pouring light into the room. His fingers itched with excitement.

That day, when Miss Rivers asked who in the class knew when the Declaration of Independence was written, Sam shot up his hand and answered, waiting for the moment when his chair would be kicked, but there was no kick, and when he turned around, Fred Morgan, who usually sneered at him, gave him a thumbs-up.

Sam walked home through the park, his camera looped about his neck, hoping he might run into Isabelle. Maybe his father didn't want him to see Isabelle anymore, but Sam couldn't be blamed if they just sort of bumped into each other, could he? Maybe he wasn't allowed to ask Isabelle about his mother, but no one said he couldn't ask her about photography, and he had a million questions he wanted to ask her about depth and framing a shot. Sometimes, as he walked, he'd just whirl around and take a picture.

You never knew who might be in it.

⁓ Eleven ⁓

It was blustery and cold, and Charlie stood outside the school, looking for Sam, thinking he might surprise him. Like April, he thought, then brushed the thought away. The kids spilled out, shouting and jumping around, their winter coats flung open, their heads without hats. They ran to their parents' waiting cars or headed for the park. He scanned the crowd for Sam, but he knew he had time because Sam always came out last, and he was almost always alone.

"Hey, Dad!" Charlie looked to the sound, and to his surprise, there was Sam, and miracle of miracles, he was grinning. The sturdy little used Canon was slung around his neck, and when he saw Charlie, he lifted the camera and took Charlie's photo. "F-eight and be there!" Sam said. "That's photographer talk about the f-stop, Daddy!"

Charlie hugged Sam to him, leading him to the car. "I got sixty chips because my homework was so good," Sam told him. "I used half for free time while everyone else had to practice their cursive."

"That calls for extra dessert tonight."

"Cool."

Charlie was glad he had bought Sam the camera, which seemed to focus him. Sam seemed happier.

His homework was now done on time. So he didn't have a lot of play dates. Who did, when you thought about it?

"I was wondering," Charlie said, "if you'd like to take a photography class."

"Maybe," Sam said.

As soon as they got home, Sam ran to get his collection of photographs. He sat in the center of the living room, his legs splayed out, his whole body hunched over. Sam was so intent, he didn't even see Charlie, not until his dad stooped to get a better look, and then he started.

"Did I surprise you?" Charlie asked, and then he moved to the other side of Sam where he could get a better look, and he felt himself reeling. Sam had taken pictures of cars moving away, of empty, winding roads. Just like the ones that April had been killed on. Every shot looked like the newspaper accident scene. All that was missing was a white chalk line for the body. Charlie felt like crying.

"Why do you keep taking pictures like that?" he asked quietly.

Sam stared at him, not moving. Charlie bent down, and that was when he saw the photo Sam was trying to hide under one of his legs. That was when he saw Isabelle's face. Her coat flying out behind her, her features in shadows.

Charlie pulled the photo free.

"That's mine!" Sam cried, grabbing for it.

"What's this?" Charlie said sharply, holding it away from Sam.

"I took it." Charlie noticed how Sam's eyes began to fill with light. "It's mine."

"When?"

Sam hesitated. "Last week. I saw Isabelle in the park."

Charlie stared at the photo. He couldn't believe what he was seeing, what he was hearing.

Sam stood up, shifting his weight from one untied sneaker to the other. "Don't you like them? Don't you think I'm good at this? I can do this. I can do this really well." He lifted his chin. "Isabelle thinks I have talent. She taught me things. She developed them for me—and there's even one she took herself." He lifted up one of the bigger prints that had a brown tone, a shot of Sam in profile. "It's called sepia," Sam said. "I like that word, sepia."

"Didn't I tell you to stay away from her? Next time, you give the film to me."

"But you don't know anything about photography!" Sam stabbed a finger at a picture. "You don't know that that's called perspective!"

"Look, I'm glad you're taking pictures. That's not the point. I'm thrilled you love photography. I really am. But I don't want you dealing with Isabelle! If you like taking pictures so much, do it on your own. Or maybe we can find you a class."

Sam shook his head, confused. "But I don't want to take a class!"

"I thought you said you did!"

"I said maybe! That's not the same as saying yes!"

"A class can help you get better," Charlie said. His head suddenly hurt and he wanted to sit down. "They can show you how to fix those blurry spots there."

"That's the best part of the pictures!"

"A class can help you photograph lots of different things besides roads and cars."

"You're supposed to snap what catches your eye!" Sam cried. "You take what you want to take, not what someone else tells you to take!"

Charlie looked down at the photographs again. The long, empty roads. The cars. The sense of yearning in the photographs, made all the stronger by what he knew wasn't there.

Sam grabbed the photographs, glaring at Charlie. "You don't know anything!" he said.

Sam ran to his room, slamming the door. Charlie heard the music going on, then the *pop pop pop* of Sam's video game on his computer, and he put his head in his hands. Sam was right. He didn't know anything. He didn't know how his life had unraveled so completely. He didn't know how to live without April or how to be a single father or what to do with the roiling helplessness he felt each and every day.

• • •

THE NEXT MORNING, after Sam had left for school, Charlie felt tense and restless. He didn't have to work today and he wasn't sure what to do with himself. He walked into the living room. No matter how many times he told Sam, that kid never put anything away, and even when he did, things always ended up in the wrong place. He put away some books. He put Sam's writing notebook on the table where he wouldn't forget it, and then he saw the big yellow envelope of Sam's photos.

Charlie sat down and pulled out the pictures. He never would have thought of photography for Sam. April used to buy kits—tie dye and pottery—for both her and Sam, but nine times out of ten, Sam would make a gallant try and then give up. "Not your thing, huh?" April would tease, and she'd let it go. But photography was something that Sam seemed to truly love, and if Charlie were going to thank someone for it, he would have to thank Isabelle Stein.

Still, the photos were unnerving. The empty roads! Charlie sighed and pulled out the photo Isabelle had taken of Sam. It was good, he had to admit. He looked at another photo, and when the picture began to tremble, it took him a minute to realize that his hands were shaking.

It was the photo of Isabelle. He shut his eyes for a moment, as if to clear his vision. The wrong woman was in Sam's photo. It should have been

249

April there, with Sam beside her. He left the photo on the table, feeling himself unraveling. Let Sam put away his own things.

Time stretched out in front of him like an endless roll of blank paper. He glanced at his watch. Eight in the morning. He grabbed his car keys. Sam was staying after school today to finish a project and wouldn't be home until four. He had eight more hours before Sam would be back. He'd take a drive.

CHARLIE HAD BEEN driving two hours when he began to feel like a shadow behind the wheel. His stomach was hot and tense and his hands were clammy. There were a thousand things he could be doing today other than this fool's mission—working, doing laundry, cleaning. Everything inside him told him to turn back and head home, but he kept going, as if the car were propelling him forward, as if he had no control. When he got to the turnoff road, he was sweating, and when he made the turn, he felt as if someone had stapled his heart. He pulled over to one shoulder and parked, waiting a minute for his pulse to slow down. He took deep, long gulps of air.

He got out of the car. It was just an ordinary road, black top, yellow lines slashing the center. It had been almost four months now. The white chalk lines were long gone, the stars of blood. The road was clear and empty. You wouldn't know anything terrible had happened here. You wouldn't know that this was where his wife had died.

Charlie breathed in more deeply. The sky looked hard and bright. He could feel a chill of wind on his back. "Come back," he said, his voice cracking, and then he started to cry because he knew instantly then that he shouldn't have come here, that it wasn't going to make anything better, that April was never coming back.

He was still crying when he got back into the car, wiping at his eyes, digging in his pocket for a tissue to blow his nose. He couldn't think straight enough to drive all the way home, but he couldn't sit here in the car, on this road, a second longer.

Charlie started the car and drove slowly. There was really nothing around here for miles, nothing except an old Ready Diner, the lights glowing even in the daylight. Ready, ready. Ready for what?

There were only a few cars in the lot. As he pulled up in front, he leaned over the steering wheel and glanced up at the windows. It seemed bright and cheerful inside, and he started to look forward to going in. He noticed a woman sitting at a booth, right by the window, her hands covering her face. When she lifted her face, Charlie saw, to his shock, that it was Isabelle Stein and she was crying.

He couldn't move for a moment. Then he shrank

down in his seat, not wanting her to see him. He watched Isabelle rising, putting money down. Her face was raw with grief and she looked dazed and exhausted. There were shadows under her eyes, and he felt his heart plummet. The front door of the diner opened and Isabelle walked out, stumbling slightly, never seeing him. She headed for a car, got inside, and said something to the driver, who was young. As soon as the car was gone, he parked his car and went inside the diner.

Charlie slid into a clean booth, and the waitress came over, a bouncy young blonde slapping down a glossy menu. "That woman who was crying—" Charlie said.

"What am I, a dating service?" the waitress said. "What'll you have?"

Charlie scanned the menu. Nothing looked good to him, but he ordered an omelet and coffee. "The woman—" Charlie said again, and the waitress sighed.

Charlie shook his head. "It's not what you think. I know her already," he said. "I'm—I'm just concerned. I just want to make sure she's all right."

The waitress studied Charlie, as if she were deciding something about him. "She's been here a few times," she finally said. "She always comes and goes in the same car and the kid always waits for her. Always orders pie and coffee and never touches it. She tips big and she always cries. And that's all I know. Now, you want anything else?"

Charlie shook his head and the waitress whisked away. Charlie dropped his head in his hands. He couldn't get rid of the image of Isabelle weeping, her face haunted. He wondered if he went back to the road if he'd see her there, too. She couldn't let go of it. Like him, she just couldn't let go.

The waitress set down the plate of eggs, steaming, flecked with parsley, and Charlie's stomach clenched. He pushed the plate away. "Just the check," he said.

"You're just like her," the waitress said, shaking her head. "The both of you. You come in here like ghosts and you don't eat a thing."

When Charlie got home, Sam was in the living room, surrounded by his photos. Sam started to push them into an envelope, but Charlie crouched down and stopped him. "I know you love taking photos, and you keep doing it," Charlie said. "And you can look at these all you want and you don't have to take a class." Sam lifted his face to Charlie. "I missed you," Charlie said, and held him close.

ISABELLE CRIED IN the back of the car, holding a tissue to her nose, her breath coming in small skips. She'd taken a Valium, which made her so tired she could hardly hold her head up. Her legs felt like noodles. Her panic was muted, and the strange, strong grief now felt distant, like it wasn't quite her own. This all felt like too much of a dream.

She pinched at the skin over her wrist, trying to reclaim herself. She sat hard against the seat, pushing to feel the fake leather against her back.

The driver, a college kid with dreadlocks, kept sneaking worried glances at her in the rearview mirror, and when she blew her nose yet again, he stretched his arm back and handed her a brand new handkerchief. "You can keep it," he said.

She took the handkerchief. "Thank you, Dirk."

This was only the third time she had asked him to drive her here, and after today, she knew it was her last. She had thought she needed to come back to the scene to pay her respects. Or maybe she had really thought that, coming here, she might sense April, a sudden warm shiver of air that might mean forgiveness, a ghost waving at her to let go.

When Isabelle had blurted to Lora that she wanted to come here, Lora hadn't been pleased. "Is this wise, Isabelle?" she said. "It's a very long way and what's to be gained by it? Why would you want to torture yourself with this?"

"I think I'll feel better," Isabelle said.

"Better? By blaming yourself? You're acting like a murderer returning to the scene of the crime. And how will you be a passenger in a car for that long? You need to start out slow, with little local trips, not three hours away. Think about what you're doing."

Isabelle did think. She couldn't afford a cab, couldn't ask her friends to drive her, but then she found a flyer on one of the kiosks in town: DRIVER! CHEAP! it said, and there were five tags with a phone number fluttering underneath and a nice simple name: DIRK. Surely, this could be considered a sign, couldn't it?

She had called Dirk, who said he'd do it for just a hundred dollars a pop.

Three times she had been here, and every time she'd thought it would be different, but it never was. Instead, it brought that day back to her, a thousand times worse.

No more, she told herself. No more. If there were ghosts, they weren't speaking with her. If there was forgiveness, it wasn't here on this muddy patch of road.

AFTER THAT, ISABELLE kept busy. She kept her appointments with Lora every week, and she even walked into a church one evening, to talk to a priest, but as soon as she told him about the accident, she saw his face change. "It wasn't your fault," he said finally, but she could see how his eyebrow was twitching when he said it.

"Can't you give me something to say or do? Aren't there novenas you say?"

"Novenas?" He looked at her curiously.

"I'm sorry, I'm Jewish, I don't know the right term."

"You're Jewish?" he said, quickly standing up. "What on earth are you doing here?"

She called a rabbi who told her he'd be happy to talk with her but she had to join the temple first. Isabelle hung up.

Every time she was working at home, she half expected Sam to show up. She kept her place clean. When she went shopping at the Thrift-T-Mart, she bought cookies and grapes and vanilla soda, kid food. She poured herself a glass of the soda and drank it herself. One Saturday afternoon, she got the cookies and watched *Blade Runner* on TV and when Sean Young found out she was a replicant and not human at all, that everything she had believed about herself and her world was now turned on its head, Isabelle began to cry. "I know how you feel," she wept, and reached for another cookie.

She couldn't just stay here eating cookies. She'd get up and walk on the beach. She'd clear her head, and then she'd come home and work.

THE BEACH WAS COLD and empty, the thin, late-afternoon light barely skimming the water, but Isabelle wasn't ready to go home yet. Somehow, walking the bumpy sand relaxed her. She bundled into her jacket, lifting up the collar.

"Hey!"

She turned around and there was Sam, a scarf bundled over his face, running toward her, his hair flying under his hat, a camera around his neck. Stay away from him, Charlie had told her, but here he was again, his eyes like stars, his face expectant and happy, and she felt something tugging at her heart.

"What are you doing here?" she said. She glanced at the camera and whistled. "A Canon! That's pretty special."

Sam beamed. "It's a film camera! Like yours!" He lowered his scarf a bit. "I'm not cold at all and if I breathe through this, it's really warm. You should try it."

Isabelle smiled at him. "You're taking pictures of the beach?" She lifted his camera to her eyes. "I'd ramp up the shutter speed. If you wanted to catch one of those gulls in flight, you could."

Sam peered down and then moved the shutter dial up. He lifted the camera to his face, pointing it at the ocean, and took a shot of one of the gray gulls skimming over the whitecaps.

"There you go!" Isabelle said enthusiastically, and Sam beamed.

"I come here to skip stones, too." Sam picked up one of the flat stones in the sand. "I come here all the time."

He drew back his arm and flung the stone over the choppy water, bouncing it over the surface. "Look at that! Four times! You really need a smooth lake for it to make ripples, but I like to do it here, anyway. It's more of a challenge."

"I have a confession. I'm a terrible stone-skipper," Isabelle said.

"No, no, don't say that! I'll teach you." He scanned the ground. "I have to find the perfect stones for you," he said, his voice so clear and earnest that she wanted to hug him.

He handed her two smooth white stones, and then he demonstrated how she should move her arm. "Some people just throw the stone any which way, but that's not right. You have to aim. You have to see the skips before you even make them. I'm up to ten, but the world record is fifty-one skips."

"That's amazing," she said.

"Yes, it is. People can get good at it just the way they do at soccer. And it's a sport, too. A real sport." He looked at her hopefully.

"Of course it is," she said.

"Come on. We'll do it together," he assured her, and then Isabelle drew back her arm, the way he showed her, and the stones skimmed along the water one, two, three, and then stopped, making her feel embarrassed. "Oh, that wasn't so hot, was it?" she said.

"No, no, that was a really great start! And you can do even better!"

It killed her the way he helped her, how he would reposition her arm gently or urge her on, how he'd clap when her stones actually made a skip. Sometimes he said, "There you go!" the way she had to him when he took the photo of the gulls. She couldn't hide how happy she felt to be with him. Occasionally, he'd skip a stone, too, and they'd both stop and watch it leap over the water. "What a thing of beauty," Isabelle said, and Sam flushed, pleased. They must have gone through twenty stones, and then she noticed how dark it was getting.

She pointed at the sky. "Hey. Sun's gone."

"I guess I'd better go."

"I'll walk you," she said, and he brightened.

"Really? You will? You'd do that?"

"Of course I will."

The whole walk to his house, he didn't stop talking. At first, he asked her lots of photography questions. Could he capture even a stone in midair? "Yup," she said. "Put the shutter speed up to one thousandth. You can stop the action." How could he get more of what he wanted in a shot? "Zoom lens would give you a really tight shot of the bird," she told him. "If you use a wide-angle lens, the bird will look like an ant against the sky!" He nodded, his small face serious. But then, Sam began talking about other things, as if he were widening his world to her. He told her that in school they were studying Native Americans, but not the gross stuff, like scalping. He said he was taking more and more photographs. "I'm trying to really see things, the way you told me," he said. His whole body was bright with excitement, and he kept making these little jumps beside her. "Wasn't it fun skipping stones?" he asked. "Didn't you have a great time?"

"I did," she said. "Come on, let's cross the street while we have the light." She was striding out into the street, when he reached out and grabbed her hand. She felt those small fingers in hers and she looked down at him, amazed and delighted, not taking her eyes away until he let go of her hand again.

When they got to his house, she hesitated. If Charlie saw her, no matter that she had walked Sam home just to make sure he was safe, he would be upset.

"My dad's not home yet," Sam said, "but I have my own key." He showed it to her, proudly. She waited for him to get to the porch. He turned at the door and gave her a salute, which made her laugh, and then he went into the house. She stood there, watching, waiting until the lights had turned on, warming the rooms inside.

At least for tonight, she didn't have to worry about him.

SHE WENT BACK to the beach the next few Saturdays, half for herself, half hoping to see Sam, but he wasn't there. She skipped stones, but when she managed to get four skips, it felt a little empty because Sam wasn't there to share the pleasure with her. She missed him but knew that he wasn't hers to miss.

Well, maybe it was for the best.

A FEW WEEKS LATER, just after New Year's, Isabelle was at Beautiful Baby, closing up late one night, when she found Sam sleeping on the wooden bench by the front door. She bent down, astonished. "Sam," she said, gently, and his eyes flew open. He shivered in the cold. "What are you doing here?" she said. "It's much too cold to be outside like this! You must be freezing!"

"I wanted to see you." He yawned and his lids fluttered shut again.

Isabelle took out her cell to call Charlie, gently pushing Sam over and settling down beside him. She was too tired to care that Charlie would probably blame her for his son's running off to find her. She couldn't tell Sam not to come see her, either, because seeing him was exactly the thing she wanted most. "I was just coming out of work and he was asleep on a bench," she told Charlie. She looked down at Sam, at the way his mouth was dropping open as he breathed.

"Sleeping on a bench? Is he okay?" Isabelle heard the panic in his voice. "He was supposed to be at a friend's! He never even called me!"

"He's fine."

"I'll be right there. Don't go anywhere. Don't move. Beautiful Baby's on Denten Street, right?"

She waited with Sam on the bench. She tried to imagine how Sam had known where she worked, when he might have followed her, and how it was possible that she hadn't felt him trailing behind her. He moved in his sleep, pressing closer against her. Her hand hovered over his hair, and then she let herself stroke it back. "It's okay," she said.

It didn't take Charlie long to get there. He leaped out of the car and came toward them, his shirt askew, his hair a mess, and for a minute, she braced herself. This time, though, he looked at her. He actually saw her. And then his eyes swept over Sam and he scooped his son up in his arms. "It's okay," he said in a low voice. "It's okay."

He looked up at her again, so forcefully that she stepped back. "I'm just glad you were here," he said, and she nodded. He carried Sam to the car, buckling him into the backseat.

"I'll be going, too," she said.

He looked around. "Where's your car?"

"I walked."

"No, no. Don't be silly. It's cold out. I'll drive you home," he said.

She didn't want to tell him that she had trouble being a passenger in a car. "I like walking," she said. "Even in winter."

"Look, I know this is awkward. For both of us. But please. Let me drive you. I thought Sam was at a sleepover. I'm just glad you were here."

She hesitated. It was later than she usually

walked, and in the distance, she heard some kids catcalling. Sam was dozing, but Charlie watched her. He was standing so close to her, she could have reached out and touched the side of his face. She swallowed hard. If she said no, he'd leave with Sam. She wouldn't have more time with him. But if she said yes, she'd have to get in a car and she'd have to do it without the help of a pill.

The ride was only five minutes. People could die in seconds. They could drown in three inches of water. She thought of how her mother had once told her that all good things had a price. She looked at Charlie, at the way his hair fell into the back of his collar, at the smooth line where his neck met his shoulder. "Okay," she said finally.

He opened the door for her. When she bent to get in the car, she took a deep breath. I can do this, she told herself. He put his hand over her head so she wouldn't bump it, a gesture so simple and startling that, for a moment, she couldn't move. She wanted to put her hand over his, and when he took it away, she missed it. When she sat down, he got in the car and then leaned across her. She could smell the leather of his jacket. "Seat belt," he said, pulling it out for her.

She waited for the motor to go on, for the moment when she would feel as if she were suffocating. Her throat locked. Charlie turned on the radio. "Is music okay?" he asked. "Sam sleeps through everything. Movies, even fireworks. Ever since he was a baby."

She glanced at the backseat. Sam's shoulders were rising and falling, his eyes were rolling with dreams. "That's a gift to be able to sleep like that," she said.

"Once he's asleep, he stays asleep," Charlie said. Charlie was a careful driver. He took his time, as if he were considering the road. He didn't care or get angry when another car beeped at him and when a dog ran out into the street, Charlie slowed to a stop, waiting until he saw the dog was safely on the other side. When he turned down the road, Isabelle saw the group of kids who had been catcalling, six of them waving beer bottles at the car, and one of them threw the bottle, so she heard the crash of glass on the street. If she had walked home, she would have run right into them. She circled her arms about herself. "Cold?" Charlie asked, and she put her arms back down in her lap.

"I'm fine," she said.

He drove past the bowling alley and the diner, and the streets began to look and feel more deserted. Isabelle couldn't remember the night ever being so quiet. She tried to think of something to say.

She thought of all the times she had driven with Luke. He kept the radio up loud and liked to sing along rather than talk to her. When she did talk, he'd say, "Let me just hear the rest of this song," or he'd want to talk about the bar.

"Your photograph was good," Charlie said quietly. He turned the wheel, gliding the car into another lane.

"You saw the one of Sam?" Isabelle looked at him cautiously.

"I did," Charlie said.

She had never talked about her work all that much with Luke. She'd show him her best photos and he'd praise them, and her, but he never really understood what she was trying to do, or why a picture was good; and when she tried to explain, he'd say, "I just love them because I love you," which didn't feel like enough.

"Sam showed me. All he wants to do is take pictures now."

"What I do for work isn't really taking pictures. I work at a kid factory. People come in off the street when they want snapshots. Sometimes I do schools, weddings, sweet sixteens. No one really cares if the pictures are any good. They just want nice pictures of their kid." Her voice trailed. She turned around and glanced at Sam. His head lolled. "He's dreaming," Isabelle said, "but the strap is too close around his neck." She unbuckled herself for a moment and leaned over to adjust it and then sat back down, quickly strapping herself back in.

"That was nice, what you just did," Charlie said, and Isabelle felt a pleased flush.

He turned down another road. "I saw the pictures. And I saw you. At the Ready Diner, by the accident. That's a really long trip."

Isabelle froze. She tried to speak but no words came out. Panic rose in her like steam. "I needed to go there," she finally said.

"So did I," Charlie said.

They were both silent for a moment.

"Let's be honest," Charlie blurted, and she turned to look at him. "This is really about Sam. I don't know what to do about any of this that's going on with Sam. I don't know what's the right thing to do or the wrong thing. All I know is that I would think you would be the last person in the world Sam would want to be close to, and instead he wants to be with you all the time. He seems to need you and I just don't understand why."

Isabelle felt as if her tongue were weighted with stones. "I know you don't want him near me, and I understand that—"

Charlie shook his head. "No, you don't understand. He's doing better. I bought him a camera and it makes him so goddamned happy. And what I want to say is . . . how can I care about his being with you if he's doing better? Isn't that what's most important? Sam? It doesn't matter what I think or feel anymore. It's all about my son. So maybe it's all right. As long as you let me know when he comes to see you."

For the first time since she had gotten into the

car, Isabelle turned to look at Charlie. He was watching the road, not her. She could imagine what saying this cost him. Then she thought of being able to see Sam any time she wanted, of not having to wander around the parks and the bookstore, yearning for a glimpse. Everything out in the open.

"I'll let you know every time," she said.

He stopped, pulling in at a diner.

"Is something wrong?" she said.

"Would you like some tea?"

She nodded. She sat in the car, swiveling around so she could watch Sam sleep, amazed that he didn't stir. Carefully, she reached around and brushed his hair out of his eyes. Charlie came back with two cups, packets of sugar, four kinds of tea, and a plastic tube of honey. "I didn't know what you'd like," he said. "So I brought everything."

"A choice! That's so kind," she said.

They sat, drinking the hot tea and talking. Charlie told her about his work, how he had uncovered a fireplace stuffed with beer cans, how a light fixture a client was about to throw out because it was painted black got a spot of stripper dripped on it and revealed it was solid brass. When he talked about renovations, his whole face lit up, and it made Isabelle think about what Charlie must have been like before the accident.

"You wouldn't love where I live now," Isabelle said. "It's just a rental."

"Even a rental can be beautiful."

They finished their tea. In the backseat, Sam snored faintly, and for a moment, Isabelle felt there was nobody else in the world, just her and this man and this sleeping boy.

When he dropped her off, she was about to bound out, but he got out of the car faster than she did and ran around to open the door for her. She started, surprised. He didn't tell her he'd see her again, or that he had a nice time. He simply helped her out of the car, his hand along her back for just a moment. Then he waited by the car and watched her to make sure she got inside.

When he was gone, it felt as if a spell had broken. She stood in her apartment, her feet planted on the floor. She had ridden in a car and not broken into shards. She hadn't felt her habitual nausea. The world hadn't ended. It wasn't the car or a pill that made her feel safe. It was Charlie.

ISABELLE GOT USED to seeing Sam. He'd show up at her apartment, sometimes only staying for a glass of juice. She'd see him in the park with his camera and they'd talk. Once she set up a timer and took a quick picture of the two of them together, laughing into the lens. Each encounter was too brief for her, and every time she was about to call Charlie to tell him Sam was there, Sam somehow had to leave. "I'll tell him," Sam promised. She never said "Stay." She never dared to ask for more than what she was lucky enough to have.

It wasn't just Sam who kept showing up. Charlie seemed to materialize as well. Just that morning, she had seen him bundling groceries into his car by the superette when she biked past on her way to the bookstore, and it had made her feel ridiculously better to think that he was buying lots of food, that he was taking care of Sam. Another time, she had spotted Charlie and Sam walking with what looked like Sam's class, and she felt a wash of relief that he was back in the routine of school. It always startled her, seeing them, and it always somehow hurt, like having a splinter. More than anything, she wanted to stop, to talk to Sam, to see how Charlie was, but she thought better of it. She kept going.

One afternoon, in the bookstore, Isabelle wandered to the self-help area. Earlier, Lora had told her how important it was to push ahead. "Right now, you have to work at happiness," Lora told her. "Then, after a while, it might feel normal."

But looking at the bookshelves, at all the titles, made everything feel worse. When she saw *I Am a Good Person, I Am a Bad Person,* Isabelle wondered, What if you couldn't tell which one you were? There was a book about talking with the dead: What would April say to her that she could bear to hear? There were courses in how to make miracles in your life, but the one she wished for—that the accident had never taken place—was an impossible one, and she didn't think there were any more miracles for her. She couldn't drive anymore. Her husband had impregnated his lover and her marriage was finished. She was in a dead-end job, living in a place she didn't like, and she couldn't leave because she was obsessed with Charlie and his son. Were there any books that could help her with that?

"You could take a class, you know," her friend Michelle had told her. "Study French and take yourself to Paris. Take more lit classes."

"With what money?"

"Take out a loan. Everyone does."

Isabelle was silent, considering.

"And you should date," Michelle said. "It isn't too soon to let yourself be happy." To jump-start things, Michelle had given Isabelle's number to some guy named Jason, and when Isabelle protested, Michelle had narrowed her eyes at her. "Luke is history. It won't kill you to have a nice time. At least talk to him. He teaches high school history. He's nice."

But Isabelle had real reservations about dating. After what she had done, how could she ever possibly have a normal life? When Jason called, they had a perfectly pleasant conversation, about films they liked, about books, and Isabelle was almost imagining she could go out—that she could pretend to be normal—when he gave a nervous laugh. "So," he said. "I admit I'm fascinated. I saw your photograph in the papers. That must have been terrible about that accident."

Instantly, Isabelle shut down. "I'd rather talk about anything else," she said. But he persisted. "I'd love to hear how it changed you." He laughed. "I love drama."

Isabelle didn't laugh, and after that, she wouldn't go out with him. She told Michelle it was nothing personal, but she wasn't ready.

Well, here she was, out in a bookstore, wasn't she? She wasn't stuck in the house crying the way she used to, was she? She had gone to a New Year's Eve party. She went to the gym. And like Lora had advised, she had even made a list of the things she was going to do, goals written down so she could see them: Drive. Leave the Cape. Get a better job. Go back to school. Written down like that, they didn't seem so impossible. Isabelle roamed the aisles, and when she rounded a corner, she saw Charlie in the café with Sam. She stopped, thrusting her hands deep into her pockets.

Sam was talking, and Charlie was looking at him, not the distracted way some adults did when kids talked, but as if nothing were more interesting in the world. That made her like him. There was a stack of kids' books on the table and a muffin in front of Sam. And then suddenly, Sam laughed, and then Charlie did, and she felt giddy. They were here at a bookstore, just as if it were an ordinary day, and they were laughing. Charlie reached over and stroked Sam's hair, so gently that it made Isabelle swallow hard. Charlie looked up, not seeing her, and for the first time she noticed how blue his eyes were. His hair so glossy. She had driven all the way home with him, but she hadn't noticed anything except that she had felt safe. Now, though, she felt flooded. She wanted to touch his face and she felt a strange, restless knocking in her head.

Isabelle stepped back. It was crazy what she was feeling. It was just grief and loneliness, that was all. He had been kind to her in the car and she was just responding to that. Or maybe it was seeing Charlie being tender with Sam. What did it matter what it was? She needed to leave before they saw her, before she felt anything more that she had no business feeling. Isabelle sighed and headed for the door, passing a bulletin board, when something stopped her.

Study Photography with Master Photographers in New York.

She pulled down a brochure. The cover showed a bunch of people with cameras, all of them crouched on a busy urban street, shooting photos. New York. Where she had always wanted to be. It was a special program you applied for, two years of intense study, and scholarships were available.

All she needed was to get a portfolio together, write a statement of purpose, and apply. No one would care that she had dropped out of high school and only had her GED, that she had let money and location keep her from college. No one would know that she had killed a woman and ruined lives.

Still, she knew these programs. Most of them were rip-offs. You paid money and some hack showed you what to do and then you were no better off than where you had started. Well, maybe she'd apply anyway. It could be something. It would get her to New York. A good thing replacing a bad. Was that forgiveness? Her mother would think so, and even Luke would call it karma. "Walk through every door that opens," Lora had told her. "Try everything," Jane had said. It was just paper, a promise that would probably never be kept. She glanced at it again. The deadline to apply was March. They would let you know by early summer if you got in for the fall. She tucked it in her purse and then started walking home.

"I'M HOME!" SHE CALLED, when she got inside.

As soon as she flicked on the lights, she heard rustling in Nelson's tank. His head poked out from under the newspaper and then on short, sturdy legs, he moved to the edge of the glass tank, watching her. You couldn't tell her that tortoises didn't talk, because Nelson was making a clicking sound with his jaws that was so strange and insistent and wonderful—and, well, *loud*—that she knew he was trying to say something. "I'm glad I'm home, too," she told him, stroking the smooth, silky top of his head. He moved his head closer against her palm. She got up and got a piece of cheese. God knows why he liked it. It wasn't as if tortoises had dairy products in the wild. Stretching his neck, he snapped. "Oh, you'd bite the hand that feeds you, would you?" she laughed. "I guess you're family then."

Judy at Beautiful Baby had made fun of Isabelle for having a tortoise. "He doesn't even know you're alive," Judy said. But Isabelle knew Judy was wrong. She had lived with Luke for nearly twenty years, but most times when she got home from work, their house had been empty, with a Post-it stuck on the cupboard. "See you later!" No x's for kisses. Not even a smiley face. She had felt so lonely she had flooded the room with the TV or the radio. She took Nelson out of the tank and put him on the table. He lifted his head and stared at her and clicked his jaw. "Thank you for the lovely welcome," she told him.

She got up and looked through some of her photographs. There was the one she had taken of Sam, his small shoulders hunched, his face filling the shot. She held the photo up to the light. She liked this one. Maybe it was good enough to get her into that photography school. She could stay in tonight and get her whole portfolio together, fill out the damned application, and see what might happen. She could take it all to the post office first thing in the morning.

Who knew? Maybe she was due for a miracle.

~ TWELVE ~

IT WAS FEBRUARY and freezing, and Charlie was shopping for a Valentine's Day card for Sam. He picked up a funny one with a monkey dressed in a heart-printed T-shirt, and then he saw one with a woman with long, black, curly hair and there he was, thinking about Isabelle again.

Charlie hated how much she came into his mind. He kept picturing her weeping at the diner. He kept replaying the drive home with her. When he and April had taken drives, the energy used to crackle in the air like sparks as they speed talked, breaking into each other's conversation. But Isabelle listened to him so intently, it was palpable. When she spoke, her words were slow and thoughtful. The drive with Isabelle had been quiet and gentle, as if the world were somehow full of grace.

He shook it off, tried to forget that night. It was all ridiculous. But then he kept seeing her around town, bundled up against the chill on her bike, once leaving a supermarket the moment he was walking in. He saw her walking with a man on New Year's Day, the two of them in glittery party hats, her skin rosy with cold, and he had stared hard, but she hadn't turned around.

He bought the monkey card and headed for work. All that afternoon, he worked on a kitchen for a second-grade teacher, and though he should be concentrating on pointing the bricks, he kept remembering the drive with Isabelle, Sam sleeping peacefully in the back, the way they had talked. He thought of the way she kept turning around in the car to look at Sam, how she had even stretched around to adjust his seat belt. April used to just jump in the car and urge, "Go, go, go." She was always looking at the road ahead.

So Isabelle was maternal. So what? So she liked Sam. He'd feel this way about anyone who was kind to his son, and you could argue that she was being so kind out of guilt, couldn't you? Charlie repointed another brick. He had to stop thinking about this. It was just because she grieved about the accident, too, because she adjusted his son's seat belt. It had nothing to do with anything else.

He took a sip of his coffee and put it down. It tasted like antifreeze.

It was just loneliness, he told himself. Just human need. And maybe, he told himself, it was good that he felt something, because it meant he was getting better, that he was ready to move on. If it was just him, he probably wouldn't care as much, but he had Sam to think about. "We're new men," he kept telling Sam, every time he brought home new clothes, new dishes, anything that felt as if they were pushing ahead.

That night, after Sam was asleep, Charlie walked quietly into his room and watched him. He was so beautiful, this child, so perfect. No one ever told him he'd feel this intensely about his child. No one ever told him that his wife would be gone.

Charlie went and stood out on the porch. What would it be like to have another woman in his life? Would he ever love anyone the way he had April? He used to draw her to him and tell her, "Look at that. Perfect fit." He used to plan on how they'd travel when Sam was at college, how they'd sit on the porch at ninety, still holding hands. Had that all been a lie? A knot balled in his stomach. How could it have been perfect if she had left with his son and he didn't have a clue why?

He tried to imagine himself on that porch at ninety, holding the hand of a woman he didn't know yet, but all he saw was empty space.

THE NEXT MORNING, Charlie went into Sam's room to clean. Sam was supposed to make his bed, but here it was, sheets awry, an Etch-A-Sketch flung on the floor. Charlie smoothed the comforter over the bed and saw something poking up under the pillow and pulled it out.

A photo. Sam and Isabelle together on the beach, which must have been done with a timer. A flicker of unease swam through him. When had this been taken and why hadn't he known about it? Hadn't he and Isabelle agreed that she'd call when Sam was with her?

A halo of light was hitting Isabelle's hair, and she had this faint smile on her face, as if she knew something special and was just about to tell you. Her hair. Look at her hair. April used to cut her hair every week with the nail scissors to keep it short and spiky, and though he had thought April was beautiful, he couldn't stop looking at the thicket of Isabelle's curls. How black they were. How shiny. The person who crashed into his wife could have been a fifty-year-old woman coming home from a mah jong game. It could have been a businessman speeding to a marketing meeting, not paying attention, or a teenager joyriding. But instead—and for some reason this hurt and angered him more—she was this enigmatic, beautiful woman.

Charlie let the photo fall from his hand. What did it matter what she looked like? Sam was a kid and Charlie needed to know where he was. Sam couldn't be expected to be responsible all the time, but Isabelle was an adult. Why hadn't she respected his wishes and told him when Sam came to see her? Why couldn't she understand that not knowing where his wife was going was horrible enough, but not knowing where his son might be was infinitely worse? The more he thought about it, the sicker he felt. He'd go see her. He'd tell her she'd done enough. She'd given Sam photography and that was wonderful, but now they needed her out of their lives because he just couldn't worry about this anymore.

He got in the car and drove to Isabelle's.

When Isabelle buzzed him in, he took the stairs two at a time, one flight up, and when he got to the top of the stairs, he was panting.

She was standing in her doorway, in jeans and a white shirt with red buttons, her hair in a big, loose braid down her back, tendrils curling from it, and as soon as she saw him, she stepped back, alarmed. He averted his face so he wouldn't look at her eyes, as luminous and deep as pools.

"I need to talk to you," he said, struggling to catch his breath, wishing he hadn't run up all those stairs. She invited him in, but he was too keyed up to sit down. Words were bubbling up before he could stop them. He swallowed hard. "This has to stop, this relationship between you and Sam," he said quickly. "I thought you were going to let me know when you saw him."

Isabelle shook her head. "He just comes over. I tell him not to, but he keeps showing up. Sometimes he's only here for five minutes, so calling would make no sense. What am I supposed to do? Send him away?"

"That's an idea," Charlie said. "I saw a photo. You two at the beach."

Isabelle sat down on the couch and Charlie was about to sit, too, when she grabbed his sleeve. "Careful," she said, pointing to the floor.

A tortoise was walking around. He stopped and ate a piece of lint on the braided rug, which disconcerted Charlie. "That's Nelson. I lct him out of his tank to walk around. I hope you don't mind," Isabelle said.

He sat down carefully on the couch. "It's your house." Charlie frowned. "Why you? Why is my son so drawn to you?" Even as he said it, he couldn't stop looking at the base of her throat, at the dark curly loops of her hair. He wanted to touch them, to thread his fingers through them.

"We talked about this." Isabelle said. "Do you think this is easy for me?"

"He still photographs roads and cars!"

"And maybe he'll eventually stop! Maybe that's his way of letting it all go!" Isabelle's voice rose. "All I'm doing is giving him little minutes of kindness. How can you not give your okay to that?"

"Because you're the wrong person to give it! Because you're the cause of his misery!" As soon as he said it, he felt a stab of regret. He didn't want to be yelling at her. What was he thinking, coming here? Why was he thinking about her? It was all mixed up, all wrong.

Her face flushed and she looked abruptly away from him, and then she turned and bent down to pick up the tortoise. "I think you'd better go," she said, her voice strained, and then the tortoise lunged and bit one of the red buttons on her shirt, making her gasp.

"Hey!" She tried to gently pull back and

Nelson's jaws tightened. His nails scraped against her shirt.

"Are you all right? Why won't he let go?" Charlie stood up and touched the tortoise.

"It's the red—he thinks it's food," she said helplessly. She tickled the tortoise's leg, which he drew into his shell, but his jaw stayed clamped shut. She supported Nelson with her hands, keeping him away from her body, holding him like a soup bowl. She looked so uncomfortable, Charlie began to be worried.

"Can he hurt you?"

"He once bit a pencil in two."

Gingerly, he tried to help. He stretched out Nelson's leg, but all that happened was the tortoise hissed through his nose and opened his eyes wider, glaring at Charlie.

"Wait, I know what to do," Isabelle said. She stood up. "You have to help me. Can you run water in the bathtub?"

He stood there. "Charlie, please," she said. "This isn't good."

He followed her into the bathroom. "Can you fill the tub for me?" She waited while he turned on the water. "Make it warm," she said, and when the tub was half full, she turned to Charlie. "Help me again," she said. "Can you slide my shirt off?"

"What?"

"Just please help me," she said, getting more

agitated. "I'll hold Nelson away from me so he won't bite, if you can just get my shirt off."

She held the tortoise as far away as she could, tenting out her shirt. Charlie's mouth went dry. He didn't want to do this, didn't want to be here, but he held the edges of Isabelle's shirt and slowly lifted them up, over her shoulders, over her head, until she was bare except for a stretchy black bra.

Charlie swallowed. He took in her pale, creamy skin, but she wasn't looking at him. She carefully lowered the shirt and Nelson into the tub, finally shimmying her arms out of the sleeves, dunking his head under the water, and the tortoise's mouth shot open and then he was swimming, his eyes open. Isabelle lunged as he gracefully paddled, grabbing the shirt out of the water, dripping it into the sink, then she turned to Charlie, and laughed. The water was draining out of the tub, so that Nelson was now walking in damp puddles, snapping at shadows on the porcelain.

Isabelle stepped back, leaning against the sink, and her braid brushed along Charlie's arms. She smelled like pine and lemon. "Charlie?" she said, and he felt caught in a dream. He swore he heard the whisper of the ocean. April was nowhere around. There was just him and Isabelle. She wasn't moving and then he took two steps toward her and without thinking, kissed her mouth. She hesitated, and then kissed him back.

• • •

ISABELLE WOKE, SQUINTING at the light coming in through the blinds. She was tangled in the sheets, and beside her, Charlie slept, his beautiful face calm and still.

She didn't dare believe this had all really happened. That she and Charlie had lowered themselves to the bathroom floor and then somehow had made it from there to her bed. That he had taken off her clothes so gently it had felt as if he were unwrapping her. He had touched her stomach and kissed her thighs, all the while looking at her as if he were drinking her in, as if he couldn't get enough of her. The whole time they were making love, she had kept placing her hand on his lips, not so that he would kiss her fingers—which he did—but so he wouldn't speak, so she wouldn't have to hear him say, "This is a mistake."

Charlie's arm was still around her, the heat of his body making her warmer. She tried to ease herself up from bed to look at the clock, mindful not to disturb Charlie. One in the afternoon. Nelson was still in the bathtub and she was here in bed with Charlie and both facts seemed somehow equally strange and miraculous. But she needed to get up. She needed to pee and dress, feed Nelson and put him back in his tank, and get to Beautiful Baby. She tried to move, but then Charlie's eyes fluttered open and he saw her and she couldn't help it, she flinched. For a moment, she was afraid to move.

"Hey," he said, and then he gave her a smile. "I can't believe this."

The tone seemed friendly, but a voice was hissing in her head, like a danger signal.

He stroked back her hair, tucking a strand behind her ear.

"Who would have thought," Isabelle said lamely.

They both got out of bed and started pulling on clothes. Isabelle had been unselfconsciously naked in bed, but now she felt shy and dressed as quickly as she could. Charlie stood there, watching her.

"Are you really all right about this?" Isabelle asked quietly.

He looked at her, surprised. "Aren't you?"

"I am, but . . . we don't really know each other."

"We know the same things."

Isabelle nodded, turning slightly away so he wouldn't see how relieved she was.

Charlie's cell phone rang, startling them both so that Isabelle felt her heart jump, and when he reached for the phone, she saw that his hands were trembling.

"Work," he said reluctantly. "I have to go."

"Oh," Isabelle said. The day stretched out tight in front of her like a rubber band about to snap. "Can I see you again?" she blurted, and was instantly mortified. "I'm sorry," she said, waving her hand, but he caught it in midair.

"God, of course," he said, "I want to see you again," and Isabelle swallowed.

When he got to the door, he stopped, as if he had forgotten something. He started to open his mouth as if he were about to speak, and she was desperate to kiss him, but then he opened the door and was gone.

FOR A WHILE after Charlie left, she just stood at the door. Any moment he might come back to see her again, or to tell her, "I changed my mind. This is a bad idea." She couldn't believe this had happened, that she had slept with Charlie.

It was crazy what she was feeling, these jolts of need like she was on fire. What have I done? she thought. What happens now?

She went to the bathroom, flooding the sink with cold water, dunking her face in, and when she straightened, she saw Nelson in the mirror, high-stepping daintily along the bottom of the tub.

CHARLIE COULDN'T CONCENTRATE on studding the wall or tiling the Robinsons' kitchen. All he could think about was Isabelle. The deep green of her eyes. And her hair. He'd never seen hair so black. It smelled like mint tea. He thought of how silky her skin had been, how she had arched her back up to meet him, and then he felt a bolt of pain and swore. Shit. He'd whacked his thumb with the hammer, something he hadn't done since the first year he took up construction. He rubbed at his thumb, massaging the ache, telling himself he had to concentrate.

Shortly after April's death, Rae Hanks, one of his neighbors, had told Charlie that April would be watching over him, that she'd send someone to take her place, to take care of him and Sam. "She won't let you stay unhappy," Rae had told him. Charlie had thought it was a bunch of hooey. The dead didn't watch over the living. There were no ghosts. And in any case, he knew better than anyone that while April might have been loving, she was also jealous as hell. She watched him when they were at the beach to see if he was looking at anyone in a bikini. At parties, if he joked with women he knew, she would come and glue herself to his side. "Do you love me?" she kept asking him, over and over. "Do you love me?" And of course he did, Jesus, any person could see that. But April was April. She'd no more send him anyone else to love than she would have bayed at the moon.

How could he dare to trust another woman with his son—or with himself? He had been happy with April. He had thought he made her happy, too, but she had left him. Isabelle seemed wonderful, but everybody seemed wonderful in the beginning, didn't they? How could he be sure?

How could he be sure she wouldn't harm him and Sam the way April had?

But it was more than that. It was the whole notion of being happy like this, of daring to think it might be real. He thought of this friend he'd had, a woman named Viva, whose fiancé, Bobby, had died the day of their wedding. She grieved so terribly that she didn't eat or sleep, but three months after the funeral, she was living with another guy, a jerk who yelled at her in public, who told her at dinner that she was too fat. Viva never stopped smiling. Her eyes stayed as bright as mica, right up until she finally broke it off two years later, and then she fell apart again. "This was what I was afraid of," she told Charlie, sobbing into a bloom of tissues. "He kept me busy so I didn't have time to think. He kept the grief at bay, and now here it is, back again."

Well, who could blame her for staying one step ahead of her grief? But was Charlie just grabbing at happiness, not caring if it was real or how long it might last? And did Isabelle really care about him and Sam, or did she just want forgiveness?

He dug into his pocket for his cell phone and called information, his heart galloping in his chest. He had said the wrong words to April. He'd have to be more careful to say the right ones to Isabelle. He'd take everything very slow so neither one of them would be harmed. "Do you have a number for Isabelle Stein?" he asked.

ISABELLE HAD NEVER dated anyone but Luke, and back then she had been sixteen and you could have told her it was common for couples to make love while jet skiing and she would have believed it. But now, she didn't know what to expect. They had only slept together once, but was this the start of something or was it a fluke she'd do best to forget? She didn't know what to call what they had. Were they dating now? She called her friend Michelle and blurted out what happened. "How do I do this?" she said.

"Well, what do you want?" Michelle said quietly. In the background, Isabelle could hear Michelle's daughter, Andi, happily babbling. She heard Michelle's husband, Barry, laughing, a big, goofy guy who had proposed to Michelle on their second date.

"I want to see Charlie," Isabelle admitted.

There was a pause. "I can fix you up with someone, if you want. A nice guy, too. Works in accounting. Smart, kind, no baggage," Michelle said.

"No. I want to see Charlie." Isabelle sighed.

"Well, just take it slow and don't count on anything," Michelle advised.

"Why not?" Isabelle blurted. "You did. You got engaged on your second date."

Michelle sighed. "That was so different," she said.

"How?" Isabelle bit down on her lip. "I'm moving on, exploring options. Isn't that what I should be doing? I even applied to photography school in New York."

"You did? Well, that's really great, but look, I care about you. Right now, I don't want you to get hurt. And honestly, this is insane. Just promise me that you'll go slow."

"I promise," Isabelle lied.

She hung up the phone, feeling prickly and irritated with Michelle. How could she not count on something when she was already feverish about seeing him again? How could she not want to grab her jacket and go over there? And how could she not feel guilty about all of it? The phone rang and she plucked it up.

"Hi, remember me?" Charlie said, and she laughed out loud.

~ THIRTEEN ~

BY THE TIME it was March, Sam was certain Isabelle would let him talk to his mother. At first he had thought that Isabelle would make this happen much sooner, but then the angel books he was reading kept talking about how everything was "in God's time," which they said was very different than the time on a wristwatch.

Meanwhile, he was learning more and more about angels. They had their own language, and it wasn't always in words. An angel could point you to a special number, like eight, which was his mom's favorite, to let you know she was around. Or they could make a song come on the radio that told you what to expect, like "Good Day Sunshine," which came on one day when Sam was at Isabelle's and he had just about died with excitement. "Oh, you like this song, too?" Isabelle said, as if she didn't really know what was going on. Lately, Sam caught Isabelle looking just beyond him, as if she were seeing something, and he whipped around, and for a moment, he was sure he saw a flash of yellow hair like his mother's. He was almost certain he could hear his mom, whispering to him. Sometimes, too, Isabelle would stare at him, her mouth opening, as if she had something to tell him, and when she closed it again, he told himself it just wasn't the right time.

He bet she was trying to teach him to be patient, and he would be. He could wait forever as long as he could talk to his mother again, as long as he could maybe even see her, just one more time.

He didn't care that people might say it was impossible. Lots of things were impossible. At school, Mr. Moto, his science teacher, told them how light could be both a wave and a particle, which was supposed to be impossible. You could go to a distant planet and somehow come back younger than you were when you left because the laws of time went all screwy.

Sam knew what his mom cared about. He did his school work. He brushed his teeth twenty times on each side the way she'd told him too. He combed his hair and he took lots of pictures of himself so maybe Isabelle could show his mom and she would know what she missed.

One day, Isabelle even talked his dad into building him a darkroom in the spare bathroom, with its own little red safety light, though Charlie, worried that the chemicals might cause his asthma to flare, insisted on calling Sam's doctor for an okay first. "I can teach him," Isabelle said. "Plus, he'll be at home."

The first time she took him into the darkroom, he was so jazzed he could hardly stand it. Here he was alone in this small room, with just him and Isabelle! He loved the way she let him touch everything, the way she put her hand on his back to guide him over to the corner of the room. He wanted to touch her back, to see if he could feel her wings, but he wasn't sure he was supposed to, so instead he gave her what his mom used to say were love taps: feathery touches on her arms, her hands. "Are you tickling me?" Isabelle said, putting her hands on her hips, but she was laughing when she said it.

But then she turned out the light and suddenly it was so dark. Darker than his room at night. Darker than when he swam underwater with his eyes shut. He was disoriented and couldn't figure out where the door was. He stretched out his hand for Isabelle, and he touched air. For a moment, he heard the beating of wings, roaring in his ears. "Isabelle!" he shouted, and then he felt her touch him. But he couldn't calm down until she finally opened the door and took him outside, the two of them shading their eyes against the sudden light.

"Was it the dark?" she said, crouching by him. "Lots of people get spooked by it."

"I couldn't see you! I couldn't find you!" He leaned closer to her so the warmth of her body seemed to surround him. He snuggled against her side.

She stroked back his hair. "But I was right there. I was there all the time."

He snuffled. "Where do you go when you aren't with us?"

She startled. "I go to work. I'm home. I'm all sorts of places."

He wondered if she was with his mom, but he didn't ask. Was he allowed to?

When she was ready to leave, he got nervous. "Could I have some water?" he asked.

"It's your house, honey. You can't get it yourself?"

"I can't reach the glass."

"Sure, I will." As soon as she was gone, he took off his watch and tucked it in the pocket of her jacket. She'd find it when she got home, and then she'd have to bring it back, visit them again.

"Here you go," she said, handing him the water. He gulped it down, suddenly thirsty.

"See you later, alligator," she said.

Sam grabbed up her jacket, his watch making a soft weight in the pocket. "Don't forget your jacket!" he said, handing it to her.

She took it, and then she smiled, turning her palm to her face and kissing her fingers and then turning her hand around and waving the kiss to him as she went out the door. Transfixed, he stood as still as he could be, right in the spot where her kiss was, letting it sparkle all over him.

THE NEXT DAY, right in the morning, when Sam was at the kitchen table drawing a picture of a volcano for a school project, the phone rang and Charlie picked it up. "Of course, come by later with it," he said.

Sam felt a rush of heat go through his body. He looked at Charlie, expectant. "Isabelle," Charlie said casually. "She found your watch in her jacket. She'll bring it over around dinnertime the day after tomorrow."

"Maybe when she comes over, we can all go to the pizza place, too," Sam said. "And to a movie." He picked up a black crayon, the color of Isabelle's hair, and studied it. It wasn't the right color for lava, but he wanted to use it, anyway. He wanted to draw her beside the volcano. He looked up at the clock. There was a lot of time to get through before he saw Isabelle again, but at least he would see her.

IT WAS ALMOST spring again, the sort of soggy April that usually wreaked havoc with Sam's asthma, but for some reason he felt better. Maybe it was because he was happy, because every weekend now, he, his dad, and Isabelle would do something. Sometimes they went to Leaning Tower of Pizza and got a pie, and Sam always got to choose the kind. Other times they went bowling, and now that the weather was nicer, they sometimes walked on the beach and all three of them skipped stones. His father didn't have that tense look on his face that he used to have when Isabelle was around, and some days, right in the middle of the week, it was even his dad who suggested that Isabelle come over and join them for dinner or board games, which delighted Sam.

One evening, when they were all on the couch watching a movie, a western about a cowboy and his dog, Sam drowsed against Isabelle. He was in that half-sleep stage when he wasn't sure whether he was dreaming or not. Isabelle's hair floated around one of his shoulders like a blanket, and even though he could hear her talking to his dad, he could hear her wings rustling. She smelled like cookies and maple syrup, and she was so warm and comfortable, he just wanted to stay like this forever.

"He's asleep," his dad said, "maybe I'll take him to his bed."

Sam, eyes still closed, began to spread himself out on the couch, so that his head was in Isabelle's lap. He reached for her hand and held it, his eyes still shut, and then he heard Isabelle's voice, soft as music.

"And maybe you won't," she said to Charlie, laughing. She stroked Sam's hair, making him shiver, but he pretended to be asleep, to see what she might do or say next. "I love this boy," she said quietly, and Sam held her hand tighter.

THE NEXT DAY, Sam was at school finishing his poster on the solar system when Teddy leaned over the desk, lightly punching Sam in the shoulder. "Hey," Teddy said. "How about you come over to my house after school?" Just like that, they were friends again.

At Teddy's, Sam sprawled over the big brown chair, picking at the fraying buttons. He didn't know what to do with himself and he felt as if a thousand bees were buzzing inside of him. They had played cards and made grilled cheese, and both of them were restless and bored. Teddy was flipping the cards and then he threw them in the air. "I'm getting sick of rummy," he said.

Sam didn't even care anymore if Teddy's mother came home suddenly because at least it would be something. Let her yell at him. Let her do whatever she wanted. He could handle it.

"We can go to my house, you know. My dad's not there," Sam said.

Teddy raised one brow. "Oh, yeah? What's cool about your house?"

Sam bristled. "My dad built me a darkroom to develop film for prints. Isabelle showed him how."

"Are they like boyfriend and girlfriend?"

"Of course not," Sam said indignantly. Isabelle and his dad had been friends for a long time, it seemed. All three of them went to the beach together and to the movies, and they had even gone ice skating this winter, until Sam had started coughing and they had all had to go home. They were together except for the times that were just Sam and his dad. But his dad and Isabelle didn't kiss, they didn't hug or touch. And anyway, Isabelle was an angel. "They're just friends," Sam decided.

"You sure about that?" Teddy said. "How much do you know about her, anyway?"

"A lot. She's my friend, too."

"Oh, yeah? No grownup is a kid's friend unless he wants something. Trust me."

Sam shrugged, but he felt something knocking along his spine. Teddy could say whatever he wanted, but he didn't know Isabelle. And as much as Sam sort of wanted to tell him, he'd never mention to Teddy that Isabelle was an angel, because you had to keep things like that secret. You had to have faith. Still, he could feel Teddy's doubts, like a jellyfish sting. "What could she want from me?"

Teddy stood up. "That's for her to know and us to find out," Teddy said.

Sam didn't like the way Teddy was grinning at him. "She's nice," Sam said.

"Well, then we need to know that, too." Teddy tapped his fingers on the table. He grabbed his jacket. "Come on," he said. "I just figured out what we can do today. The lock was broken on the back door of the movie theater and I bet we can sneak right in."

⁓ Fourteen ⁓

THE FIRST FEW MONTHS of their courtship, Isabelle felt dazed. She knew enough not to depend on anything, but she couldn't help feeling a thrill when another week passed, and then two months and then three, and here it was May and they were still together. Every time she saw Charlie, her heart jumped about her ribs, and she noticed, too, how his whole being seemed to light up when he saw her. He brought her little gifts: a perfect iris, a roll of film, and once a wind-up camera with two little legs. "This relationship is impossible," he kept saying, but he smiled when he said it. He always kissed her nose, and lately, he called her every night before he went to sleep.

At first, they saw each other only when Sam was in school, grabbing lunch together, taking a walk. "We have to take this slow and careful. He's been traumatized," Charlie said. "I just want to make sure this is going to be something real before we tell Sam. That makes sense, doesn't it?"

"Of course," Isabelle said, running the words *something real* through her mind.

They hung out with Sam more and more, but were careful not to act like anything but friends. At the movies, on the street, Sam was always in between them. When Charlie dropped Isabelle off at night, he waved at her, the way he might to the postman. Still, she was so happy. What a thing, to feel good again! The next time she was in Lora's office, Isabelle blurted that she wanted to stop therapy.

Lora raised a brow. "Why?"

"It's a chance for me, now," Isabelle said. "A way to feel good without the weight of all that examination and thinking. It just finally feels right to stop."

"Don't you think examination and thinking have value? Especially now, in a new relationship? Especially considering who this new relationship is with?"

Isabelle thought of Charlie, the way he looked, sleeping in her bed, one arm thrown over her waist. She thought of the expression on Lora's face when she had told her, like a door slamming shut. She couldn't help it—she sighed, and then she looked up at Lora. "I think sometimes you just have to go by how you feel."

"Well, then," Lora said, standing up. "You can always come back," she said, but Isabelle, walking outside, thought only of Charlie.

ONE DAY, THEY were having lunch at the Mermaid diner by the beach. Isabelle, sitting in a booth across from Charlie, ordered fries and a coke. She reached out and took Charlie's hand, and then she felt something, like a disturbance in the air. She turned around to see Luke with his girlfriend, who was hugely pregnant in a blue dress. Luke leaned down to nuzzle her neck, to kiss her mouth, and she laughed delightedly. Isabelle swallowed and held Charlie's hand tighter. "What?" Charlie said.

"Hello, Luke," Isabelle said, and then Luke looked over at her, and his whole body tensed. His girlfriend awkwardly put her hand on her belly.

"Isabelle," Luke said. "Nice to see you," and then he put his arm back around his girlfriend and guided her away and Isabelle felt suddenly as if she had been slapped.

"They're unfriendly," Charlie said.

"That's my ex," Isabelle said.

"Are you okay?"

Isabelle nodded. Seeing Luke had hurt, but not the way she thought it might have. She didn't want to be the woman beside him, not anymore, and that was a relief. But seeing him so loose and easy with his girlfriend, so devoted, made her unsettled. Would she and Charlie ever be as bonded as that?

She traced her hand along Charlie's arm and he took both her hands in his. "Don't be upset. You're here with me," he told her. "And tonight, we'll take Sam to the movies. Any one you want to see." He studied her. "How come you and Luke never had kids? You're such a natural with Sam."

Isabelle pushed her fries away. "We couldn't. I can't have any." She waited for Charlie to say what people always said: "You can adopt"; "It doesn't matter." Or once, most horribly, "Aren't you too old to have kids anyway?" But instead Charlie reached up and cupped her face. "I'm sorry," he said, and it somehow made her feel better.

When the waitress came by with a dessert menu, a tall blonde with a name tag that said Joey, she glanced at Isabelle as if she knew her. Isabelle pretended to be studying the forty varieties of ice cream they had listed on the menu. The accident had been a while ago. No one in the town talked about it anymore, and sometimes, if she was lucky, she even had whole days when she didn't think about it at all herself. So why, when she saw the waitress giving her and Charlie the once-over, did Isabelle feel so guilty? Why did she feel as if she were committing a great, unpardonable crime that she needed to apologize for? She glided out of there as if the huge tip she insisted on leaving wasn't a bribe to have the waitress on her side.

She thought of how her mother used up her whole life after Isabelle's father died. She wouldn't date, even though suitable men called her up with invitations so sweet they made Nora's women friends swoon. Nora, though, couldn't let go of that one great love. Eventually, she was able to replace it with a love that was even greater, and to Isabelle's shock and dismay, that love was for Jesus. If Luke had died, would it have been as simple for Isabelle to give him up? Death made you look differently at the people you loved. Their real selves weren't there to contradict your beliefs about them. The dead became a whole other person.

"What movie should we see?" she asked Charlie, as they walked through the parking lot. Charlie opened his mouth and then he looked up and started waving at someone in the distance. "Fred!" he waved, and a man in a baseball cap turned around and waved back and started coming toward them.

She waited while Charlie talked animatedly to Fred about sheet rock and Italian tile, and the whole time Fred kept glancing at her and then at Charlie, and Isabelle felt unnerved. "I was so sorry to hear about April," Fred said abruptly, and Isabelle felt Charlie fading beside her. She wanted to reach out and grab his hand, but he seemed miles away. "I always adored that woman," Fred said quietly. "I was just nuts about her. What a shock. I still think I'm going to see her walking around the corner."

"I'm Isabelle," she blurted, and both men looked at her. She held out her hand until Fred shook it and she felt her face flushing.

Fred didn't stay very long after that. He mentioned a restaurant he was redoing, and when he left, he shook Isabelle's hand again. "Bye, you," he said.

"Isabelle," she called after him.

"Why didn't you introduce me?" she asked Charlie after Fred had gone.

"It wasn't a slight," he said. "I was just caught up in seeing him."

He walked beside her. On the corner, a man cupped a woman's face in his hands and dotted her face with kisses. Across the street a girl whooped and leaped up into her boyfriend's arms, nuzzling his neck.

Isabelle took Charlie's hand again and held it.

ONE DAY, CHARLIE came home to find a note from Sam, asking if he could stay the night at his friend's house. "Call me if it's okay," Sam's note said. A sleepover, Sam's first since the accident. Usually, because of his asthma, Sam didn't get to go on overnights. The last time, Charlie had received a call at two in the morning because Sam was wheezing and the inhaler wasn't helping. The parents were frantic and unsure what to do. "Should I call an ambulance?" the father asked, his voice tight with fear, and Charlie had grabbed for his keys. "Call," he said. "I'll be right there."

Sam had spent the rest of the evening in the ER, hooked to an IV, and after that, the kid had never invited Sam over again; and every time Charlie ran into the father, the guy seemed uncomfortable, like he couldn't wait to get the hell away.

This time, though, Sam was at his friend Kit's

house, and Kit's father was a doctor. He called the number Sam left and talked to Kit's mom. "We're so glad Sam can stay. We'll take good care of him," she said, and her voice was so sincere that Charlie could have hugged her.

Still, without Sam, the house felt empty and cold. He knew he could invite Isabelle over, but he didn't know how he felt having her here, in April's house, just yet. He went out again, by himself.

Charlie walked down the main drag, just a small street full of shops and restaurants, scattered with wood benches and a few scrubby trees. He and April used to love to take walks when they were courting, and later, when they had Sam, they'd take him with them everywhere. He had loved the small-town quality of the place, the feel of community, the way everyone seemed to know everyone else. But now, he was stunned by the new stores. When had there ever been an Italian restaurant there? When had the toy store he and April had loved closed? Where was their favorite indie bookstore? It was as if April had taken parts of the town with her when she died. Charlie passed by the soccer field. There was the Blue Cupcake team in their jerseys. Sam hadn't gone back to the team since his mother had died. He hadn't wanted to play anymore. Not that they ever really let him do anything more than hand out water or carry the ball, anyway.

His cell phone rang and he lifted it up. Isabelle.

At first, he felt that heady flash of joy. But then his heart felt clipped. Could he really love her the way he had April? Could he trust her? Was this a good thing for him—and more important, for Sam?

"Hello?" he said, but the line went dead. Isabelle, he thought. Isabelle. He glanced down at the phone, pained.

She hadn't left a message.

ONE NIGHT, WHEN Charlie didn't call her, Isabelle couldn't sit still. Oh, she knew it was probably that he was just busy with Sam, or maybe something had come up. Still, she got up and biked around the dark streets.

She glided to Charlie's street, and stopped in front of his house. One light upstairs was on, and the rest was dark. She stared at the house. Another minute, and then she would bike back home, and then the door opened and Charlie came out in his pajamas and robe. He strode across the street until he got to her.

She said it for him. "What am I doing here?"

"Don't go," he said.

"What about Sam?"

"We'll lock the door. We'll set the alarm. You'll be gone before he wakes up." He nuzzled her neck and she felt her stomach tighten with desire. "Please," he said.

Isabelle stayed the night. She left early in the morning, way before anyone was up. The air was sharp and clear and no one was around, except for a neighbor who knew Isabelle from the days when she used to stalk the house. "Good morning!" Isabelle called, and the woman lazily waved as if there was nothing startling about Isabelle being up and about at six in the morning, as if Isabelle was just another person who was part of the neighborhood. When Isabelle took off on her bike, the wind sang in her ears.

SHE GOT USED to seeing him, two, three times a week, and sometimes, Charlie just showed up. When they were with Sam, they were careful not to hold hands or touch. The one time Charlie put his arm about Isabelle and Sam looked over, Charlie pretended he was suddenly brushing lint off her shoulder. "Got it," he said, his fingers lingering.

Isabelle was running out of her apartment, late for work, and there he was, holding up a basket of food. "I brought a snack," he said. One night, she was at the greengrocers buying oranges to juice and she bumped into Charlie by the cheeses. "I'm taking Sam bowling tonight. Come with us," he said.

One evening, when they were all set to go out to a play, she heard Sam's lungs faintly whistling. "Go ahead and we'll meet you," Charlie told her, his voice rushed, but Isabelle saw how stricken Sam looked and she shook her head. "Let's get your rescue meds, cookie," Isabelle said, and she sat with Sam on the couch, quietly talking to him until the medicine kicked in and he could take long, even breaths. "There you go," Isabelle said, giving him a hug. When she finally looked up from Sam, she saw Charlie watching her, a look of amazement on his face. "What?" she asked.

He shook his head. "You were so calm," he said.

Nowadays she had less work, and though it gave her more time with Charlie and Sam, it made her nervous. "Take time off," Chuck kept telling her. "In fact, let me call you when we have work. That's a better idea. Let's do that."

Isabelle sat, stunned. She got paid for only the days she worked. When she took a vacation, it was never a paid one, but she took so few that it hadn't really mattered. It was one thing to go in and try to look busy, going through old prints, trying not to see the funny looks customers still sometimes gave her when they found out who she was, but it was another to be told not to come in at all.

What if the work really dried up?

She riffled through the bills. She hadn't made enough money to cover them this month, and what about next month, and the month after that? Where would she go and what would happen to her? She couldn't ask Luke for a loan, and even if she could muster up her courage, would he give it to her? And how would she pay it back? If she got into photography school, they might give her a stipend, but she wouldn't hear anything about that until the summer, and she knew how foolish it was to count on something like that.

If she told Charlie, he'd offer her sympathy and try to make her laugh. But it wasn't what she wanted and she wasn't even sure what she really needed anymore. Everything seemed in flux, Charlie, her job, her whole life.

She told herself they were a couple. He didn't see other women, and she certainly wasn't interested in other men. But sometimes Isabelle wasn't so sure she understood what was going on. One night, when Sam was sleeping over at a friend's, Charlie invited her to the house for dinner. It felt new to her, and special. They were grilling salmon, and Charlie put her in charge of making the salad, when the wall phone rang.

"Got it," he said, reaching for the receiver. She heard Charlie's voice change. "Charlie, what is it?" she said. "Is Sam okay?" He turned slightly away from her.

"Where?" he said into the phone. "No. No, she didn't have that."

Isabelle waited. Charlie hung up the phone. "It was Hank, the detective I hired," he said. "For April. He thought he had a lead. A doctor in Santa Fe said he had seen a woman who wanted her whole appearance changed two weeks before the accident, but she had three tiny moles on her back." Charlie swallowed. "It wasn't April."

"I'm sorry." She kissed his face. After dinner, she he took him out for tea and cupcakes at the Blue Cupcake, and though he laughed and joked with her, she could still see that phone call hanging over him. Isabelle knew he needed to know what had happened, but she knew, too, that as long as he had that need, he wasn't letting go of April, that she was still part of their lives.

Isabelle knew that if she had met him in any other circumstances, she'd still want to be with him, and why not? He was kind, he doted on his son. He was smart and sexy. Every time she saw him coming toward her, the air seemed to sparkle.

"Do you love this guy?" Michelle asked, and Isabelle hesitated. She had been in love with Luke full throttle from the moment she laid eyes on him, but this with Charlie was different. Slower. More cautious. She didn't know where she stood with him, and sometimes she didn't care. She just wanted to be with him.

"What if I said yes?" Isabelle said quietly, and Michelle sighed.

"Then I really give up," Michelle said.

Isabelle didn't give up, though. It made sense, didn't it, that they would protect Sam, that they would protect themselves by taking things really, really slow? There would be a right moment and they would somehow know it, and then it would all come together. Wouldn't it?

• • •

ONE AFTERNOON, ISABELLE was photographing a wedding, a job she had gotten through an old client. It was the beginning of June; the sky, as hard and blue as a sapphire. As soon as she had walked into the reception space, a headache bloomed. The room was huge and covered with mirrors. Flowers dripped from the stairways and tables. Isabelle had dressed up a bit to blend in with the guests, but even in her fancy green silk, her hair clipped with a rhinestone pin, she was underdressed. She had asked Charlie if he wanted to come with her, if he wanted to bring Sam. "To a wedding?" he said, as if she had asked him if he wanted to fly to Spain that night, and though she had shrugged it off, she had felt a little stung.

She thought of her marriage to Luke, the two of them standing up in front of a justice of the peace. No guests, no parents, nothing but each other. The only flowers Isabelle carried were the wild ones she had plucked impulsively from the side of the road. Her ring was a simple band, and Luke hadn't even worn one until she fussed. "It destroys the natural beauty of the hand," he insisted. She hadn't cared then that no one was there to see them make their commitment. But that had been a kids' wedding, not an adult one, and she couldn't help but feel that maybe that had something to do with why their marriage hadn't made it to forever.

She scanned the room. Ah, there was the bride.

She was Isabelle's age, and a little overweight, in a white dress pouffed out like a meringue. When she noticed Isabelle taking a photograph, the bride beamed and then came over, holding up the heavy edges of her dress, showing off her sparkly white shoes. "I can't believe how happy I am," she told Isabelle. "Do you have a guy?"

"I do," Isabelle said, but even she could hear the doubt in her own voice, and she turned her face away from the rush of sympathy she saw in the bride's eyes. "He has a young son. We're taking it slow," Isabelle said.

"Ah, a stepparenting issue," the bride said knowingly.

"He lost his mom. We've only been a couple five months." Five months! She knew Charlie wanted to give Sam more time, and she didn't want to push him, but somehow in her mind, five months seemed like the magic number to her. The day of reckoning.

The bride touched Isabelle's shoulder, so gently that Isabelle felt like throwing herself into her arms. "I'll throw you the bridal bouquet," the bride said conspiratorially. "It always works. How do you think I got my Dave?"

"You don't have to do that," Isabelle said, but the bride was gone, and there was Dave, tall and balding with green eyes like a go signal, making his way toward his bride.

It was midnight when she got to Charlie's. Sam

would be asleep, and she'd be gone before he woke up. She felt dense and uneasy, and despite the bride's aiming the bouquet at her, Isabelle had let the flower girl catch it.

She lifted the rock for the key. She could probably make a copy for herself and somehow so could Charlie, but neither one had, and the more she thought about it, the sicker she felt. She was here every night, but she didn't even have a dresser drawer of her own.

Charlie was in the living room, watching a black-and-white movie, his wire-rimmed glasses settled on his nose. "Hey," he said happily when he saw her. Edward G. Robinson flickered on the screen, yearning after Joan Bennett. "*Scarlet Street*," he told her. "A she-done-him-wrong. An avenging angel."

Isabelle sat down. "What?" Charlie said. He flicked off the movie. "Hungry?" he asked, and she shook her head.

"I'm full of wedding food." She peered at Charlie in the dim light, trying to see him more clearly.

"You look so tired. Was it an awful wedding?"

She took off her shoes, rubbing her toes. Her ears still felt stuffy from the noise. "It was lovely. I really liked the bride. She was really nice." Isabelle kept rubbing her toes until Charlie pulled her feet into his lap and rubbed them for her. "She said the moment she met her husband, she knew."

"Everyone talks like that at a wedding, don't they?"

"She wanted me to catch the bridal bouquet."

"Ah, she wanted you to cut her a deal on the pictures."

Isabelle pulled her legs down and tucked them under her. "That's not it," she said. "She wasn't that way and neither was her husband." She bent toward Charlie and kissed him, the way the bride had kissed Dave. She pressed against him, putting her hands into the back of his shirt. "I love you," she said, and he nuzzled the line of her shoulder. His hands slid over her breasts, and then she felt April, a force field between them, and she kissed him harder.

Isabelle pulled him to the floor so roughly, she banged her elbow. She pulled him into her, but then she made the mistake of looking at his face, and she saw, shocked, that he was crying.

Stunned, she got up and began putting her shoes on. Charlie tried to reach for her, but she stepped away.

He leaned against the wall, dazed. "I'm sorry."

"You're crying about her."

"I'm so sorry," he said, quietly.

"Charlie, what are we doing?"

"What do you mean?"

"I don't know where you are. Or maybe I do. I know you loved her. I know love doesn't die just because a person does. I know she was your wife,

314

she was Sam's mother, but can't there be room for someone else? Can't you love me, too?"

Charlie took her hand and this time she let him. "We just need more time."

Isabelle let go of his hand. "What more about me do you need to know? What more can I possibly show you about me that I haven't shown you already? Charlie, I was leaving here that day. But I stayed because of you and Sam. I'm staying here now because of you and Sam."

"Have a little faith in me."

"What do you think about?"

He drew her closer. She leaned against his chest and she felt his hair tickling her cheek. "I think about Sam a lot. His asthma. Whether he misses his mother." He swallowed. "I think about whether he knew what he was doing going away with April."

"You think about April," she said quietly. "Of course."

"I think about my *family,*" Charlie said. "That sense of permanence, of possibility. I think about how wonderful a thing that was. And I think about how I wish to God I could know what happened. How I just want to know something, anything, how it drives me crazy, the not knowing, the crazy scenarios I imagine."

Isabelle felt something swirling around her chest. She knew all about what ifs, the not knowing. She had spent all this time wondering what might have happened if she had taken a train instead of driving, if she had taken ten more minutes to pack, if she hadn't gone down that road at all. Would she be in New York now and happy? Would Luke have come for her and would she be back here, passing Charlie and Sam on the street, maybe even standing behind April in line at the local superette, both of them buying bread and eggs and butter, as normal as pie? How could you ever know what choice was the right one to make and what opportunity might be a mistake you would regret all your life?

She thought of the way Dave had dipped the bride, the clear joy in his face every time he looked at her. Isabelle had glanced at the bridesmaids and seen how young they all were, how she was the oldest single woman there. Charlie was right here beside her, and she felt the most alone that she ever had.

"What else do you think about?" she asked.

"Oh, God, everything," Charlie said, with real feeling. "I think about my parents getting old and how hard it is to watch. I think about their frosty marriage. I think about being able to protect Sam from every bad thing in the world. How I'd wrap him up in cotton batting if I could, but I know I can't."

"What else?" Isabelle said.

"Work, life. I just try to keep all the pieces in place."

Isabelle stood up. The room was spinning, but she grabbed her shoes, buckling them tightly. In the back of her mind, she heard a drift of music from the wedding, a song the bride had written for the groom, corny and cloying, and so beautiful, so rich with love, that Isabelle couldn't stop smiling when she heard it.

"What are you doing?" Charlie moved in front of her. "Look at me. What just happened that I'm missing?"

"You think about everything," she said. "Everything that matters to you. But where am I in the conversation in your head? Where am I, Charlie? You won't let me in there!"

He drew her to him and kissed her mouth. "You're here," he said, and then he kissed her harder. He kissed her neck and she felt something loosening in her chest. "And here," he said, kissing her shoulder. "You're right here with me."

ISABELLE WAS SLEEPING when he woke up. Charlie watched her. What would it be like to come home every day and find her here? To wake up beside her, with her hair spread out across his shoulders and hers? This wasn't just a Band-Aid against pain. This could be real, and the only way to find out would be to really test it. You could love many people in your life. Maybe love didn't die even when a person did, but that didn't mean there might not be room for someone else in your heart.

"Hey." Isabelle stirred and stretched and then pulled the sheet up to her chin. "Was I snoring?" she asked.

"You were talking in your sleep," he said.

"I was? What did I say?" She sat up, a little embarrassed.

"I don't know exactly, but you said it with such passion." He looked so grave.

"What's wrong? Is something the matter?"

"I want us to be together more."

She sat up. "Charlie, are you sure?"

"Are you?" he asked. "Is it really me you want?"

She nodded and then he nodded, too. "Then, I need to talk to Sam," he said.

That evening after dinner, Charlie ladled big glossy scoops of banana pudding into glass bowls. He watched Sam digging in, and then Charlie put a hand on the back of Sam's head, ruffling his hair.

"I saw Isabelle today," Charlie said casually. "She's a lot of fun, isn't she?"

Sam's spoon stopped clattering. He nodded his head. "Uh-huh."

"You like her, right?"

Sam nodded.

"Well, so do I." Charlie struggled. What was he supposed to say next?

"You know no one can ever replace your mom."

Sam frowned.

"You know how sad we've both been. Well, sometimes, when a really important relationship ends, people stay sad for too long. Sometimes, even though you don't forget that person, it's good to explore new relationships, to branch out. Especially when it's with people you already know and like."

Sam pushed the bowl away. "But relationships don't end when people die."

Charlie started. "Who told you that?"

"I read it in a book." Sam dug his spoon to the bottom of the glass bowl, not looking at Charlie.

Helplessly, Charlie watched the tense way Sam's shoulders were hunching. "Let's talk about Isabelle for a second," Charlie said.

Sam looked up, stitching his brows. "You said we could still see her! You said it was okay! You can't go back on your promise! Not now!"

"And it is okay! And we can see her! I know you like her, and I do, too, and I thought—well, sometimes relationships can change."

Sam pushed up from the table. His breath came in little pants. "No, no! I don't want it to change! Please! Please! You can't change it! Not now!"

Charlie reached for Sam and swept his hair from his eyes. "Okay," he said quietly. "We don't have to talk about it. Okay."

Charlie couldn't sleep that night. He thought of how upset Sam had become and luckily, Charlie had been able to pull back before he really said anything about how he felt about Isabelle. It was too soon for Sam and that was that.

He rubbed his eyes. Sam didn't want anything to change, but Charlie, ah, that was a different story. He wanted the dull ache in his belly to change. He wanted his sleepless nights to change. He thought of how he felt when he walked up to Isabelle and there was that funny crook in her smile and all he wanted to do was kiss it. He didn't expect blind happiness anymore, certainly not all the time, but to have it, to feel it, just for a few minutes a day, seemed like a paradise to him.

He shifted in the bed. Sam wasn't ready, and maybe as much as he yearned to be, maybe the truth was that he himself wasn't quite ready, either. If he was, would he still sometimes see April out of the corner of his eye? Would he still have dreams about the accident, where April walked away and came home to him as if nothing had happened?

Nothing stayed the same. That was scientific fact. He wouldn't do anything to push things in a new direction, but he knew that one way or another, life eventually would.

~ Fifteen ~

"My stomach hurts," Sam said. He and Teddy were standing in front of Isabelle's building. The air had gone thick and dark and heavy, and Sam glanced anxiously at the sky. Even his toes felt clammy. Teddy was pressing all the buttons, flattening his thumb on buzzer after buzzer.

"It does not. Admit it, don't you want to go inside? Look around her place? You wouldn't have told me her address if you didn't," Teddy said.

"I've been inside Isabelle's apartment lots of times," Sam said. "Lots."

"But not when she hasn't been there. That's totally different. My mom always hides the empty wine bottles when she knows people are coming over."

"Who is it?" a voice scratched through the intercom.

"Delivery!" Teddy boomed, lowering his voice, and the buzzer rang. "There's always a jerk who lets you in," Teddy said, rolling his eyes and pulling the door open.

The whole way up the stairs, Sam wanted to turn right around and run back to Teddy's. What if a door opened and someone asked them what they were doing there? What if a cop lived in the building and arrested them?

Reluctantly, Sam pointed to Isabelle's door. Teddy took out a credit card. "One of my mom's boyfriends showed me how to do this."

The whole time Teddy was working on the door, Sam wanted to yell at him to stop, to turn back, but he couldn't manage the words. Part of him wanted to know what they might find in her apartment, what secrets she would hide.

Teddy jiggered the credit card again, and then there was an odd click and the door swung open. "Bingo!" Teddy said, and ushered Sam in.

"What are we looking for?" Sam whispered.

"No one's here, dummy, you don't have to whisper," Teddy said, but he was barely speaking above a hush himself.

Sam walked on tiptoes. As soon as they walked into her apartment, his mouth turned dry and sour and his body felt shaky. Isabelle's apartment smelled like vanilla cookies, the way she did, and he suddenly didn't want Teddy there. He saw Isabelle's books, her table, the chairs, and he wanted to touch all of them, to rest his head on her couch, to pick up the flowers she had in the vase and smell them, just for a minute, but he didn't like the way Teddy was staring at things, the dark, greedy look in his eyes. "We should go," Sam said. "There's nothing here."

"God, look at that!" Teddy said, noticing the big glass turtle tank on the dining room table. He tapped on the glass and the tortoise lifted his head, staring at Teddy. "It's like a freaking dinosaur!"

"That's Nelson," Sam said. "And he bites, so be careful. Don't even touch his shell."

"You don't touch the turtle?" Teddy looked at Sam askance. "You couldn't feed him or nothing?"

"I told you, he bites."

"Bullshit, she just didn't want you touching her turtle." Teddy laughed, but Sam didn't see what was so funny. "Let's take him out," Teddy said. "I want to see him move."

"He doesn't move! He doesn't do anything!" Sam said, but Teddy already was pulling up a chair out so he could reach into the tank. He thrust his hands in and lifted the tortoise up, so Nelson's long legs swung back and forth as if they were boneless. "Wait!" Sam cried, "you'll hurt him! Let me take him!" He reached out and then Nelson stretched his long neck around and bit at the air.

It felt funny holding Nelson. He was as light as a box of popcorn, cool and dry and leathery, and Sam made sure to keep him away from his body. He was about to put Nelson down when Teddy grabbed his sleeve.

"I bet she has something hidden in here," Teddy said, pointing to the bedroom, and Sam crept up behind him, still holding Nelson carefully.

Teddy flung open the door. Sam didn't know what to expect, but not this.

Isabelle's room was spare and clean, the bed

neatly made, the surface of her dresser shining. Teddy picked up one of the photographs nested on Isabelle's night table. "Hey, that's you," he said, and Sam glanced over and there he was, standing beside Isabelle and there were Isabelle's eyes looking out at him from the picture, as if she knew what he was doing. He turned away so abruptly that Nelson snapped at the air.

Sam wasn't sure what he should be looking for, but Teddy was rummaging through Isabelle's drawers. He put Nelson down on the floor, and the tortoise headed for the shadows under the dresser, his nails making small skittering sounds against the wood.

"Better go get that thing before he vanishes," Teddy said.

Sam bent and picked up Nelson again, but Teddy grabbed his arm, making Sam lose his grip. Nelson hit the ground with a cracking sound. Sam flew back, his eyes wide with shock. Nelson wasn't moving. "Why'd you do that!" Sam shouted.

"Oh, shit, now you did it! You freaking killed him!" Teddy said.

Terrified, Sam crouched beside the tortoise. "I was trying to put him back!" Sam cried. Nelson's eyes were shut. His whole body was wedged deep into the shell so you could barely see it. Sam tried to touch the edge of Nelson's leg. It felt cold and it didn't move. "Nelson!" Sam cried. "Nelson!"

"We better get out of here," Teddy said. "You're really in trouble now."

"You told me to come here!" Sam screamed. "You told me!"

Teddy's mouth dropped open. "Get out!" Sam screamed, shoving Teddy, who shoved him back.

"Fine, I'm going. You stay here and deal with it!" Teddy said. And then, just like that, the front door slammed and Teddy was gone. Sam could hear his heart galloping in his chest. The apartment was so silent, his breathing seemed magnified. He crouched and gently picked Nelson up, placing him back in his tank, covering him with the hollow log. He'd killed Nelson. Killed him like he'd killed his mother. It was all his fault and no one would ever forgive him, and he wouldn't blame them.

"I'm sorry!" Sam cried, and then he ran out of the apartment, too.

Outside the storm clouds were so thick that if he hadn't known better, he would have thought it was nighttime. Teddy was long gone and the streets were empty. Sam didn't know where to go or what to do, but he started walking home, and there at the end of the block, right before the intersection, was his father's car and inside his dad and Isabelle were quietly talking.

Sam panicked. They were on the same side of the street! What if they saw him and wanted to know what he was doing here and then later, when they saw Nelson, when they saw how anxious Sam was, they put two and two together? His heart began that odd hammering in his chest, and he swayed on his feet, and then his father leaned over to Isabelle and kissed her on the mouth.

Something roared in Sam's ears. His father and Isabelle continued to kiss and he suddenly knew just how much was wrong, just how much he had fooled himself. He thought of Teddy, the way he kept harping that something was going on and Sam was too dense to know it. He remembered his father always asking him, "You like Isabelle, don't you?"

For a moment, he was dizzy with shock. Everything he had ever thought about Isabelle was a lie. She wasn't bringing his mother back so he could talk to her. She wasn't making things right again. She didn't care about him and she wasn't here for him—it was all about his dad! She was sitting there kissing his dad, and it was all his fault for bringing them together. He squeezed his eyes shut, but something was wrong with his senses. He couldn't see clearly, he couldn't hear. She wasn't an angel!

"Mommy!" he screamed, and then he couldn't stop the hot scald of his tears, the way all his bones had turned to ice. He bolted into the street, running into the intersection just as a car entered it. "Hey, kid!" the driver shouted, furiously beeping his horn, and then Sam saw his father and

Isabelle look up. He saw the way they pulled apart, the way their faces changed, and then he heard their car doors fly open, his father calling, "Sam! Sam!"

Sam ran harder. Every step he took, the air seemed to thicken. He sucked in air, shuddering.

It felt as if no one was in the world but him right now. The streets were empty, and there were no lights in any of the houses. No cars traveled past him. He heard a crash of lightning, the sudden boom of thunder, and then the sky split open into a thousand jagged pieces and there was a shower of cold rain. His steps smacked against the pavement. A scrap of paper from the sidewalk caught in the wind and rose up in the sky like a giant bird.

Sam's heart was beating too fast. His pants were already so wet that they were dragging on the ground, and he was shivering hard. Bits of something flew into his face, biting his skin, shooting into his eyes so he had to snap his lids shut.

"When you're scared, think of the facts," Charlie had told him, but every fact he knew frightened him even more. Lightning could strike you while you were in the shower. It could race through the pipes, lighting you up like a firecracker. People had been struck by lightning and some people had lived, but some people hadn't. Sam ran faster, slipping on the sidewalk, skinning a hole in his pants. He was alone in the world. Isabelle wasn't an angel. His mother was really dead.

"Mommy!" He screamed, but no one answered. No one would ever answer, not now. He thought of his mother's face, her hands, the way she tickled him under the ribs, and every thought tore him in two. "Mommy!" The wind covered up his voice. Sam tugged himself up and ran again. The lightning seemed to be coming closer, following him, punctuating every step with a sonic boom of thunder. Yellow sizzled in the sky, and he felt his bones turn to water.

"Dad!" he screamed, but the wind gulped down his voice. Fear pinballed inside him. He sucked at the air and it felt like he was inhaling a wet washcloth. His lungs were crunching up. Sam felt for his inhaler, but it wasn't there, and that made him panic even more.

His hair sluiced against his face. Running into the wind, he pushed on. There was a big tree up ahead, the branches like arms scratching at the sky. Then he heard a sound, like the world splitting open.

The cracking sound grew louder and then he heard a whooshing, and there was a bolt of lightning tearing across the sky, zigzagging and connecting with the tree. He craned his head, staring, frozen in place and the whole tree seemed to light up. One of the branches shimmied with light as it broke off. Sam felt something crash against his side, toppling him to the ground. A hot sting zoomed through him.

He glanced down and saw a flash of red streaming down his arm. Blood. There was blood. He bolted up, his arm throbbing, and it was then that he saw the tree branch, like an extra arm, fallen beside him, and a huge open gash in the tree. He ran, not thinking, grabbing his arm, stopping the blood with his fingers. *Don't cry, don't cry, don't look.* He ran with his eyes closed. He told himself not to think about the pain, not to think about his mom or his dad or Isabelle. All he had to do was get to someplace safe and he had to do it fast. *I can't breathe!* he thought. *I can't breathe!* He gulped at air.

The school loomed in front of him. He had an extra inhaler there, locked in the nurse's office. He banged on the door, screaming. "It's Sam! It's Sam!" The pain made him shake and wheeze so that he couldn't shout anymore. He couldn't bang on the door as hard. "It's Sam!" he tried to scream again, but the world suddenly began to suck him down until everything narrowed into black.

~ Sixteen ~

THEY SCREAMED SAM'S name, all the windows of the car open, the rain pelting in and soaking them as they drove. How had he run so fast? Before she had seen him, Isabelle had felt something, like a charge in the air, and then she had pulled free of Charlie and there was Sam, standing there with his mouth open, and her heart had broken.

"We should have told him," Isabelle said. "We should never have kept things so secret."

"He wasn't ready!" Charlie said.

"But this makes it worse! How can we explain it to him now?"

Helpless, Charlie turned another corner. "He's nine years old."

Isabelle glanced out the window, the booms of thunder so loud they seemed to crack open the sky. "We'll find him," she said.

They left a note for Sam at home. They drove to the places Sam loved: the beach, where the sand was wet and heavy; the diner, which had closed because of the weather; the playground, which was deserted. They couldn't find him anywhere.

Charlie called home every few minutes. They went to the police with a photograph. "He's severely asthmatic! He's nine years old!" Charlie screamed.

The officer looked at Charlie. "We'll get right on it," he said.

They got back in the car, the rain drumming against the windows. Charlie dialed one hospital after another, and with every call, his voice seemed more faded. He couldn't let go of Isabelle's hand. "Do you have a nine-year-old boy there, an asthmatic?" Charlie cried into the phone and Isabelle moved closer to him, trying to hear what the voice on the other end might be saying. Charlie nodded yes, and he listened.

"He's okay," Charlie said, finally, hanging up the phone. "They have him. He's in an oxygen tent. Cuts and scratches, but he's okay."

"Let's go. We'll be there in five minutes," she said, but he shook his head.

"I'll drive you home. I can't think straight. I'll call you."

"Charlie, please! Let me go with you! Don't you think I'm worried, too?"

A sheet of rain poured across the car. The windshield wipers squeaked. "I know you're worried, but he's got to be furious with both of us. It's better if it's just me right now."

He put one hand on her shoulder and she felt a shiver of cold. She looked out the window. The streets were empty. "Why? Why is it better?" she said quietly.

His whole body seemed to be shaking. "Isabelle, my son is in the hospital! I can't have a conversation about this now. I'll call you when I can," he said. And then he started the car, and the whole way to her place, neither one of them spoke. When Charlie dropped Isabelle off, he pulled away almost immediately and she was left standing in the soaking rain.

SAM WOKE UP with a thick plastic oxygen tent around him and his arm glowing with pain. Doctors ringed his bed. He turned his head away from the light. "You're one lucky boy," one of the faces said. Sam bit down on his lip so he wouldn't cry, because after all that had happened, how could anyone in his right mind ever say that Sam was lucky?

"Oh, yes," said another face. "I'm Doctor Stamper. The school janitor found you. He knew who you were and he knew what to do. He drove you here. We gave you something for your asthma and the oxygen should help, too. But this arm! Your arm's been hurt before, buddy, hasn't it?"

For a moment, Sam was back in that day, his mother wheeling around the car, yelling at him to get back inside the car. "I fell," he lied.

"Looks like some of these cuts are right at the same spot," the doctor said. "Now what's the chance of that happening, I ask you?"

Dr. Stamper patted Sam's shoulder. "Your father's coming," he told him. Then he reached under the plastic and gave Sam a shot, making him woozy. The room was floating. He kept craning his neck, looking around for his dad.

He slept off and on, but he didn't dream, and every time he woke up, it was a shock to be back in the hospital. And then the door flew open and there was his father, soaking wet, and there was no Isabelle. There was no Mom. It was only then that Sam began to cry as if he would never stop.

His father drew a chair close beside Sam and took his hand. "I'm so sorry," Charlie said.

"Mommy's dead!" Sam wailed, "She's not coming back!"

His father swallowed. "I know," he said.

"I thought I could talk to her, just one more time! I thought I could see her!"

His father moved in closer, so that Sam could see the droplets of water sparkling on his skin. "You know that isn't possible."

"You and Isabelle lied to me!"

His father rubbed Sam's hands between his. "This is all my fault. I should have told you that I was seeing Isabelle," his dad said. "I should have let you know what was going on."

"Do you like her more than Mom?" Sam blurted.

His father gave him a pained look. "Sam, no one can replace your mom for me."

"Then why did you like Isabelle that way?"

"I was just trying to move on. I was trying to

make you and me happy again. I'm so sorry. I'm so sorry."

Sam struggled to sit up in bed. "Nelson . . ." he said, pained.

Charlie looked surprised. "Nelson is at home."

"He's okay?" Sam could hardly dare to believe it.

"Of course, he's okay."

Sam tugged himself up further, wincing. "No, no, rest," his father said.

"I have to tell you something," Sam said.

Sam told his father everything about the day of the accident. It all spilled out of him—how he had hidden in the car that morning with his mother, how it was surely his fault because if he hadn't had asthma, she wouldn't have stopped. "She wouldn't have died," he said.

His father looked as if he were frozen to the chair. "She wasn't taking you?"

"I hid! And then I had an attack and I spoiled everything!"

His father looked dazed. "It's not your fault," his father said, but his skin had no color and he wouldn't stop looking at Sam as if he somehow didn't know him. "None of it is your fault," he repeated.

But it was his fault. Of course it was his fault, and then there was nothing left for Sam to do but tell his father more of the story. How he had seen Isabelle at the accident, how he had thought she was an angel and how sure he was that she would know where his mom went, that she would let him talk to her.

"But Mom's dead!" Sam's voiced tore from his lungs, flooding with tears. "She isn't coming back! She's dead! She's dead! And Isabelle can't help us talk to her!"

Charlie moved his chair closer to the bed, stunned. "You thought Isabelle was an angel?" He took Sam's hands in his. "Why didn't you tell me? Why didn't you tell Isabelle?"

"You wouldn't have believed me. And the books I read said you're not supposed to tell, you're not supposed to talk about it."

"Kiddo," Charlie's voice was pained. "Isabelle isn't an angel. She's just a person, like you and me. She doesn't have any secret knowledge and she can't bring your mother back in any way. No one can."

"But I saw—she had a halo! I heard wings!"

"Sometimes you think you see things that aren't there," Charlie said quietly. "Sometimes you wish for them to be there so much, you believe that they are."

Sam stared down at the hospital sheets, threading his fingers tightly together. Then he looked back up at his dad.

"Do you hate me for the accident?"

Then, to Sam's surprise, his father climbed up onto the bed and lay beside him, just outside the oxygen tent, but still so close that Sam could smell the soap he used, right through the plastic sheet. Charlie wrapped as much of Sam as he could in his arms and rocked him. "I love you," he said. "Wherever you are, whatever you do. I'll always love you."

THE NEXT DAY, Isabelle rode the elevator up to the children's ward. What a horrible thing, a children's ward of a hospital. How could anyone work here and not have their heart broken every day? The walls were painted with brightly colored murals of animals. The staff all wore smocks with teddy bears on them, and though everyone was smiling, Isabelle still felt affronted.

Sam shouldn't be here. Not in this place.

She was tense and worried. Charlie had called her only once, rushed and apologetic. "I'll call you back," he promised, and when he hadn't, she called the hospital herself.

"We can only give information to family members," a stern voice said.

Isabelle protested but the voice was unmoved. She hadn't wanted to call Charlie, but she couldn't just sit around, so she grabbed her jacket and now here she was.

She rounded a corner, toward Sam's room, and saw Charlie in the waiting room. He looked terrible. His hair was lank, his clothes rumpled. When he saw her, he glanced at her as if he didn't know who she was.

She sat down beside him, and when she touched his arm, he looked at her. "What are you doing here?" he said wearily.

"I came to see Sam, I came to see you." Something about him seemed suddenly missing to her. If she touched him right now, she wasn't sure he wouldn't dissolve under her fingers.

"You can't see him. He's in an oxygen tent," Charlie said.

"Then I'll sit out here with you. I love him, Charlie, and I love you."

Charlie met her eyes and for a moment she thought he was going to stand up and take her into his arms, but instead, he sank lower into his chair. "He looks so little in that bed." He half shut his eyes. "I haven't slept, I can't eat. His asthma's getting worse and they don't know why. All I keep thinking is that if we hadn't been together, this wouldn't have happened. That it was my fault."

Isabelle touched Charlie's hand, but his fingers didn't reach for hers. "Please don't shut me out of this." She pulled up a chair and sat beside him.

He shook his head. "I'm not shutting you out. I just don't have a lot of room right now for anyone but Sam."

"Charlie, please."

"He told me he thought you were an angel, that you were some link between him and his mom so he could talk to her, that you could make her manifest so he could see her."

"What?" Isabelle started. "I never told him anything like that!"

"The day of the accident. He said you had a halo of light, that it looked like the pictures of angels in books. He said he heard your wings."

"Oh my God. I wish I had known. I wish he had told me!"

Charlie swallowed. "He told me something else about the day of the accident. April wasn't taking him. He hid in the back of the car to surprise her. She was leaving both of us. Both of us!"

Isabelle felt herself dissolving. She tried to touch Charlie again, but he moved back, almost apologetically. She was about to try to pull him back to her, when a doctor came into the room. "Mr. Nash? Could you come in Sam's room for a moment, please?"

Charlie stood up, but when Isabelle stood up and started to follow him, he stopped and touched her shoulder. He cupped her chin, just for a moment, before he let her go again. "Please. I'll call you when I know something," he said.

All that day, Sam seemed to get worse. They gave him nebulizer treatments and started him on prednisone. By supper time, though, his breathing had calmed, and by late evening, he was sleeping, his small chest rising and falling. Charlie sat by his bed. He thought of April, the way some crackpot had told her that children with asthma are souls uncertain about staying here, and so she had climbed into Sam's bed and whispered to him not to leave.

Charlie took Sam's small hand in his. "Stay," he told Sam, just as a nurse whisked into the room.

"Go home," the nurse said.

"No, I should stay."

"It's three o'clock in the morning. Sam is out for the night and all that's going to happen if you stay is that you'll be a mess in the morning. Go get some sleep. You won't be any good to your son if you get sick, too."

The nurse shooed him, the way she might a dog. Charlie slowly got up and walked to his car.

Then he drove. The whole world seemed to have emptied out. The streets were dark and there were only a few cars on the road. Occasionally he saw someone walking. A man with his head bent low, crying. A couple with their arms slung about each other. The only people out were either miserable or in love.

Charlie thought about going home, sleeping on the couch because to get to his bedroom he'd have to walk past Sam's empty room and he couldn't bear that. He thought about Sam, so tiny in that hospital bed, and then he thought about Isabelle and felt a tug of yearning.

He wanted to talk to her, to touch her face, to just be with her. He thought of the curve of her neck, and how she leaned forward as if she wanted to scoop up every word. And then he thought about how he had been so short with her at the hospital. He had seen the way her whole body flinched, and though he had ached to hold her, to tell her it was all right, it didn't feel right.

He parked in front of her apartment and buzzed.

"Charlie?" Her voice was soft with sleep.

"Please . . ." He couldn't get the words out. He rested his face against the door and then she buzzed him up. By the time he got to the top of her stairs, she was on the landing, walking toward him in her robe, then resting her head against his shoulder.

They lay spooned together on Isabelle's bed, Charlie's head against her shoulders, her heart beating against him. Then she turned to face him, taking his face in her hands. She kissed his nose and then each of his eyes. "It's going to be all right," she said. "Try to sleep."

When he woke, she was still beside him, still in his arms, her eyes open. "You slept," she said. "I'm so glad. I watched you."

"Then you didn't sleep," he said, kissing her.

They both got up slowly. He had forgotten how much he loved just seeing her move, the slow, easy way she lifted up her hair and knotted it, the way she tilted her head when she listened to him.

She was making them French toast, squeezing juice. He grabbed his pants from the living room floor and pulled out his cell to call the hospital.

"We tried to call you last night," the doctor said. "Sam's not doing well."

His heart jammed. Had he been so involved with Isabelle that he hadn't heard his phone from the other room? "I'll be there right away."

"It's Sam," he said to Isabelle, reaching for his clothes. Why did he leave the hospital? How could he have been so stupid? He didn't have to listen to that nurse. He could have stayed. He could have been there when Sam got worse. His son didn't have to be alone and scared. He could have been home to get the call. But instead he had gone to Isabelle.

He was lacing his shoes when he noticed that Isabelle had turned the burner off, that she was standing there, helpless.

"I know I can't come with you," she said, her voice sad.

"I'll call you as soon as I can," Charlie said, and then he grabbed his jacket and was gone.

ALL THAT WEEK, she waited for Charlie to call. Isabelle told herself he was at the hospital, he was busy with Sam, and when he was home, he must be exhausted. But sometimes, too, she wondered why she couldn't go through this with him. Why did they have to deal with it as if they were on separate coasts of the country?

She thought about how April could have driven away without her son. Isabelle had driven away from a husband, too, but Luke had been cheating on her. He had fathered a child with another woman. She could understand leaving a husband like that, but a son? How could you leave your own child? She thought of April in her red dress, shrouded by fog, staring at Isabelle as if she knew what was coming, and then Isabelle leaped up and grabbed the phone, calling the hospital to ask about Sam.

"Discharged," said a rushed voice, and Isabelle felt a shock of pain because she hadn't known, because Charlie hadn't thought to tell her.

She called Charlie. "Why didn't you tell me?" she asked.

"I'm sorry. I've just been so overwhelmed that I haven't had a second. It's all I can do to take care of Sam," he said. "He's still not doing so hot, but at least he's home."

"I could help you."

There was that funny silence again. "I want to see you," he said. "I know you're worried, but every time I pick up the phone, I think about what it might do to Sam. I feel like I'm padding on this very thin layer of ice and I can't even see the cracks."

"We can protect him together."

"I saw him being born," Charlie said. His voice sounded far away, and she gripped the receiver tighter against her ear. "Some fathers don't want to go into the delivery room, but I did. I saw him curled up, as tiny as a minute. I heard his first cry. When he came home, I used to sleep beside him, even though April was worried I'd smother him. I just loved staring at him. Having a child is, well, it's just profound. Even as they grow, you just stop and look at them and you keep thinking in absolute wonderment, Where did you come from? How is it possible you're here?" He was quiet for a moment. "I'm sorry, I have to go. I have to get Sam's medicine. I'll call you later," he said, and then hung up.

Isabelle curled up in the sheets. She thought about Charlie tending his son, about the way he'd look at Sam with pure amazement that he existed, and then she thought about all the babies she would never have. All the names she had picked out. They were ghost babies.

And there was Sam.

And right now, she didn't have either one.

All that week, Isabelle called to get reports about Sam, but it was always the same. Sam was wheezing. Or Sam was on a new medication or having to use an oxygen tank. And then he began to do better, to respond to the medication. "He's turned a corner," Charlie said finally, and she could hear the relief in his voice. "He's back to normal."

"Can I come by, then?" she asked.

"Not yet," Charlie said. "Sam refuses to even talk about you right now." He was quiet for a moment. "It was such a close call," he finally said.

She wrapped her arms about her body, stung. "At least he's better," she said. "At least he's going to be fine."

SHE WENT OUT for a walk, and when she came home, there were two messages on her answering machine, Michelle and a wrong number. Nothing from work. What was she going to do if she couldn't get some income? How would she live? She picked up the paper and scanned the help-wanteds. She knew she wasn't exactly old, but she wasn't twenty, either, and she didn't have a college degree. The kinds of jobs she'd be competing for might not even want her—not that she truly, deeply wanted them herself. Photo-graphing pots and pans for a department store, where the most creative thing she might do would be to put a plastic banana in a glass fruit bowl, or spread a robe across a well-made bed—that wasn't for her. She scanned the ads. She could work at Sears, but it would be Beautiful Baby all over again, and they paid even less and didn't offer full benefits, and how could she afford that?

Breathe, she told herself. But all she felt was panic. If she had to, who could she even stay with until she got on her feet? Michelle had the baby and a husband. Her other friends had boyfriends or studios so tiny there wouldn't be room for even an extra houseplant. The summer people were starting to arrive, and even on one-room studios the prices were already skyrocketing. And she couldn't ask Charlie. Not now.

Going through the mail didn't help. Her electric bill was due, her rent. She still owed her dentist five hundred dollars for a chipped tooth he had repaired. And then a white envelope slid forward. She picked it up and suddenly felt sick, as if she needed to brace herself for another blow. The photography school. She had completely forgotten that she had applied. They had said on the brochure they'd let her know by summer, and now here it was.

Bad news comes in threes, Nora used to tell her, but she had said it after Isabelle's father had died young, after Nora had lost her job at the library for repeatedly refusing to let kids take out books she felt were antireligious, and Isabelle had begun sneaking out to see Luke, a boy Nora considered pure poison. But now, here it was again. One, two, three. Charlie, her job, and probably a polite little letter: *Dear Isabelle Stein, We're sorry you weren't good enough for us. We told you not to count on anything, didn't we, but as usual, you refused to listen.*

She slid the letter on the table and then picked it up again and opened it. There it was in her hand. Her future.

ISABELLE WAS PANTING when she got to Charlie's. She flung her bike on the grass and bounded up the stairs. She had to see Charlie, she wanted to see Sam. The world had suddenly opened up for her and she had to share it.

She buzzed and then the door opened and there was Charlie.

"Isabelle!" Charlie said. "What are you doing here?" He looked tired and shaggy, but the house was quiet. "Sam couldn't sleep last night, but he's finally napping," he said. Charlie stepped outside onto the porch. "He'll be out for a few hours," he said. "It's good school's almost out. He won't miss too much." He touched Isabelle's hair. "Stay a bit. Sit out on the porch with me."

"I'm too excited to sit." Hands shaking, she showed him the paper.

"What's this?" He took the paper but his eyes stayed on her.

"I got in! They want me!" Isabelle cried. "They gave me a scholarship!"

He studied the paper. "This is for photography school?"

"You don't understand—I never really graduated high school. I just have my crummy little GED, so most programs wouldn't even want me. But this! This is the real thing, this is credentials. I could go someplace with this!"

"It says it's in New York." Charlie gave her a funny look. "You're leaving us?"

Isabelle paced excitedly. "Charlie, remember you once said that you could imagine us being

346

together for real?" She swallowed and then she decided to just say it, to just take the leap. "We could all leave. Go to New York together."

"I have a house here. A business."

"You could rent out your house. You could find work in New York or maybe you could come back here a few days a week. We could all see how we felt being really together."

"Sam just got better! He just found out we're a couple. I can't spring it on him that we're all moving to New York!"

"Nobody is springing anything! We all work this out together! And when Sam gets well, we can make real decisions about us."

"I don't know," Charlie said slowly. "Kids with asthma don't get well. This is chronic. Anything could set him off. Sometimes I think that if I wasn't so intent on moving on, Sam would have been safer."

"Charlie, that's crazy. You always put Sam first!"

"Is it crazy? He could have died."

"But he's all right now. And Sam knows about us now, we don't have to sneak around."

The way Charlie was looking at her made Isabelle step back. "You're not saying, Isabelle, what a brilliant idea," she said.

"Sam just told me that his mother wasn't driving away with him, that she meant to go alone, and now you tell me you're leaving? How can you do this to us?"

"I don't want to leave you! I want you to come with me!"

"I don't want you to leave! We need you here. I know it's been rough, but things will get better. Can't you at least wait until Sam is a little older? Can't you give us more time? I can't make a decision like this with all that's going on now!"

"I don't have more time! My money's just about gone. Work is drying up at Beautiful Baby. I never intended to stay here for good."

"But you have stayed."

"Because of you. And Sam." Isabelle dug her hands in her pockets. "Charlie, I don't have anything else. I've been combing the want ads, making myself insane. This is my shot for a real future and I want you and Sam in it."

Charlie rested his hands on the porch railing. "I built this porch the summer before Sam was born. This is our *home*. This is what Sam knows. And we can't live in New York. The pollution there is terrible for asthma. It's hard enough when Sam goes to visit his grandparents there. He can't be exposed to more of that."

His hair was so long now, it fell like a wing. She wanted to cup his face. She wanted to kiss his beautiful mouth and then his throat. She swallowed. "If I stayed, Charlie, I'd have to give up this chance. I don't know if I could get in again or if there might be other chances for me. Would you really want me to do that?"

His face turned tense and miserable.

"And if I stayed, if I did give it up, what would happen?" She pushed on, unable to stop herself. "Do you love me, Charlie?"

"How can you even ask such a question? Don't you know how I feel?"

"I have to know there's a place for me here. You keep asking me to wait, but for how long? I want more. I need more."

As soon as she said it, she knew she had made a mistake. Charlie looked at her as if she had just struck him, and she felt suddenly hot and shamed.

"You don't understand," Charlie said. "Last night, I mentioned your name and Sam had an asthma attack. If I tell him you and I are serious—or if I tell him you're leaving—I don't know what could happen. How can I promise you anything? I just have to take things moment by moment right now. Please—we need you here. I need you."

She took a step closer to him. She thought of Michelle and her husband, who had known he was going to marry her the second he had met her. Then she thought of Sam, who was so angry with her now he didn't want to see her—who would never really be hers because Charlie couldn't trust her enough to let them try.

She thought of all the ways she was going to be lonely from now on. "I can't stay here any longer. I can't be just on the edges of your life," she said.

"I love you. I love Sam. I want you to come with me. And I have to do this."

"Is this it?" he asked, shocked. "You're really leaving?"

As soon as he said it, she felt an emptiness, like her bones had filled with air.

"What about Sam?" Charlie said.

"I'll talk to him. I'll explain. I have to say good-bye to Sam. And you have to let me."

Charlie stared at her as if he didn't know her.

Isabelle stepped back from him. "I don't understand a single thing about what's happening here. Some people fall in love at first sight and stay that way their whole lives. Is that you with April? Is there really no room for anyone else? For me?"

"And some people fall in love and the timing is wrong and nothing they do can ever fix it. My son's in the middle here, and you're asking me to jeopardize him to find out if we could be together. You're asking me to bet on all these what-ifs, and I can't, Isabelle, I just can't. Sam was almost killed leaving with his mother. And he'll be almost killed by your leaving."

Isabelle grabbed her purse. "I love him. I love you. And I have to go," she said.

AFTER ISABELLE LEFT, Charlie sat on the porch. This couldn't be happening, not like this. Not again.

He went in to check on Sam. He was sleeping. Charlie gently pushed the hair away from his face. You're all I have, he thought. Charlie put his head in his hands. He felt something, like a whisper at the back of his neck, and he looked up, but all he saw was the room, sparkling with light.

Charlie got out a rag and began to dust. He thought about the day April left, the morning when all he had to do was say different words and she might have stayed. None of this might have happened and she'd still be here. If he had held his tongue, if he had run back into the house and apologized, he'd still have his family. And now Isabelle was leaving and he had said everything he could think of to get her to stay. He had no idea what to do differently, what else to say.

He used to work with a sheetrock guy whose wife and child had died in a plane crash. The man never got over it, and it used to irritate Charlie the way Hank would say, "I dreamed about Jean and Suzie last night," and everyone would look sort of stricken, wondering, Why doesn't he get over it already? But that was the secret, wasn't it? You never got over what you lost. You always carried it with you, stitched to you like Peter Pan's shadow. And you never wanted to get over it, because who wanted to forget a time that had been so important? No, the truth was, you wanted to remember it always.

Charlie sat heavily on the couch in the living

room, where he used to cuddle with April and watch old movies, where he had spooned with Isabelle as if they were teenagers. He had begged her to stay. He had pleaded for more time. But she was going.

He had Sam. No matter what, he still had Sam.

~ SEVENTEEN ~

ISABELLE DIDN'T CALL CHARLIE. She had already said good-bye, and she didn't need to hurt either of them any more. A part of her kept expecting him to show up at her door, telling her he had changed his mind, that he and Sam were already packed; but all that happened was that the June days got hotter and hotter. There were more summer people on the streets, and when she walked past the school playground, she saw that the sturdy black gate was locked, the windows of the school shut until fall.

She packed and planned, marking off one week on her calendar and then another, and then went to Beautiful Baby to give Chuck her notice. He was in his office on the phone, and when he saw her, he yawned. "Oh, Isabelle," he said, as if he had just remembered who she was. "I'll get right back to you."

She waited at the door, not moving, even when he kept giving her pointed looks. Finally, he hung up the phone, and shuffling some papers, waved her in. He motioned for her to sit. "So," he said. "We need to talk about you and Beautiful Baby."

"I quit," she said.

He sat up straighter. "Aren't you being a little dramatic?"

"I'm going to photography school in Manhattan."

She had wanted him to be impressed or excited, but his face was impassive. His eyes glazed over as if she had just told him she was going food shopping.

"Well, good for you," he said finally. For a moment, she wished he didn't look so relieved. He pumped her hand. "You want a good-bye party?"

"No, I don't think so."

She stood up and shook his hand and as soon as she left the office, she heard him pick up the phone again. "Because the order was due today, that's why," he snapped.

It wasn't until she was outside, her skin prickling in the hot sun, that she realized he hadn't asked her why, or when she was going, or even if she would keep in touch.

ISABELLE DECIDED TO take a walk. Luke used to insist that if she ever left the Cape, she'd miss it, but she didn't think so. If she went to New York, she'd never go to Coney Island. She'd never miss salty air or pine trees.

She still hated the Cape. The endless beaches, the sand that always got into everything, even the sheets. She hated the tide of summer people, the way the town seemed to fill up and empty out with the seasons. No matter how long she lived here, she'd never really feel that she belonged. She knew she'd never really be a part of Charlie's family, not with Charlie still living with the ghost of April. Sam would never really be her son. She knew she needed a new life because this one didn't really have a place for her.

SHE CALLED MICHELLE to talk. "Listen," Michelle said. "You're doing the right thing. You need to move on. This is your chance. And guess what? Remember that illegal sublet you were supposed to get last year? I was just talking to my friend Dora and she said the guy renting it moved out. It's available again, but you'd have to take it now."

"What?" Isabelle wrapped the phone cord around her wrist.

"Say the word and I'll call Dora. And even better, I'm driving down to Manhattan next week to see about starting a jewelry business from home. I'd love the company."

Isabelle tried to think. Next week. Photography school didn't start until September, but was there any more reason to stay here? Could she afford to pass up on this sublet and a ride to the city? She would have to get a job as soon as she got to Manhattan. Waitressing, something part-time. She'd start to save so she could work less when her classes started, which were supposed to be intensive. Could she do this? "Yes," she said. She hung up, and then without thinking, she called her mother.

"Oh, the prodigal daughter," Nora said dryly, and then Isabelle told her she was going back to school. She told her about Charlie and Sam, and her mother was silent.

"That's good, what you're doing," Nora finally said.

"It is? I thought you'd disapprove, because of my age. I thought you'd think because of my divorce, I was a failure."

She heard Nora sigh on the phone. "I never liked Luke. You knew that. And you know what? Marriage is a funny thing. I put my whole trust in your dad instead of God, and your dad was the one who broke my heart. I used to see the same thing happening with you and Luke, but you wouldn't listen."

"It wasn't the same," Isabelle said. "Dad adored you. I adored Luke. It took me a while to figure out that Luke adored himself."

"Listen to me now. I'm apologizing. I was wrong to be so hard on you. I have to forgive myself every day for it, and I ask God for forgiveness, too. But you did the right thing with this Charlie person. You couldn't lose more of your life for another man, especially not for a man who won't lose some of his life for you."

"Mom. I can't believe you think this."

"Sometimes marriage isn't such a sacred covenant. There. I said it."

"Why didn't you ever answer my letters? I sent

a million of them. I made a thousand calls. You never responded."

"I couldn't. Not while you were with Luke. I couldn't have been any part of it." Isabelle heard something in the background, a hum of voices, a TV turning on. "But now that you're going to school, maybe I can visit. If you want. We're still family."

"I want," said Isabelle.

THE MORNING OF Isabelle's departure, the radio was warning about traffic jams. "Everyone's headed back to the Cape!" the announcer boomed. How many times had Isabelle heard that and yearned to leave as fast as she could, and now, here she was and leaving wasn't anything like she ever had imagined.

She had one last call to make. Luke. When he picked up, she heard a baby crying in the background, a female voice soothing. For a moment, her stomach tightened, but she didn't feel like running away. Instead, she was running to something.

"You're leaving!" Luke said. "Well, good for you."

They talked a bit about where she would live, what she was going to do, even about Chloe, his sunny little baby. And then, just as she was going to ask about his job, he grew so quiet. She felt something dissolving through the wires. "I'm so sorry, Iz," he said. "About everything."

357

"You don't have to apologize. All that feels like such a long time ago."

The baby's laugh sparkled in the background. "I hope everything is wonderful for you," he said.

"For you, too," she said. "But it sounds like it already is."

When she hung up, her jumpy heart was more about getting ready to leave than about Luke. She spent all morning looking for a special photograph she wanted to give Sam. She had enlarged it to 8 x 12, and it was black and white and full of shadows. It was a photograph of the two of them, her favorite, and though they weren't looking at each other in the picture, you could tell how connected they were. She turned it over and carefully wrote "Some connections are never broken." She packed the photograph in a box with an old zoom lens that she knew Sam would love, with directions on how to press the button to get the old lens off and put this new one on. Then she wrote a letter to him. It took her several tries to get it right.

Dear Sam, I had to leave to go to school, but it's not forever. No matter what, you have to know that I love you. That that love will always be there for you. That I didn't leave because of you or because of your dad. I left because I had a chance to go to school. This is my new address and I will have a phone number soon that I will get to you, and I hope you'll call and visit and write. I'm sorry I wasn't an angel, but that doesn't meant there isn't magic in the world.

Love, Isabelle

P.S. The zoom lens is for your Canon. You can see much more with it.

Michelle was coming to pick her up in two hours, so she still had a little time. Her apartment was empty.

The day was clear and hot, the sky like watercolor wash. During the whole walk to Sam's house she missed him so much, it felt like a wound.

The house was quiet, the shades drawn. She sneaked around to Sam's window, which was halfway open. Standing on tiptoes, peering up from under his plastic blind, she could see him sleeping, the damp, soft sleep of boys. His mouth was slightly open and his eyes were rolling with dreams. She ached to kiss his forehead and take his hand, to hear his raspy little voice. Instead, as she wavered on her tiptoes, she tried to memorize him, imprinting him like a snapshot she'd never forget.

She crept to the front of the house. She could

knock on the door and demand to see him. She could rap on his window and wake him up. She could stand here and scream for them both to come outside and listen to her, just for one minute.

Gingerly, she stepped over the new young plants, Charlie's bright, hopeful splashes of color. He could open up to nature, but with her, he was closed, and how could she stay with someone like that? Plus, there was all this Cape Cod, all this place that was like a single finger pointing at her, reminding her of what had happened, of what she had done. She turned back to the window. Charlie was a heavy sleeper. Carefully, heart sprinting, Isabelle tapped on the window. Sam started and then just as he was pulling the plastic shade angrily down on her, she beckoned him to the window.

He opened the window fully.

"We don't have time for you to pretend to be mad at me," Isabelle said.

"I'm not pretending. I am mad."

"I know." She tried to touch his hair, but he stepped pointedly away from her.

"Why don't you just leave if you're leaving?"

"I came to say good-bye." She handed the package through the window. "I wrote something for you. And inside is a camera lens. A good one. And a photograph I wanted you to have."

He blinked really hard. "I hate you. Go away."

"Listen to me, Sam," she said. "I know you

don't hate me. Well, maybe today you do, but you won't always. I will always love you. I will always want to know how you are. I will always try to call and write you and you can call and write me. I wrote down my address and as soon as I get my own phone, when I get settled, I'll send that to you, too."

"I'll never call you," he said. "I'll never write."

She heard something. The slam of a screen door, a neighbor next door. Any moment Charlie could come up, and if he found her here, there would be an argument. She reached out to touch his face, but he pushed her hand away. "You're not an angel," he snapped.

"I never said I was. You write me," she whispered. "You call if you need to. I love you, Sam. I love you."

She started walking and then she heard feet, and then she turned and Sam was climbing out of his window, and then he was running after her in his bare feet. She stopped and crouched down, and when he flung himself on her, she wrapped her arms around him. His shoulders shook with sobs.

"Don't go," he pleaded. "I won't tell my dad you were here. I won't tell him anything you don't want me to! I won't try to find anything out ever again! I don't care if you're an angel, just please don't go!"

She brushed his hair back so she could look at his face. She quietly blotted his tears with her fingers. "Sam, what are you talking about?" She walked him back to his room, and boosted him back and watched while he tucked himself back under the covers. She pointed to the sky. "I just can't stay, honey. But you know how far away the sun is out there? That's how much I love you," she told him.

A couple of hours later, Isabelle loaded Michelle's car with her suitcases and her boxes, and then together they wedged Nelson's tank in the backseat. Isabelle climbed into the front. "You ready?" Michelle asked, and she nodded. "You're doing the right thing. The only thing," Michelle said. "This will be a whole new life."

"I'm ready," Isabelle said. Michelle peeled around the corner and headed for the highway.

For a moment, Isabelle heard a buzz, the same as the day of the accident, and she looked anxiously at the corners of the car. "I hear a bee," she said.

"No bees in here," Michelle said. The humming sound had vanished.

It was the first time she was a passenger in a car with someone who wasn't Charlie and she didn't feel like jumping out. She was traveling to a new life and somehow, all her old responses seemed wrong to her now. They didn't fit. She held up her hands. They weren't shaking. Her skin was cool and dry.

"You okay?" Michelle said.

Isabelle opened her window a bit, so the breeze blew in, ruffling her hair. She'd remember all that she was leaving behind, as indelible as if she had photographed it.

She turned and smiled weakly at Michelle. "I'm going to be fine."

~ Eighteen ~

IT HAD BEEN three weeks since his argument with Isabelle, and Charlie, standing at the bathroom sink, still felt terrible. He didn't know what to do, but he hoped time would sort it out, that Isabelle would come to her senses and realize that this was a thorny time for all of them and she wouldn't actually leave.

Charlie couldn't shave. He couldn't bear to look in the mirror and see his own face. His hands shook, even when he pressed them under his armpits to steady them. He shaved slowly, carefully, and cut himself, anyway. He washed his face and the soap stung his eyes.

He heard Sam crying in his room. When he walked in, to his surprise, Sam was sitting on the bed with a big camera lens and what looked like a letter on his lap. "Where did that come from?" Charlie asked, and Sam cried harder, kicking the lens off the bed, throwing the letter to the end of the bed where Charlie was. "I don't want this stupid camera lens, so don't try to make me take it!" Sam said. "I'm never taking photos again!"

Charlie stared at the lens, his mind in knots. He glanced down at the letter and as soon as he saw Isabelle's handwriting, his whole body ached. "Sam," he said, steadying his voice. "Was Isabelle here? When did you get this lens?"

He saw the window, opened wide, and he sank onto Sam's bed. "She shouldn't have come to see you," he said quietly, but he couldn't help wondering, if she was brash enough to come see Sam, why hadn't she come to see him as well? Why hadn't she called or at least knocked on the front door? "I'll call her," he decided.

"You can't call her!" Sam wailed. "She's gone! She moved to New York!"

Something twisted in Charlie's stomach. He reached for Isabelle's letter, reading it in a rush. Each word was like a burr in his throat. He let the letter fall back onto the bed, astounded. She had left. She had really left them. Sam hiccoughed, rubbing fiercely at his eyes, and then staring at Charlie. Charlie knew he should have something comforting to say to Sam, something reasonable and solid, but he was afraid if he opened his mouth, he might start weeping. Instead, all he could do was touch Sam's shoulder, and even then, Sam wrenched away. "Leave me alone!" Sam said. "Get out of my room!"

He nodded. "It's going to be okay," he said, but he couldn't keep the hollowness out of his voice. He walked out of the room and then he heard the sound of paper tearing over and over. Then Sam slammed his bedroom door shut.

Charlie felt as if he were sleepwalking. He knew he could call her. He could find her. But it wouldn't make any difference. She had decided to leave them.

TWO DAYS LATER, Sam was outside, sitting on the front porch of his house. School was out, and though usually he went to a special camp for kids with asthma, this year he told his dad he wanted to stay home. "I'll find things to do," he insisted. His dad had asked him if he wanted to invite a friend for dinner, but ever since that day at Isabelle's apartment, Teddy barely spoke to Sam anymore, which was all right with Sam, because he wasn't sure he wanted to be friends with Teddy anymore, anyway. Next year, in fifth grade, maybe they wouldn't even be in the same class. He'd never have to even look at Teddy. He wouldn't have to remember.

Sam didn't want a lot of things anymore. Not the tenth birthday party in July that his father suggested, not a trip somewhere special. He wouldn't come in when Charlie told him it was time for lunch. When the mailman came, Sam ran to him, but all that arrived were bills and his father's magazines. The only time Sam moved was when he heard the phone and then he tensed, expectant. He stood up and tried to listen. "Wrong number," his father said, and Sam's face grew dark and angry again. Why didn't she write or call?

Sam dug into his pocket and pulled out an old grocery list of Isabelle's that he had saved. Blue scribbles on a page she had actually torn out of a book: "Goat cheese. Sun-dried tomatoes. Basil. Arugula. White beans." He put it to his face but it didn't smell like vanilla, like her. His father, walking by, stopped. "What are you doing?" his father asked quietly.

"Trying to figure out what dinner was that day," Sam said.

Sam saw the odd way his father was cocking his head. Sam left her list on his dresser, and two days later, it was gone. Sam tore his room apart. "Did you see her list?" he cried.

"I don't know where you put your things," Charlie told him.

THE LONGER ISABELLE was gone, the more frantic Sam was and the worse his asthma got. He began wheezing more and more. He used his albuterol rescue inhaler so often that Charlie began to panic. It was as if Isabelle had taken all Sam's air along with her.

"You need to learn to listen better to your body," the doctor in the ER had told Sam. "When you get a slight wheeze, don't wait. When you feel out of breath, take action. Take your rescue medicine right away, and if it doesn't work, go and tell your dad." Sam hadn't wanted to talk about it further; he just nodded and acted like he understood. He knew what his body was telling him. It was the only thing he ever heard. Punished. You were bad and now you are being punished.

One day, when Sam was walking home from the park, he passed the Grey Goose Market. It was one of the few places that still had a phone booth inside. Sam turned back and went into the market. He felt as though he were sleepwalking. It was like one of the math problems his teacher gave that seemed completely unsolvable until you thought harder and then there it was, the perfect solution to your problem floating past you like a feather. He knew exactly what to do now. He walked to the pay phone, dug out change from his pants, the Velcro making a *shush*ing sound, and he called information for New York. "Do you have a phone number for Isabelle Stein?" he said, and his own voice surprised him. He told her the address Isabelle had given him.

"Please hold," said a voice, and then there came the number. Sam quickly dug out a pen and wrote it clumsily across his hand, careful not to smear it.

He dialed, his heart thudding sickly in his chest. "Hello?" a voice said. The voice sounded really far away, but he knew it was her. He felt as if everything were zipping ahead of him. "Hello," he said, and he felt his lungs tightening. He heard the wheeze in his voice. Everything he had been thinking and feeling jammed up inside him.

"Sam?" Isabelle said. "Sam, is that really you?" She sounded glad, but she sounded, too, like she might be crying and that made Sam want to cry, too.

"Why did you leave us?" Sam cried. "Please come back!" His shoulders tightened and he felt his lungs folding in. "I don't care that you aren't an angel! I don't care!"

"Where are you? Is Charlie with you?"

"Don't you love us? Don't you love me?" He was struggling to catch his breath. His lungs were growing smaller in his chest, balling up into a fist, even as the air was turning into chunks he couldn't breathe in. "Listen to your body," the doctor had told him. "Take your rescue medicine." He didn't care who saw him, who was around. He had to breathe. He grabbed open his Velcroed pocket and pulled out his inhaler. He sucked on it, one puff and then two, but his lungs didn't clear. Instead, his heart banged harder in his chest. His head swam from the medication. He gripped the phone so tightly his knuckles turned white, and when he turned around he saw that a woman in a flowery dress was staring at him. "Are you all right?" she said, and she sounded angry, as if it were his fault. Sam gasped into the phone and then the phone clattered out of his hand. His legs buckled and he slid to the ground, even as he was stretching himself up, trying to force open his lungs. The woman shouted, "Manager! Manager!" and then more people crowded around him and he wanted to say "Stop, stop," because they were using up his air. He saw the dangling receiver, he imagined Isabelle, in New York City, hearing what was going on, calling out to him, but he didn't have the air left to call back to her. Then, the woman in the flowery dress picked up the receiver and hung it up, and Sam cried out for her to stop, stop, but no sound came out except for the gasp of his breath.

"We need an ambulance!" someone said, and then the woman nearest Sam touched his shoulder. "Don't cry," she said. "Someone's coming for you."

HE WAS IN the hospital two days this time. He lay in the bed while doctors buzzed around him. They had him breathe through a special green nebulizer every few hours. They gave him prednisone and took an X-ray. They put him in one of those stupid blue Johnnys that opened in the back like a dress, and when he was dozing, he woke up to find, panicked, that Isabelle's phone number was no longer there on his hand. If he stared, he could make out the tag end of one or two numbers. "Where did it go?" he cried, "Why did you wash off the number?" He tried to remember the numbers—567, was that it? Or was it 657?

The nurse touched his shoulder, soothing. "I didn't wash anything off. Just on your arm where we put in your IV." She whisked out as a new doctor came in.

"What do you think caused this?" the doctor asked Sam.

"The supermarket was really cold and sometimes cold bothers my lungs," Sam said finally, but he knew it was a lie. He lied to his father, too, when Charlie rushed into the room to see him, when he asked what Sam was doing in the supermarket. "I was thirsty. I went to buy a juice box," Sam said. His father didn't ask about the phone call, and Sam sure wasn't going to tell.

Every time the door opened, he sat up, expectant, but it was never Isabelle. It was always a nurse wanting blood or an orderly with some sort of mystery food he was supposed to eat because they said it would make him stronger.

He knew she'd come. He just knew it. He had done what he had to. He had set things in motion. He felt dizzy with relief, hot and sweaty under the hospital blankets.

The next day, Sam asked the nurse why there was no phone in his room. "What do you need a phone for?" the nurse said. When he saw his father, he threw his arms around him. "Did anyone call for me?" he asked his father, watching him carefully. "Everyone," his father said. "Your friends, your grandparents."

"Anyone else?" Sam said.

His father looked away from Sam for a moment. But when he looked up again, he had a fake kind of grin on his face that made Sam suspicious. "What, friends and family aren't enough?"

"Did you wash my hands?" Sam asked, and his father smoothed the cover.

"No, kiddo, I didn't," his father said.

Sam stared at the door again. Why wasn't she coming? What had he done that she wasn't here?

AS SUMMER PRESSED on, Sam began to realize that Isabelle wasn't going to call. She wasn't going to show up and surprise them. The phone rang and rang, but it was never her and after a while, Sam stopped picking it up.

One day, though, when Charlie was in the shower, Sam impulsively called information for Isabelle's number. Where were you? Where have you been? Why haven't you called me? He felt angry and desperate all at once. But when he said her name, the woman at information told him there was no such number. "Check again. Please check again," Sam said. "I know she's living there."

"I'm sorry, but I'm showing nothing," said the woman.

Stunned, Sam leaned against the wall. He heard the dial tone, the steady *blip blip blip*. Isabelle had disappeared, and it seemed clear that she didn't want to be found.

"Look outside the frame," Isabelle had told him, when she was teaching him to take pictures, but now there was just empty space.

For the rest of July and into August, Sam was on

high doses of prednisone. It made him restless and hungry and so full of energy, he couldn't sleep at night. It made his face and body puffy so he couldn't button his jeans, and even worse, it made him lose some of his hair. He stared at the patchy spot at the side of his head, trying to cover it with the hair he had left. "It's almost over," his father promised. "You just have to get weaned off it." But almost seemed like forever to Sam.

Most of the time, he didn't know what to do with himself. His father worked less so he could be with Sam, and during the day, Sam was allowed to stay home by himself, or go over to a friend's, but it all felt lonely and sad, as though he were slogging through mud.

One day, Sam was staring out at the front window when he noticed a cat sunning itself on the sidewalk, and he couldn't help it; like instinct, he drew his hands up and framed a shot. He made a clicking sound with his tongue, like the snap of a camera, and suddenly, he knew what he wanted to do that day.

He went to the hall closet and rummaged behind the winter coats, separating them until he saw the shelf. There it was. The Canon, glinting out at him, and behind it was the zoom lens Isabelle had given him. He pulled them both out. There was a fresh roll of film in the camera, and he took off the old lens and fit the new one on easily. It was just a camera. Just glass and metal and mirrors and shutters. All the magic of it was gone. If he wanted, he could take the camera and take pictures again. He could become a famous photographer and then Isabelle might see his photos and wish she had been kinder to him. Looking at his photos, she would see all that she was missing.

Sam held up the camera and went out onto the front porch. He must have taken pictures of this road a thousand times, but now, with the new lens, everything looked different, bigger somehow and more important. He pointed the camera at the cat, which was still lazily lolling on the sidewalk. As soon as he took the picture, he felt something spark inside of him. All that afternoon, Sam took shots of the neighborhood. He snapped the park where Isabelle loved to walk, the gourmet grocery where she'd sometimes bought them yogurt-covered raisins to share, and the beach where he had taught her how to skip stones. He used up almost the entire roll of film. When his father came home, Sam was sitting on the front porch, waiting with the camera. "You're taking pictures again!" his dad said, brightening. Just to prove how happy his dad was without Isabelle, Sam lifted up the camera to his eye and took his father's picture. "Got you," Sam said, and for the first time in weeks, his father smiled.

The next day, Sam was in the park with his camera, trying to frame a shot of kids on the swing sets, when he felt a little wheezy. He didn't want to stop to get his inhaler, to miss the shot, so he snapped it, and to his surprise, as soon as he did, his lungs seemed to clear. How could this be? He took another shot of the swings, and then of the trees bordering the park, and the more pictures he took, the easier his breathing became.

He watched kids playing basketball on one of the courts and took a photo of them, too. He had never been able to play with other kids, running like that, jumping so high, not without wheezing so hard he had to go to the school nurse, not without the other kids mocking him, clutching their chests dramatically and making little gasping noises. He kept thinking about what it would be like to move so fast, so freely, and he began to walk really fast toward home, and then he was running, the camera banging against his chest, his arms pumping.

His lungs stayed clear and he ran a little faster, exhilarated by the way the houses seemed to be smearing past him. When he got to his house, he felt buoyant. He had run all this way without wheezing! He was so excited, he laughed out loud.

Sam didn't know whether he should be exhilarated or terrified, but he kept his seemingly asthma-free existence to himself, studying his breathing the way a scientist would. He wasn't a total fool. He took his Pulmicort inhaled steroid every morning, sucking out the powder, waiting for his heart to race, which meant it was working. He popped a theophylline tablet even though he hated how jittery it made him feel. He still carried his rescue inhaler in his pocket just in case.

Every day Sam carried the camera, he seemed to get better. His photographs got better, too, sharper and richer. On his birthday, his dad took him to Aruba, and when he developed those shots, they were so good, he put them in a special album.

One day, Sam stopped taking his Pulmicort. When he had gone a week without once using any medicines, when he was sleeping through the night and waking with clear lungs, he was certain that something had happened to him that couldn't be taken away, sure that it was some kind of miracle. He dumped his pills out so his dad wouldn't know he wasn't taking them. He let his dad go get the refills, too. It was September, right before school started, when he finally told his dad that he had stopped taking his meds.

Charlie stood completely still. "That's not a good idea," he said.

It didn't do any good to argue with his father, to tell him he didn't need the medicine anymore. Sam knew his father was remembering all the times they had had to rush him to the ER, the times he had gotten so sick he had to sleep at the hospital. "That was then, this is now," Sam insisted.

"We can't be sure of that." Charlie rubbed his temple.

"Yes, we can! I'm the proof!" Sam insisted.

Charlie looked thoughtfully at Sam. "Okay, look," he said. "Let's do this. I want you to go see Pete, tell him what you told me. You do that and then I'll relax."

Pete, the same pulmonologist he'd had since he was a baby, frowned when Sam told him he hadn't taken meds in months, hadn't even felt a tightness in his lungs, let alone a wheeze. He made Sam take a lung function test, clipping Sam's nose, making him breathe into a special and complicated machine.

"I don't think I need to come here anymore," Sam said proudly.

"When did you go to medical school?" Pete said. "Let's take a listen."

The stethoscope was warm. Pete tapped Sam's chest and then listened. Sam was exhilarated, the way he was when he took a math exam and knew he had just aced it. "Gone, right?" Sam said.

"Get dressed, come into my office, and we'll all talk," Pete told him.

Sitting in Pete's office, his dad beside him on the leather sofa, Sam smiled expectantly.

Pete tapped his pen. "Your asthma's not gone," Pete told him, folding his arms across his chest. "That's the thing with asthma. Even if you don't see it, it's still there. It's in the structure of your lungs, which, whether you know it or not, are damaged. You think you're breathing just fine, but the machine tells us something different." He pushed a piece of paper across the desk at Sam and tapped his pen on the sloping lines. "See? The blue line is normal, the red line is yours. They don't quite match up."

"I grew out of my asthma," Sam said.

Pete waved his hand. "Well, that can happen, but usually to kids who aren't as sick as you've been. You can't go thinking you don't need your maintenance medicine. Those are the people who *die.*" He raised his hand when he said the word "die," all the while looking at Sam, and Sam felt his father flinch beside him.

"So, what should we do?" his dad asked Pete.

Pete scribbled something on a piece of paper. "I want you, Sam, to still take your meds. And I want you to breathe every morning into the peak-flow meter. Any time it goes below four, you call me. Deal? And don't you dare not follow my instructions."

Sam nodded but he wasn't really listening. Already he was a million miles away. He was already thinking of pants without pockets, of what it would be like to walk outside and not have to carry anything else but a house key.

A week later, Sam was back in school, and though he carried his inhaler in his pocket, he didn't use it. He marked off months on his calendar. All of September, he didn't have to use it. October he was okay. November. By December, even Sam's father noticed how healthy Sam was. "Asthma's gone," Sam said.

His father knocked on wood. "It seems that way. I can't believe how healthy you are."

"Maybe I'm a superhero," he told his father.

"What's your super power?"

Sam thought of the photos, of how Isabelle had faded from them. He thought of how he used to hear the beating of wings, and now there was only deafening silence.

"I survive things," he said.

~ Nineteen ~

ISABELLE WAS IN SoHo, crushed in a too small borrowed party dress, in the middle of a New Year's Eve party she hadn't really wanted to go to. A year and a half in New York City and she still wasn't used to the pop and zing of the city, the way everything seemed to be speeding past her. She was surrounded by people all the time, and still she was lonely. "Everything you could ever want is here," her New York friends told her. They pointed out the all-night diners, the twenty-four-hour gyms, the gurus and the clubs, but finding what Isabelle wanted was far more complicated.

She stood by the food table, between a woman in red high heels and black jeans and a man with a bald head and a silver earring. She took another sip of her wine, looking around her. The air smelled like burned popcorn, cigarette smoke, and too much perfume.

The party was thrown by Michelle's friend Dora, who had provided the illegal sublet. The apartment was better than Isabelle had expected, a huge loft in Hell's Kitchen that Dora had gotten way back in the sixties and was now worth the price of a small country. Dora was the one, too, who had found Isabelle a job as a night-shift proofreader at a law office, who had even helped her with the proofreading test, so that she could make enough money to live on while she went to school.

Isabelle finished her wine. Dora grabbed her arm and tapped the bald guy. "Stan, Isabelle," she said. "Painter. Photographer." Dora nodded at Isabelle encouragingly and then slid back into the crowd. Stan smiled at Isabelle. "Dora told me all about you," he said, and Isabelle sipped her wine.

"What did she tell you?" she asked.

"That you're in photography school. That you have one of the all-time great sublets. And that you have a tortoise." He smiled at her and she relaxed. People were always interested in her tortoise, which always struck her as funny. Still, he didn't say, "Oh, the woman from the accident," or give her a look of pity.

"I just got out of rehab," he said, and Isabelle's wine glass tipped in her hand, sloshing a starry splash of red on her skirt. He turned and began talking to a woman with platinum spiked hair.

In fact, as the party wore on, as she began to talk with more and more people—"Connect!" Dora had urged her—she began to realize that everyone she met seemed to have stories of their own, most of which were just as complicated as hers. The only difference that Isabelle could perceive between herself and these other people was that they wanted to tell her their stories and she could barely bring herself to think about her own.

No one would have batted an eye if Isabelle had

told them she had accidentally killed a woman, that fool that she was, she had even fallen in love with the survivors, a husband and son she had foolishly dared to consider her own. In fact, she suspected that telling her story might have actually made her more interesting to this crowd. The party was filled with couples, and watching a man cup a woman's face for a kiss made Isabelle realize how lonely she was, how she still missed Charlie.

For weeks after she'd left the Cape, she'd had to stop herself from picking up the phone and calling him. She had torn up a letter and returned a gift she had bought for Sam, because what was the point? When was enough enough? She had done damage to them. She had thought she could redeem herself but ended up making things worse for everyone.

She tried to heal. She went to three therapists in three months, but as soon as she walked into their offices, she wanted to leave again. One doctor peppered her with questions, another told her to get over it in a kind of tough-love therapy, and none of it mattered. She left each office feeling as terrible as she had when she arrived. If anything, talking about what had happened made her feel worse.

I killed a woman. It was an accident. I love the victims. It was an accident.

After a while, she stopped going altogether.

Instead, she buried herself in work. Her friends fixed her up, but they didn't really have to. Men stopped her in the supermarket and on the street, teasing and playful, wanting her number, and most times she gave it. Although all the men were perfectly nice, nothing seemed to take. They liked her, she thought, for her mystery, for the part of her she kept hidden. They thought there was something dramatic about her and that they'd be the ones who could unlock her. And if they could, she thought, maybe all they'd find would be an empty room. It was as if love was this season that had already passed her by.

She moved toward the door, glancing at her watch. It was only 11:30 and she didn't know if she wanted to wait around for the New Year, for the kisses from strangers. She glanced at a woman by the window, who had brought her child with her, a sunny little boy with a shock of red hair, and she felt pierced by sadness. The two of them were dancing, holding hands and laughing so hard, the woman had her head thrown back. Happy as clams, Nora would say.

Isabelle knew this phenomenon. Be tortured by something and the world was sure to serve it up to you. Since she had moved to New York, she saw mothers and sons everywhere on the street. She could be in an empty movie theater and a parent with a child was sure to sit in the row right next to her. In the Korean greengrocers, little boys would whisk ahead of her in line to grab for candy, and sometimes, she'd just abandon her groceries and walk out. She missed Sam so much, every little bit hurt her.

She must have been staring, because the woman and the child at the party suddenly stopped dancing and looked at her. The woman smiled and waved, and then her little boy waved, too. Isabelle waved back, and then drained the last of her wine, set her glass down, and headed for the door. Good-bye. Good-bye.

Outside, the air was thick and heavy, the sky carpeted with clouds. Isabelle walked west on Prince Street, buzzed from the wine. She stumbled a bit, righting herself by bracing her hand on the building wall. Low tolerance. "The perfect wife for the owner of a bar," Luke used to joke, and sometimes he'd brag about it to his customers, even though it always made Isabelle vaguely uncomfortable.

People crowded the streets, some of them in party hats, a few blowing paper horns. All around her the city hummed, giving off a vibration she swore was a message, if only you could learn to read it. Well, she hadn't been here very long. She'd figure it out.

What she did love about New York was her classes. Imagine, going to school to learn the thing she loved! The light here was different, somehow sharper and more complex. She shot black and white because it seemed more real to her, all those shades of gray, like moving through a fog.

She had wanted to keep her world small, but it kept expanding on her. She was busier than she thought she'd be, and she made a point of taking her camera everywhere. She looked at the sky, something Dora told her never to do because it would mark you as a tourist and present you like a blinking green light to all the hucksters prowling about. Isabelle didn't care. Nothing could have made her stop looking. Even with all the clouds and the dimming sky, it was still a beauty of a night. Everywhere you looked there were these huge, busy buildings and throngs of people, and they all looked interesting to her. She wanted to photograph nearly every face she saw.

She turned up the collar of her jacket against the nip in the evening air. Thinking about the boy at the party, she dug her hands deeper into her pockets.

Isabelle had never stopped aching for Sam. She remembered the feel of him on her lap, the silk of his hair, the lilt of his voice. She sent Sam photographs of the city, and books, and though they never came back, she never heard back, either. She had called a few times and Charlie told her that Sam couldn't come to the phone, that he was in and out of the hospital with serious asthma, and even though Charlie never said so, she felt that he blamed her somehow. When she missed

Sam most, she went to Central Park Lake and skipped stones, just the way he had taught her. A million times she thought about visiting, just showing up, but her course workload was so heavy and her bankbook so light, she couldn't get away. And more than that, Charlie never asked her to come.

She knew that Sam came to visit his grandparents twice a year, at Thanksgiving and spring break, and she was always wondering if she'd run into him. "My ex lives a block away and in five years, I've never seen him," Dora had told her, meaning to be consoling. Isabelle had never met Charlie's parents. She had certainly seen enough photographs to be able to pick them out, and though she knew it was nuts, she kept looking for them in the city, running over in her mind what she might say if she did. Yes, I'm doing fine. How are you? How is Charlie? How is Sam? Sometimes, she imagined they would be sympathetic to her, that Charlie's mother would pat her hand. Other times, she thought they'd be dismissive, that they'd still somehow consider her a murderess, though Charlie had told her they had been cool to April, too, that perhaps they'd be frosty to any woman he chose. She knew they lived on the Upper East Side, and one day, when she felt especially lonely, she had taken the uptown train to their block, walking past their apartment building, a huge limestone structure with gargoyles carved in the side, a doorman in a uniform stationed in the front. She took her time walking by, she pretended to be admiring the building, which was certainly beautiful. She wondered if they'd come out and if they'd know who she was, or if she'd recognize them. Of course, all that happened was that she hovered in front of the building so long that the doorman asked, "Are you lost, ma'am?"

"Yes," she said. "I am." And then she walked away and never went back.

Isabelle leaned against a building now and shut her eyes for a moment. She shouldn't have had the wine. Maybe she shouldn't have gone to the party. She was drunk and lonely and felt as if everything she wanted were a thousand miles away. A knot of tears formed in her stomach, and she wrenched herself away from the building.

The day she had left the Cape, sitting beside Michelle in the car, she had felt numb with grief. Her first few weeks in New York had been chaotic. There were a million things to do. She had to set up her apartment, get Nelson settled, and get a phone. She had to register at the school, find a darkroom, and change her address, sending the cards to everyone, even her mother, who sent her a card with a big cross on it and the inscription Faith Will Find the Way. She had cried all the time. Once, on the street right in front of Macy's, on a bright, sunny day, she had been unable to stop crying. No one even turned to acknowledge her. People calmly walked by as if she were invisible, and to her surprise, that made her feel better. She began to feel that New York was just what she needed.

When the phone didn't ring with a call from Charlie or Sam, when no letters came for her, she told herself that maybe it was for the best. Sometimes she dreamed different versions of her life: Charlie would call and tell her that he was free of his demons, that all he wanted was for her to come home and marry him; Charlie and Sam would show up on her doorstep, saying, "We can't live without you." Or even just Charlie, finding her to say, "We have to talk our way through this. We have to figure this out. We can do this, I know we can."

Now a headache was forming, as small and hard as a Brazil nut. Alcohol was supposed to wear off, but instead, Isabelle seemed to be feeling drunker. She tried to walk a straight line and wobbled. She didn't want to go back to her empty apartment or call a friend who would look at her with rich sympathy, and in any case, most of the friends she had now were still at parties. She felt in her purse for her cell phone. Her heart was racing and she felt sick, but she dialed.

She let it ring, four times, five, hypnotized, before she hung up. What would she say if Charlie or Sam answered? How could it possibly make anything better?

Isabelle put the phone back into her purse.

• • •

SHE WALKED OVER to Houston and then headed up Hudson Street. It began to snow. Instantly, she was covered with flakes. The thin, fancy red flats she had bought for the party skidded on the damp sidewalk. A woman ran past Isabelle, her hair dappled with white, and she glared at Isabelle as if she blamed her for both the terrible weather and her tragic hair.

Isabelle felt woozy and hungry and her headache was worse. In two more months, she'd be thirty-nine.

A cab zipped by, the top light on, but it was packed with people. She crossed Fourteenth Street, past Twenty-sixth Street. She was still ten blocks from her apartment, an easy walk in nice weather, an even better run, but she needed to take a break. Coffee, maybe. Or hot chocolate cooled with cream. She ducked into the first café she saw. It was a small space, with ten cozy, pale wood tables and everything lit with candles, and there wasn't a single person in there. Empty restaurants weren't a good sign in New York, but she was cold and hungry, and she sat down.

As soon as she scraped her chair out, a man popped out from the back, a white apron about his waist. "The electricity's out," he apologized. "Actually, everything's out. I can't even scramble you an egg, and I just sent the waitstaff home."

She looked up at him. He was all shades of black and white. Pale skin. Black T-shirt, sneakers, and jeans. He had a ruckus of black hair and a weathered-looking face. "Can I just sit here for a bit?" she said. "It's beginning to snow harder out there."

"Absolutely," he said. "Be my guest." He studied her for a moment and then abruptly disappeared into the back room.

She began to relax, watching the glow of the candles. She felt weightless, as if the merest rush of air would float her away. The snow fluttered and stuck against the window, so all she could see was what was here, inside. She stretched her legs and then he appeared again and set a plate in front of her. Three kinds of hard cheese, some crusty bread, and red grapes. She looked up at him. "Oh, I didn't order," she said.

He waved his hand. "It's a cold feast, but it's on the house," he said. He poured her a cup of coffee. "This is what you need," he said kindly. "It's actually still hot."

She stared at the food.

"If you don't eat it, it'll just spoil, so you're actually doing me a favor," he said.

She nodded. "You're so kind," she said, and he looked at her, surprised.

She didn't realize how hungry she was until she picked up her fork. Her stomach roiled and her mouth began to water. The food was delicious, the cheese sharp and dotted with bits of cranberry and orange. He looked at her happily as she ate. He went to the boombox behind the bar and put on some music, an Italian aria. "Thank goodness for batteries," he said. "Now we have atmosphere," he said.

"You don't have to do all this for me," she said.

"Why not? I do this for all my customers."

"It's getting nastier out there," she said. "We both should go home."

He shrugged and she noticed that his eyes were this eerie electric blue and for a moment, she wondered how old he was. Forty-five, maybe. Fifty tops.

"I'll let you in on a little secret," he said. "This isn't really my restaurant. I'm babysitting it for a friend tonight, a silent partner for my own restaurant." He dug into the pocket of his apron and handed her a bright green card. Frank's, it said. "All my life all I wanted to do was cook," he said. "I was that weird little kid who made his own breakfast and took fancy lunches to school that everyone else made fun of." He looked at her with interest and she suddenly was aware of her hair, damp from the snow, and she flushed. "What do you do?" he asked. "I know you're not supposed to ask a question like that, but you look like you do something interesting."

When Isabelle told him she was a photographer, that she was in school, he sat up straighter. "Well, what do you know?" he said. "Would you photograph me in front of my restaurant? I'm doing this new package for investors and I need a picture of myself. I hate being photographed. I'd pay you, of course. And I'd make you a real dinner."

"Don't you want to see my work first?" she asked, and he waved his hand. "You haven't seen my work yet, either, so we both can be surprised," he said. "And anyway, I trust you."

"You don't know me."

"I can read people. I'm a good judge of character."

"This is for real?"

"Why would I make it up?"

"Deal," she said, and when he took her hand to seal the deal, she felt a jolt of heat.

All that week, Isabelle kept thinking about Frank. How easy his kindness had been, how he hadn't thought twice about taking her in and bringing her food, how he hadn't once asked what had brought her into the café alone on New Year's Eve.

THE DAY ISABELLE photographed Frank was blisteringly cold. She tried on two pairs of jeans before leaving the apartment. She brushed her hair until it gleamed.

Frank's restaurant was on West Eighteenth Street. It was all windows and greenery, and inside were polished wood tables and flowers. Frank wore chef's whites, which made him look both older and funnier, and as soon as he saw her, he smiled. "It's a little cold out," he said. He was alert and snapping with energy, and it made her feel more lively, too.

"Doesn't matter," she said. "We'll take some inside shots first and then a few outside. I promise I'll work quickly." As soon as she started photographing him, she forgot how nervous she had been. She searched out the best, most natural light, over by a window, and had him lean against it. She forbade him to pose with his arms folded, the way most chefs did. "Talk to me," she ordered, moving back, crouching behind her camera, and when he started telling her about his childhood, his six brothers and sisters in a tiny town in Michigan and how his sister had liked to dress up the family guinea pig in doll clothes, she began snapping.

She went through ten rolls of film. She had him stand in front of the window and in the kitchen, sitting on one of the tables and standing by the counter. The whole time, he didn't complain once. He didn't ask her "Are you done yet?" or suggest that his right side was his best, and anything she asked him to do, he did. "Done," she said finally, standing and stretching.

"Beautiful," he said, and she thought he meant beautiful that she was finished, but he was looking at her when he said it, and for a moment, before she remembered just who she really was and how she could never ever be that lucky, not after what she had done, she felt the world shimmering all around her.

~ TWENTY ~

IT WAS SPRING again and Charlie was sifting through bills. The gas company wanted money. The mortgage was due. There was an invitation to a bowling birthday party for Sam, which made him happy because he worried that Sam at ten was still too solitary, that he didn't have enough playdates, didn't even seem to want them, no matter how Charlie coaxed. There was junk mail from a mattress factory and a Cheese-of-the-Month Club invitation, and then, stuck in the middle, was a single gray envelope. Curious, he pulled it out. For one stupid moment, he thought it might be from Isabelle, but he brushed it aside. They hadn't heard from her in months. No. That life was gone.

He looked at the envelope again. It was hand addressed to April. It was postmarked Pittsburgh, which gave Charlie a jolt. He flipped it over.

No name, though. No return address.

He tore it open, letting the letter fall out into his hands. It was a single sheet of white letterhead paper, carefully folded into thirds. Bill Thrommer, it said on top. There was the same sloppy handwriting that had been on the envelope, and the paper seemed worn, as if someone had folded and unfolded it over and over, deliberating whether to send it or not.

April,
I've written this letter a dozen times to you, and ripped it up a dozen more. I'm taking a chance sending it. Breaking our rules, but what does it matter now?

Maybe you've forgiven me.
Or maybe I'm the one forgiving you.
I loved you. I really did. And I just wanted you to know that.

Your Bill

Charlie's hands shook. He scanned it again. Thrommer. Bill Thrommer. *Your Bill.*

He reached for the phone and called Hank Williams, his detective. "You don't say?" said Hank, when Charlie told him about the letter.

"Can you follow up on this for me?"

"I suppose I could." Hank's cautious tone irritated Charlie. Why couldn't Hank jump on this, and then Charlie thought, why did he really need Hank to do it at all? He had a name. He could call information and get a phone number. Why couldn't he do this himself?

"You know what, never mind," Charlie said.

"Good for you. You're doing the right thing. Getting on with your life," Hank said, and as soon as Hank hung up, Charlie reached for the phone and called information, and a minute after he said

Bill Thrommer's name, he had a phone number and an address.

He was afraid this Bill might not talk to him on the phone if he called. Besides, Charlie wanted to see him. He'd ask his parents to come and watch Sam, and then he'd go to Pittsburgh.

CHARLIE'S PARENTS WERE thrilled to have Sam to themselves. "It's just for two days," Charlie told them. "Just business." He lied so easily. He said he had to go to a building conference. He'd call every night and every morning, and he'd be back before anyone knew it. Charlie didn't even know how long it would take. It could be two minutes, long enough for Bill to slam the door in his face and refuse to come out. Or it could be two days, where Bill might talk and talk and show him a whole life with April that Charlie didn't know could possibly exist. The horrible thing was that Charlie didn't know which of the possibilities would make him feel worse.

"Why can't I go with you?" Sam said.

"You'd be bored silly. All that talk about drywall. And think what fun you'll have with Grandma and Gramps. All those cookies. Movies."

Sam's face lightened. Ever since Charlie had found out about Bill, he had felt this burning in his stomach, as if he had swallowed lighted matches. Where did Bill fit in? Judging from the letter, the relationship was over.

Would it do any good to know?

He couldn't bear to think of another man spending time with his son, and he couldn't bring himself to ask Sam if he'd ever met Bill. But did he know him? Did Bill act like a father to him? A friend? Did he bribe him with presents? Tell him knock-knock jokes?

CHARLIE WAS ON a plane halfway to Pittsburgh when he began to worry that what had seemed like such a good idea now seemed like a fool's mission. What did he expect? He didn't even know if Bill was home. He could be on vacation or out of the country. He could have a family. "What will it take to put it to rest?" Hank Williams had once asked Charlie. Isabelle had asked him the same thing. The truth was, Charlie didn't know.

By the time he arrived, it was almost lunch time. Charlie rented a car, got some maps, and drove out into a day golden with light. He didn't know what he had expected, but he had thought the skies might be murky with soot, that the city would be ugly and cramped. Instead, he was surprised at how pretty Pittsburgh was, how green and hilly. The sky was vast, like a chip of the ocean, and when he reached Oakland, it was lively with people.

There, halfway down a green, leafy street, was Bill's house, a beautiful little Colonial with blue shutters and a wraparound porch. Tasteful. You could look at this house and just know what it was like inside. Lots of wood floors, he bet. A staircase. An Oriental rug or two. There weren't any kids' bikes or toys in the yard.

He heard music. An itchy slide of jazz. A trombone. His father used to tell him, when Charlie said he wasn't a jazz fan, that the most intelligent people in the world loved jazz, that it took smarts to appreciate it. Charlie parked the car. If a woman answered, a wife or a girlfriend, he'd ask to see Bill alone. He wouldn't say why he was there until they were out of her range. He didn't want to hurt anyone.

He rang the bell, and before he could turn and leave, before he could decide this was a mistake, he heard footsteps, and then the door opened and there was a man with a wooden cooking spoon in his hand.

Charlie's mouth opened. Was this him? This guy didn't look like someone April would love or even notice if he walked past her on the street. He had a face as ordinary and unhandsome as a baked potato. He was just a guy in a faded black T-shirt and blue jeans and sneakers, with thinning dark hair and a squint. He was older than Charlie by at least ten years. He could have been anybody, but oh God, he wasn't. And then Bill lifted his other hand to scratch his face and that was when Charlie saw his glinting wedding band, as thin as a wire around his finger. "Bill?" he said, and the man nodded.

"And you are . . . ?" Bill said. The wood spoon was red at the tip. Tomato sauce, Charlie thought. He suddenly noticed the air was spicy with basil.

"I'm Charlie Nash," Charlie said, and the man frowned.

"Excuse me, who?"

"Charlie Nash." He looked beyond Bill. There was a blue shag rug in the living room, a clutter of magazines spread across it. "April Nash's husband."

Bill's face changed. "Hold on," he said, and then he stepped back inside, and for a moment, Charlie thought he was going to shut the door on him and lock it. That he'd refuse to see Charlie or tell him anything. The music stopped. And then Bill was back and the spoon was gone. "Please," he said. "Come in."

Bill took him into the kitchen, a bright yellow room with wood floors. "Coffee?" he asked, holding up a pot. Charlie nodded, though he didn't think he could do more than sip. His appetite had died a long time ago. Plus, he didn't like how friendly Bill was. He didn't want to like this man.

Bill glanced at his watch. "I don't have to be at work until three." Bill gestured to two seats at the Formica table. Bill's wedding band glinted in the sun. "Your wife," Charlie said, taking a seat. "Where is she?"

Charlie put his hands around the cup, warming them. He smelled cinnamon in the coffee, and he thought of April, sifting cinnamon over her morning toast.

"Surgical nurse," Bill said finally. "McGee Hospital for Women. Met her in an emergency room when I had this kidney infection. Married her a year later." He took a long, slow sip of coffee. "That was twenty years ago."

Bill squeezed his eyes shut, so that a fan of wrinkles bloomed in the corners. "Let's be honest," he said. "How is April?"

Charlie looked at Bill closely. He saw the tiny scar across Bill's cheek and wondered if April had kissed it. He saw the way Bill kept tapping one finger on the table, as if he were waiting for something. Charlie had a thousand things he wanted to ask him, how had they met, what had Bill said that made April step out of her life and into his, why had April been drawn to him, and what had even happened? Were they good friends? Were they lovers? April had once told Charlie that she could forgive anything but the one unpardonable sin: infidelity. "You can't forget that one," she said.

"April's dead," Charlie said.

Bill's finger stopped tapping.

"She died in a car crash," Charlie said.

He heard Bill swallow. "When . . ."

"It'll be two years September second," Charlie said.

"What are you saying?" Bill put one hand on his forehead.

"There was a suitcase in the car," Charlie said, leaning forward. "For the longest time I didn't know a single fucking thing about you, and now I do and I'm not sure I'm better off for knowing any of it."

And then, to Charlie's horror, Bill began to weep.

Charlie didn't know what to do. Bill didn't bother sluicing the tears from his eyes. He didn't cover his face. Instead, he sat crying, a sight so surprising, Charlie averted his eyes. Bill stopped as abruptly as he had begun. He dug out a handkerchief from his pocket and blew his nose. "How?" he asked.

The whole time Charlie was telling him, Bill didn't move. "She was stopped in the middle of the road, her car turned around. It was a really foggy day and another car was coming. Sam got out of the car last minute, and I think that's what saved him."

Bill lay both his hands flat on the table. "Sam?" he said.

The sip of coffee Charlie had taken churned in his stomach. "Sam. My—our son, Sam."

Bill scraped his chair away from the table and stared at Charlie. "She took Sam?" he said. "He was in the car that day?"

Charlie felt sickened. *That day.* You didn't say

that day unless you knew about what was going on then, unless you were a part of it. "Where were you supposed to meet?" Charlie said thickly.

Bill didn't speak, but the way he looked down at his shoes made Charlie know what the truth was, and it didn't matter whether he wanted to hear it or know it, because there it was. And then, Charlie dug out his wallet and took out the plastic binder, and, hands shaking, pulled out a photo. There were the three of them, Charlie, April, and Sam, standing by a big tree in the park, the three of them laughing. It hurt him to look at it now, and he suddenly didn't want Bill touching it, so he held the photo up so Bill could see, and when Bill reached for it, Charlie jerked it away.

"I can't believe she brought Sam," Bill said.

"You knew my son?"

Bill shook his head. "No. No, I didn't know him. We never even talked about kids. I don't have them—I never wanted them. It was never a question with us and that was such a relief not to ever have that conversation, not to even think about it. All the places we went—they weren't for kids. Casinos. Nightclubs."

"You went to casinos?" Charlie asked flatly.

"There were never any kids around. And if there were, she never even looked at them."

"Did you leave when you saw Sam in the car? Is that what happened? Did that make you fucking change your mind? That she brought Sam with her?"

"Charlie, you don't understand. I didn't see Sam—"

"I bet you don't think you do, but you fucking owe me." Charlie felt his voice rising. "She was *married* to me. She had a *son*. We were a *family.* Or didn't that mean anything to you?"

Bill took a long swig of coffee. "I told you, we never talked about Sam."

"What did you talk about, then? Quantum physics? Literature? Did you talk about her husband? Did you talk about me?" Charlie pushed his coffee out of the way so fiercely, some of it sloshed onto the table. He leaned toward Bill. "So you tell me. You tell me everything. How you fucked up my life. How you fucked up hers. How there's a ten-year-old boy who misses his mom because of goddamned you. Because I really want to know. I came all the way out here and now you fucking tell me what you know."

Bill spread one hand across his face. When he removed it, he looked like a different person to Charlie, like a person to whom something terrible had happened.

"It was an accident," Bill said.

BILL DIDN'T KNOW how his life took a turn. He was on business on Boylston Street in Boston, paging his wife Ellen at the hospital because he missed her. "I'm kind of busy right now," she said, her voice offhanded. She didn't say she'd call him back or that she missed him, too. When he hung up, something was buzzing in his head.

He passed an art gallery. It was bright and inviting, and splashed full of sunlight. The paintings were big and colorful, but that wasn't what stopped him. He looked up and there was this woman like an apparition, floating by him in a long filmy dress, looking at the paintings. Suddenly he began to want things he hadn't wanted in a very long time.

He went inside and it smelled like cinnamon and honey and vanilla. He saw the woman more clearly and she was even more beautiful. Then she looked up at him, like an invitation, and it seemed like the most natural thing in the world to go up to her. "Great paintings, aren't they?" he said. "Should we buy everything up?"

She laughed. He had a wedding band, but she did, too. My wife doesn't understand me, he thought, and then he laughed at himself, at the cliché.

"April," she said.

"Bill."

They walked around the small gallery. He stopped in front of a painting that was all skyscrapers tangled together, almost as if they were holding hands. He thrust his hands in his pockets. "I like this," he said.

"Me, too." She kept her eyes on the painting.

She told him that she lived on the Cape, that she'd come to Boston just to have a day to herself, popping on a train because it was faster than driving.

"Isn't that kind of crazy?" he said, "Coming all this way just for a day?" and she gave him this sad, broken little half smile, and that was when he began to fall in love. "Do you want to tell me what's wrong?" he said quietly.

"You have no idea how much it helps just that you asked," she said. "But I just want to feel good today. I don't want to think about anything else but that." She looked outside. "Want to walk with me?"

They walked outside, stopping to look at the windows of the shops. It was growing cooler, darker, and they both had to be going. She thrust out her hand for him to shake and he felt the heat rise up from her skin. "It was nice to meet you, Bill," she said, and that sad little smile was gone. Her voice had music in it. "You made my day," she said.

"Maybe we'll meet again," he said. "April."

When he came home, everything seemed different. He felt unmoored. He wandered into a Thrift-T-Mart for Lifesavers, and when the girl rang him up—bored, with scraggly dishwater hair—he looked past her at the sky. "Boy, doesn't a day like today make you wish you were on the

Cape?" he blurted, and she yawned. "The Cape's for tourists," she said. "Jamaica, mon. That's where I want to be."

He walked past a man on a bench reading a book about modern art. "I come here the third Wednesday of every month," April had said. The man noticed his stare and looked up. "You an art lover?" he said.

"A friend of mine is," Bill said, and he thrilled at the word, *friend,* because it was and wasn't the truth. "She goes to this one art gallery in Boston every month."

"Lucky her," the man said, and returned to his book.

He felt discombobulated. He went in to work and told his boss how well the Boston trip had gone. "I think it's smart to have me there," he said.

"I'm glad you're taking the reins," his boss said. "Don't think I haven't noticed."

At dinner, Ellen talked about vacation. She wanted to go to Paris or London.

"What about the Cape?" Bill said. "We could go for the whole month." He glanced at her over his baked potato, his heart banging in his chest.

She chewed thoughtfully. "We could do that," she said. "It might be nice."

"It would be great," he said.

It didn't take long for Bill and April to have a routine. They didn't set a time, but they began to meet at the gallery, and then headed over to a café nearby, staying longer and longer until the waitresses began to know them, to call them by name, to place their usual order in front of them before they'd even asked for it. And they began to know each other. She told him she was a volunteer at the community beach clean-up, that she worked at the Blue Cupcake bakery, which had won "Boston's Best" three years in a row, and that sometimes she made special cupcakes for the kids with allergies, who always clamored for thirds. "Asthmatics," she said.

He waved his hand and looked around the café. "I'm glad there are no kids here. It'd be too noisy. I couldn't concentrate just on you."

"Don't you like kids?" she said, surprised.

"Sure I do," he said. "In other people's homes. Inside schools. At kids' matinees."

She rolled her cup in her hands. "People can change," she said quietly. "Can't they?"

He thought of Ellen, how crazy he had been about her. "Yes," he said. "They can."

We're just friends, he told himself, but he never mentioned April's name at home when Ellen asked him about his trip. Still, every time he came to Boston, he wore his best shirts. He began getting his hair cut at the most expensive place in Pittsburgh, and when the stylist asked if he wanted a manicure, he didn't laugh the way he would have before. He held out his hands. "Make them look great," he said.

"You're looking awfully spiffy," Ellen said.

"I'm trying to get a promotion," he said. "You know, you look more like the boss, he's more apt to promote you."

"Well, I like it," she said, resting her head on his shoulder. "It's very sexy."

He leaned away from her, feeling woozy, as if he were in the wrong place. At night, for the first time in a long while, Ellen reached for him. He heard a rustling in the bed. He saw April's face, April's body. He felt April whispering to him, and Ellen held him tighter.

He cut his time at the Boston office shorter and shorter, which seemed to make the staff there as happy as it made him, because, really, all he did there was hover over everybody and make them uncomfortable.

"There's a lot to take care of," Bill told his boss. "It's better if I go up more often."

"Good man," said his boss. "That's what I like to hear. Someone right on the ball."

April began to come up twice a month, and then, so did Bill. He breezed into the Boston office and talked to the key people. He looked at some mock-up ads, talked to some clients, and then he was out of there. "Call me on the cell if you need me," he said, and then the whole day with April spread out before him and nothing else mattered. The few times the phone rang, he felt so happy that he said yes to whatever anyone from the office asked him.

New mock-ups? Yes. A change in the tagline? Absolutely.

Once, he came to the café and she was sitting there with her head in her hands. "Hello?" he called, and she looked up at him and started to cry. He didn't ask her what was going on. Instead, he poured her tea, pulled his chair close to hers, and sat beside her. "Tea," he urged. He took her hand and held it. He kissed her fingers. And then, when she rested her head on his shoulder, he let her cry as long as she needed to.

"I'm fine now," she told him, smiling weakly, and he didn't press. She'd tell him if she wanted to. He knew people had secrets and he respected that. Plus who was he to judge? "I just want you to know that whatever it is, I understand," he murmured, and she gave him a look of pure gratitude.

"I think you might actually mean that," she said quietly.

He and April got in the rental car and they drove for hours. He wasn't sure where he was going, and after a while, he knew they were lost. He kept driving farther out, feeling more and more addled, as if clouds were drifting through his head, but instead of being annoyed, he felt wildly happy.

"Are we lost?" April said.

He pulled over to the side of the road and leaned across her to open the glove compartment, which was stuffed with maps. He dug a few out, and smoothed them across his lap. "Ah, here we go."

He couldn't make anything of the road lines and symbols. "Help," he ordered and she slid over on the seat toward him, so close he could feel the heat from her body, the steady moving silk of her hair sliding against his cheek. "There we are," she said, touching the map, "We're not lost at all." Her face was so close to his that all he had to do was turn and kiss it.

It was the simplest thing in the world to check into a hotel. It changed everything and both of them knew it. He checked them in as Terry and Celia Spring and then grinned at her. "And to think that kiss was an accident!" he said.

"There are no accidents," April informed him.

He was used to Ellen coming to bed in her T-shirt and panties, exhausted, reaching for him in the middle of the night. Ellen was gone by morning, already at the hospital. April slowly undid the buttons of her shirt and then she undid his. She lay beside him on the bed so they could look at each other, and when he touched her, he felt small shocks through his fingers. When he reached for the lights, April stayed his hand. "No, I want to see everything now," she said. April whispered to him the whole time they were making love and he began whispering to her. Yes, I love that. Oh, there, that's nice. Yes, do that. More, please. More.

I love that.

I love you.

They were never really finished with each other, not when they woke, not when they got up from the bed, slow and reluctant, dazed. They dressed and splashed cold water on their faces. They made their way to the car, and although Bill played the loudest music he could find on the radio, April leaned back against the headrest and closed her eyes. "Don't wake me. I like this dream."

"It's not a dream."

There were rules, of course. They never called each other or e-mailed, though he kept imagining calling her a thousand times a day just to hear her voice.

One day, he came into work and his boss, Buddy, called him in.

Buddy tapped one finger on the desk, as if he were pointing something out. "I'm puzzled, here, Bill," he said quietly. "Maybe you can help me out a little."

"Sure," Bill said. "I'm your man."

"Are you? Are you my man?"

"Excuse me?"

"You haven't been at the Boston office in weeks."

"Sure I have." Bill shifted position.

Buddy shook his head. "If you had, you'd know about the brushfire I had to put out last week. About the disaster that started this week. You'd also be aware of the client who called me up screaming this morning and gave me an earful before he fired us." Buddy stood up. "The Dining Delights account is gone, Bill."

"What brushfire?" Bill's skin was hot.

"That's just what I'm talking about. You don't even know, do you?" Buddy stood up. "This just isn't going to work. I have to have people I can depend upon."

Buddy didn't want to listen to any of Bill's explanations. He held up his hand. "Enough," he said. They gave him three months severance and let him collect his things in a little brown box under security supervision, which was humiliating. He took everything, even the paperclips on his desk. He didn't say good-bye to anyone, not because he didn't have friends at his job, but because he didn't want to see the sympathy in their faces.

He let the guard walk him out, all the while staring straight ahead.

As soon as he was home, he dumped the box in the trash. Then he called Ellen, but quickly hung up because how could he explain this to her? She'd want to know why they had fired him. She'd want to call their lawyer and get the facts and then what would he do? He wished for April's number. How could he make a living? Maybe he could work out of his house. Maybe he could call in some favors.

Maybe he could set up business in Boston.

It was easy to keep being fired a secret from Ellen, because she never asked. While she was at work, he looked for work, or he took himself to the movies, sitting for hours watching whatever was playing. And then, that Wednesday, just as he always did, he packed his bag and went to Boston. "Have a productive time," Ellen said.

"WHY, THAT'S JUST INSANE," April told him when he told her he had been fired, and then she touched his hand.

"Why don't we run away?" he said, surprising himself as soon as he said it.

Her face turned quiet and serious, and something felt like it was uncurling in his heart. "We could start new lives," he said quietly. "We could leave it all behind us. Why shouldn't we grab at happiness if we can?"

"What about your wife? What about my— husband?" Her voice was so soft he had to lean forward to hear her.

"Why shouldn't we think that people might be happier without us? Ellen never says 'I love you' to me anymore. Does your husband?" He paused. "It isn't often people get a second chance," he finally said. "Don't we deserve to be happy? And admit it, everyone will be happier without us. Better off."

She looked past him. "My husband never says I

414

love you," she told him. "When I ask, he says 'You know how I feel.'"

He reached for her. "I love you," he told her. "I love you, I love you."

"Tell me again," she said, and she curled alongside him and for the first time that day, he felt a point of light, far off in the distance, like a star guiding him home.

They were in love. It was a fact of his life. He thought about it when he woke up and kissed his wife, and saw her like a postcard that had been sent him from another life. He thought about it when he walked into Oakland and wandered through the Carnegie Museum and he realized he wouldn't be back here. Good-bye, good-bye, good-bye.

They made plans. They couldn't wait. They'd meet in New York and then fly to San Francisco together. They'd figure out what to do. They'd buy their tickets at the gate so that by the time they were discovered missing, well, they'd already be long gone. He hadn't touched most of the accounts he and Ellen had, but he had taken half of the savings, enough to live on for a year if they were careful. He tried to imagine Ellen without him. She'd be the same she always was, working early and leaving late. Who knew, maybe she'd meet a doctor and fall in love again herself. He'd be happy in a one-room studio with April, but April kept insisting that they needed an extra room for guests. "Who needs guests when we have each other?" he said.

"We have to have a guest room," she said, and she looked so suddenly panicked that he took her hands in his. "You want a guest room? You got a guest room," he said.

"Good," she said, and the tight way she was holding her shoulders loosened.

And then, two weeks before he was due to meet April, he got a call from an advertising agency in Boston for a job. A man named Marc Ryser told him they were looking for a vice president of Thoroughbred, a boutique agency with some high-end clients. It was in Boston, but they had branches all over the place, in Pittsburgh and California, which gave him a surge of hope. He'd be crazy not to interview, but the only day he could get it was for the day he was to meet April. Well, it was early in the morning. He'd be done before ten, and then who knew? Maybe they could leave with a job waiting for him, the perfect segue to a new life.

The fog was beginning when he got to Boston. He had kissed Ellen in the morning, leaving the house after she did so she wouldn't see the suitcase he was taking, the letter he was leaving for her, the cab that would take him to the airport. Thoroughbred was in the Prudential Building, on the twentieth floor. Bill looked around at the photos. The usual framed diplomas, white parchment against black wood. There, on the desk, a photo of Marc Ryser and his wife, a toothy brunette in a red dress, and a few kids and then in the back, a big colored photo of a bunch of kids in soccer uniforms, "The Blue Cupcake" in script across the jerseys. Bill leaned forward, his heart jumping. Synergy. He had read about the universe making connections for you, showing you that not only were there coincidences, but they had real meanings and importance. "That's quite a photo," Bill said.

"Soccer," said Marc. "You got a kid who plays?"

Bill shook his head. "No kids." He had heard that companies wanted you to have kids, wanted you to be a family man. He hoped it wasn't the case here.

"Really? Kids are the future."

Bill couldn't take his eyes off the photo and when he looked up, he saw Marc eyeing him curiously. "Oh, I know someone who used to work at the Cupcake," Bill said.

"Really?" Marc sat down at his desk. "Who?"

Bill heard the tick of the clock. For a minute he wasn't sure what to do, and then he couldn't help his smile. "April Nash," he said. It was the first time he had ever said her name out loud to another person and he felt the sound of it thrum in the air.

"Oh, April," Marc said. "Of course. How'd you know April?"

Bill's grin grew. "Just a friend of a friend," he

said. And then quickly, "Don't they have the best cupcakes, there, though?"

Marc laughed. "They do, indeed." Marc pointed a finger at one of the boys in the picture, a small boy with a thatch of hair, who was swimming out of his uniform. "See that kid there?"

Bill glanced over. A scrawny little boy with way too much hair. He felt a stab of pity. Must be Marc's son. "That's your boy? Fantastic," he said quickly.

"No, no. My boy is over here—there, that's Roger," he pointed to a tall, sandy-haired kid holding a soccer ball. "That one over there is April's son."

The clock on Marc's desk grew louder. Bill tried to speak. "That's April Nash's kid?" He swallowed. "You sure? She doesn't have a son, does she?"

"Sure she does," Marc said. "Ever meet him? Nice kid. He has such terrible asthma, he never plays, but they let him put on the uniform and be in the team. Sort of a nice community thing they do there."

Marc snapped his fingers. "Sam. That's his name. Sam. Too bad about his being so sickly, though. Terrible thing, asthma." He looked back at Bill. "So," he said. "Have a seat. Let's talk about what you can bring to Thoroughbred."

Bill couldn't concentrate on the rest of the interview. Marc had to repeat questions twice because Bill wasn't listening. Bill couldn't remember the clients he had worked for, the jobs he had done. He felt his palms, damp and sticky. "Sorry, I'm fighting a cold," he lied and Marc nodded. By the end of the interview, Marc's disinterest was palpable, and Bill knew that he hadn't gotten the job. "We'll be in touch," Marc said, and dismissed him.

Outside on the sidewalk, the fog was thicker. He glanced at his watch. In a few more hours, he would meet April. She had lied to him.

She had a kid, and for Bill, that changed everything. It wasn't just the lying, though that certainly put a crimp in things. It was having a *child.* Bill thought it was one thing leaving a spouse you had stopped loving, but how could you leave a child? Especially one who was sick? What kind of a person could do that? He felt as if he didn't know her at all, as if everything about them had been some kind of lie.

His hands were shaking. He remembered suddenly all her talk about a guest room. Was she planning on bringing the kid, springing it on him like an unwelcome surprise? Did she just want the kid to visit? And if she wanted the kid there so much, did that mean that she'd soon want him to have a kid with her, too? He felt a flash of anger. He hunched his shoulders and kept moving through the crowd. What else about her had been a lie? Did she love him or did she just want to leave and he seemed like an easy meal ticket? And if she could leave her kid, would she leave him, too?

He went to a diner to get coffee, sitting by the window, which was almost opaque with fog, and he was listening to this couple fighting. "What color are my eyes?" the woman kept shouting, and when the man said, "Brown," she wept. "Blue," he said, and she cried harder. And it struck him because he couldn't remember what color April's eyes were. What did he really know about her? He had never called her house, had never seen a photograph of her husband, or really ever known what kind of woman she was. He had only known her from their time in Boston. Suddenly, things didn't seem so simple anymore.

He was supposed to catch a shuttle to New York, where April was waiting for him. He thought of how lovely she was, how she liked to pull her body around his after they had made love. He thought of all the promises they had made to each other.

Abruptly, he changed his mind. When he got to the airport, he bought a ticket for home. He didn't look at his watch until he was back in Pittsburgh, and then he saw it was past three. Two hours after he was supposed to meet April, he noticed his wedding band, how he had never taken it off. He began crying so hard, he had to fumble for his sunglasses and slip them onto his face.

He took a cab home and went into the house and there was Ellen lying on the couch in her robe, blooms of tissue scattered around her. He looked past her and saw the note he had left her, fallen by the bookshelf, unopened. He bent and scooped it up, crumpling it deep into his pocket. "I got a cold!" she said, and pointed to the stack of DVDs near her. She patted the couch. "I had them deliver all these old film noirs. Come cuddle up and watch them with me," she said.

He walked to her and as soon as he touched her, he felt his eyes welling up again. He thought of April. She might cry, but she also might buy herself a ticket and get on the plane without him and go and disappear into another life and never look back. He felt his cheeks growing damp, his eyes pooling with tears.

"Oh Jesus, what?" Ellen said, alarmed. She sat up, drawing her robe around her. "You're scaring me. What's going on?"

"I lost my job," he blurted, because it was the only thing he could tell her, because he didn't want any more lies in his life, and she moved closer to him. She smelled like cough drops and Vicks and maple sugar. He told her how hard he had been looking, how he hadn't told her because he didn't want her to worry. A thousand tiny cracks earthquaked across his heart.

"What a mess," she said quietly. She stroked the back of his neck. "Fuck them," she said. "You were too good for that place anyway. You'll find something good now, you'll see. Something you love." She bent and kissed him and he looked up at her, at her soft little nose that was all pink with her cold.

"Yeah," he whispered. "Who cares," and then he glanced up, and there was the big clock pointing to five, just the time when he and April imagined they'd be on a plane soaring away from the New York skyline. He turned back to Ellen, took her hand, and held on tight.

After that, things had gotten better. Not right away, but in a few months he finally found a new job, one with a growing company. He looked at Ellen with fresh eyes, appreciating all the things he'd forgotten about her. He half expected April to call him or write, and he had to admit, every time the phone rang, he felt unnerved. But when she didn't, he gradually started to relax, until she had faded into mirage. A dream he had made up and then awakened from.

WHEN BILL FINISHED SPEAKING, he couldn't look at Charlie. He stared at his hands.

"She planned it," Charlie said, amazed. "She planned out a whole new life."

"We both did."

"You wrote her a letter," Charlie said.

"Everyone has relapses," he said. "And I thought if I knew what had happened to her, well then, I could finally forget her once and for all." He put the tips of both hands together, like a church steeple. "Sometimes, believe it or not, you get a second chance in life and you do whatever you can not to mess it up."

"You said you loved her."

Bill took another swig of coffee and looked at Charlie.

"What are you going to do," Bill said. "We're all fucked."

CHARLIE SAT IN the airplane, staring out the window. Beside him, a young woman with a blond Afro was tapping on her laptop, occasionally glancing at him. Charlie looked at the sky, black and sprigged with stars. Sam was young enough to still think there was Heaven—that living among the clouds was a God who made sense of the things that you could not. Now the sky was dark with night, and try as he might, the only thing Charlie sensed was the ghost of his family.

April had left him and maybe that was his fault somehow, maybe he could have changed if she had let him, if he had seen the signs brewing. He thought of the night before the accident, how she had wanted him to wake up. "Let's talk," she had said. That was her last night with them, and April, his impulsive April, had known it, had planned it all out for months. Who knew what she would have said to him? Maybe she had wanted to say good-bye, or maybe she had started to have cold feet about leaving. That had been his moment to change everything and he hadn't.

He couldn't forgive her for unraveling their family. She had calculated her departure, had orchestrated a whole future with Bill, too, insisting on a guest room, but how could she imagine Sam could only be a guest in her life? Or had she thought she could have more? Had she changed her mind that day in the car and planned on bringing Sam with her? He'd never know what to believe.

All that time with Isabelle, Charlie had felt he was being unfaithful to April. He hadn't been able to let April go, but now he knew that April had been the one who was unfaithful. His loyalty to her had kept him from letting Isabelle in, and now he knew how rare it was, what they had. Now that was gone, too.

Well, he didn't blame himself anymore for April's leaving. All you had of a person was what they showed you. He thought of the way she was always playing with Sam, giving him this wild adventure of a life, making sure he knew he was someone special. Then he thought of Isabelle, quietly helping Sam with his photography. "Look inside," she'd say to him. "Go deeper. See what's right there in a new way. Find the magic of the real moment."

There was no real moment with April.

April had left abruptly, without even a letter, but Isabelle had refused to leave without a good-bye. Isabelle had left Sam an expensive lens, and she'd made sure he knew how much she loved him.

People had always told Charlie to follow the road signs in life, not to get lost. Was meeting Bill a sign? Was he about to be lost in his life again? Or could he find the magic of the real moment again? Could he find Isabelle?

He thought of the smell of Isabelle's hair, the feel of her skin. He suddenly ached to hear her voice. He wanted to tell her all about Bill and April and what had happened, and then he wanted to talk to her about movies and books and what they were having for dinner, all those little moments that made up a life.

The night, after seeing his parents off and having dinner with Sam, Charlie made a decision. He let Sam watch a movie after dinner, and then when it was dark enough, when the stars were bright enough, he went to the closet and took down the box of April's ashes. He beckoned Sam to the front door. "Come on," he whispered, as if there were someone else in the house. They went out to the backyard, and it wasn't until they were right by the garden that Charlie opened the box and showed Sam what was inside.

"What's that?" Sam asked.

"Your mom was cremated," he told Sam. "She

never wanted her body to be buried in the ground. These are her ashes."

Sam bit down on his lower lip.

"It's okay," Charlie told him gently. "We can scatter her ashes here in the garden, and then she'll be a part of the whole world."

Sam stepped back. "Will you do it?"

Charlie nodded. He sifted some of the ashes out, strewing them among the tiger lillies, and did the one thing he had been so sure he would never be able to do:

He let her go.

— Twenty-one —

CHARLIE SAT AT the midtown café, on a sunny May day, waiting for Isabelle. It all felt so strange, so upside down. His parents were at the Cape with Sam, and he was here. She hadn't been hard to find. As soon as he heard her voice, he realized how stupid he had been, how much he missed her.

"Charlie!"

He had forgotten how beautiful she was. Even though she was just wearing a simple, loose summery dress, Isabelle looked exotic to him. There was something different and familiar about her, something he couldn't quite pinpoint that unsettled him. She was beaming, but didn't touch him. "Charlie," she said happily. "Oh, Charlie."

A waiter hustled over and they both ordered omelets, though Charlie wasn't hungry.

"Is Sam here?" she asked, and when he said no, that Sam was with his parents at the Cape, she looked deflated.

"But he's good, he's good." Charlie leaned forward. "His asthma is gone."

Isabelle started. "How can that be?"

"I don't know. The doctor said sometimes kids grow out of it." The waiter set down two glasses of water.

"Is he still taking pictures?"

"Not so much anymore."

"Oh, no! I'm so sorry to hear he stopped. He was good, wasn't he?" she asked.

"Yeah. He took these great shots of the road." As soon as he saw Isabelle flinch, he regretted saying it. "He took dogs, the neighborhood. He had a great eye but a lot of the shots were blurry."

"He could have learned to fix that," Isabelle said. She took a sip of water and then looked at Charlie. "Do you have pictures of him?"

He took a school picture out of his wallet. Sam had long hair now, like a Beatle boy. Charlie handed the photo to Isabelle and when she didn't give it back, he didn't ask for it. It passed through their hands like an understanding. She nodded, some of the shine gone from her. "Well, it's been a long time," she said.

They talked about their lives and then, slowly, he told her about April, about how he had found out she was planning to run away with her lover, how she was going to have a guest room, which made it seem as though she were planning to get Sam, at least for visits. He told Isabelle about going to see Bill and that Bill hadn't known about Sam. "He didn't want her because of Sam," Charlie said.

"Then he's a fool," Isabelle said. "And so was April. What they both lost. What they both gave up." She put her fork down. "Does she still haunt you?"

"I can't forgive what she did, and I can't understand it."

"Neither can I," Isabelle said quietly.

"She doesn't haunt me anymore." He reached across the table and took Isabelle's hand, making her drop her fork. "But you do."

Isabelle slid her hand away from his. "For months I waited for you to call," Isabelle said slowly. "I kept expecting you to visit, and I kept seeing you in the city. Once, in a supermarket, I ran after a man with long, dark hair like yours and grabbed his arm. Of course, it wasn't you. It never was you. Every time I saw a boy, I felt something coming undone inside me. You told me not to call Sam anymore because he was getting sicker, and I didn't. It just felt like every time I came into your lives, I was creating another accident."

"I know, I know—forgive me. Forgive us."

"You found your answers, Charlie, and I'm glad. I'm really glad. Now you can move on and put it behind you. And I'm so happy Sam's asthma is gone. But Charlie, I moved on, too."

"You told me to come see you when I called. You said you wanted to see me."

"I did want to see you." She swallowed. "I'm seeing someone. Frank. He's a chef."

Something clipped at Charlie's heart. "Serious?" he asked.

She was quiet for a moment. "I want you to be happy, too," she said. "Are you seeing anyone?"

He shook his head. Frank. A name like a bite out of an apple. He tried to imagine it, a chef cooking for her, a man who wooed her with fresh pasta and fine wine. "My timing is terrible, isn't it," Charlie said. "I never should have let you leave, but I thought it was the right thing to do at the time. Now, seeing you . . ." he swallowed. A piece of bacon was stuck in his throat, and he took a gulp of water. "Right now, it just feels as if the whole nightmare is over," he said. He put his fork down. "Maybe we should try again."

She was so silent that he began to be a little scared.

"You don't still love me," he said.

Isabelle drew her hands from the table. "I'm getting married," she said quietly.

Charlie felt suddenly dizzy.

·She reached across and took his hand, and again, he felt that same, strange heat.

"How could you marry this guy?" Charlie said. "How long have you even known him?"

"Since January."

He looked at her. "You're not crazy in love. I can tell by looking at you."

"How do you know? And what does what I feel or want have to do with anything? He's good to me. He doesn't obsess. He's steady and there aren't any other women in his life. This isn't the movies. Everything doesn't turn out all tied up in a neat bow the way you want."

His heart rushed against his ribs. "Why can't it turn out the way we want?" he said.

"Because I'm pregnant," she said.

That was why he recognized that look. He had seen it in April when she was pregnant with Sam, the way she had seemed as if she were carrying another secret self around that she wasn't quite ready to reveal yet. That was when Isabelle's loose dress began to make sense to him, the glow of her.

"Five months," she said. She smoothed the dress against her and he saw, suddenly, the swell of her stomach.

"I thought you couldn't . . ." Charlie said.

"I thought so, too," she said. "Every doctor, every specialist I've ever seen has told me I couldn't. I gave up trying a long time ago. I knew it was something I couldn't even dare to hope for. And right away, it just happened. I was a basket case at first, just waiting to miscarry, plus it was a brand-new relationship, but everything has been good. It's almost like it's meant to be." She folded her napkin, motioned for the waitress, and then turned to Charlie. "I'm having a little girl," she said.

After lunch, they started walking to Hell's Kitchen where she lived with Frank now. She pointed out her favorite shops and restaurants. Charlie tried to concentrate, but all he could think about was that he was here with the woman he most wanted, and she was pregnant by someone else.

"The city has a buzz, doesn't it?" she said. "Look at that." She pointed to a man walking down the street with a tree branch tied around his back with purple ribbons, but the only thing Charlie could pay attention to was her. The air seemed charged around her. Colors seemed brighter. "My parents always thought I belonged here," Charlie said.

"Do you think you do?"

The buzz Isabelle loved sounded like tinnitus to him, but he didn't want to hurt her feelings by saying so.

"Come to dinner. Meet him," she said, and he shook his head.

"I don't think I can meet Frank," Charlie said.

"Want to keep walking?"

Several blocks later, they were winding their way toward SoHo, when she stopped in front of a hotel, hesitating. The Mercer. She didn't say anything to him, but she didn't have to. He followed her inside and he paid for the room, using their real names.

AS SOON AS they were in the room, she leaned toward Charlie and kissed him. Isabelle slipped her shirt down and he saw the soft swell of her belly and he leaned down and kissed it. You be good to her, he wanted to whisper to the baby.

She slid out of her clothes. Every time he had touched her before, he had felt that he was cheating on April. Now there was nothing but this room, this bed with the squeaky springs. There was nothing but Isabelle's pale skin and the way she sighed when he touched her. He reached for the lights, but Isabelle pulled at his hand. "No, I want to see you," she said, and the whole time they were making love, she kept her eyes wide open. When Charlie shut his, she whispered, "Look at me," and he did. He wrapped her hair around his hand and pulled her closer to him. He studied Isabelle and she touched his mouth. "I love you," he said.

Her mouth moved. "You never said that to me before."

"Yes, I did. All the time. Just not out loud." He kissed her shoulder. "I love you," he said again. "I always will."

Afterward, they sat naked in bed and ordered room service. A salad plate, crusty bread, and sparkling water, because she was being careful not to eat a single thing that was bad for her. They littered the sheets with their crumbs. Isabelle looked up. "Hear that?" she said. "All that traffic noise. It's getting late."

"I don't hear anything," Charlie said, reaching for her, but Isabelle got out of the bed. She began putting her clothes on. "We should get going," she said.

"Stay," he said, trying to pull her back onto the bed. She smiled and kept dressing. He got up and started dressing, too. He helped her smooth the sheets, as if no one had been in the bed at all.

Outside was still bright and hot and Charlie's mouth was dry. He rested his hand along the side of a building for a moment. Isabelle walked him all the way back to his car. He saw her mouth wobble, just for a moment, before she smiled at him.

"Come with me," he said. "Come back to the Cape with me. Come see Sam. I love you. I know you love me." He grabbed her arm and held it and there was that fierce heat again and he felt like crying. "You can call Frank from Massachusetts. We can work all this out." He thought of their whole life, like this big stretching picture. Every cell in his body was pulling toward her, like magnets. "I made a mistake," he said, cupping her face in his hands. "Let me fix it. We can be a family. I'll love your baby like my own. Like you love Sam."

And then she pulled her hand away and folded it on her belly. Her lower lip trembled. "I can't," Isabelle said. She stepped back from him. "Please, Charlie. Please don't make this harder."

"You don't love me?"

"I didn't say that."

He felt a pull of desperation. "Maybe I could stay a few more days."

"Please. Just go," she said. "You have to go."

Charlie got in the car. You could think you understood things, but the truth was that you could never see the full picture of someone else's life. Not April's, not Isabelle's. He wasn't even sure about his own life now. He looked back at her. Her hair was lush and full and shimmering. He wanted to jump out again and grab her and tell her she had to come with him. He wanted to kiss her mouth, her neck, the slope of her shoulders. He drove slowly, and even though he knew it was crazy, he half expected her to run after the car, waving her beautiful hands, calling to him to stop, stop, because she had changed her mind, she couldn't live without him, either. He knew she loved him. He thought of April, always holding something back, and then he thought of Isabelle, in the hotel room with him, her luminous skin, the smell of her hair. The way she kept her eyes open while they made love, the way every time he turned away, she would whisper to him, "Look at me."

And he had. He had really seen who she was.

Charlie let himself look in the rearview mirror. The street was teeming with people, but Isabelle was gone. It was then that he started to cry.

AFTER CHARLIE LEFT, when she was sure he wouldn't see her, Isabelle started crying right there on the street. She leaned against a building and sobbed into her hands and when she finally stopped, she dug out her sunglasses and then walked to the curb and hailed a cab. As soon as she was seated in the back, she blew her nose and then carefully put on a little makeup, assuring herself that by the time she got to her building, she'd look as if nothing had ever happened to her.

"How was your day, beautiful girl?" Frank was home, standing in the kitchen, in jeans and a denim shirt, stirring a red sauce in the pot. "I gave Nelson scallops," he laughed. "Sautéed them, too." Then he glanced at her, and his face filled with alarm. "Allergies again?" he said, and Isabelle nodded. The house smelled of basil and garlic. "I made something special," he said. He turned, looking at her. "God, you are beautiful. I am so lucky," he said.

"I'm starving," Isabelle lied, and when she went to kiss him, she closed her eyes.

That night, Isabelle bolted awake. She'd been dreaming that she had said yes to Charlie, that she had driven away with him to the Cape, flushed with happiness, and Sam was there and she had hugged Sam so hard, she had thought she might never let him go. She sat up, disoriented, seeing the contours of the oak dresser Frank had found for her, the framed photo of his restaurant. For a moment, staring at Frank, she didn't know who he was. "Szzth," Frank muttered. She glanced at the clock. Three in the morning. She got up to make some peppermint tea, one hand on her belly. She was terrified because the baby hadn't kicked yet, and though her obstetrician told her it was nothing to worry about, that the baby had a heartbeat like a firecracker, she couldn't help but be unnerved. She walked past the den, hearing Nelson rustling in his tank. She went into the kitchen and switched on the light. Outside, an alley cat was yowling, a strange, fierce cry in the night. She poured the tea and sat down. She thought of how Frank had made her a special dinner, how he sang sweet, silly songs to her when she called him on the phone, how surely he deserved someone better and kinder than she was, someone who loved him the way he loved her. "You should see the way he looks at you!" one of her friends had told her. Every night he rested his head against her belly and spoke Italian to the baby. *Ciao. Linguini.* Food words that made her laugh.

Charlie. Her heart raced and she suddenly felt sick. She was pregnant and she had slept with Charlie. She thought she heard Frank moving around, getting up. Any moment he'd come in and give her that worried look. He'd make her broth from scratch, he'd rub her back. If she said to him, I'm in love with someone else, he would tell her to go and be with that person, and he would be kind about it. She would ruin his life. And maybe she would ruin her own in the process. She touched the phone. She'd call just to hear Charlie's voice and hang up. She'd call just because she could. She started to dial and then just as she punched in the last digit, she felt a tiny flutter in her belly, like someone was tickling her from inside. Her hands froze and she let the receiver clatter onto the table. She felt it again.

"Frank!" she shouted. "Frank!" Her voice was like a kite, rushing the sky. She heard his footsteps and when he tumbled into the kitchen, his face tight with fear, she was laughing out loud. She was standing in the middle of the floor in her nightgown, her hand on her belly. She reached for his hand and put it there, there on the side, where life was kicking. He kept his hand there, staring at her in wonder.

THE FOLLOWING SPRING, after the baby was born, a beautiful sunny girl named Elaine, Isabelle began taking driving lessons. She hadn't been anxious about being a passenger in a car for a long time, but driving had been a hurdle she hadn't mastered yet. "Are you sure?" Frank said. "We have plenty of money for cabs, and most everything's walkable, anyway." Isabelle kept thinking of her baby, of what might happen if she needed to be the one driving Elaine to something. To a doctor or a playdate. You couldn't spend your life being afraid. "I'll teach you," Frank offered, but Isabelle wanted someone neutral.

Every Tuesday and Thursday, a man named Ramon drove up and took her out. She was sick to her stomach for hours before he showed up, alarming Frank so much he begged her to reconsider. As soon as she sat in the driver's seat, she broke out into a cold sweat. She gripped the wheel so tightly, her knuckles turned pale. "Relax," said Ramon. He was wearing dark glasses and there was music in the car. "I haven't lost a driver yet."

He had a lot of crazy ideas. "Hit the break like a sponge," he told her. He also told her to think of a spot ahead of her that was drawing her forward. She felt as if the world had narrowed, as if there wasn't enough space for her to drive through. Hunching her shoulders, she struggled to breathe, and then panicking, she stopped and rested her head on the wheel. "Maybe some people aren't meant to drive," she said.

"What? Are you crazy? Who told you such a ridiculous thing? You drive like a pro. When you want to get your license?"

When she told him why she had stopped driving, he didn't say anything. He studied her for a minute, tapping one hand against the wheel. "I taught a man to drive who had run over his baby daughter in the driveway," he said quietly. "He hadn't been looking. I taught a woman to drive again after she had been in an accident with her fiancé and he had died and she had survived.

Drunken driver." He looked at her. "People who are frightened, who don't know where they're going," he said. "They're my best students."

Isabelle put her hands on the wheel and sat up straighter. "I don't want to be frightened anymore," she told him, "and I want to know where I'm going," and then she stepped gently on the gas.

～ TWENTY-TWO ～

TWO WEEKS BEFORE his thirtieth birthday, Sam Nash was getting ready to make the four-hour drive from Boston to upstate New York to see Isabelle for the first time in nearly twenty years. Everything was set. Another obstetrician was going to be on call for his patients, though if any of them had been due for delivery, he wouldn't have even thought of going.

"I'll be back in a few days," he told Lisa, the woman he loved. Lisa was already dressed in the extra pair of hospital scrubs she kept at his place, on her way to do a morning gall bladder surgery, but she lingered at the door with him. "I'll leave the cell on all the time," he said. She nodded.

"It's good you're doing this," she said.

"Are you still mad at me?" he asked.

She shrugged. "A little." She lifted up a brown paper sack. "Lunch," she said, and when he stepped toward her, she pushed him away. "This doesn't mean I'm not still mad," she said. "I'm just giving you lunch out of your own refrigerator." He took it, grateful, and she gave him a quick kiss that tasted like strawberry jam.

He watched her through the rearview mirror. She stood on the front porch, waving at him, while he drove away. He knew her. She wouldn't go inside until his car disappeared from her sight.

The whole first half hour of his drive, Sam's head swam and he felt as if he had swallowed stones, which were now a sour lump in his stomach. He wasn't even gone, and already he missed Lisa. He pulled down the sun visor. There, clipped inside, was his favorite photograph of her. She was drowsy, smiling, totally herself. He touched it, tracing her face, and then put the visor back up.

They had argued the night before. Lisa was on call and had to rush to the hospital to look at a patient with bleeding ulcers, but she couldn't find a clean shirt in the closet. "God, if all my clothes were here, I wouldn't have to go through this circus every time," she said, and then she grew silent again. She finally pulled on a blue T-shirt of Sam's and then pulled the V-neck top of her scrubs over it. "There, you look pretty," Sam said, but Lisa, frowning, wouldn't look at him.

She buttoned her coat and tied her shoes, snapping the laces. She finally turned back to him. "What are we doing?" she said quietly. "What are you afraid of?"

"I'm not afraid."

"Really?" She lifted the newspapers from the couch. "Real estate section's right here. You want to look? Here's a three bedroom. Here's a whole house. Belmont. Newton. Waltham. Back Bay. Anywhere we want." She waited one beat, and then two, and when Sam didn't move, when he staycd thcrc, paralyzed, she flung the paper back down on the floor. "I rest my case," she said.

Lisa turned away from him, shaking her head, refusing to meet his eyes. "I have to be at the hospital," she said curtly, reaching for the front door. She turned to look at him, her gaze hard. "Sometimes I wish I didn't love you," she said. After she left, he sat on the porch with his head in his hands; and when she finally came back, two hours later, she just shook her head at him.

Sam turned onto the highway, merging into the left lane. What *was* he doing? He'd been with Lisa for five years. "Imagine us together for that long!" he exulted to her once.

"Imagine us married," she said wistfully, and then she stroked his arm. "I know this is hard for you," she said.

He brought Lisa flowers every week, jonquils, her favorites. He brought her funny little presents that he thought she might love, tucking them into places where he knew she'd find them. A wedge of smoked Gouda cheese. A piece of imported chocolate with orange cream inside. He called her four times a day, and every time she opened a present from him and he saw her face, bright and expectant with hope, he felt a line of guilt. "Are you happy?" he asked, and when she paused before answering, he shivered. "Of course I am," she said. They were still good together, he told himself. He just wanted more time. He wanted her to be sure she wasn't making a mistake with him.

Lisa sometimes chided him for being at the hospital too much, for getting up out of bed too many times to tend to other women, even if it was just to talk to one of his patients over the phone and soothe her because she hadn't gone into labor yet. "But that's what you yourself would want in a doctor!" he insisted.

"From my doctor, not from my boyfriend," said Lisa, rolling over. "I want you to tend to me, too," she said, and then she pulled the covers over her head so all that showed were the points on her dark hair.

Sam turned onto an exit ramp and was trapped in traffic. Summer was probably the worst time to travel anywhere, but there was no right time if you were a doctor. Sam had checked all his patients before he left. He knew their due dates as well as his own birthday, and he told himself that if he needed to, he could get back here in time for a delivery.

It was the end of June, and Sam rolled the windows down, resting his arm on the top of the door. There it was. After all these years, it still surprised him. His scar, a jagged line of silver all the way up his arm. For years he had worn long sleeves even in the hottest weather because he didn't want people asking him why his arm was so chewed up. He didn't like feeling that people were staring at him.

A car honked and Sam merged into another lane. He and Lisa would go together to the Cape in another month, at the height of the season. They'd slather on sun block and swim in the ocean and eat enough fresh seafood to grow gills. They'd stay with his father and his girlfriend, Lucy, who would be insulted if they even thought of a hotel.

Sam opened up the thermos and took a swig of the coffee. It was sweet and black, the way he loved it. He opened the lunch Lisa had packed and took a bite. Spicy chicken, arugula, and peppers, on a seeded roll. A wake-up sandwich, Lisa would call it.

Lisa. The night he met her, it was three in the morning.

He'd just lost a patient, one of his favorites, a bright, cheerful forty-year-old woman named Eleanor who had gone into cardiac arrest just as she delivered her first baby, and though he had tried his best to save her, she hadn't lived long enough to hold her own child.

Sam had sat with the stunned father until relatives appeared, and then he had gone to the cafeteria, sitting in the bright, florid lights. He felt like hell. He kept thinking he'd go back upstairs, make sure the father was okay. He'd make sure the baby was all right. Eleanor probably would have said, Well, at least I got to be pregnant. At least I got a chance to give birth. At least I got a chance to be this happy.

She was probably in the morgue by now.

He was draining his cup, the hospital coffee dark and sludgy from being in the pot too long, when a young doctor stumbled in. She wore a white coat over a turquoise dress, her short, dark hair matted. She looked as terrible as he knew he did. To his surprise, she sat right at his table and took some of his carton of milk for her coffee. "Don't mind me, I'm having a nervous breakdown and can't be trusted to sit by myself," she said, swirling her spoon in her cup, making parabolas of milk.

"My milk carton is your milk carton," he said. It felt funny to hear his own voice after being silent for so long.

"Okay if I stay?" she asked.

He shrugged, because really, what did it matter? He could use the company, himself, especially from someone who wouldn't take it personally if he didn't want to talk.

He glanced at the ID pinned to her lab coat. Lisa Jean Miller. He couldn't remember seeing her around the hospital. She stirred more milk into her coffee and then told him that she was a gastroenterologist and she had just lost a patient. "Inoperable cancer. Stage four," she said quietly.

Sam stopped drinking his coffee. "Me, too," he said and she started. "I lost a patient, I mean," he told her.

Sam had loved women in his life, but it had always been a cautious thing, like at the beach when he would splash water on his chest before he would dare to dunk in. But with Lisa, he fell in love instantly.

They talked quietly in the cafeteria, about work and then about life. All around them, people kept coming and going like a tide. Lisa told Sam how she had been at Mass General only two years now, but she liked it fine. She loved the city and couldn't imagine living anywhere else. She was one of eight kids from a big Nebraskan family, the only girl, and her parents had been saving since she was a baby so she could go to college; she became the only one in the family who didn't stay to farm. "My brothers all feel sorry for me," she laughed. "They don't understand how I could be happy living in a city."

Sam's heart was beating ridiculously fast. When Lisa got up to leave, it was the most natural thing in the world for him to get up, too. Not a word was said about it, but they walked out to his car, Lisa opened the door and slid into the seat without looking at him, and when he pulled up to her place, she simply took his hand and led him inside. He didn't leave until the next morning, and even then the only way he could leave was because she was heading out for the hospital, too. By the end of that month, they were living out of each other's apartments.

"How did I get so lucky?" he asked her, cupping her face.

"Luck never has anything to do with love," she said, and he thought of his mother.

"Luck has everything to do with everything," he told her. "Especially love."

Now, he grabbed the phone and called her, but got her voicemail. He glanced at the road signs, made a right turn, and then he picked up the phone again. Another doctor was taking his patients, but still, he wanted to make sure everything was all right. He called his service but there were no messages.

Well. Sam had been a doctor for several years and he had never stopped marveling at how lucky his life had turned out. Isabelle used to tell him you could look at anything any number of ways and angles, so you might as well look at it the good way, the way that was most meaningful to you personally.

HE WAS GETTING tired now from driving. The winking lights of a diner shone up ahead: Tick Tock. The sign winked at him.

Sam stopped and got out of the car. The parking lot was full of cars. He needed to stretch his legs. He liked diners. They always reminded him of all those years when his mother used to take him on adventures, the two of them pretending to be all sorts of other people. He remembered one of the last conversations when they were driving. "Always remember," she had told him. "When you're grown up, I want you to take your girlfriend, or your wife, or boyfriend—whoever it is you love—and you make sure they know you so well they can read your mind. You don't even have to tell them what you need, because they already know it. If they don't—well, it isn't love."

Sam felt a sudden flash of sorrow. He hadn't really known what she had been talking about back then, though he had tried to get her to read his mind. In the car, sitting beside his mother that day, he had thought so hard, Go home, Go home, that it made his brain ache, and of course, she hadn't. She had kept going forward.

Maybe he'd have some coffee and pie, soak up the atmosphere, have a story to tell later. Before he went inside the diner, he tried Lisa again on his phone. This time, she answered and he felt something switching on inside him. "I wish you were with me," he said. "I'm sorry about what happened."

She was quiet for a moment.

"When you come home, we'll talk," she said.

He went into the diner and ate a plate of fries and a burger—the worst thing for his health and the most delicious—and he overtipped the waitress so much, she ran after him, asking if there had been some mistake. "Keep it," he told her.

He got back in the car. He had another half hour before he reached Woodstock, where Isabelle now lived. Woodstock was full of old hippies and people who wanted lively shops and movies but not the buzz and hum of the city. He never expected Isabelle would have moved up here from New York City, and most of all, he had never expected he would see her again after twenty years.

She was the one who had contacted him. Her letter had been a shock. It came to the hospital two weeks after there had been a short piece about him in the paper, a series on the best doctors in Boston. A reporter had come to his office to talk to him because of all the patients who kept singing his praises. A photographer had posed him by the window, his white lab coat jauntily thrown open, his face laughing. "The Doctor Every Woman Loves," the headline ran, and for weeks afterward, his colleagues teased him mercilessly.

As soon as he saw her handwriting, he had to sit down. His head was thumping and he couldn't quite breathe. For a moment, he thought his asthma might have returned. "I read about you," Isabelle wrote. "I wanted to call but I thought this would be easier for you." Her handwriting was still the same uneven tumble, the scrawl his father used to joke about because no one but Isabelle could ever read it. She was married. She had two children, one of them adopted from China. "It's been over two decades. Do you think we could see each other?" she wrote.

No, he thought. Of course the answer was no. She had left him when he was nine years old. She had never called, never written, and gradually just vanished into the ether the same way his mother had. He tucked her letter into the pocket of his lab coat, unsure what to do. It had been so long. He felt the letter when he went on his rounds. He swore he heard her rustling when he leaned over a patient to check her heart. He felt it when he sat down to gulp some coffee, and he felt it when he came back home and told Lisa. "What could she possibly want, after all this time?" he said.

"Maybe she doesn't want anything. Maybe you should see her," Lisa said.

He startled. "See her? She vanished when I was a little kid. Now she contacts me with this letter."

"You should at least call her," Lisa said. She rubbed his arm. "Aren't you at least a little curious?"

"I don't know," Sam said, waving his hands. "I don't know, I don't know."

"You don't have to do it *now*," Lisa said.

It was like a mosquito bite that he couldn't help scratching. He didn't call, though he kept the number by the phone in the bedroom, and after he had picked up the paper so many times to look at it, he had the number memorized. He didn't know if he should tell his father or not, so he kept silent.

Then, one night at the hospital, he had three deliveries and none of the mothers had really dilated yet. A few nurses padded down the hall, talking to one another. Patients were asleep. He passed the waiting room and a woman was sitting there, avidly reading a picture book, *The Runaway Bunny*, to a boy leaning against her. His mother had read him that book all the time, though she hadn't been a fan of it. He still remembered the story, about a baby rabbit that kept threatening to run away, changing into clouds or mountains or whatever he needed to be to escape his mom. The mom rabbit kept insisting that she would always find her baby, that if her baby morphed into a cloud, she'd become the sky. If he was a fish, she would be the ocean. She'd be anything, just so she could be with him. "Now that's pathological," his mother had said, but Sam had loved the book. He had asked for it every night.

Sam dug his hand in his pocket and there was Isabelle's phone number. He couldn't deny that he missed her. That she had been important to him. That at one point in his life he had thought she was an angel, a conduit between him and his mother. Well. People believed in angels when they were most in trouble, when there was nothing else they could do. His patients whose babies died comforted themselves with the thought that the babies were angels. But he was a doctor now, and he knew there was no such thing.

He took out his cell phone and, before he could change his mind, called Isabelle, his fingers gripped around the phone.

"Hello?" she said, and hearing that voice, he pressed the receiver against his forehead and shut his eyes. His whole life came back to him. "It's Sam," he said.

"Sam!" She sighed his name. "I didn't know if you'd call. I'm so glad you did."

"I almost didn't." Behind him, a nurse was whistling. "But here I am."

"That article about you! You're all grown up." She was silent for a minute.

"I haven't been a child in a long time."

"I know that."

"So. Why didn't you write before this? Why didn't you call?" He knew it sounded rude, but he couldn't help himself.

"Oh, not on the phone," she said. "I can't do this on the phone. Please. Can we see each other?"

Talking was hard enough. He couldn't imagine what it would be like to actually see her, how he might feel. He tapped his fingers on the phone. Behind him, he heard two people arguing. "They charged me for an aspirin!" a voice said.

Did he really want to see her? Was this really a good idea? He could hang up and tear up her number and that would be that. He could pretend she had never called him and his life would go on the way it always had. He'd have his father still. He'd have Lisa and his work.

"Sam?"

He could pretend this had never happened.

"I'll come to you," he said. "Just for a few hours."

Babies in the womb got their senses mixed up. There was an eerie phenomenon where they could hear colors. They could see sounds. He felt as if he finally understood what that must be like, because surely, every sense of his had gone awry. He went to his house and dug out the old Canon. He had stopped taking pictures with it years ago; now he used a digital that required nothing but a steady hand. Still, he had kept it. He traced the camera with his hands.

He made plans. He called his father, attempting to be casual. "Isabelle wrote me," he said, and Charlie was silent.

"I'm going to visit her. Would you like to come?" Sam asked.

"Another time," he said. Sam's father would never talk about Isabelle with him, no matter how many questions Sam would ask. "Did you love her? Did you love her the way you loved Mom?" Sam kept asking. "Why did she leave us?" over and over until he was old enough to see how such questions hurt Charlie, how his father would retreat into the other room, how maybe there really weren't any good answers, and only then did he stop.

Still, the day before Sam left, Charlie called. His father coughed into the phone and Sam felt the hesitation. "You tell her hello from me," Charlie said.

BY THE TIME Sam got to Woodstock, it was midafternoon. It was a lively little town, full of shops and restaurants and people ambling on the street. He turned down a road, following the directions she had given him, and there was her house, a big white Colonial with a green lawn, and as soon as he saw the child's jump rope, like a squiggle, his legs buckled. He wondered if he had made a terrible mistake, if it wasn't too late to turn around and go home.

He sat in the car, tense and angry, with the motor running. He could be back before Lisa got off her shift. He could go home and pretend none of this happened. He felt nine years old. He had thought she had wings. He put his hand on the gear shift, and then the front door opened and Isabelle flew out.

Her hair was still long but mostly gray now, which somehow made her even more arresting to look at. She was still thin, but her features were softer, and there were fine lines around her eyes.

She was still beautiful.

Slowly, he got out of the car. She hugged him close, but he couldn't bring himself to put his arms up around her, and instead, he forcibly stepped back. She was crying, but his heart still felt hard. "I've missed you so much," she said. "I can't stop looking at you."

"You wouldn't have missed me if you'd kept in touch."

She startled. "Do I deserve that, Sam?" she said quietly.

He shifted his weight. Something was burning inside his stomach. "Why did you want to see me?" he said finally.

"Come inside and meet everyone," she said. "Then we'll talk."

Everyone, he thought. Who was everyone? As soon as he stepped inside, he heard music, something jazzy, and there were voices in the back. It wasn't raining, his shoes were clean, but he stamped his feet on her rug. The house was big and roomy. Everything was polished wood and white walls, which were full of her photos. They were all black-and-white images of peoples' faces, and in every photo a different part of the face was hidden in shadow. Then, there, toward the back, there was an enlarged one of him, at nine, set slightly apart from the others. Maybe she'd hung it up just before he got there. Did she really think that that would make him believe she had cared? There were photos of Nelson, too, his mouth open and yawning. "Nelson," Sam said. "He was a great tortoise."

"What do you mean was? He still is. Want to see him?"

"He's alive?"

"He's going to outlive us all," she assured him. She led him to a small room in the back and showed him the tank. Nelson arched his neck when Sam came in, and for a moment, Sam felt that same crazy disorientation. "Remember me?" Sam said, touching Nelson's smooth shell. Nelson hissed and slid his head back into his shell, making Isabelle laugh.

"Nelson's unsociable as always," she said, and then she turned back to Sam. "Are you taking photographs these days?"

"I stopped taking them when I was a kid."

She put her hand to her face. "How is Charlie?" she asked, and her voice got all funny.

"He's seeing someone now. She teaches Spanish at Oakrose High."

Isabelle nodded. "Good. I'm glad. Is he happy?"

Sam thought of his father and Lucy, his new girlfriend. Did they seem happy? Or was it more just a kind of contentment? The last time he had visited, Lucy cooked paella and kissed Charlie and held his hand across the table, but Sam noted that they still kept separate addresses.

"He's as happy as anyone," Sam finally said.

Isabelle looked as if she were about to say

something, but then a big wooly black dog sprang out from the kitchen, and then a little girl tumbled out, too, Chinese, with almond eyes and straight black hair cascading down her back. Isabelle gave a half smile. "Ah, here's Grace," Isabelle said. "She's six. Elaine, my oldest, is at college." A man came out, balding and steel-haired, grinning. "You must be Sam," he said, and he draped an arm about Isabelle, drawing her close, kissing the curly top of her head.

Dinner was long and delicious. Grace had to be coaxed to eat vegetables. "Please don't eat your zucchini," said Frank. "Because I really want it for myself!" Grace giggled and grabbed a bite. "And don't even think of touching the carrots," he said meaningfully.

Grace shot a glance over at Sam and then pronged a carrot with her fork, popping it into her mouth.

All through dinner, Sam compared Isabelle's husband to Charlie. Frank was probably the last kind of person he'd expect Isabelle to end up with, big and boisterous, and clearly older than she was. But even though he tried not to, Sam liked Frank. Frank told him how a critic had come in with a fake mustache that had fallen into his soup, how the pastry chef had inadvertently lost her ring in a cupcake and served it to a young woman who thought her boyfriend was proposing. ("He proposed anyway." Frank laughed.) Frank asked

Sam a million questions about his job, about his life. The whole dinner, no one mentioned Charlie at all, but he seemed a presence, anyway.

After dinner, Sam helped with the cleanup. "Why don't you show Sam the park?" Frank asked Isabelle. "Gracie and I can man the fort here."

Isabelle nodded. "Go," he said.

The park was green and leafy, with a fenced-off playground of jungle gyms and swings and a big sign, NO ADULTS WITHOUT CHILDREN ALLOWED INSIDE. He felt Isabelle's eyes on him. "What?" he said.

"Can I take your picture?" Isabelle asked, lifting the camera.

"You're now too rich and famous for my budget."

"Hardly," she smiled. She moved to another angle and the camera whirred. "Still not using a digital?" Sam asked, and Isabelle laughed.

"I like film," she said. "It captures every detail. It's a shame you don't take photographs anymore. You had a good eye."

She crouched and he felt prickles all over his skin as she focused on him. When he was a kid, he used to love it when she took his picture. He loved all the hours in the darkroom with Isabelle, not seeing her, but knowing all he had to do was reach out and he could touch her. Watching her, he felt a pulse of anger.

Still crouching, she took another shot. "I'll send you the prints," she said, and then she asked, "How is Charlie, really?" Her face was hidden by the camera.

"He's good. I told you. He loves the Cape. He's still working. He has Lucy."

Isabelle stood up, and looked down at her camera. "One of these days I'm going to just show up to see him."

"Maybe you should."

She stared down into the camera again. "Is he happy?" she said carefully.

"Are you?"

"Why wouldn't I be?" She took two more photos in rapid succession and then stood up, putting the camera away. She shielded her eyes from the sun. "God, it goes so fast, doesn't it?" she said wistfully.

"I almost didn't come," Sam blurted, and Isabelle turned to face him.

"For a long time, I didn't want to, I was so angry," Sam said. He felt it all building up inside him, all over again, all the feelings he had tamped down.

She was about to say something, but Sam held up his hand. "I was a little kid when you left," he said. "I couldn't believe you would just go like that, that you didn't write or call or want to see me. That you wouldn't even answer my letters. All I ever got from you was one phone call, Isabelle, and then I got sick—remember that day when I called you and I was wheezing so hard I couldn't talk? I kept waiting for you to come see me. How could you do that? Didn't you even want to contact the hospital to see if I was okay?" he said.

"Sam—" Her face grew pained.

"How could you just leave me? I was a *kid*. I loved you. Do you know what it did to me? How I blamed myself when you vanished?"

She opened her mouth to speak but no sound came out, and he was suddenly so hopeless with anger, he had to shut his eyes for a moment. He swallowed, and when he looked at her again, she looked as if a layer had been peeled away from her, as if she were a thousand years old, all her beauty gone.

She put the camera down against her body, and he saw her hands were shaking. "It didn't happen that way," Isabelle said.

"What didn't?"

Isabelle shook her head. "I'm so sorry, but that's wrong, Sam—"

"I thought we'd always be friends," Sam said. "How was it so easy for you to vanish? Do you know what it was like for me? For my dad? Especially after all that had happened?"

"I was always your friend. And it was far from easy."

"No. You weren't a friend. You left."

Isabelle stared past Sam. Her fingers moved on

her camera, as if she were reading it like Braille. "You really don't know, do you?" she said quietly.

"Know what?"

"I called the store," she said. "I called every hospital on the Cape until I found where you were admitted. I called Charlie." She grabbed for Sam's arm and he stepped away from her. "Sam, I was ready to get on a plane and go there, but Charlie saw my phone number scribbled on your hand and got to me first. He told me to stay away. He was so scared you would call me and get worse that he scrubbed my number off."

"What?" Sam looked at her, astonished. He remembered the numbers he had inked on his hand, how frantic he had been when he had found them gone.

"Sam, I'm so sorry."

"Why can't you take responsibility?" Sam said. He felt his voice tightening. "Why can't you just admit that you did something wrong?"

Isabelle shook her head violently. "You don't understand! They couldn't get the asthma under control and Charlie was terrified you might die!" She swiped at her eyes. "Every time I wrote you, every time Charlie even mentioned my name, you were ending up in the ER. Emotions can exacerbate asthma, you know that. Charlie begged me to just stay away. And when I did, he told me that your asthma disappeared. I knew asthma sometimes disappeared, but it seemed so sudden, so miraculous. How could I not think that my not being there was making you better? How could I tempt that?"

Sam tried to swallow but he couldn't. His head swam. He tried to imagine his father doing such a thing, knowing how Sam had waited for the phone, the mail, how he had run crying after the postman, sure there must be a letter for him. He thought of his father sleeping on a cot by his bed in the hospital and every time Sam woke up, his father was awake, too, and watching him, his eyes damp.

"He thought you were going to die, Sam!"

"I didn't die."

"Did you know that I wanted the two of you to come to New York with me? Didn't Charlie tell you?"

"My father wouldn't lie to me."

"I suppose he was protecting you."

Sam felt his anger burning like a match flare. His mother used to bend the truth as easily. His father used to tell him that the worst thing a person could do was to be dishonest and now Isabelle was telling him how his father had lied.

He was furious with his father, furious with her, and even angrier at himself for thinking that coming up here might be a good idea. "You could have stayed on the Cape. You had a life there, too."

"No, I didn't. You were the only reason I stayed.

Both of you. And then I was losing my job and my money was dwindling. All I had was you, and I was losing that. I was making things worse for everyone, and this school opportunity came up for me in New York." She wet her lips. "I loved your father. I loved you. But I was making you sick. What else was I supposed to do, Sam?"

Sam tried to remember. The late-night phone calls his father made to Isabelle. The way Sam would sometimes wake up and find Charlie pacing, or baking loaves of bread at four in the morning that no one ever ate. Once he found his father scrubbing the kitchen floor, tile by tile, even though the cleaning lady had been there just the day before. He remembered how sad his father was, and how he had thought it was because Isabelle had left them both.

A headache pulsed behind Sam's eyes. He sat down heavily on a bench.

"Your father felt he had to choose between the two of us, and you know what? We both chose you and we did the right thing." She grabbed his arm but he tugged it free. "Don't you think I think about the accident and your mother dying every single day? I do. I wanted to make things right for both of you. I fell in love with both of you, but it wasn't enough."

"No one said you were responsible for the accident."

"Really? That's not what the newspapers said.

Or a whole lot of people. And how do you know? How do you know for sure?"

"You were driving below the speed limit on the right side of the road!"

"I was driving in the fog! I couldn't see!"

"Jesus, it wasn't your fault!" Sam shouted.

"And it wasn't yours, either!" she cried. "Not your mother leaving, not the accident, not what happened with your father and me! You just think it is!"

Sam didn't realize the keening noise he heard was coming from him, until Isabelle sat down beside him and put her arms around him and then he cried and cried and cried.

IN THE END, Sam stayed only one more day at her house. He watched how Frank brought Isabelle coffee with her breakfast, how every time she came into the room, Frank's whole body seemed to light up. He watched, too, how Grace would curl into Isabelle's lap. That evening, they ate at Frank's restaurant, a busy, boisterous place filled with plants. She had a life, a family, and it made him feel for his father.

"What will you tell Charlie?" Isabelle asked.

"That I saw you. That you have this great, happy life."

She nodded. "Tell him I asked about him, too."

Before he left, Frank insisted on giving Sam something for the road. A care package of bread and vegetable spread he had made himself, some grapes that would be easy to eat in the car, and a thermos of herb tea. "See, now you have to come back to return the thermos," Frank said. "See how cagey I can be?"

It was strange being the one to leave her, the one to get in the car and drive away, and for one moment, Sam couldn't do it. He sat with his hands on the steering wheel and glanced at Isabelle in the rearview mirror. She was waiting for him to go, waiting to get back to her family, to her life, shifting weight from one foot to the other. That morning, she had put his address and phone number into her computer. "We're not going to have just this day," she told him. "You're stuck with me in your life. I want to meet Lisa. I want to see you at work. I want to know all about you."

He studied Isabelle, framing her as if she were going to be a photograph, frozen in time. She leaned against Frank and rested her head on his shoulder, and for a moment, he wanted to weep.

He rolled down the window so he could see them without the pane of glass.

Frank and Grace went back in the house, leaving Isabelle standing in the middle of the road. Time seemed all mixed up and he wasn't sure where he was or what year it was. Only that there was Isabelle in the road watching him leave, one hand uplifted, not moving, growing smaller and smaller in his mirror as he drove away from her. Staying there in that house, where, if he wanted to, he could always find her.

AROUND DUSK, HE was at the Tick Tock Diner, and the other familiar points. It was still a good hour before he would be home, but he stopped, pulling into the parking lot. He got coffee, and then took it back to the car, but before he got back in, he leaned against the front door and he called Lisa.

Her voice was soft with sleep. "How did it go?" she said.

"I want . . ." he said. He felt a frisson of fear, real and familiar. Would his whole life be perfect or just this moment? And wouldn't that be enough?

"You want what?"

"I want to. With you. I want to." He swallowed.

He looked outside and he saw there was a moon out now, full and white in the dark sky. He held the phone close to his face, and then, he waited for her to answer. He held his breath.

Acknowledgments

EVERY WRITER DESERVES a dream agent like Gail Hochman, whose enthusiasm, warmth, and advice make me grateful every day. Huge thanks, too, to Bill Contardi and Maya Ziv and everyone at the agency. Thanks to every amazing person at Algonquin and to my editor Andra Miller, who made working together exhilarating, illuminating, and fun.

For help getting facts straight: Peter J. Salzano and Sue O'Doherty on how kids deal with grief, Lissa Rankin for medical information, Eric and Andrew Johnston on funeral homes, Linda Matlow on photography, and Lynn Reed Baragona on the legal ramifications of a car crash.

For friendship, reading, advice, and support: Leora Skolkin-Smith, Katharine Weber, Kate Maloy, Jennifer Gooch Hummer, Liza Nelson, Robb Forman Dew, Rochelle Jewell Shapiro, Jeff Lyons, Jane Bernstein, Jeff Tamarkin, Victoria Zackheim, Beth Ann Bauman, Lisa Cron, Lindy Judge, Jane Praeger, Jessica Brilliant Keener, M. J. Rose, Marlene Quinn, Cara Mayrick, Jo Fisher, Linda Corcoran, James Lambros, John Truby, Leslie Lehr, Masha Hamilton, Clea Simon, Carole Parker, Barney Lichenstein, Jo-Ann Mapson, Helen Leavitt, Ruth Rogers, and Susan Ito. Thanks, too, to the Bellevue Literary Review, who published the short story that jump-started this novel, and to UCLA Writers' Program online, where I teach.

Most of all, I owe everything to the two guys who sing me songs, surprise me with cupcakes, and fill my world with love: Jeff and Max.

The Writer as Reviewer

A NOTE FROM THE AUTHOR

"DON'T DO IT, it'll kill your writing," a writer friend warned me when, seven years ago, I first mentioned I was going to be a book critic for the *Boston Globe*. I can't say I was that surprised by her response; a lot of writers I know won't review books at all. They don't want to risk reading a book they may not like, having to give another writer the kind of review we've all gotten at one time or another—you know, the one that makes you feel that maybe it's not too late to give it up and go to dental school. A writer writing reviews is incestuous, I'm told. Shouldn't we really just be concentrating on our *own* writing rather than taking apart someone else's for all the world to see?

Ah, I beg to differ.

I want to review because I'm passionate about books and writers. And for me, reviewing opens up writing in ways one wouldn't expect. Having to read critically, instead of for the pure, dizzy enjoyment of being lost in a read, forces me to look at a book differently: I notice what's working and why, and what is leaving me adrift. This, in turn, impacts how I write. Writing is *always* challenging—but I've slowed down, gotten more meticulous, because of everything I'm learning from reading other writers critically. I take note of a great first line, a reveal I never expected—and I begin to tuck those techniques into my own author's toolbox. Reading as a reviewer is like seeing the scaffolding of a building, the bones beneath the skin. Reviewing actually makes me more conscious of not just how and why books work but how and why I want my *own* to work.

While I knew I could learn a lot from reviewing great books, I was happy to see I could learn even more from the ones that faltered. Recognizing a flaw in someone else's work can prevent me from making that gaffe in my own. Having to read flowery, fussy language makes me stop every time I think about adding what seems like a perfectly good adjective. Closing a book unsatisfied because the ending ties everything up in a neat bow makes me work harder at my own grand finales, making sure they're more open ended, that they provide more of a never-ending story that makes you wonder about the character's next step even after you've shut the book. I've learned that if I don't love a book by the first twenty pages, chances are I'm not going to love it for the next three hundred. This means I spend months on my own first chapter, honing it, getting it exactly right. What I most love are the books that aren't afraid to break a few rules.

Λ meditative chapter might not advance the story, but you know the book would be less without it. A character who leaps into a book midstream, tells his story, and then vanishes can somehow tie the book together. These things give me the courage to wander, to take risks in my own novels.

It's awful to have to give a bad review, but even bad reviews can be helpful. I realize no one sets out deliberately to write a bad book (and I know that most of my writer friends and I are always terrified that we somehow have), but sometimes a bad review gives helpful feedback. For example, a line in a *New York Times* review for my first novel, *Meeting Rozzy Halfway*, mentioned that my "back-story was sparkling while the front story faded." This taught me how to pay more attention to making things more immediate. I try to give the same sort of critical help, because I feel that all writers are in the trenches together and we should do what we can to help one another. Plus, false praise is disrespectful to another writer, like telling a friend he looks terrific even though there is that bit of salad greenery lodged in his teeth that he could easily get rid of if someone would gently point it out.

I love reviewing. When I'm desperate to figure out my story, I always study what worked for other writers I've reviewed—and what didn't. But when I'm deep in the writing zone, engaged in my character's struggles, I don't consciously think about anything but the world I'm lost in creating. It's then that I hope that all those techniques and tools will emerge, organic as seedlings and just waiting to sprout on my pages.

Questions for Discussion

1. Why do you think Leavitt describes the events surrounding the pivotal accident in the book three times, from the points of view of Isabelle, Sam, and then Bill? What do you think this is saying about how we see events in our lives and whether or not we can ever really know the whole truth? Do you personally think anyone can ever really know the truth?

2. What's different about the ways in which April and Isabelle are running away? What do you think would have happened with April if she had not made the choice to leave? And why do you think she was really outside the car?

3. Some of the characters in *Pictures of You* engage in magical or wishful thinking. Sam believes he has seen an angel. Isabelle is told she has a special gift to foresee the future lives of the children she photographs. How do you think this magical thinking helps and hinders the characters, and have you ever used such thinking in your own life to get through a painful situation?

4. Sam's asthma impacts his life, April's, and Charlie's. At one point, on page 97, April tells Charlie that she heard that "breathing is our contract to remain here on this planet," that people with respiratory problems are "troubled souls." If this is so, why do you think that Sam's asthma vanishes? What made Sam want to stay on earth and survive?

5. At one point, on page 105, Charlie asks, "Was any parent perfect?" Discuss the ways April and Charlie were both good and also highly imperfect parents. Was there anything they could or should have done differently, given Sam's illness? Do you think parenting ever turns out the way we expect it to?

6. Sam remembers how he and his mother used to go on short trips and pretend to be other people with other lives. Why do you think people need to create different realities for themselves? How can it be both helpful and harmful?

7. As Isabelle teaches Sam about photography, she explains that photographs sometimes show things that aren't there. She tells him that he has to learn to look deeper, to see what might be hidden, and in a way, she's really

talking about people, as well as photographs. How much do you think we can ever really know about the people we love?

8. Leavitt's book explores many different kinds of love: the love of a mother for her child, the love of husband and wife, and some unexpected kinds, too, such as Isabelle's devotion to Nelson, her tortoise. Why do you think Isabelle's love for her tortoise is so important to her?

9. How did you react to Bill's story about what really happened the day of the accident? How did you feel about his ultimate decision? Why do you think he tried to find April after all that time?

10. Why do you think Leavitt chose to flash forward thirty years and show Sam as an adult? How would the novel have been different if it ended with Sam as a child? Was Sam's life what you expected it might be, or were you surprised by his choices?

11. Leavitt has said that the novel is about the stories we tell ourselves about the ones we love. How do these stories keep each character from truly seeing the ones they love?

12. On page 440, Isabelle's driving teacher tells her that "people who are frightened, who don't know where they're going . . . are my best students." Why, in the context of the book, do you think this is true?

13. The novel asks, can we forgive the unforgivable? Do you think Charlie ever really forgives April? Do *you?*

14. At the end of the novel, on page 467, Sam wonders if his whole life might be perfect, "or just this moment? And wouldn't that be enough?" What do you think he means? And what do you think the answer to that question might say about Sam's worldview?

15. Leavitt has said that she wanted to create a never-ending story that would make readers wonder about the characters long after they turned the last page. What do you think happens to Sam? Do you think Charlie and Isabelle ever meet again?

Caroline Leavitt is the award-winning author of eight novels. Leavitt's essays and stories have been included in *New York Magazine*, *Psychology Today*, *More*, *Parenting*, *Redbook*, *Salon*, and several anthologies. A book critic for the *Boston Globe* and *People*, she is a senior writing instructor at UCLA online. Her Web site is www.carolineleavitt.com.

Center Point Publishing
600 Brooks Road • PO Box 1
Thorndike ME 04986-0001 USA

(207) 568-3717

US & Canada:
1 800 929-9108
www.centerpointlargeprint.com